# The Travels of Dr. Rebecca Harper

## A Matter of Time

### Book 1

**Elizabeth Woolsey**

Elizabeth Woolsey Horse Doctor Press

ISBN: 979-8-9869111-5-1



The Travels of Dr. Rebecca Harper: A Matter of Time, is a work of fiction. Any similarities

to places or. persons, living or dead, is coincidental.

Cover design by Natalie Keller Reinert

Published in the United States

ewoolseydvm@gmail.com

https://elizabethwoolsey.com/

For
My children
Quincy Andrus
The staff at Adelaide Plains Equine Clinic
My mother, for her love of the written language
The many Western television characters,
who inspired both my passion for horses and my ethics.
Finally, to my father, who taught me to fly fish and inspired
my love of veterinary medicine.

# PROLOGUE

I have always liked geometry and trigonometry. My love for these subjects came from Mr. Thompson in my sophomore and junior years in high school. He could make me understand the rules of geometry that, once learned, would stand me in good stead for the rest of my life. The real savior was my best friend, Quincy Charter. She was a total brainiac, and she had great ways of remembering things. Her specialty was mnemonics, which are little sayings to help you remember long lists. Quincy wasn't around when I learned the cranial nerves in vet school: on old Olympus towering tops...olfactory, optic, oculomotor, trochlear, trigeminal. It goes on. Only a few mnemonics have stood the test of time for me. One came from trigonometry to figure triangles by measuring the length of their sides.

In veterinary medicine, and especially in horses, angles are critical in assessing conformation.

Sine: saddle our horses, or the sine of an angle is equal to the length of the opposite over the hypotenuse length.

Cosine: canter away happily, or the cosine of an angle is equal to the length of the adjacent over the length of the hypotenuse.

Tangent: toward other adventures, the tangent of an angle is equal to the length of the opposite over the length of the adjacent.

Saddle our horses,

Canter away happily,

Toward other adventures,

How could you forget?

Those numbers can be found in my grandfather's little red arithmetic book, and the angle can be derived from that.

I have always pictured time in a long continuous line. In contrast, others have suggested that time may be better considered in parallel, as in a parallel universe. My story begins when the earth's parallel lines are shifted by an unknown force, and the realignment causes two previously parallel lines to converge.

So here it is.

Yours truly,

Becky Harper DVM

# PART 1

1981-1847

# CHAPTER 1

Graduation 1981—Oh my God, I'm a vet. A real vet. No more practicing writing my name as Rebecca Ann Harper, DVM—or better yet, Dr. Rebecca Harper—in the margins of my class notes. No more calculating my GPA daily in my spiral notebook while Dr. Fitzgerald drones on about accreditation exams. Considering the last three years, this is a miracle. I have it all.

With my diploma in hand and Pomp and Circumstance droning from the loudspeaker, I rushed off the graduation stage. I walked past my beaming husband, Jeff. He had Lauren, our three-year-old daughter, in tow and intended to keep her from screaming as I walked past without a hug.

Jeff and I met when he started his residency in equine reproduction four years ago. A kinder man, you will never meet. "He's tall, muscular, sandy-haired, and the best husband and father you could ever ask for. The cliché is gag-worthy, but it's true." He opted out of his theriogenology residency program for one year with only a few months to go, so I could continue my schooling.

He'd been in practice at a small, rural veterinary clinic when he realized his passion for all things repro needed to be satisfied. We met when he came to the vet school to complete his doctorate and residency in equine reproduction. Now, Jeff has only six months left to complete his studies, and then we are out of here. Well, I'm out of here next week.

Don't get me wrong. Vet school has been the best part of my life so far. I'm a bit slow, so it took me longer than most to be accepted into vet school, but, once that happened, I became a student with a passion. I graduated with honors and received plenty of job offers.

Like Jeff, horses are my passion.

I grew up on a horse ranch with my older sister, Sherry, and my parents. Well, up until I was fifteen, when my mom died. Septicemia from a ruptured appendix caused her death, but she'd had problems for years. I just pray I haven't inherited her gastric intolerance. Sherry went off the deep end after that, and we don't even know where she is. In the end, it was Dad and me, and now just Dad.

Our ranch is in the high country of Montana, so I'm accustomed to rough winters and the hardships of rural life. We had cattle, but Dad's primary income was from horses. We bred ranch stock. Most were quarter horses, but we had a bit of everything. Dad had three stallions and about twenty mares. He had around fifteen foals every year. My father also accepted outside horses for breaking. Well-known for having a way with horses, he even did training for a few movies and one long-running T.V. show. It may have been *Gunsmoke.*

Dad was in the graduation audience, and I looked around to find him in the crowd. I waved at him, and he beamed back at me. I was the first college graduate in the family. When I married and became pregnant, I think he thought the gig was up. I knew he loved me, but I could hear the yelling four states away when I hung up after telling him, "Dad, I'll go back and finish. I promise." He was not persuaded. I think he considered coming down to castrate Jeff. He performed all the colt castrations on our ranch, where we lived. Thankfully for all concerned, we were going to come and assume that job.

Jeff loved the ranch and the streams. We both loved to fish. Up in that remote area of Montana, the fishing was easy. Jeff was a fly fisherman, and he was showing me how to cast a line the summer before I got pregnant. Well, I graduated on time, and because Jeff sacrificed his studies so I could finish mine, my dad put away the emasculators when he came to see our beautiful daughter. When he heard we might move to Nevada, the fight was on again for one and all.

"I didn't raise you and put you through college so you could run off and live a thousand miles away. I have a right to see my granddaughter at least once a month, and I'm not getting any younger. I'm gonna need help this spring, and I don't mean a few days of vaccinating, castrating, and floating teeth." If you don't know about horses, floating teeth means filing down the sharp points on the molars.

"Dad, there isn't enough work in Mountain Laurel to support a vet, and you know it. I'm going to pay you and the bank back. I have six months until the student loan payments start. Jeff is still receiving a pitiful salary as a resident.

I'm trying. Please believe me. If we could find jobs closer to you, we would. Besides, we are even farther from Jeff's family. Like it or not, I have two families now."

A truce was declared. The plan was for me to visit a mixed practice with a significant horse component near Lake Tahoe. I would go the week after graduation and check out the Nevada veterinary practice. The owners were Mac and Julie Smyth. They were both vets, but Julie had not worked as a vet in twenty years. She gave up practice when their kids were born. She ran the office and raised the kids while Mac did the rest. An up-and-coming vet had planned to take over the veterinary practice in three years, but one kick to the shoulder and the young vet checked out of the clinic and never returned. Mac had a progressive neurological condition and would not be around much longer.

The practice was put on the market for a song. Mac and Julie had done well and had properties and investments all over the area. Selling the veterinary practice was not a retirement deal. They loved their staff and clients, and they wanted to make sure all their staff and clients were looked after. Mac figured he had a year or two to do the things he'd never done. He was going to take Julie and the kids to ride the John Muir Trail. If that went well, he and Julie were doing the Pacific Crest Trail the following year.

The Smyths knew we couldn't afford to buy anything. They just wanted out. They asked us to take over the practice this summer, so they could get the John Muir done. They would hire me and provide a nanny, and Jeff would join us in January. We would buy the practice, and they would finance it. Mac was a well-respected vet. He was up-to-date and even knew the correct dosage for penicillin. Lots of vets were still using ten milliliters once a day. Try three times that dose twice daily.

It seemed like a dream come true. We would be close to big cities and yet still be in the mountains. Jeff loved to ski and hike and fish, and I just wanted to be a vet. A second child was in the short plan as Jeff was twelve years older than me. Yep, I go for the old geezers.

Jeff's uncle was a famous horse vet in Vermont. His uncle advised him to find a practice where he could get away for a few hours and then get back to work. Jeff spent his summers and vacations with his uncle working long hours, and to Jeff, the Tahoe practice seemed ideal. He could leave work and play with our kids and be just as happy. He was always putting a long stick in Lauren's hand and pretending to cast a fly. I had no hope. She was Daddy's girl. I was just the milk bar, and even that was long over.

Jeff still loved the reproduction side of things, but that was seasonal, and so he wanted to plan the next child for mid-to-late summer. He could be the stay-at-home dad, at least a few days a week. All systems are go for launch. The only glitch in the system was a somewhat unplanned celebratory activity the night of the graduation. Worst-case scenario, by the time I was six months preggers, Jeff would be with me to take over the dangerous stuff. The day I left for Nevada, my fears were allayed, and I was once again a free agent. Phew, close call.

After graduation, I prepared for the trip to Reno and then went out to see the vet clinic. I was surprised at how dry the area was, but I saw several ranches on the way to the clinic. I drove up to the office, and a woman in a blue scrub top greeted me. She said little as she took me into the main office. She barely acknowledged me. I thought I heard her mutter something about my being a girl. I knew I was breaking the stereotype for a rural veterinary practice. The vet they wanted was Jeff. I guessed the woman was expressing what she had heard from her bosses.

A plump woman with very unnatural blonde hair was barking orders on a two-way radio. "No, you idiot, it's Box 218, not 128. Mac, it's a good thing you're retiring. You're going to take us to rack and ruin with these sidetrack adventures. Hazel's waiting at the gate if she hasn't died of old age."

"I'm going to leave you up on Mount Whitney if you don't stop squawking, woman. I see her. Has the lass arrived?" Mac yelled back on the two-way.

"I think so. She looks green and eager. Doubt she'll look this good next year," Julie Smyth announced, looking over her shoulder at me and smiling.

So, this was 'Mrs.' Dr. Smyth, and obviously, 'Mr.' Dr. Smyth was on the other end of this conversation.

"Dr. Green, reporting for duty," I joked. "Well, some folks call me Becky." I extended my hand and introduced myself. The woman stood up and reached over the counter to shake my hand.

"Well, well. Aren't you tiny? I hope you've got some muscles under that shirt."

"Yes, ma'am, dozens of them." I still hadn't shed the baby fat after my daughter Lauren's birth, so I was slightly bigger than usual. Even so, I was accustomed to people judging me for my short stature. In her day, to be a woman vet, she had to be tough and twice as bright as the guys in her class. These days, not that difficult. I was in a class of seventy-eight, and thirty-five were women. It wasn't easy, and for sure, there was a two-tiered system. I'd worked at the school as a vet technician, so the faculty accepted me more than they did the other female students.

The scrub-topped greeter waited at the door. It was then I could see that she might be intellectually disabled. I suspected Down syndrome. She did not talk to me or even offer a small friendly gesture.

"Rosa, this is the new young vet, Becky." Turning to me, Julie asked if I minded being called by my first name.

"No, of course not." *Well, the 'Dr. Harper' name didn't last long.*

"Don't take any mind of Rosa. She's the backbone of this practice, but she is the strong, silent type." Rosa smiled at Julie while she emptied the wastebaskets. "Rosa is our firstborn."

"Oh, got it." I could see she was definitely challenged. Jeff and I were so lucky to have a healthy and bright child. I could not imagine having a son or daughter with a disability. Julie could read my thoughts.

"Rosa is independent. She lives at the clinic, and she pays her way. You'll be lucky if Rosa stays and helps you when we retire. She cleans the barn and the clinic and cares for our personal horses. She has a way with animals that I don't understand."

"That's great. We'll keep Rosa if we can afford her rates."

"She's also awesome with small children, and she practically raised our younger two."

"Hired! A job for life." I wasn't going to let that go. Julie smiled, and I thought I'd just passed a test.

Mac arrived back at the clinic an hour later. He walked in, slapped Julie on the backside, and shouted for Rosa to restock his truck. Only a few things were missing, and she went to the storeroom to get more vaccines, Banamine, which is used for pain relief in horses, and syringes. I observed her with her dad and could see they were devoted. Mac's hand shook slightly. He had early Parkinson's disease. He shook my hand with a firm grip and crushed it in the process.

"How's the dean? You know, we used to call him Stinky." I gave Mac a quizzical look.

"Oh, he fell in a hog pen in his second year of vet school, and he never lived it down. He's a good guy, though. I hear he has big dollars coming into the school. Well, the football team's record might have a hand in the donations too, but he is one smart man. Did he tell you we were in the same class? It was his recommendation that made us look at you and your husband as potential successors to our clinic."

"Yes, sir. He mentioned that you even beat him in awards."

"Oh, bullshit. Stinky was the top dog. I just got the one award he wanted for the best equine vet student. He won four other awards and was at the top of the class. Oh, and don't call me sir. That was my grandfather, and he's long gone. I'm Mac to everyone but my kids."

I could see he was a man who was easy in his clothes. He and Julie had no pretensions. They were just folks, and I had a lot to learn from them in a short time. They planned to go in two weeks if we could come to terms, and Jeff and I agreed to start work for them. I would have to talk to Jeff about this plan. The feel of the practice was good, but six months on my own, just out of school, was daunting. Actually, it was frightening—Hershey swirls in the pants kind of scary.

While I was applying to vet schools nationwide, I worked at the college in the large animal clinic. I knew a bit more than the average recent graduate, but that was a damned sight less than Julie and Mac. I was good at horse wrangling, and tough horses were not intimidating. *Thanks, Dad.*

Happily, I spent a week riding in the vet truck with Mac. It was real vet work. We performed castrations, floated teeth, and fixed a hernia on a Belgium filly. He had me pick the anesthesia protocol and do most of the fine work that was becoming difficult for him. I sutured a large shoulder laceration, and we saw two colics. Horses are prone to abdominal pain for various reasons, which is commonly called colic.

At the end of the week, Julie told Mac she was stealing me for the afternoon. She wanted to take me on a ride up in the mountains and show me the backcountry. The horses needed to get fit for the first ride on the John Muir Trail.

It was a beautiful summer day. We took the horses a few miles in the trailer to the trailhead and saddled up. The pines and other conifers were tall and fresh and made the blue sky look even bluer. The smell of pines permeated the air. Julie could have stopped there. I loved the mountains.

"No smog or pollution up here, Becky," she commented as she observed me inhaling the smell of pine. It was hot in the valley, but as we climbed out and up the well-worn trail lined with conifers, the temperature dropped. I could feel how pleasant it was in the coolness of the mountains.

After an hour's climb, I could look back and see the valley and the small ranches and roads below. Julie pointed out some of their clients' properties.

Pointing to an old house in what appeared to be a ghost town, she said, "They used to film a few of the *Comstock* episodes over there, but mostly it was a tourist attraction."

"Really, were you around? Did you meet any of the actors? Did you take care of the horses?" I was fascinated. I watched *Comstock* every Sunday night. I remember visiting my grandmother when we came out of the mountains, and we saw it in color once.

My father was not impressed. He would say, "You know the saddles are all plastic, so they show up better on the screen, and the horses are all lame. I don't know what you girls see in that program, anyway. You've got the real deal right out your back door." Whether the rumor of the plastic gear was true, I don't know. I have to say, Sherry and I looked hard to see if we could confirm the story.

Julie replied, "I met Colin Chandler in the pharmacy once. He seemed nice enough. We saw the paint horse that Danny rode for a foot abscess. Mostly, they had the studio people doing what they needed. When they closed, it was a death sentence to our town, though. Who was your favorite, Bec?"

"Oh, that's a hard one ... Gee Ling." We both laughed. "I know where my bread is buttered."

"That Clint was a dreamboat. I was sure sad when he left the series," answered Julie.

We climbed some steep embankments. We snaked along a granite ledge that had a long drop to the bottom and was just as far from the top. Below was a river or a creek. I could see the rock-lined pools, and I looked for signs of trout. We stopped for a minute so Julie could take a nature break. I held her horse as she went around the bend for some privacy. Some rocks came down from above. I looked up and thought it looked rather precarious. I shouted to her that the side of the mountain looked dangerous. She laughed and said that was what she had told Mac the first time they came up here. "This trail is more than one hundred years old, Becky." She returned from around the corner. "A few small slides occur almost every year, but nothing really to worry about. I've been coming up here for thirty years, and the trail is rock solid."

I was dubious, but the allure of the trout down below attracted my attention. Julie stood up on a large boulder and remounted. "Come on, slowpoke. I want to show you my favorite spot in the entire world."

Since I had the baby, I was not used to riding, and my legs were getting weak and sore. I gritted my teeth and rode on, following her buckskin gelding. My gelding was a smaller, gray Arabian. I chose him as they said he was the best-footed horse they had. He was solid and never put a hoof out of place. The granite shelf was glaring, and I was glad to have a hat and dark glasses. The forest below was thick, and I could see bushes that might have blackberries. I was hungry.

We had almost reached the end of the trail along the rocky cliff when I heard a tremendous roar. My gelding swung his head and looked up above the track. I was grabbing for anything I could. Julie was ahead of me, and she yelled but was drowned out by the noise of a massive rockslide coming down between us. I saw her horse bolt, and Julie fell to the ground. Large boulders started falling all around me, and the trail gave way. The whole mountainside was crumbling. The noise was deafening. My gelding buckled, went down on his knees, and came out from under me. I was thrown back, which was the last thing I remember.

# CHAPTER 2

The crushing weight of the rocks pressed down on my chest. I had dirt in my mouth, and I was bleeding. I tasted the metallic sensation of blood as my teeth crunched the gritty soil in my mouth. I tried to recall what I'd been doing. I thought I was dying. I couldn't speak, and I was too weak to move. The sun was on the horizon, but there was so much grit in my eyes. The light was dim. Was it dawn or dusk? My eyes stung, and the lids were swollen, offering me only a slit to see my surroundings. I wasn't sure if it was morning or night.

Where was I, and what had happened? The effort of thinking was too much. I was so tired and so sore. I could feel something on the back of my head. I reached around with my left hand and touched a gaping wound that I could feel through my blood-matted hair. *Whoa, too much* blood. Was I going to die?

I remembered my husband and daughter. Was I going to see them again? I had to see my little Lauren grow up. *Oh*

*God, please let me live.* It was too much, and I could not resist the comfort of closing my eyes and drifting away. Far, far away.

Sometime later, I awoke to see what may have been dawn. I wasn't sure. My lips were dry and cracking, and my thirst was overwhelming. I was still not sure where I was or how I got there. The blood had congealed and was matted in the hair on the back of my head. My tongue was swollen and dry. I tried to call for help, but the sounds were like slurred groans. I coughed, but even that was muffled as saliva mixed with sand in my mouth, which prevented any deep breaths from expelling what was in my trachea.

I lay there and listened for any signs of life or help. I thought long and hard about who I was and how I'd ended up in this position. Large rocks trapped my right arm, but I could lift my left hand, and I tried to move it over to my face. The pain was excruciating. At least I could feel my arm. In fact, I felt both my legs and pelvis.

"Help me. Anyone. Please" sounded like "hepma ameon plas." I could hear, and while there was sand in my ears, I recognized the sounds of a bird. I lay there and watched the decreasing dark blue turn to the yellow glow of the sky behind me. I heard a second bird. It must have been dawn. It was so cold, and I was shivering. I was sure I heard a car in the distance. *How did I get here? Why is no one coming? Did I drive off a bank?*

I took stock of what I knew. I was in an accident. I had a father, but I was sure he was far away. I rode horses. I thought I smelled a horse. Turning my head, I could see a saddle about twenty yards away. I must have fallen off a horse. The saddle was immersed in water. *Water!* I needed water. It was so close.

"Hep, hep." I raised my voice. I was near a stream, but it would be hard to get to the water. Pain shot through my back, which was in spasm. I could move one leg. I used that leg to kick a large piece of slate that pinned down my other limb. The effort cost me precious energy, and after freeing the pinned leg, I had to rest. I must have dozed off, and when I next gazed around, the sun was up, and I could hear many birds. My eyes burned from the sand. I was so thirsty and cold. My right arm was still sandwiched between a large flat granite slab and another large boulder. If I could move the rock, I could free myself. I was sure help was coming. I thought more about how I got there and what I knew. The saddle meant I was riding. I must have fallen off. Was I alone? Where was I? *Oh my God, I need water. I need water.*

I tried to think about how I could get the last boulder off my arm. There was a stick within reach. I grabbed it with my left hand and shoved the end into the gap that pinned my arm. It made my arm even more painful, but I rolled onto my side, and with both my arm and leg leaning on the wedged stick, the boulder rolled just far enough away to release my arm. I was free.

Now I had to make my way down to the creek. I could only crawl. It took me an hour to reach the stream, and every part of my body either stung or ached for the effort.

When I reached the water, I slowly immersed my face into the icy liquid. The joy of getting water to help rinse my mouth of the sand and dirt was unbelievable. I washed and gulped and washed some more. My teeth all appeared as if they were in the right place. I felt my body expand, and I had more energy from the rehydration than I could imagine. I drank until I felt satiated and then drank more. I washed my eyes and tried to dab the back of my head. The water was clean and so cold. I lay back on a sandbar and fell asleep again.

It was dark when I woke up. I was shaking uncontrollably, and I could feel my exposed arms and legs. I had to pee, and I was busting. I was wearing Levi's 501s. Those damn buttons that normally unbuttoned so quickly were unmoving in my icy hands. I had to let go. I wet my pants — trading fifteen seconds of warmth for an entire night of stiff, wet pants. I didn't dare take them off. I would wash them in the morning. I tested my voice. It was still raspy. I shouted, "Somebody help me, please." In return, I heard a coyote yelp. I immediately realized what a stupid thing that was to do. I was alone in the woods, and I could summon a bear, mountain lion, or possibly a crazy mountain man.

I could feel something jabbing me in the butt. I reached into my pants pocket and touched a pocketknife and a small piece of paper. The joy of finding something that might protect me made me forget the paper note. I looked for something to give me warmth, but I found nothing. I sat up, clutched my knees, and rocked. I was still too sore, too exhausted, and too disoriented to do anything else. I wondered how long it had been since all this had happened. My hand was black and swollen, my thoughts were muddled, and I suspected I had suffered a concussion. I remembered things, and then I didn't. I was having difficulty recalling things I knew I should remember. At one stage, I looked at the gold band on my finger and could not relate this to my current state of mind. I knew medical stuff, for sure. I knew that peeing meant my kidneys were functioning. The fog was lifting, but only slowly. I rocked for hours. I was too afraid to go to sleep, but my next recollection was of the sun and a hint of warmth.

I looked around and saw what looked like a massive rockslide above me. Trees were sideways, and there was no sign this was any older than a few days. It went from the top of the cliff face to the creek where I rested. It had to be several hundred feet and equally wide. I thought this must be why I was here. I looked around and found some dead tree branches several yards down the creek. I had not stood, but I could crawl. I wanted to call for help, but I wasn't sure if that would bring unwanted guests.

By crawling, I could gather enough wood to start a fire. I checked my pockets for matches. It was a considerable long shot, but what if I had some? I didn't, of course. I felt the paper in my pocket and thought it would help to get a fire started. I pulled the piece out and saw a picture of a man and baby on one side. Stuck to it was a driver's license — my license. I gasped. A flood of memories returned. I knew who I was and now realized where I was and why I was here.

I immediately shouted for Julie. I called until my voice ran out. There was no response. I looked over the large rockslide and the enormity of this set in. Julie was dead. Her horse was buried, and who knew what had happened to the gelding she'd lent me. I was devastated. I wanted my husband and daughter, and I wanted out. I sat and cried. I cried until I could no longer cry. Looking up the cliff face, I knew my only way out was to climb up and get back on the trail. Julie's husband did not know where we were going. I'd asked her if she ever was afraid of this trail, and she said no, and that was why it was her favorite place in the world. It was her secret retreat from her family and work life.

I had to get out, or no one would find me. My pants stank, and I was feeling the need to pee again. I took off my pants and undies and dropped them in a small side pool along the creek. I shimmied in and submersed myself quickly as it was cold. I remembered when I was riding, I'd looked down and noted the shadows of trout in the stream. The creek was not flowing now, which was different. I guessed the slide had dammed the stream on the other side. I wrung out my pants and undies and set them on a bush to dry. I hoped no one would come in the next hour or two as I was naked from the waist down and was only wearing my bra. Oh, hell, I would kiss anyone who showed up even if I were naked. My legs were swollen and bruised, my butt was one big purple mass, and my knees stung from crawling around on them. I was going to stand. I crawled over to a tree and, using the branches, stood up and wavered for several minutes. I was weak and sore, but I could not feel any broken bones. My ribs might be broken, but that was it. Getting out required climbing up the cliff face and then getting back on the trail. I yelled twice and staggered around. I looked for a search plane that might fly overhead. There were no sounds of human activity.

Hunger was next on my mind. I recalled passing blackberries as we rode along the trail. I salivated at the thought. I slowly walked along the creek bed that was drying out and noticed some bushes with berries. It was much farther down the creek, and I might be able to walk down to them. I didn't think I would have the energy to walk back toward the berry bushes. I knew the back of my head had dried blood, and I wondered if the smell would attract bears or mountain lions. This was a bit too au naturel for me, and I put on all my clothes, which were still quite wet. Getting my jeans on was difficult. I was so sore and bruised that it took forever to pull them over my swollen legs. I knew I needed food for the energy to attempt a climb up the cliff face.

I remembered it was a long way until the trail came even close to the creek. I was not sure, but I thought it might have been two days since this happened and maybe even more. I needed food. I slowly walked along the rocky creek bed until I came to a pool that held substantial water. My eyes were still stinging from the dust, and my eyesight was slightly blurry. I could see several trout might be trapped in this pool. I sat and watched and tried to figure out how I was going to get one. It looked like too much work, so I went farther down the creek bed to the bushes. Blackberries! Not a lot, but enough for a meal. I put one into my mouth. It was painful from the previous gravel in my mouth. Still, possibly the best taste I'd ever experienced — almost orgasmic. I ate a handful. I looked around upon hearing a distinct crunching noise in the woods directly behind me. It was loud enough to be an enormous animal or person. Of course, I thought about a bear with the berries and decided it would be wise to get a meal and leave. I'm smarter than the average bear.

I turned to the noise and was preparing for an encounter, but nothing appeared. After an eternity and no additional ominous sounds, I returned to the berries and ate some more. My stomach had a cramping feeling. I was envisioning diarrhea.

I knew I would not get out before nightfall. I had my pocketknife, and I needed to prepare for another night in the woods. I decided that the best plan was staying down near the creek for one more night. My guts were really churning. I was alarmingly sure diarrhea was imminent. My shirt was almost dry, but my pants had a way to go. The wet cloth chaffed against my bruised legs.

The sun was getting lower. I needed to start a fire and ready myself for another night in the woods. I couldn't understand why no one was coming for me. I wondered if Jeff was on a plane coming here to help in the search. I couldn't wait to be in his arms again. The baby would never remember this or understand, but holding her once again was my reason to stay alive.

I gathered enough wood to build a campfire to last through the night. I also wanted to make a spear for protection. I'd never made a fire without a match in my life. I'd seen it done on television, but I was not a pioneer woman. I may have been raised in the mountains, but I was never a Girl Scout, and my ability to survive in the woods was limited, to say the least.

I tried several techniques of rubbing sticks and banging rocks together. I finally saw smoke by twirling a branch against a stone. After a discouraging hour and some pauses for calls to nature, which I now suspected resulted from a combination of giardia and the blackberries, I gave up and kicked the whole thing in frustration. Julie had warned me not to drink the water. Knowing giardia had invaded most western streams in the last twenty-five years, she'd brought a canteen. I reassembled the sticks and had another go at the twirling branch, and, mother of God, I got a brief flame.

It took about three more attempts, and I had a fire, which then increased to a campfire that would make a Boy Scout proud.

Despite the gastro issues, I was hungry, which I was guessing was a good sign. I was now walking with confidence and went back to the creek to reassess the fish. The water was only three feet or so deep, but the fish were spooked. I spent a short time making a spear. It took until it was almost dark. After sharpening my knife several times on a granite rock and using a long tree branch, I had a nice four-foot-long spear.

I went hungry that night. I thought about making a net, but that would require wading and getting wet or getting naked. I would think about it tonight. I curled myself up as close to the fire as possible and slept fitfully, turning myself from side to side for warmth. I woke with a shock. A bear had moved into the area between me and the creek. I could barely see him in the dim early light, but it was watching the fish. The water level had dropped, and the bear waded into the water. It looked like a grizzly bear, but I was sure the grizzly population had been decimated, so I hoped it was just a bear that was not too scary. I grabbed a large branch from my reserve pile that I used to keep the fire going. This branch had pinecones and quickly was alight. The bear turned to me and appeared to be getting ready to charge. It reared up on its hind legs and roared. I was almost paralyzed with fright, but I waved the flaming branch toward him. The animal reared back and stopped, looked, turned, and trotted off.

No more sleep for me. I was climbing out of this hellhole today. I didn't care how much I hurt or how hungry I was. My gastrointestinal issues were getting better. I was stronger, and I had no option but to drink the water and suffer the consequences. I ate a few berries and looked once again at the trout in the pool. I had nothing to make a hook. I wondered if I could use my shirt to trap just one of the fish. I took off everything but my bra and undies. I looked down at the front clasp on my bra and realized the metal hooks might just work. I undid the seam and made a simple line. I dug near the water and found small grub-like creatures and slid one onto the metal hook I had fashioned from the bra. Bingo! I caught a nice trout. It was enough for breakfast and dinner, and that was it. The hook I had created from the clasp broke, as did the second one before I even got it off the bra. I must buy some new bras with my first paycheck. I slipped on my last attempt to catch another trout, and once again, I was immersed in the freezing water. This time I could dry the few clothes that were wet with a fire.

This made me think about the reason I was even in this situation. I was sure Julie was dead. I wondered if Mac would sell his practice now. I still had several bras. Obviously, my brain had turned to mush. I was clearly delirious, worrying about bras when I was in such a desperate situation. I thought about the reunion with Jeff and Lauren. I allowed myself to cry for a minute. The trout was cooked and eaten by the time the sun hit the water next to me. I picked a few more berries as I slowly walked past the bushes and started my ascent of the cliff face. I can also say I'm not a climber. I didn't have a fear of heights, but I had no experience going up rock faces. I went up what looked like a straightforward path only to be stopped with impassable obstacles, or I quickly slid back. That frightened me much more, as I saw how easily the eminent slide had occurred a few days previously.

After hours of ascents and descents, I made it up to the trail. It looked much smaller and rougher than I remembered. In fact, I wasn't sure it was the same track, but it headed along the side of the cliff back out of the mountainous forest.

I finally came to a clearing where Julie and I had observed the valley. Again, it wasn't the same. The fields had no fences. I saw no signs of irrigated pastures, and the area where Julie said *Comstock* had been filmed no longer looked like a ghost town. I figured it would take me another day to walk there. I gave a small sob thinking about spending one more night alone in the woods.

"Grow a set" was a common phrase the guys in my class would say. Jimmy Bond was one of the rougher guys, and he would say that to the shy, quiet girls to get them riled up. They would always turn red-faced, and, finally, one day, one of them said something like, "According to all the girls on campus, Jimmy, you're the one who needs to grow a set." Jimmy did not utter that phrase again. So, in honor of Jimmy, I told myself to grow a set. I had my spear, and I now knew how to make a fire. I would make it out alive.

Looking down on the *Comstock* set, I was perplexed. Clearly, the town was alive with people. They must be making a movie or another television series there. What I couldn't see was the large parking lot I was sure was there when we rode into the forest. I couldn't see any cars. How was I going to get back to the clinic after I made it down there? Maybe a helicopter would come to transport me. I would find out tomorrow. I only had to survive one more night.

With no water and no food, I was still warmer. I started my fire for protection and lay on the flat ground, feeling my aching limbs. There were no unwanted visitors, so I slept. Weak from lack of food and water and diarrhea, I put out the fire and started down the rough trail at daylight.

I reached the edge of the pretend town by noon or early afternoon. Walking down the main street, I observed a series of tepee-like huts on the edge of town. I noticed small children playing around the structures. They scurried into the tents as I approached. The children were well-cast as Native Americans. I decided this must be a movie set. It was a bit too realistic for a traditional television program.

I wandered farther into the town center, where the next block had only dilapidated lean-tos and canvas tents. The actors were all Asian. I remembered the street scene in Comstock. Two Chinese actors were arguing or chatting as one looked toward the town center. I wondered if I was disturbing the filming, although I didn't see any cameras. They might be hidden inside the walls of the structure?

In the middle of the street, I found a water trough. I was so thirsty that I didn't care if I shared it with horses. It had a pump, and I lifted the lever up and down. Actual water came out. I cupped one hand to drink and pumped with the other. Ducking my aching head under the running water, I cleaned my putrid head wound. I felt feverish and hoped this was not giardia, but I knew an infected wound was not good either. I needed antibiotics and probably a doctor. I wanted food, and I needed a ride back to the veterinary clinic. I knew there was currently an army of searchers.

I wondered if Jeff was among them. I was counting the minutes until I was reunited with him and Lauren. I was feeling dizzy. There were only a few people out on the main street. It was about noon, and I assumed everyone else was inside having lunch. My mouth watered at the thought. I closed my eyes and waited for someone to come to me.

# Chapter 3

## Chapter 3

I was unsure how long I was there, but a man sat beside me and asked me if I was all right. I opened my eyes and said, "No, I need food and a doctor and a phone."

"I can help with the food and doctor, but you have me with the phone," he replied

"I need to make a call to my husband."

"Oh, you mean a telegraph." His quizzical look was familiar. He was about six feet tall and had dark curly hair and black clothing. He kind of looked and sounded like Clint Buchanan of the *Comstock* series, but he was much younger. This actor was the spitting image of a young Clint — great casting.

"Where's everyone? I think I need some help." I looked down the street and only saw possibly three men and no women. The men were all in Western costumes. They were dressed in old-time clothes of the 1800s. "Are you making a movie, or is this a television show?"

He looked perplexed and replied, "I'm not sure what you're talking about, ma'am. Most of the men are in the saloon. There was a strike, and everyone's celebrating."

"Why would men celebrate a strike? Isn't that bad for the production?"

He looked at me again and yelled to a young man with his back turned to us across the street. "Hank, can you come over and help this..." he looked me up and down, "lady?"

*Ah, so this was a remake of Comstock.* These guys really took it seriously. I couldn't imagine them using their stage names when they weren't shooting. From a distance, the second man looked like the character "Hank" on *Comstock*. He was tall, had a green shirt, brown vest, and large high-crowned felt hat, but this man was much younger.

"There was a rockslide up in the mountains." I pointed to the area, which could be seen from where we sat on a bench. "My friend Julie and I were separated. I'm pretty sure she and our horses are dead. I have a laceration on the back of my head, and I need antibiotics and food. I've been up there for three or four days. I'm not sure. I ate some trout, but I need food. I must contact my husband and Julie's husband, too." I almost cried.

The actor playing Hank came over. "Ma'am, can we help you?"

"Will you take me to a doctor? Do you have one on the set?"

They looked at me and then at one another.

"Look, I know who you are supposed to be. You're Clint Buchanan, and you're Hank Buchanan, but you need to step back from the acting, and please get me some help." I stood up, and each man grabbed my arm, which was painful due to the bruising.

"You have us at a disadvantage. You seem to know us, but we don't know who you are. "The actor playing a young Clint looked at the man playing young Hank with another puzzled look. "Who are you?"

"Clint, she's deranged. Let's get her over to the Doc's." The man, really a boy, playing Hank, turned me around and started to almost frog-march me to the small white building on the opposite side from the saloon. I was relieved.

"My name is Rebecca. I'm here in the county to interview for a position as a vet at the clinic outside Tahoe. I was riding with the clinic owner, Julie Smyth, when a rockslide occurred. I saw her go down, and I think she's probably dead. I need to get back to town."

"Woman vet?" The Clint character looked at me, then at the man playing Hank, and shook his head.

"Ain't no such thing, is there, Clint?" replied the Hank character.

I was so weak I buckled. The two boys locked arms behind my back and propelled me to the doctor's office. There was a sign that read "Dr. Sullivan" hanging on a shingle outside the door. We entered, and they sat me down on a chair. The Hank character knocked on a second door and called out for Mrs. Sullivan. She opened the door, looked at the boys and me, and instructed them to bring me in. They helped me stand up, took me to a room with a bed, and laid me down.

"Mrs. Sullivan, she was just sitting by the horse trough, and she isn't making sense. She has a nasty gash behind her head. She thinks someone is dead in the mountains. She wants to send a message to her husband. She says she's a vet."

I looked around. It was a simple room with a bed, desk, and chair. Mrs. Sullivan appeared to be in her fifties. She was plump, with gray hair and a kind smile.

"Do you have some food? I don't have any money, but my husband can pay you when he gets here." They looked concerned, but I could see they thought I wasn't making sense, so typical of actors and actresses today. "I can give you his number, and you can call him."

Mrs. Sullivan looked at the junior versions of the Buchanans and shook her head. "Can you boys call the sheriff?"

"Oh, thank you." *Finally, some progress.* "I'm sure they'll sort it out. I just need to get home."

The young male actors left the office, and Mrs. Sullivan suggested I get out of my clothes and into a shift hanging on a hook near the bed. "Paul will be back shortly. He just went to have a quick drink with the boys. Did you hear there was a strike?"

This situation was just plain weird. "What do you mean by a strike?" I wasn't so sure that she meant an industrial strike.

"Silver, my dear. The town will be awash in money in no time. Quite a few townsfolk owe us money. We're just about broke. You can eat only so many chickens and eggs. The miners are on their knees today."

Mrs. Sullivan left the room, and I slipped into the gown. I was careful to hide both my knife and the picture of Jeff and Lauren, along with my driver's license.

She brought chicken and potato soup. It was the most delicious meal I have ever eaten without a single spice. She had me lie with my face down on the bed and cleaned and dress the gash on the back of my head. "My husband will look at this soon. You may have cracked your skull. Why don't you rest a bit until he gets back? I'll try to clean your clothes for you."

"Thank you, ma'am."

She said something more, but I was asleep. Exhaustion overtook any other needs. I woke to total darkness. I was alone in a clean bed and with clean clothes. I would request a shower in the morning. I could feel my aches and pains, but had renewed energy. I was sure Jeff would be there when it was daylight. I fell asleep again and woke up mid-morning.

An older man sat at a desk across the room, reading a newspaper. Perched on the edge of the desk was another man in a light-brown plaid wool shirt with a badge on his vest.

"Welcome back." The man in the chair smiled. "I'm Dr. Sullivan, and this is Deputy sheriff Frasier."

The man with the badge tipped his hat. "Howdy, ma'am, you seem to be in a state. Can you tell us how you got here and where you're from?"

I retold my story, but something made me stop. I could see the men adopted a Twilight Zone look. I played the music in my mind. I needed to be careful. It was as if I were in another century—about a hundred years earlier. I laughed to myself. Everyone was dressed and acted as if they were in the 1800s. I was the odd one. I must be dreaming.

Was I dreaming or dead? Was this place heaven? I knew I had a mild concussion, but surely this was all imagined.

"My name is Rebecca Harper. I'm originally from Montana, but I have been attending college back East. I'm here to work. I was with a friend, and we were separated from each other in a rockfall. I'm almost certain she and our horses were all killed in the slide. I don't remember what the trail is called, but it's in the mountains. I'm trying to get back home. My husband is Jeff Harper, and I have a daughter who is only three years old. I would like to contact them."

I left it at that. I doubted this was a movie set. I was now thinking about a cult. I was worried about what they believed about me and my story. I remembered the cult that killed all its members in Guyana. I was nervous. I was glad I'd put my picture and driver's license in my boot. The idea of the cult was growing in my mind. I had to consider that it might be a bad dream as well. I almost chuckled at that thought. *Wake me up.*

"Young lady, do you know where you are?" The sheriff walked toward the bed and placed his hand on my forehead. "Doc, she's feverish. Maybe we should see if she comes out of this before I send out any telegrams."

"Do you have any antibiotics?" I inquired. The sheriff looked at the doctor, and they both shrugged.

"I packed your wound with sulfur, so let's just hope the lockjaw doesn't set in."

"I had my shots." Again, the quizzical looks. I was sure these people lived in a time warp of their own making — kind of like the Mennonites or another sect.

After the sheriff left, the doctor also came over and felt my head. He told me I felt feverish, and he would make something for me. He left the room but returned soon with his wife. They sat me up and gave me something very bitter to drink. They closed the shades and suggested I try to sleep.

I felt I was being held captive. I was apprehensive. These people seemed to be honestly concerned. I thought they were trying to help, but the doctor knew little about medicine. I became drowsy, and a kind of euphoric feeling washed over me. Mrs. Sullivan held my hand until I drifted off to sleep.

I awoke in the pre-dawn morning. A full moon provided enough light to read. I climbed out of bed and walked over to the desk. I picked up the newspaper to determine what was happening in the world. Sadly, it was not the U.S. News. It was a local paper. The headline read, "Cattleman Gets the Contract to Feed the Army." It continued to talk about Sam Buchanan of the Cattle Creek Ranch winning the contract to sell nine hundred cattle to the U.S. Army engaged in the Indian Wars.

I could not for the life of me put this publication into my reality. I looked at a few other short stories about the Nevada Territory. Finally, I saw the date: June 15th, 1857.

# CHAPTER 4

I reread the headlines and dates. I opened the paper to the next page. The society page mentioned the church news, as well as the new judge who would begin riding the circuit from Reno to other towns. It made little sense. *I must be dreaming.* Was I living in a world of the Buchanans and the Cattle Creek Ranch? They were not even real in the 1800s in Virginia City. Was I dead? I just wanted to get home to my husband and child. *Oh, please let me wake up.*

I looked for my clothes. I was going to walk out of this town, and the dream — this nightmare — would end. I walked to the window. I needed to pee. Where was the bathroom? Did I have to use an outhouse? I wanted to leave now. I went to open the door, and it was locked. Oh my God, they were holding me as a prisoner. I had just a nightgown and my boots on, but I was getting out. I went to the window and found I could open it. Because I was on the ground floor, I eased over the windowsill and slid down. It was early, and I assumed the town was sleeping off yesterday's strike celebrations.

I needed food before I made my way out of town. I walked behind what I'd thought were facades of the main street. They were, in fact, actual houses. They were not as fancy as I remembered on *Comstock*, but real, nonetheless. I saw what I thought was a cellar and wondered if people kept their produce in there. I would like to say I'd never steal, but these were desperate times. There were onions, carrots, potatoes, and jars of peaches. I took some carrots and a jar of peaches, and I headed out of the still-sleeping town. A dog barked for a few seconds but stopped when I passed it. I turned and smiled at it, and the dog sheepishly wagged its tail and wandered off. The Indian village was stirring. Women peeked out of their tepees and stared in my direction. These women didn't show any interest in me, except for my apparent lack of clothing. The last place I passed was a hovel where a clothesline with a family's wash hung on the line. I was going to start my career in crime with a bang. I grabbed boys' pants, shirts, and even a jacket. As I returned to the road that led me into town, I remembered I'd left my spear a mile or so up the road. I retrieved it and used the nightgown to stow my booty from my life of crime. I was incredibly excited about the glass jar.

I planned to retrace my steps, up to where I had come, and try the other road to head back to where we parked Julie's vehicle. I stopped for nature's call. I continued on my way back to the place where we'd left the truck and trailer. I was sure I could find my way. After several hours, my assurance was waning. I doubted my memory. I could hear what sounded like a horse and wagon, so I stepped off the path to hide. I would not be held hostage again. I watched two men on a long buckboard driving four horses. They moved at a trot. One horse was noticeably lame.

The driver pulled up, got off, and examined the leg while I watched from behind a tree. He was tall, with salt-and-pepper hair. His companion was a smaller, stocky Chinese man. The older man yelled to the smaller man to hold the reins tight.

"Yes, Mister Sam, you know Gee Ling will do his best," I heard him say.

The taller man turned toward where I hid. For an instant, I thought I was looking at Colin Chandler or a very young Sam Buchanan. I watched the man pick up the leg of the lame horse. He went to the buckboard and retrieved a metal hook. He used the implement to pry a large stone out of the hoof. The bigger man jumped up on the buckboard, and they walked the horses for a few feet and watched the lame horse, which now was only mildly limping. They resumed their fast pace heading toward the town. My heart was pounding. *I've now seen younger versions of the three Buchanans and Gee Ling. Wake me up, please.*

# Chapter 5

The ascent of the mountain and my aching body made progress slow. I ate some carrots and what might have been a beetroot. Shaking from the effort, I finally reached the branch in the road where I needed to turn toward the truck and trailer. I was sure there were no signs when Julie and I were heading out. Still, now I could see a wooden sign with an arrow pointing to town, another pointing to Lake Tahoe, and one that led to the Cattle Creek Ranch. I muttered to myself, *Toto, I don't think we're in Kansas.*

I was sure the road to the truck and trailer was the same as the path that headed to the Cattle Creek Ranch. I was confused, but I was convinced that was the way I needed to go. My legs ached. The clothes I stole were way too big and chafed against my body, and I had no bra. After breastfeeding, let's just say firm and perky had gone out the window. I was still carrying a bit of baby fat, but I had lost a considerable amount of weight in the last few days. Much of that was in the milk bar area, so the nipples were particularly swinging, and friction took its toll on them. I needed a bra. I was no hippie. I needed support — lots of support. I had gone from a double A cup to a good C cup. With any luck, there was no going back.

It was late in the afternoon. While I had food, I was contemplating another night in the woods. Clouds gathered overhead. I had more protection from the trees, but a night without a fire, if it rained, and spending a soaking night in the forest were frightening prospects. I kind of gasped when I saw lightning. Okay, I may have actually cried. I kept pinching myself and wanting to wake up from this nightmare. More lightning and a pummeling rain drowned out the sound of an approaching wagon and horses coming from behind me. I knew for sure I'd been spotted this time. I stepped to the side for them to pass, but they pulled up and offered me a ride. A large canvas covered them. It was young Sam Buchanan and Gee Ling whom I'd seen earlier. I weighed the options. I could either spend a night out in the rain or a night in a dry barn of — dare I dream — the Cattle Creek Ranch?

"Thanks, yes." I climbed into the back of the buckboard, but young Sam, or should I say, Mr. Buchanan, said, "No." He extended his hand and told me to climb up in between him and Gee Ling.

"I'm Sam Buchanan, and this is my cook, Gee Ling. Are you Rebecca? My boys described a woman they met in town, and your departure from the town has sparked some discussion." He looked at me wryly.

I shrunk in the seat. I responded, "Guilty." I think honesty is usually the best policy. "I'm lost and trying to get back to where I took off a few days ago. There was a rockslide." I pointed behind me. "I was with another woman, and I'm fairly certain she and our horses are dead." I could feel the tears and exhaustion welling up, but I was fighting it. Whoever this guy was, I could tell he was uncomfortable with female emotions. I stopped for a few seconds. "I'm trying to get back to my husband and baby. If I can return to where I started, I'm sure I can reach them." That was all the info I was offering until I knew where I was and the date. Was I in the 1800s or 1900s?

"We still have an hour, but you're welcome to stay at the Cattle Creek Ranch tonight."

I could not believe my ears. The Cattle Creek Ranch! I was shocked and intrigued all at once. This was a mythical television family and was never part of history. The two men on each side of me were fictional television characters, and yet they were as real as real could be. I could feel, touch, and certainly smell them. I heard his words. My mind was exploding. I could feel a headache coming on, which only added to my aching body.

"Well, if I could just stay in the barn, that would be appreciated."

"Mister Sam, she can sleep in my bed." I turned to Gee Ling and looked gratefully at him.

"Rebecca can stay in the guest room. What's your last name?" He looked ten years younger than he did when he was the television version of Sam Buchanan. There was more dark hair than gray, and he had a youthful appearance. Gee Ling looked much younger, too. He had the spicy smell that you would expect of a Chinese cook.

"It's Harper, and the barn will be fine. I must tell you I have no money. I have no way of repaying you." I could not see the point in mentioning I was a vet, but maybe he'd already heard that from his sons.

"Miss Rebecca can help me in the cookhouse, Mr. Sam." Gee Ling pulled out a paper, rolled a cigarette, and lit it with a flint.

"You smoke?" I blurted out. "That's not good for you." Oh, damn, what was I saying? I looked down and tried to make myself disappear. Both men shrugged. Now that I thought about it, I could smell sweet tobacco on both men. I remembered the television Sam Buchanan smoked a pipe.

"I think we can find something for her to do for a day or so," replied the young Sam Buchanan.

"It will be just for tonight. I'll be gone by daylight."

In the warmth of the two men and the cessation of conversation, I drowsed. I woke up leaning on Gee Ling, with drool slipping down my cheek. I lurched up and realized I was at the Cattle Creek Ranch.

We pulled up in front of the house and next to the barn. This was not the same barn as on the television show. The jasmine bush, so prominent in the television series, extending up to the roof of the first story, was just a tiny bush in front of the house. Even the house seemed smaller than the one shown on the television program, but the structure was unmistakable. The men each descended off the buckboard. They both appeared ready to catch me and help me down, but I turned and climbed down, facing away from them. I was too sore to jump, but I slid down to the ground. I staggered backward and bumped into Sam Buchanan. He placed his hands on my shoulder and asked if I was all right.

"Yes, of course." But really, I wasn't at all. I needed to go; I was cold, and I ached. I looked at the barn and just wanted to go in and lie down.

They pointed to the outhouse. "Come into the house after."

As I walked, or even half ran, to the outhouse, I could see three young men come out of the house. They didn't see me. They were pulling back the tarp and unloading provisions. I heard one ask, "Did you see her?" I saw Sam Buchanan pointing toward me and to the outhouse.

I walked out and saw the boys carrying the wooden crates into the side of the house. Gee Ling was examining the contents of each box and directing the boys to either the kitchen or around the back to a cellar.

I walked to the back of the buckboard when they were all inside and grabbed a box. As I walked toward the house, a teenage boy confronted me. He was clearly a youthful Danny. "Ma'am, I'll take that." I handed him the box and went back to the buckboard, and grabbed another. All the men came out and told me to go inside and sit down. It was raining again, and a flash of light indicated thunder was imminent.

Before I went in, I looked at the horse that had stepped on a rock. I had noticed he was limping again. I ran my hand down his leg and felt for a pulse. He was still harnessed. His entire cannon and pastern areas were swollen. I picked up his leg and palpated his tendons. The deep digital flexor tendon was painful to palpation. Icing would be good. Did they have ice? I saw Hank paint liniment on horses' legs in many episodes. In my dream, was there going to be some in the barn?

I looked at Hank and Danny as they returned to the buckboard for the last of the boxes. Hank came around to unhitch the horses and saw me looking at the lame gelding.

"Hank, do you have any liniment in the barn?" I asked. "Your horse has a bowed tendon on his right-front leg."

I pointed to the leg, and Hank said, "Oh, ma'am, that's an old bow, but it looks like it might have flared up a bit. I have something in the barn."

It was pouring rain. I helped Hank unharness that gelding and took him into the barn. Hank brought the other three, put them away, and gave them some hay. I held the injured gelding, and Hank returned with the liniment. The label read, "Doctor Chester Horse Elixir" and claimed it was good for colic, heaves, and 'all' leg ailments. It contained camphor, but the other smells were strange. Hank applied it to the gelding's leg.

"Do you have a bandage?"

"Yes, ma'am." He returned with a cotton roll from the cabinet. I bandaged the leg and pinned it. I would say that Hank might have been impressed with my neat bandage, but I might kid myself.

I looked at a foal in a stall with knocked-kneed legs. In vet school, I'd learned that the condition is called carpal valgus. It's seen in some newborn foals. There is a surgical procedure, but I didn't mention it. I knew that rasping the feet would help. I didn't elaborate. I asked Hank what he was doing with the foal, and he said he was hoping the legs would straighten on their own.

"I can smell Gee Ling's cooking. You don't want to be late for dinner at the Cattle Creek Ranch, ma'am," said Hank.

"I'll stay out here in the barn, but thanks," I replied.

"My pa would skin me if I didn't get you in the house. Anyway, I think you just earned your dinner. How'd you become a lady vet, anyhow?" he asked.

I wasn't sure if any vet schools existed. I thought about it and said, "My father was a vet, and he taught me." I thought that was a pretty plausible explanation if this were in the 1800s.

"Let's go." The rain was making it hard to hear in the barn, but it was warm and dry. I hesitated, and Hank grabbed me by the hand and pulled me under his jacket, which he had taken off to spread over our heads. I slipped in the mud, and he caught me before I went down. I winced when he grabbed my back.

"Oh, sorry, ma'am," he shouted above the thunder that was almost non-stop. We stopped on the porch and re-moved our boots. I no longer had socks, and the bruises on my feet were evident to anyone who looked.

"Oh, Lord, ma'am," Hank said. "Can I help you?"

"No. I know the bruises look bad, but they don't hurt anymore. It's just bruising. It'll be fine." The most delicious and pungent smell hit me. I almost swooned at the sight of a roast, potatoes, and corn.

"I'm fairly proud of my cooking since Gee Ling wasn't here today," said Danny.

"Danny, you should be," I replied.

A puzzled look came over my host.

"Well, I was going to introduce my youngest son, but perhaps you've already met?" Sam Buchanan held out a chair for me at the end of the table. I sat down and clearly blushed and stammered.

"I think Mrs. Sullivan told me about him." I was going to have to watch myself. I believed this was not an era when witches were hanged, but I pretty much would fit the category.

They said grace, and the boys fought over serving me this delicious meal. As per the *Comstock* television series, Gee Ling served the food and ate in the kitchen. Many of the commentators of my day were critical of his role as a Chinese cook. He appeared to be happy, and he was probably in an enviable position. Still, I didn't approve.

While I had the perspective of time, I would not rock the boat. One meal, one sleep, and I was off to another century. I hoped. The thought made me almost cry. I caught myself and hoped no one noticed.

"Dr. Harper, where are your husband and child?" Clint seemed to question my circumstances.

I looked at him and knew he was even younger than I was in this instance. I had watched him age on television, first as Clint Buchanan and then as a television police sergeant. It was surreal.

"Back East." I looked at the Buchanans and realized I needed to give a slightly better account of myself. I thought of a more detailed answer.

"My husband and I are from Missouri. He and my daughter were heading out to meet me here. His train was damaged by fire, thankfully before he boarded, and they're now coming by covered wagon to meet me in Sacramento." I thought that sounded like a believable explanation that might make everything look acceptable.

"Where in Missouri?" asked Sam Buchanan as he leaned forward and put his chin on his hand, waiting for an answer. I could feel the trap.

"St. Louis. I was raised in Montana, but my husband's family is from a small town near there. He's a veterinarian, too."

"How old is your daughter?" The noose was tightening.

"Lauren is three. She's the spitting image of her father and the light of her grandmother's eye. Mrs. Harper, my mother-in-law, just adores her, and that is why I left them to come out and establish a home first. I knew she was in safe hands. I know it seems unusual, but I'm an independent person, and my husband was happy to wait for me to come first. We have a, shall we say, more modern relationship."

Oh boy, that was totally ridiculous. Why didn't I just call these men for what they were: figments of my imagination and a dream? I should have grilled them. As lovely as they were, I just wanted to get home to Jeff. The strangest aspect was that when I watched *Comstock* as a child, they were all older than me. Now, I'm closer in age to Sam Buchanan than to any of the three boys. I had to be older than Clint by at least ten years. Creepy. The television Sam Buchanan was nearly a grandfather figure, but this man was probably close to my husband's age. My head was spinning.

"Do you mind if I go back to the barn? I'm really bushed." Again, the perplexed looks. "Tired," I replied to their curious gazes. I needed to watch my language. I was leaving the Cattle Creek Ranch, but if I encountered others from this time, I would have to talk as if I were one of them.

"There will be no barn for you tonight. If you want to leave early, you can sleep down here." Sam Buchanan pointed to a room right off the dining room.

"Thank you, Mr. Buchanan. I'm so tired. I hope you won't think it rude of me to retire early?"

"Please call me Sam. No, we understand. You've been through a lot. I stopped and talked to Dr. Sullivan, and he told me about the rockslide and losing your friend and horses. I'll tell you what, if you stay the day, I'll have the boys go up and check out the slide area and find out if they can retrieve her body or anything you may have lost."

I was torn between my loyalty to Julie, whose body was probably still buried under the boulders, and my desire to get back to my family.

"Just one day, but perhaps I could be of help with your horses? I know a trick to correct the foal with knock-knees." I thought this was an old term, but they again looked confused. "Do you have a pen and paper?"

"Danny." Sam pointed to his desk.

"Right, Pa." I had to stifle a laugh. I remember that was a phrase he said so often in the television series. It was predictable. He jumped up and retrieved an ink pen and paper. I hoped I didn't look too much like a novice using this writing material. I faltered, holding the pen and wondering how to dip it in ink. While the boys were curious, Sam Buchanan showed me how the quill worked by dropping it into an inkwell. I drew the legs of the foal and asked what they would call them. They said, "Bandy-legged."

I showed them where one side of each leg grew faster than the other side. In this case, the inside grew faster. "If you frequently trimmed the hoof on the outside, it would release the pressure on the slow-growing side and maintain compression on the fast-growing side. As the foal grows, the legs will straighten to some degree." Of course, there is a modern surgical treatment where the periosteum, the tissue covering the bone, is transected on the slow-growing side, allowing a significant straightening compared to the hoof trimming method, but that was not possible now. If 'now' was what I was thinking it was: in the 1800s.

"I'm exhausted. I'm sorry. I can help Gee Ling with the dishes, and then I must retire." Gee Ling brought out two cups of coffee. I figured the boys were too young to drink coffee. Sam poured two glasses of brandy and handed one to me.

"I'm guessing such a modern woman has an after-dinner drink. Please no dishes, and this will help you sleep."

"You not do dishes on your first night here at Cattle Creek Ranch," chimed in Gee Ling.

I took a taste and coughed, but I drank it.

A chorus of "pleasant dreams" chased me to bed. A beautiful nightgown and bathrobe were on the chair next to the bed. A chamber pot was beneath the bed. How the hell do you use that? And then I was dead to the world.

# CHAPTER 6

I overslept big-time. The sun was truly up when I awoke. Again, some more suitable clothes were on the bed. I had a choice of either a fancy riding outfit or a long dress. Three guesses. I used the chamber pot reluctantly and donned the riding outfit. Still no bra, but there was a corset that I ignored.

I came out of my room and was hit by the aroma of breakfast. On the table were eggs, bacon, pancakes, and even milk. I would have settled for Rice Krispies, but what's a girl to do? Sam was sitting at the table reading a newspaper. His coffee had just been refreshed. He smiled and inquired how I had slept.

"Well, I think."

"Missy like coffee?" asked Gee Ling as he came around the corner of the kitchen.

"Oh yes, please." I realized I had not had coffee for days. Fearing insomnia, I hadn't drunk the coffee offered last night, and the smell was overwhelming.

"Where are your boys?"

"They took off early up to the spot where you said the slide happened. I thought if you don't mind, I would have you look at a few of my horses, and maybe I could show you some of the Cattle Creek Ranch while we wait for them to return."

I was feeling the dread of the interrogation, but it would be nice to repay their hospitality. "That would be lovely." Lovely, really? I'm using words like 'lovely?' I had to think about the conversation style I learned in my youth from watching *Comstock*. I thought this would be a safe but interesting test. "Does the phrase 'Comstock Lode' mean anything to you?" I asked.

"I know a Henry Comstock, or did you mean something else? Most folks call him Old Pancake. Is that who you are referring to?"

"No, just asking." I ate all I could without embarrassing myself. I figured a toothbrush was out of the question. I excused myself and went to my room. When I returned, Sam had two horses saddled and tethered to a hitching post. Of course, he had a buckskin gelding, which is what he rode in the television series. Next to the gelding was a beautiful copper chestnut mare. I walked up and patted her. I reached for the saddle and placed the stirrup under my arm to see the length of the stirrups. They were perfect.

"Oh, I judged correctly," Sam laughed.

"Yep. Where are we off to?" Was 'yep' too informal?

"The breakers are up about a mile from here. I thought we could go see a couple of the colts."

"Lead the way." I mounted quickly, despite my bruising. I wondered how I was being judged. "I can trim and rasp the foal's feet before we go if you like."

"Let's wait until the boys are back. Hank does most of that, and you can show him. You're pretty close to my wife's size. This saddle belonged to her, but I have a sidesaddle if you prefer. I never gave away her clothes. You're welcome to whatever you need. That's where she had her stirrups."

At five foot three inches, I was average in height for the 1800s but small for my time. "No, this is fine. I can't thank you enough. I hope there's something I can do to help and repay you."

"That foal over there with the bandy legs was supposed to be Cash's replacement. He's from the same dam, and the stallion is related to Cash, so I was hoping to replace Cash with this colt. When he was born, and with his crooked legs, I thought I was going to have to try again, though."

"It's not genetic." Did I just say genetic? "My father says it's from the foal cramped in the uterus." Did I just say 'uterus' to a proper Victorian man? He blushed.

I tried to remember the names of the Buchanan horses from *Comstock*, but I couldn't. I didn't see the boys' mounts. I wondered if they also rode horses that matched their television counterparts.

We rode out to a remote enclave where a modest lean-to was adjacent to a corral, and several men were milling about. There was a large paddock alongside the corral where thirty or so horses were kept. Large mounds of hay were placed in the paddock, and the horses were eating. I wondered about parasite control. How did they address that problem, or did they? Was tobacco used then?

"Morning, Mr. Buchanan," said the man leaning on the rail. "We already got the first ten ridden. The men are taking a break, and then we will get to the next set. Good news, no one's been bucked off this morning so far."

"That's because my boys are out doing other chores today," laughed Sam.

"Now, Mr. Buchanan, that youngest lad is going to be a top hand, and the other two can match any one of my men."

"Gil, you lookin' for a raise?" mused Sam.

"Always," said Gil with a wry smile.

Gil looked toward me. "Howdy, ma'am."

"Hello. I'm Becky."

"Yes, ma'am, pleased to meet you." Gil obviously wondered who I was.

"Mrs., or should I say, Dr. Harper, is on her way to meet her husband. They both care for horses. I thought she might look at some of the lame stock we culled."

"Yes, sir. I might get someone to take you to them. They are way down the way near the canyon." Gil pointed to some hills, where they joined the prairie like a grizzly bear's claws stretched out and scratching.

Sam examined the horses and seemed to be happy with them. The horses were rough compared with what I was accustomed to. Many had ewe necks, and on average, were thinner with less musculature and body fat than quarter horses of today. I laughed to myself, considering the concept of 'today.' Which today? I wondered if the black stallion with the white tip on his nose was in this herd. He had always been one of my favorite horses on the television series. But then again, I seemed to be here five or ten years before the television *Comstock* ever occurred.

"Do you have a black stallion?" I asked.

"No, but that's about all we don't have here. You name the color, and we have it."

I looked at five horses with injuries ranging from hoof problems to a fractured splint bone. Given my lack of anesthetics, syringes, and tools, I would not be able to do much. Antibiotics would have helped a mare with a laceration. I suggested packing the wound with honey. They'd been using some tar ointment.

As we rode back to the house, a young man rode up and excitedly told Sam his mare was foaling. Sam shouted, "Can you gallop?"

Can I gallop? Pfft. I grinned and nodded. We took off back to the main house. Next to the barn, in the corral, a dun mare lay panting. Three men stood over her.

"It don't look good, boss." The men were looking at her heaving flank.

I asked if her water had broken. They replied several minutes ago, but nothing was coming out. They thought they saw something white, but the mare got up and repositioned herself, and nothing had progressed since then. Sam rolled up his sleeve. Without even cleaning his arm, he stuck his hand in her vagina up to his elbow. The television Sam Buchanan would sort this out quick-smart, but the man I was looking at could not. He quickly yelled for one of the men to ride to town to get the liveryman. He apparently was the only knowledgeable horse doctor close by. It was a two-hour trip each way. We might save the mare, but the foal was going to die. No pain, no gain. No guts, no glory. God does not love a coward.

"Get me some clean water and soap." I was totally ignored. "I may be able to save this foal."

Again, the men were so busy doing nothing, and they didn't hear me. Gee Ling, who had come out to see what the yelling was about, heard me. He ran to the house. He came back with a bucket of water and soap. "Can you get me a small rope, please?"

Finally, the men looked at me as I rolled up my sleeve and washed my arms. The mare was down and was occasionally rolling on her back. If I got down flat on the ground, I would miss the hooves as she flailed around in agony. I would have killed for some anesthesia, but I entered the vagina and quickly recognized a nose and one hoof. I ran my hand down the foal's shoulder and could just feel the foal's knee flexed and stuck on the brim of the pelvis. As the mare contracted and pushed, my hand and arm were crushed against the pelvic brim. The pain was almost unbearable due to my prior injuries.

I withdrew my hand and grabbed the rope. Trying to force the end of the twine past the mare's pelvic brim along the outside of the foal's knee took several minutes, but I finally had the line down far enough to feel it on the inside of the leg. Despite my pain, I could bring out the twine and make a loop around the flexed leg. I asked the men to pull up on the rope, and I put my hand in and directed the foal's leg up and over the bony pelvic brim along with the head. The foal was big, and I thought we were going to have to pull both legs. I took the other end of the rope and made a slipknot and then a half hitch around the other leg.

The mare was quietly lying on her side, so I sat up and braced my feet on her thighs. I asked the men to help me pull the ropes and legs down toward her hocks. The head was not coming, but I could see both hooves and pasterns, so I got up, reached in, and pulled the foal's head around. Then we all pulled at once.

Whoosh. Out came a black foal with a white snip on its nose. The birthing waters gushed out as well, and I was instantly soaked in fetal fluids. The entire process lasted thirty or more minutes. During that time, hardly a word was spoken. I was wet, and my hands and arms were aching. The slippery white amnion covering the foal retreated as the colt moved. I just sat there and watched the foal become more and more lively. Someone began to move the foal, but I stopped him. "The foal's getting blood from the placenta. Don't break the cord too soon." I inched away like a crab, and Sam grabbed me and helped me stand up.

There is nothing better than a moment like this. I'd helped my dad many times. I worked in the horse barn at vet school, which was how I met my husband. I had helped half a dozen mares, but Jeff or one of his professors was always present. This was my first solo dystocia, and there would be no picture or video to show Jeff what I'd done to save the mare and foal.

I don't think I had smiled this much since the rockslide, but I couldn't wipe the grin off my face. The entire crew were smiling and patting each other's backs. My classmates had used high fives in vet school. Maybe I could give it an earlier start. Or not.

"What is it, colt or filly?" asked one of the men. The amnion was still covering the hindquarters. I didn't have to look — it was the black stallion. I turned and walked away from the men and the sternal mare and foal. I was close to tears, and I sure didn't want anyone to see me. Gee Ling did. He came up and put his arm over my shoulder. We didn't say a word. He knew I was overcome. After a minute, the mare stood up, breaking the umbilical cord.

"Have you got iodine?" I inquired with a wavering voice.

One of the men went in and brought out a bottle. I dashed a bit on the umbilicus, knowing this was not the tamed iodine I was used to. This would scald, and I tried to keep it off the foal's abdomen. "Iodine helps prevent lockjaw," I explained. "It prevents joint ill, too." I think they used that phrase back then. At that moment, I didn't care. I had just saved a life, and I could not share it with my husband.

I turned around, and Sam was behind me. I could see he was happy and yet quite confused. Sam hugged me and thanked me. He realized he'd just been baptized in placental fluids as well. "Gee Ling, will you draw a bath for our guest? Oh, and get some more of Mrs. Buchanan's clothes. It's time they saw the light of day."

"Yes, Mr. Sam. I cook big meal for Missy here. I have so much to do." He announced his dinner plans, and then his broken English turned to Cantonese.

"I can peel potatoes and cut beans and whatever else you need."

"No, missy, you guest of honor. You no help tonight."

We walked together to the house, and immediately before I entered, I heard the men say, "By gosh, it's a colt, boss. Look at him. You'll have your stallion in a few years, Mr. Buchanan."

I just smiled.

# CHAPTER 7

A small metal tub was in the room down the hall from the kitchen. Gee Ling filled it with hot water by adding boiling water to warm the water in the tub. When the copper container reached a pleasant temperature, Gee Ling handed me a hard soap with a floral smell. He'd placed a dress and undergarments for me in the room. He instructed me to leave my riding outfit outside the door, and he would wash it with my clothes from the previous day. I set them outside the door and gently eased myself down into the deliciously warm water. Gee Ling had added some fragrant salts.

This was my first bath or shower in what had probably been a week. I had to be careful with my head laceration, which was now healing. I knew Mrs. Sullivan had helped me with a sponge bath, but this was pure luxury. I could have stayed forever, but it was getting cold. Reluctantly, and I mean very reluctantly, I got out. There was a small cloth, which I assumed was used to dry myself. I looked at the undergarments and could not figure out the trusses, so I ignored them. Once again, I let things fly in the wind. The dress was a long, sheer, green single piece. I wondered if Danny would be offended that his father had lent his mother's clothes to me for the evening. All the boys had different mothers, as was not uncommon during this period due to difficulties with childbirth and other harsh conditions in the 1800s. It must have been mid-afternoon. I went out to the corral, and the men all looked at me in a new light. I'm not a dress kind of girl. My father said I was 'all the boy he ever needed.' But wearing one of the beautiful dresses featured in the Comstock series was not the worst thing.

The black colt was now cantering around his mother and aggressively nursing. Several men complimented me on my birthing skills. I was delighted, but my one regret was I could not share this moment with my husband. He would have been so proud. He was not a man who needed the glory and limelight. He would be just as happy if one of his students performed something and received the credit rather than himself. I could once again feel my eyes watering. I saved the black stallion that would someday populate the Cattle Creek Ranch herd and increase its business empire. It was then I became convinced this experience was all a dream. It was the most extended dream I ever had. I hoped it would end soon.

It was fun to meet these people, but it was time to get back. Would going back up the mountain and traveling in another direction get me there or not? Maybe I had to try something else. I lay down on the bed for a few minutes. Sleep was the tonic that seemed to save me. I dreamed I was back with Jeff and holding Lauren, who repeated, "Mama,

Mama, Mama." Oh, how I missed holding her and smelling her hair.

A knock on the door woke me up. It was Clint. "Ma'am, it's time for dinner."

I gazed around the room and realized I'd slept well beyond the thirty minutes I'd planned. It was growing dark. The house lanterns were already lit. I emerged from the room and noticed the Buchanans all formally dressed for dinner.

They pointed to the chair at the end of the table once more. I sat down, and Sam poured wine for everyone but Danny.

They raised their glasses and toasted me. "To our guest, who saved the Cattle Creek Ranch breeding lines today. Hear, hear!" exclaimed Sam.

Hank took a sip and pursed his lips. "He is one nice colt, Pa, but I sure don't know why anyone would ever like wine."

Danny reached for Hank's glass, but one look from his father, and he retracted his hand and looked down at his plate. Now, this was the family I had watched for so long. I smiled inwardly.

"Yes, he will play a big part in your lives, I'm sure," I replied. The response was polite, but I could tell I had not really convinced them. I had the advantage of watching countless episodes of Comstock, in which this colt had played a prominent role. I hoped they would now believe I was a vet, but somehow, I doubted it.

The dinner was delicious and filling. I sensed the family had news for me, and I waited with dread. After dinner, we all moved to the living area in front of the enormous fireplace. Because it was summer and hot, no fire was burning. I looked at the three boys. Clint leaned forward and clasped his hands.

"I," he hesitated and looked at his father, who nodded. "I mean, my brothers and I went up to the turnoff. We followed the track you suggested. I'm afraid we didn't find the area you described. There'd been a rockslide, but it looks as if it took place many years ago. There's nothing new. The creek was running, and we didn't see any water pools with a recent dam. We found this near the creek." He held out a stirrup that looked much more modern than the ones they were using. "I saw something like this when I was in Denver. It's unusual for these parts."

I stood up and turned away. I was sure I had directed the boys to the right spot. Clearly, I misjudged or got mixed up. Was I in a dream, or was it something else that I didn't understand? Maybe I really lived in this time? The wedding band on my finger reminded me of another life. Should I tell them the truth?

"Will you excuse me? I think I'd like to get some fresh air, and I need to think." They stood up, and I went out the front door. I'd barely stepped outside and into the trees before I retched.

Am I crazy? I knew I'd had a concussion. I realized I'd had an accident. The bruising on my back and legs and the gash on the back of my head didn't come from my imagination.

I know I'm from another time. I'm married to Jeff Harper, and I have a child named Lauren. This place and this time aren't my reality. I know facts that others who live in this time do not know. However, have I irrevocably arrived at a time in the past? Will I be able to return to my home and family? Okay, Bec. This whiny crybaby stuff has got to stop. I abhor public displays of emotion. Screw this.

I was about to turn, head into the house, and announce my departure tomorrow when Sam came out. "Rebecca, I have a proposition for you. The boys and I discussed it. We'd like you to stay with us here at the Cattle Creek Ranch until you're feeling better. When you pulled the colt out of our mare, I could see your back. I don't know what happened, but you had quite an accident. I suspect the gash on your head may have resulted in a concussion, and I think you need to rest before you leave us to meet your husband and daughter. If you give me an address, I can write to him and describe what's happened, and maybe he could come here to get you.

"In your brief stay, you've earned our gratitude. I dare say you've saved us a year or two in our herd development. If you insist on going, I thought I could ride with you to where you feel the slide occurred. We could look for your friend and perhaps recover her body, and then you could go on your way. Did you like the mare you rode today? We'd love to give her to you to pay for your advice and help with the horses."

I wasn't expecting that. I thought Sam Buchanan was going to give me some fatherly advice. But then again, the Sam Buchanan I knew from Comstock was my father's age at least. This Sam Buchanan was closer to, or maybe even younger than, Jeff.

I thought the key to getting back to my time would be near the original trailhead where Julie and I started out. I needed to find the rockslide to orient myself. I was still "befuddled," as they might say here.

I glanced down at my feet and took him up on part of the offer. "I would gratefully accept the use of the mare. I'll return the mare if I can, but now I would like to go up to where I think the slide happened. I know this sounds crazy, but you'll have to accept that I have reasons to go back."

"May I accompany you? At least as far as the slide?" Sam looked concerned, and I was touched. Now, I was getting the fatherly television response I knew.

"Mr. Buchanan," I began.

"Sam. It's Sam."

I blushed, and, thankfully, in the dark, he could not see it, but I felt it. "Sam, you're too kind, and I know you have important things to do. I'll be fine."

"Do you have a gun?" he asked.

"I have nothing. The truth is the doctor's wife, Mrs. Sullivan, took my clothes and probably burned them. I walked out. No, let's be honest. I slipped out the window in the dressing gown she lent me. I walked down the main street, and I stole the clothes I wore when you found me. I'm not poor, but I have no means to pay for anything except with my services." I was embarrassed to be in this situation, but telling the truth was cathartic. I actually laughed; so did Sam.

"Why don't you sleep on it and tell me in the morning? I really would like to help you. It's not charity. You know you saved the foal and the mare. We owe you."

"Just curious, but how much is a horse like the black colt worth?"

"Not much right now. When he's mature, the colt might be worth one hundred to five hundred dollars. It's his bloodline. He'll sire one hundred foals, and the offspring will each command top dollar in another two or three years." Sam smiled as he looked back at the mare and foal. We walked over to the corral, and the mare pinned her ears and shook her head.

"Foal proud," I stated. "Be careful around this mama for a few days. She is liable to clean your clock."

"You have some unusual sayings. Where do you get them?"

"My husband. He can really turn a phrase."

"He's a lucky man to have you."

"No, Sam, the luck is all mine."

# Chapter 8

We returned to the great room and the fire. I hoped no one noticed my red eyes. If they did, they politely ignored them. We retired to our rooms after Gee Ling's dessert and brandy.

I woke in the morning to another amazing breakfast. If I weren't married, I could fall for Gee Ling. My mare stood tied, carrying a much newer saddle and beautiful bridle. Next to her was Sam's horse, Cash. Sam was talking to one of the many men he employed. He turned and smiled when I greeted him.

"I thought I would second-guess you. I'll go only as far as the slide or where you think the slide was, and then you can go on. Gee Ling has packed you lots of food. You could take a stagecoach over the divide to Placerville and then down to Sacramento. I can send a telegraph to your husband's folks, and they could forward it if he and your daughter have already left."

He paused and looked at the clothes I'd picked out. "You'll need a few more clothes for the trip. I think I still have a good coat. It gets cold at night. I want to give you a gun. Do you know how to shoot?"

"I took riflery." I stopped myself before adding "in college." *Please, Lord, let me get back home before I am sprung as a witch.* "I mean, I have some knowledge of guns."

Sam handed me a twenty-two-caliber rifle. "It's lightweight but easy to load and shoot. It will protect you against most of what you will encounter in the woods. It might not kill a bear, but it will scare one." We both knew an injured bear could be even more dangerous.

"Thank you so much. Shall we get started?" How could I deny this man his chance to prove me wrong? I realized he genuinely didn't believe my story, but he held no malice. I knew he would want me to find Jeff and Lauren.

We headed out after saying goodbye to Gee Ling. I bid farewell to the boys up at the corral, where Danny was helping Clint to saddle a bronc. Hank was shoeing a filly, and the head wrangler, Gil, was separating out the following few horses for the morning work. They all stopped and wished me well. I left the Cattle Creek Ranch and headed back. Sam led the way as we climbed up into the east side of the Sierras. I directed him to where I'd been, as I remembered the location well. We came to the area of the slide, but there was no sign of a recent disturbance. The trail was rough compared with what I recalled. The penny dropped. The rockslide was over a hundred years later. I must have crossed over after I woke up from the event. I didn't know precisely when or why. I was in the past.

"Sam, if I keep going on this trail, where does it go?" My voice wavered, and I was sure he sensed I was at the breaking point.

"There's a beautiful valley about three miles up with a lake full of trout in a meadow. Can I take you there?"

I wanted to be alone, but since I knew I needed to turn back eventually, I agreed. We rode on, and Sam offered several excuses for my failure to find the area I was seeking. I just stared ahead and occasionally mumbled that I was convinced this was the area. I knew it was here. It just hadn't happened in this time. I had that homesick feeling with the lump in my throat and the whole nine yards. My eyes were red, and I was glad Sam didn't turn around.

We climbed over a rise and descended into the most beautiful valley I could imagine. I wished I had my dark glasses. I had taken to wearing a wide-brimmed hat for protection from the sun, rather than a bonnet as was the custom for women. Pine trees were sparse, except near the lake. The summer day was glorious, and I wished I could appreciate the warm air, the smell of the forest, and the deep-blue sky. Dense green grass covered the valley floor. Maybe twenty cows with calves dotted the valley. In the center was the most beautiful lake. The end closest to us was emerald in color, and the far end was deep blue. Julie Smyth must have been taking me here. I wondered if it had changed and whether the view of the valley from up here was now dotted with tents from backpackers.

Sam rose in the saddle, surveyed the scene, and laughed. "That's where those cows are. We've been looking all over for them. I guess we can eliminate the idea they were rustled." He turned and smiled. "Is this where you were heading?"

I nodded. "I think so." That might have been a mistake. No rockslide, so why would I be here? Clearly, I was a pathetic liar. If he caught me, he did not acknowledge it.

"This is still Cattle Creek Ranch land," was all he said. I must have been trespassing.

"Oh, maybe I'm mixed up, and it was somewhere else."

Sam stared down and squinted. "Rebecca, do you want to go down and look around?"

I needed to transport myself back to my time, and this place was enchanted. While I didn't want to waste time, it was so inviting. Frankly, what were my options?

"That would be lovely." *Oh my God, I'm still using words like 'lovely.'* I need to get back to my time.

"My friends call me Becky, or Bec, by the way."

"Becky it is," he replied, "and thanks for thinking of me as a friend."

*I'm a friend of the famous Sam Buchanan.* I pondered how I would explain that to Jeff. Young Sam was really quite attractive. He was no Jeff, but he was kind and so polite. The deep homesick feeling came over me. I wished Jeff and I could have been here descending into this beautiful valley with Lauren in tow. Sam Buchanan was an excellent substitute, though. My hands were still swollen and stiff from the prior dystocia drama. My ring was almost cutting off my circulation. I twisted it around to loosen it. Did it belong in my past or my future?

# CHAPTER 9

We arrived at the valley floor forty minutes later. As we crossed a small spring, we stopped to let the horses drink. We both filled our canteens. The water was icy and tasted sweet.

"Becky, I want to check brands, and then let's go down by the lake and have lunch."

"You're the boss."

"Yes, I am," he said sternly. I saw him smile, however.

"Yes, sir."

I was surprised the cattle allowed us to approach them. The first four cows carried the Cattle Creek Ranch brand. The following eight had brands from other ranches. I noticed Sam became silent. He kept looking up in the mountains that surrounded us.

Sam explained his cattle operation. It was like my father's ranch. It was customary for the various ranchers to take their cattle up to the mountains in the spring. The cows fed on the grass until fall, when they returned from the high country. Often, ranch cows and calves became mixed with cattle from other ranches. They were gathered, sorted, and driven back to their owner's ranches for winter feeding or driven to market on a traditional cattle drive. The calves were sorted in the fall and branded.

Some of these older calves already had brands. The brands on three calves did not match the cows they were with. I was certain Sam was thinking the worst. He mentioned he had never seen the stock come up here. I considered how remote and difficult it was to get here. I could not imagine cattle would come up here on their own. And yet, no fresh tracks could be seen on the trail.

After looking at about thirty cows, Sam pointed to the lake, which was around a twenty-minute walk away. He continually glanced up into the mountains.

"See anything?" I asked.

He was extremely quiet. "No."

We loosened the girths on our horses and tethered them so they could eat. I unpacked a lunch that Gee Ling had made from the last night's leftovers. Sam laid out a large blanket, and we both sat down and ate. After lunch, Sam reclined on the blanket and tipped his hat over his eyes. I thought he might take a nap, so I quietly got up and went away to relieve myself. I returned and sat next to him on the edge of the blanket. He didn't move or look at me. "I don't suppose you want to tell me what's really going on?"

"Well," I stammered, "no." I paused. "It's too complicated, and you wouldn't believe me, anyway. I mean you no harm, and tomorrow I'll be gone. You can have all your clothes and mare back, but I really can't explain it. If that's not enough, I'm sorry."

"You say things that make little sense, and yet it seems you know my boys and me, although we've never met you. To be honest, I can't read you. This story about a husband and daughter does not ring true, yet you certainly know about horses. I can see you are quite a horsewoman. You had to learn that somewhere. I see you are troubled, and I truly want to help you, but I can't if you don't tell me how."

I thought about what he said and the sincerity with which he spoke. I knew he was used to solving problems and offering advice. Well, that was if the television Sam Buchanan was indeed this Sam Buchanan.

"Thank you. If I thought you could assist me, trust me, I would ask for your help. You can't, and you are just going to have to believe I am an honest person, some stolen clothes and food aside." I laughed.

I gazed over and saw the faintest trace of a smile come from below his hat, which still covered his face. "If anything changes, and I'm around here," I thought, *God forbid*, "You'll be the first person I tell. But for now, I need to deal with my situation. The truth is, I have a husband and daughter, and I love them both very much. Very much."

He sat up and put his hand on my shoulder. "Will you keep in touch and let us know when you sort out your life?"

I hesitated again. "If I can, I will. I need a favor. Do you mind if I spend the night here?"

"No. I mean, I do most certainly mind. I have a feeling that rustlers may use the valley to hide stock. It's too dangerous for you to stay here by yourself."

I only wanted to explore this area and the cliffs by myself. I questioned if I could somehow get back to my own time by walking past something down here. I knew this was where Julie wanted me to come, and she even used the word magical, but I knew the commanding voice that I heard so often on *Comstock* was the law. We tightened our girths and remounted. We rode around a few more of the cows. Clearly, the calves were branded with the neighbor's brand, yet the cows were Cattle Creek Ranch stock.

I said nothing. It was obvious, and it really wasn't my business. I was a mere passerby in their lives. Like a television episode — one quick story about me, and then they got on with their lives, and I was gone. *Cue the music and credits.*

We climbed out of the valley, and as we reached the summit, I turned back and gazed at this beautiful scene. I felt the valley might be the answer, but I needed to be careful with Sam Buchanan. You didn't want to cross him too many times. We had maybe four hours of daylight. We rode to the fork where we were to go our separate ways. He talked about his plans for the Cattle Creek Ranch and his hopes for his boys. Once again, he asked me to let him know how I fared. I thanked him and offered to give everything back, but he would not hear of it. He said the trade was not fair, and he owed me more.

I turned in the direction of the parking lot, and he turned down toward the Cattle Creek Ranch. He was careful not to do anything more than shake my hand. I'm sure his usual grasp was firm to the point of pain, but noting my bruised, swollen hand, he only gently shook it. His last words were, "He is one lucky man."

"If you only knew." And we parted ways.

# CHAPTER 10

I thought about it for all of two minutes. After waiting for half an hour, I turned around and headed back to the valley. I needed to discover a place to transport myself. I hoped the beautiful valley and secluded areas might be the key. It took three hours to get back to where we had lunch. I gathered pinecones and sticks and turned my beautiful mare free.

They'd named the mare Penny and said she was well-trained and would not bolt. *Oh, please let that be true.* In fact, she ate for an hour while I wandered around, and she returned to my little makeshift camp. It was a clear day, and the last of the sun was descending. At this elevation, it was going to be a chilly night, and there might even be frost. I prepared myself for the night and did one more walk in the valley near a craggy outcrop. I explored the external remains of an old mine. I needed a flashlight. *Yeah, right?*

I would make a torch in the morning from my campfire and have a look. I enjoyed eating Gee Ling's leftovers and saved the hardtack for the following day. Now that I had a flint, I was pretty good at starting a fire. I wished I had a dog, but I wasn't long for this time, and leaving a dog would be torture. My last dog died just before graduation. I wanted to wait until we were settled in our practice before going down that puppy trail again. Lauren would not miss out on the joys of having a dog.

It was dark, and I ensured my gun was ready. I would not be surprised to see a bear in this valley. This gun would only frighten a bear, so I realized I had to be careful. I knew grizzly bears were prevalent in the 1800s but were gone from the Sierras in the 1980s. I still had to think about mountain lions. My fire was for protection. The smell of the fire and the pines was intoxicating. I knew what Julie had felt and found in this oasis. I planned to come back here when I returned to my real life.

I slept well and was warm enough. I was a light sleeper due to baby duty, but I was bushed. I felt something press on my forehead, and I heard a click. I awoke to a figure standing over me. I moved my hand, but a boot came down hard on my arm.

I had a difficult time seeing. But I knew someone was pointing a rifle barrel at my head. I want to say my life flashed before me, or I woke up from this terrible nightmare and was back in the 1980s, but no, I just lay there and waited for what seemed forever. I then heard Sam say, "Shoot her, Gil, and you won't live to hear your gun go off."

"Oh, Mr. Buchanan, is that you? I thought someone was stealing your cattle," said Gil.

"Gil put the gun down. Rebecca, pick up his gun, and come over next to me." I did as he directed. I was caught red-handed. I'd done exactly what I said I wouldn't do. I didn't speak. I was so ashamed. I was pissed too, for the truth of it.

Sam turned and addressed Gil. "Lie down on the ground and put your hands behind your back. Rebecca, hold the gun for me while I tie him up." I shook terribly while he tied Gil. Sam said nothing else.

I was in shock. Sam said nothing to me for a long time. I knew he was less than impressed. There was no excuse. I'd left nothing here. There was no logical reason for me to return. I'd risked my safety against his will. I was embarrassed.

I was close to tears. My life might have ended if Sam had not come back. Why did he return? I presumed it was the cattle.

"I guess saying I'm sorry won't be enough," I stammered.

"No," was all Sam replied for a long while.

I rebuilt the fire and made coffee, which Gee Ling had packed for me. I handed Sam the only cup.

"Rebecca, this is the West. It's not a safe place for a young woman to be alone. I have no right to tell you what to do, but I tell you these things solely for your safety. I saw you double back and followed you. I don't know who you are or what you are really searching for, but there are rules which will keep you alive, and you need to be more careful." He held out the cup for more coffee. I felt like a ten-year-old getting a scolding from my father. *Oh, earth, please swallow me.*

Gil sat against a tree. Sam did not offer to feed him. When daylight came, he told me to saddle my horse and find his and Gil's horses and bring them back. Although I offered, Sam didn't touch the food in my saddlebag. He drank one more cup of coffee and poured the rest on the campfire. Sam helped Gil up into the saddle, and we mounted. I knew he was taking Gil back to town to stand trial for cattle theft. I didn't ask, but I was reasonably sure that it would end in a hanging. I wondered if Gil had a family or any accomplices.

We broke camp and started out of the valley. I wanted to stay, but I felt this would not be the portal to get back to my time. I had no clue where the window to my time was or how I would get out. We were going past the cliff area where the slide would eventually occur. I looked down into the water below. I saw a fully running stream with the shadows of trout I had seen with Julie. No one was talking.

When we arrived at the fork where the trail branched to the Cattle Creek Ranch and town or back to the site where the horse trailer had been parked, I got off and handed Sam the reins. I didn't deserve his generosity. I thanked him and apologized, but he dismounted and took me by both shoulders. "No, you need a horse, and you need supplies. All I ask is that you take care of yourself and let me know when you have found your husband and are settled." He hugged me for a moment, turned, and remounted, and then he and poor Gil went down the mountain. I continued on my quest to return to my time. The perfect ending to a *Comstock* episode — no wedding, no attachment, unrequited love, well, on his part. *Goodbye, Sam Buchanan. In another time.*

# PART 2

## HEADING WEST 1857

# CHAPTER 11

Which trajectory do I choose now? Was I going to encounter actual 1800s people or more characters from my television dreams? James Garner, Clint Eastwood, or perhaps I would go to Dodge City and meet the *Gunsmoke* crew? How did this work? And how could I return to my real life?

At noon, I arrived where I estimated the trailer had been parked. Of course, it was a small clearing with no sign of vehicles or other advancements in civilization. I stayed overnight in a dilapidated, abandoned shack.

I considered the notion of time travel. I couldn't be the only one this had happened to. I wondered if there was anything written about it. I thought it might be best to go to a large city. Sacramento might be right, and I remembered the views of the 1800s San Francisco Bay from *Comstock*. That might be good, too. I needed money and possibly a job. Sam had given me far more than my services were worth. It could last me a month or maybe more if I were frugal. My mare would be my companion. It was probably best to get over the Sierras before fall, so I wouldn't get stuck in the snow — no Donner Party outcomes for me.

I'd eventually need warmer clothes. Did they make Levi's 501s? Didn't Levi Strauss start during the gold rush? I didn't see anyone wearing blue jeans. I hadn't even considered the Native American population. Were they a threat as depicted on television? My knowledge of history or anthropology was appalling. I'd heard about Ishi, the last member of the Yahi people found living in Northern California, but that was in the early 1900s. I supposed I might meet John Sutter, who was given credit for discovering gold in California.

I was in Sacramento by October. The trip was uneventful. I stayed in a few way stations. I met miners coming and going from the Sierra gold country and Sacramento. I met two married women who were quite wary of a woman traveling alone in such a remote area. They were rough, and their clothes were functional but not fashionable. They were from the East and were not happy about living in such harsh conditions. One was pregnant. I felt for her, but she didn't want to talk. Once Penny was saddled, I left the women and headed down the mountains through the foothills and toward Sacramento.

Sam Buchanan gave me the addresses of two boardinghouses and letters of introduction to use when I arrived both in Sacramento and San Francisco. I rode to Miss Jayne's Boardinghouse. Tiny letters on the sign read, "For women of Culture." I was pungent from days of travel. I walked up the stairway and asked for Miss Jayne. A maid looked down on me and asked me to wait at the door.

Miss Jayne, as I was told to call her, was a rotund, cheerful woman who looked as if she had never seen 'culture' in her life. She wore a bright-red satin dress, which displayed her ample cleavage with pride. Her platinum hair hid the gray. She made a Japanese geisha woman look plain in the 'war paint' department, as Jeff used to say.

"Oh, you're one of Sam's friends, are you?" Her tone made it sound as if Sam had a string of women he sent to her boardinghouse.

"Ma'am, I'm just a new acquaintance. I'm Dr. Rebecca Harper from back East. I traveled through Nevada to Sacramento to join my husband and daughter." I extended my hand to shake hers. I made sure she saw my wedding band, and happily, my bruising had resolved.

"Oh, I see," she replied in a tone that suggested she saw more than I could comprehend. She tilted her head and squinted with one eye. "You really a doctor?" In my short time in the 1800s, I'd found the term doctor did not necessarily mean a medical doctor who went to school. Most doctors were men. Lots of men might just call themselves doctors. They frequently sold elixirs or might have remote knowledge of medicine, which was learned as a trade without formal education. I would not claim to be a human doctor, at least not at this stage. "Yes, but just for animals." The term veterinarian was known but not commonly used. Best to keep it simple.

"Well, I'll be. You ain't got no animals you're trying to sneak in? This is a very fancy place." She bent over to straighten the rug and let a big one go.

"Oh, no. I can see that. No animals. I'm just traveling through. I'll be here for a short time. If I can't catch up with my husband in Sacramento, I'm sure he will be in San Francisco. We had a mix-up, and it is just a matter of time. I may try to get a job for a few weeks, but you'll barely see me." Phew. Her flatulence reminded me of pathology labs. I would have loved to ask what died but thought better of it.

Miss Jayne took me to a small room and told me the rules. The room cost thirty-five cents a day, including toast, coffee, and supper, which was served at six o'clock on the dot. On Saturdays, the neighboring boardinghouse shared a meal. "There's no smoking at the dinner table, and we observe strict manners. No spittoons at dinner." I was told I could not have a man or liquor in the room, either.

She took me upstairs. I was certain the bed had fleas. The walls were papered with pink *and green stripes, and there was a dresser, a chair, and an oil lamp. Of course, there were no electric outlets. Sheesh, this country was so backward. The good old days were not good old days.*

I left my saddlebag and a satchel that Gee Ling gave me to carry my food in my room and locked the door. I went downstairs and out on the veranda. Sacramento was not as big as I'd hoped. I took Penny to a livery stable and paid the owner for a week's board. The horses in the stable looked surprisingly well-fed and cared for. I told Mr. Slocomb, the owner, that I was good with horse ailments, and if he needed any help, I was happy to lend a hand. He gave the "yeah, sure" look. I shrugged. Again, I had a letter of introduction about my horse skills, but Mr. Slocomb could not read.

I asked him if the city had a library. Mr. Slocomb said there was one, but it wasn't open today. I walked up and down the main street. I was confident John Sutter was living in Sacramento. I also heard he liked the bottle. While I wanted to see the fort he had built, I would do that the next day. I purchased the supplies at a small shop and returned to my room.

I locked the door from within and lay down on my bedroll on the floor. I was growing accustomed to bad beds. My mother always said to my sister and me, "Where is your pioneer spirit?" when we complained during rare family camping trips. I admit I have no pioneering spirit. I took out my picture of Jeff and Lauren and had a moment of self-pity. I fell asleep until someone knocked on my door and announced supper was starting.

I splashed my face with water and came down to the dining room. Three young women, who were probably five to ten years younger than I was, were seated at the table. They all dressed in bright satin dresses with gaudy fringe. They were laughing and teasing one another. Their faces were painted like ladies of the night. *Oh my God, is this a brothel?* Had I missed the cue? Did Sam Buchanan send me to a brothel? My face reddened.

"Ladies, this is Dr. Harper. She'll stay with us for a few days. I don't think she's in the trade, so no one will use her services unless I say. Are we clear? She is a friend of a friend." Miss Jayne gave a look that meant business. A well-endowed woman stretched out her hand and introduced herself, as did the others.

"That Tom was so slow. Sorry, Miss Jayne," said another woman who arrived late. There were ham, potatoes and something green that I had never eaten before. We all served ourselves, and then Miss Jayne said grace. "God, give us strength." And with that, supper commenced.

"Who's the new girl? Isn't she a bit old for our house? What's with the riding clothes?" asked one girl with a distinctive Southern accent. The women all looked at me, and I had to think about how much to tell them.

"I'm out here scouting for a home so my husband and I can settle down. We are both animal healers. We thought with the gold rush and all the new immigrants, we could make some money by helping with the workhorses. How about you all? Are you from here? I think you must be from the South, maybe Georgia?"

"Alabama, ma'am," she drawled. "I'm here to make some money to send back to my family. My father died, and it looks like my brother will join the rebels. There's no one to feed my baby sister and mother. I had a husband, and we came over in a Conestoga, but he got kilt when Injuns attacked the train."

"I'm sorry." I had thought little about the Civil and Indian Wars. What were the dates?

Another explained, "I came out to find a man, but so far, it is just been one-night stands. The money's good, though. I'll make enough to get back home to Maine and then look around there." She had raven-red hair. She was a beauty and must have been six feet tall. Her green dress contrasted nicely with her red hair. "I like to read and sew when I'm not workin'."

"Oh, where do you get books to read? At the library?" I asked.

"No, men leave me dime novels and magazines. I ain't been to no library. Is there one here in town, Miss Jayne?"

There was the ring of a small bell at the door. "I'll bet that's Elmer. He knows we aren't open until seven. He wants an early visit, so he can get home to his missus, and she'll think he just worked late again. Who wants a quick dollar?"

One of the women made a face and said she would attend to his needs. "Honestly, he only wants a diddle. I don't know why he can't just diddle himself." She grabbed a biscuit and went to the side door.

I looked at the last two and inquisitively cocked my head. One just looked away, and a plump, unnaturally blonde woman smiled and said, "I'm here because I just like it. It's easy money with no commitment. My family is painfully uppity, and I ran away, maybe three years ago. I'm pretty sure they think I'm dead. I'm not going back to that hellhole again. Our family's got secrets, and I know what my father did with my sister. There's no way he was going to get to me. I prefer to be paid for those services." She smiled and looked quite proud. I was shocked. I tried to hide it, but I understood what she meant about her father. I knew that incest happened in all walks of life.

The last woman, a tall brunette, looked at me and said, "You don't have the money or the time for me to tell you about myself. I need at least a bottle of whiskey to get me going on this topic." She got up to prepare herself for the evening.

A young boy, who was about fourteen years old, came in and sashayed up to the plump blonde. "As soon as I finish the dishes, how about I come up for a visit?"

"You know we have rules. When you turn fifteen, I hope you let me be the first, but not until then, you little grub."

Miss Jayne grabbed a knife and pointed it toward the young boy, and he swiftly grabbed an empty plate and ran for the kitchen.

"Dr. Harper, you best go to your room and lock it unless you need money. You're a bit old for our clientele, though. You don't have much in the asset department, anyway. Either that or you need a better truss." It was true. My assets had been reduced in more ways than one. I still had money, but, looking down, I realized I had basically returned to my pre-preggers boyish self. The well-endowed looked at me and said she would help the asset department the following day.

"That would be great, thank you. God knows I could use some help." I retired to my room, and the sounds of headboard banging and whoops from men receiving pleasure lulled me to sleep. It went on until the morning when the shop shut, except for special guests like Tom and Elmer. The workers all had an early breakfast and went to bed for the day. As the brunette left the dining room, she took me aside and said to knock on her door at four in the afternoon to wake her, and we could discuss my wardrobe. "You need all the help you can get, honey." And she was gone.

I went down to the livery stable and saw Penny. She nickered as I approached. Two men were huddled over an old paint gelding. One man appeared to be slightly drunk. He smelled of booze and needed a bath. He had a black top hat, which was askew, and a ratty black coat. He slurred his words as he spoke of the virtues of this arthritic old gelding. The other man was young and appeared green, with little clear horse experience. He was looking for a mount to take him up to the hills and gold country.

"How old is he?" asked the younger man.

"Sixth if he is a day," slurred the older man.

"May I be of help?" I inquired of the younger man. He looked at me, and I could tell he didn't think I could be of any assistance in this serious negotiation. I smiled and said, "Okay, sir, ignore me at your peril." I walked away toward the stable doors.

"Madam, if I thought you could assist, I would accept your offer, but this is horse-trading." He turned to the older drunk and questioned how much for the horse.

"I would suggest you ask me why I might help you," I replied in earnest.

"Again, madam, clearly, you're out of your depth," scoffed the young man.

I walked over to the paint and opened its mouth. I pointed to the groove in the outside front tooth, or incisor. "This is Galvayne's groove. It is a good gauge of a horse's age. It starts down the tooth at roughly ten years of age. It is halfway down the tooth at fifteen and all the way down the tooth at twenty. It is like a canoe, and it will continually move down the tooth. This horse's teeth would suggest he is in his late teens. And since you asked — not that you did — I have a hard time watching someone get fleeced, and I will feel guilty. The right fore has a bowed tendon. I haven't flexed his front legs, but I suspect he will react to flexion, indicating he has advanced ringbone. We haven't got to his hind end, but his hocks are like cannonballs. He probably has spavin too, but don't mind me. I couldn't possibly know anything as I'm a girl."

A well-dressed, sophisticated man stepped out from the nearby tack room and applauded. He looked like John

Wayne, except he was younger and had a bit of a baby-face. I looked over and smiled. "Good day, gentlemen." I walked to the livery stable entrance, but I paused and listened to the conversation.

The older horse trader was furious. "Who the hell is she?"

The John Wayne doppelgänger said, "Obviously, she's a horsewoman." He finished saddling his horse and went out the back door.

I was off to the library. Is it open? I walked over to where Miss Jayne had directed me. There was a narrow door with the word 'Library' on it. A note was pinned to the door. "Out for fifteen minutes and will return in thirty minutes." What did that mean? I seated myself on the bench and enjoyed a few minutes in the warm sun.

John Wayne Jr. rode past and tipped his hat. "Howdy, ma'am."

I waved and smiled. A small, plain woman in a floral-print dress walked up to the library and pushed the door open.

"I think they are out now." I pointed to the paper on the door.

The lady smiled and said, "They is me. Can I help you with something?"

"Oh, well, yes. I want to look through your library. Do you have a reference section?"

"Not sure what you mean. Do you mean a dictionary? Yes, we have one of those." She pointed to an enormous book on a stand.

"Not exactly what I was looking for." I thought about saying, *do you have a book about time travel and witches?* Fortunately, I didn't ask. She looked at me suspiciously.

"I don't believe I've seen you around?"

"No, ma'am. I'm new in town. I'm meeting my husband in a few days. Do you have old newspapers? I've been traveling, and I'm afraid I've lost contact with the news of the world."

"Only last week's *Placer Times*."

"When is it published?" I casually asked while perusing the books. I could see no rhyme or reason for the filing system in this library. I wondered when the Dewy Decimal system started.

"Tomorrow. Are you looking for something in particular? We got a new book a few days ago. Have you heard of Moby Dick? I can't seem to interest anyone in it."

I smiled. "*Call me Ishmael.* Give the public time. I bet it will be a best seller."

"A what?"

"It will be a well-used book in a few years." I wondered when it was published.

"I don't know. Can you imagine a book all about chasing a whale?" The librarian set it down and thumbed through some dime novels. "Now, I can hardly keep these on the shelf."

I sat down and looked through The Times. There was news of more gold discovered. Sutter's mill had shut down but was now back up and working. Three men had been hanged for cattle theft, and Indians had attacked a remote ranch. About three pages in was a brief article about the Cattle Creek Ranch's cattle bringing the highest price ever paid per head. One thousand cows were driven down to New Mexico to meet a train heading east. The article reminded me I owed the Buchanans a letter.

I found nothing about time travel or even the occult in the library. I thanked the librarian and left. On the way back to the boardinghouse, I passed a women's dress shop. I'd tossed out the corset on my trip and knew the time had come. I needed to find work, and I realized I should dress more like a lady to be taken seriously. I stepped inside, and a woman greeted me with a grin and a salutation that told me she could be a friend.

"Can I help you with anything?"

I introduced myself and explained my situation. The shopkeeper understood my needs without judgment. The woman promptly found an inexpensive corset and some pantaloons for the one dress that had belonged to Danny's mother. Her name was Hattie. I asked about jobs for women, and she said that barmaids and cleaners were the only jobs she knew about.

I told her where I was staying, and she was shocked in a not too judgmental way. I explained how I boarded in a brothel. Frankly, I enjoyed seeing how the other side lived. The women were friendly and, mostly, decent, but I was pleased to meet someone who appeared to have similar values to me. The shopkeeper was a widow with five children, ranging in age from eight to sixteen. They were in school, except the oldest, who worked on a farm outside Woodland, about fifty miles away. He wanted to be a horse trainer and was apprenticed to a drover who worked for Dr. Merritt. Dr. Merritt was one of the most prominent breeders of horses and mules in the area.

"Lorenzo loves working there. The doctor has racehorses and riding horses as well as cattle and sheep. You learn little about these things unless you join the men at the race meets."

"Race meets? Do you hold horse races here?" I asked.

"Of course, we do. We're an up-and-coming city."

"Will you tell me where the racetrack is? My job at home was caring for the horses. Maybe I could get a job doing that while I wait for my husband to arrive." I had given her the basic info and was changing my story, so it didn't look so unbelievable. A woman leaving a child in the 1800s was just not done.

"The track is where they meet for races, but in the morning, some of the owners bring their horses for practice runs and training. The races are run every other week. Dr. Merritt will be there with his horses this Saturday. I'll be there so I can see Lorenzo. I miss that boy. He is the spitting image of my late husband." There was a pause. "Hey, Becky, do you want to come with us for a picnic at the races?"

"I want to go, but I'll have to be ready to do some work. I'm running out of," I paused, "grubstake." I laughed to myself for using such old language. "How about I find you and meet your children?"

"That's wonderful, Becky. Now, let's get a corset to go with your dress."

After we completed the transaction, Hattie gave me directions to the racetrack. I thanked her and left. I headed down near the riverfront, where several boats were docked. Supplies from San Francisco, destined for the minefields, were being unloaded. A couple of men tipped their hats to me. Still, I was just another woman who thankfully did not stand out, figuratively or literally.

I was not sure what I was looking for. I needed to find out if there were people who would not judge me or my story. I traveled back on another road, which was lined with tents. They must be for the miners, who were just arriving or heading out. The daytime seemed safe enough, but I would not venture out in the night. The youthful man, who looked like John Wayne, rode past again. He stopped this time and asked me if I knew where I was and if I thought it was safe to be out on my own.

"Sir, I know how to take care of myself, but thank you." I may have blushed.

"I see you know horses, but men are another species. You're new to Sacramento. Just beware. True horsewomen are rare. We'd hate to lose you." He took off his hat, circled his arm in a broad arc, and galloped away.

I thought I would return to the boardinghouse. As I passed the livery stable, the young man who had been considering purchasing the old broken-down horse stepped out of the barn and hailed me. I looked closer and noticed he was well-dressed, probably only twenty-two years old, and pockmarked, as were many young men I'd encountered.

"Madam, I'm Jonathon Marks. I'm looking for ten to twelve horses and mules for my mining company, and I wonder if I could pay you to look at a few for me. Mr. Cogburn suggested you might be invaluable to my needs. I'll pay you well."

*An intriguing idea, but why me?* "Sir, many men can do this for you. Why would you seek my help?"

"Well, I understand you're new to the area and might not have skin in the game. And Mr. Cogburn thought we could both benefit from the association. As you saw, I lack the experience to judge a good horse."

I pursed my lips together and thought for a minute. Pre-purchase examinations were routine in my time. A buyer would pay a veterinarian to look at the health and soundness of a prospective horse. It rarely entailed suitability, which was often handled by a trainer or agent. This might be my ticket.

"Who is Mr. Cogburn?"

"The man who came up to us this morning. He wore an enormous hat and chaps. He was riding a big brown horse with a white stripe on its head. You don't know him?"

"No, sir. He reminds me of someone I saw once." I left out the 'in the movies.'

"His name is Reuben Cogburn, but I hear he goes by Rooster," Jonathon replied.

This dream was becoming weirder and weirder. I could almost enjoy it if I weren't so homesick. The lump in my throat emerged, but I kept the tears at bay.

"Mr. Marks, I'd be happy to advise you." We settled on a generous compensation plan. We would meet tomorrow and start the process of finding him stock to take to the goldfields. He gave me an advance on my fee. He could probably see I required toiletries and clothes.

His company had already purchased land near the original discovery site in the foothills near Coloma. Men were up near Sutter's mill, guarding the property. I would help him find at least ten horses and two mules, and he would head up with those. I'd find more stock as needed later.

Identifying suitable horses was difficult. These horses were rarer than hens' teeth. The army required them as well as the miners, who were still showing up daily from wagon trains and down the river from San Francisco and other ports.

By four o'clock in the afternoon, I returned to find my fashion consultant awake and ready to make me into an 1850s hussy. We headed to her room, where she had laid out some of her more modest dresses. I showed her my new corset, and we began the transformation. Somehow, I was adjusting to life, including not bathing every day, every other day, or longer. She had highly diluted perfume and powder that took away the odors of her profession. She told me about her life. While she did not tell me about her past, she talked about her aspirations.

"Rebecca, this is easy money. You should think about it. It's not as if you will earn what I earn as you are," she paused, "Um, kind of lacking in, you know what."

"You mean I'm more like a boy than a girl with my flat chest? My husband hasn't complained. A handful and a mouthful."

She laughed. "Well, some men are into that. I don't want to shock you, but some men like, well, other men. I hope that doesn't offend you."

I laughed to myself. One of my good friends and classmates was gay. "No, really? I guess I have a lot to learn."

"Yes, you do. Just follow my lead," replied my fashion consultant with all sincerity. "You're so innocent. You act as if you were born in the last century."

"Yes, well, something like that. Not to change the subject, but how do you...." I planned to ask about personal safety, hygiene, and pregnancy prevention, but the dinner bell rang.

"Dinner, then duty. Let's go, Rebecca. The mayor is coming tonight. It will be a fun night for one of us. The man is a legend. I don't know how his wife puts up with him. He goes on forever."

We sat down at the table, and Miss Jayne repeated grace. "God, forgive us. And God, give us a chance to redeem ourselves for the sins we will commit tonight." She was about to go on, but 'Blondie' just grabbed a ladle and started serving everyone. Miss Jayne looked up. Realizing she was being ignored, she sat down to join in the supper.

"So, Dr. Rebecca, want to join our financial endeavors?"

"Miss Jayne, I have good news. I've been employed to vet horses for a mining company. It's probably best if I stick with what I know, given my lack of assets." I looked down. Even with the corset firmly in place, there was no cleavage to be seen.

The girls rolled their eyes and laughed. "We can't all make a living by just lying around. I guess some of us actually have to work." It was apparent the fashion consultant was a card — intelligence, a sense of humor, and assets. At another time, we could have been great friends.

After spending one day in Sacramento, I could tell I needed to move on. This was not where I was going to live the rest of my life. I would stay long enough to build up some money. I had to find someone who could get me back to the twentieth century. I was still nervous about telling anyone my story. Thankfully, the conversation at the dinner table turned to tonight's activities and who was going to serve whom. Now that they knew I did not need to use my body to make money, I was of little interest to these women tonight. I was taking up precious space, and I felt they would want me to leave soon. Miss Jayne politely asked how much longer I would be staying.

"Miss Jayne, I can leave tomorrow if you need the room. Do you have a suggestion of a boardinghouse that might suit me better?"

"Just down the street is the one Mr. Buchanan was suggesting," she smirked.

"Huh?" I was perplexed.

"You came to one of two boardinghouses on this street. I'm fairly sure Mr. Buchanan meant the boarding house two blocks down the way. I had an empty room, and I'm always looking for new talent. I checked while you were out. Several rooms are available."

"I'll be out tomorrow. Thank you for your hospitality." I was externally polite but fuming internally. I thought about it for a minute, and then I laughed out loud. They were all in on it from the start. The women laughed as well.

"The joke is on me. You all ought to be shot."

"Oh, we love outside company. We still haven't heard your story," said one of the girls.

"You don't have enough money or liquor to drag that out of me, ladies. I will say I am a doctor, but of animals, and that is the sum of it."

The doorbell rang to a chorus of, "Elmer." Dinner was over, and I returned to my bedroll on the floor of my room. My evil thoughts about Sam Buchanan sending me to a brothel vanished. Dare I write to him and thank him for the introduction to the whorehouse?

# Chapter 12

My thoughts returned to Jeff and Lauren. I looked at
the picture I still had hidden. I wanted the comforting touch of my husband, the sound of my daughter, and
the smell of her hair as she sat in my lap. I wondered if Jeff
had accepted my death or was he still searching for me. After a moment of self-pity, I fell into a fitful sleep, serenaded
by the sounds of copulation throughout the night.

In the morning, I walked down the road to the other
boardinghouse. It was for men only, and I was directed to a
house with a front veranda, another street down from the
brothel. Mrs. Findlay was sweeping the porch and singing a
familiar tune. I introduced myself just as Rebecca Harper.
I explained I was in town for only a month, and I needed a
place to stay while I was here. I produced the same letter of
introduction. This woman could read and beamed fondly.
"Ah, Mr. Buchanan. My husband worked for him until he
got sick. We moved down here to be near my boys before
Harold passed some three years ago." She sighed. "How is

he? How do you know him? How are the boys? How is the cook?"

I passed on the little information I knew. I was shown to a nice, clean room on the second story. The going rate was quite a bit more, but I could come and go as needed. There was a stable out back if I needed to bring my horse. Dinner was served at six o'clock sharp, and my room was cleaned daily. The social room displayed books and other reading material.

I left after paying a week's rent and retrieved my belongings from Miss Jayne's establishment. The girls were all asleep. I was sure I would see them again on the street. We didn't come from such different backgrounds. *There but for the grace of God—and lack of assets—go I.*

Eager to be on the road, Jonathon Marks was already waiting when I arrived. He'd selected several horses for me to examine outside of the city limits. During the ride, he told me the story about his adventure around the Horn of South America and up to San Francisco. His family had several businesses in Boston, and his great-grandfather was in the original tea party. He was 'old Boston.' He traveled from the San Francisco Bay through the delta on a riverboat to Sacramento, where his father and uncle sent him to start a mining business.

"My father wanted to toughen me up. My brothers were already working in the mills and clothing factories." His sister had married a banker, and she was well on her way to giving his mother a brood of grandchildren. Jonathon was not needed in the family business. "So here I am, ready to make the family richer than they already are. They're prepared to spend more money if I can just get this parcel outfitted and ready to mine, or we can dredge the creek that runs through the property."

I cringed at the thought of all the damage to the Sierras that would ensue in the next few years. "Mr. Marks, I'll help you all I can to get you up to your claim as soon as possible."

He laid a hand on my thigh. I lifted his hand off my thigh. He put his hand back. Once again, I removed it. "I'm old enough to be your mother, Mr. Marks."

"I meant nothing untoward, Miss Harper. I assure you."

"All I want is a professional relationship. I'm a married woman, I'll remind you."

"Yes, ma'am, but I meant no harm. It was just a reassuring, friendly gesture."

"Mr. Marks, I castrate horses for a living." Nothing more needed to be said.

We arrived at a corral and shack about five miles from central Sacramento. The horses were of all varieties. Most were inexperienced and untested breakers and not ready for serious hard work. By prearrangement, Jonathon was to do all the talking. I was there only to assist. Jonathon introduced me as his aunt. "My aunt is here for the ride and to help me. She is not much of a horse person, but she loves looking at them." I nodded and looked away.

"How do, ma'am?"

"Very well. How do you do?" I responded.

The stockman was about my age and was missing several teeth. He wore a bandana around his forehead. Turning to Jonathon and ignoring me, he described what he had.

"This here is a Cattle Creek Ranch gelding," he said, pointing to a bay potbellied horse. I casually looked at the horse. He didn't have the Cattle Creek Ranch brand.

"Oh, I've heard of that ranch. They have wonderful stock." Jonathon seemed to be mesmerized by the name. The gelding had a knocked-down hip. At some point, he had torn his sacroiliac ligament.

"Jonathon, I know you are the boss, but I don't really like his color," I said sweetly.

This went on until I saw one that would be a good workhorse. I never said what the problem was with the various horses. In the end, we bought two, which were to be delivered to the livery stable the next day. This was going to be a long, drawn-out process. As we drove the horse and buggy back to the livery stable, Jonathon questioned my reasons for rejecting most horses. "So, what was wrong with the first horse?"

"He's not from the Cattle Creek Ranch. The brand is wrong, and he has a sacroiliac luxation. If you look from behind, one hip is much higher than the other. We probably need a signal. It's best if we keep my role just between us around these men. They'll resent the interference of a woman quick-smart." Of course, my assumption was based on watching television, which, in my opinion, was a totally reliable source. Maybe it wasn't as bad as I thought, but it might be worse. I was playing a role that would befit any *Comstock* episode.

"We can look at the other place you suggested tomorrow, but I learned about a breeder in Woodland. I think we should go there on Monday. It'll probably be an overnight trip, so you may choose to bring a bedroll."

Jonathon was not impressed. I thought he was hitting the brothels at night. A night away with a woman who was less than interested in him was probably not high on his list of things to do.

"Well, let's hope we have better luck tomorrow." Jonathon flicked the reins.

"You and me both." I needed the money, but this was taking up a significant amount of time that I could use in finding the window back to my era. I needed to be back at the boardinghouse in an hour for dinner at Mrs. Findlay's. I wanted to go to the Chinatown area to see if anyone might help me find a way back to Jeff and Lauren.

Gee Ling had mentioned a distant cousin, who he said was an honest person, to translate for me. After leaving Jonathon at the livery stable, I walked down to the area in the Chinese section of Sacramento that looked like the right place for my hunt for mystical travel. I asked for Gee Ling's cousin and was directed to a canvas tent. Many men dressed in traditional clothes were standing near a large kettle. They looked similar to fieldworkers in the twentieth century, except their conical rice hats were wider. I was a babe in the woods, but I was sure they were all smoking opium. I asked again for the cousin. He was away but would be back next week. I could see the suspicion on their countenances. I mentioned that Gee Ling, the cook from the Cattle Creek Ranch, had sent me, and they relaxed.

"You come back next week. Next week. No, cousin today."

After leaving the Chinatown section of Sacramento, I stopped by the livery stable again. I asked Mr. Slocomb if Mr. Cogburn was around. I thought he might be a suitable source for horses.

"Mrs. Harper, Reuben left for the army yesterday. He is a character, isn't he? I bet he'll be famous someday."

"I think you can bet on it." I laughed. "I would believe he is a man of true grit."

"Yes, ma'am." Mr. Slocomb turned away and begun feeding the horses their evening hay.

The meal at the new boardinghouse was delicious. Meat and three vegetables were traditional meals, and Mrs. Findlay was no slouch. She reminded me of my mother. It was worth the extra money as it included a bug-free bed. I'd made double my room and board today, and it was a comfort to have my finances going in the other direction again. I still didn't feel right about the money the Buchanans gave me. I knew the black stallion would play a significant role in their lives. However, I was confusing the reality of the present with an old television program. What was real? I honestly didn't know. The other dinner guests were a varied group. One of the boarders was a salesman from back East. He was selling mining equipment. His company had sent him out to sell stock to the mining supply companies.

Another man worked on Sutter's home. He was an immense man with a cheerful smile and disposition. He was from San Francisco and went home every two weeks to see his wife and three children. There was also a woman who taught school and was probably in her fifties, and sadly, by all measurements, lacked a sense of humor. I guess teaching will do that to you. She had lived in Mrs. Findlay's house for several years as the school board paid for her lodgings. She eyed me suspiciously. I got the heebie-jeebies from her. In reply to her questions about where I came from, I replied,

"Back East, and I'm waiting to join my husband." I didn't even mention Lauren.

The last guest was a traveling preacher. He was young and easy on the eyes. Very easy. He reached out and shook my hand vigorously. "Pleased to make your acquaintance, ma'am." He was polite and well-educated. He made a circuit in the mining towns and came back once in a while to Sacramento to see his mother and sister. There was no room in their house for him to stay, and he didn't get along with his brother-in-law.

"It's just best we keep our distance." He was courting a woman who was a widow with children. This situation did not sit right with his mother. He left shortly after dinner to see the woman and then his mother.

I retired early to bed. I spoke briefly to Mrs. Findlay and told her I planned to be gone for a few days on a horse-scouting trip. I would leave on Monday. She said she would pack me a lunch and inquired whether I needed anything else—what a difference from Miss Jayne. I felt as if I had a mother.

The following day with Jonathon was more of the same, with mostly unsuitable horses. Total wheeler dealers with little in the substance department. We worked out a signal. If I thought the horse was suitable, I would smile and say what a lovely bay, chestnut, or whatever color it was. If I didn't like the horse, I said nothing. Jonathon was no fool. He caught on quickly and became a better judge of horses.

As we rode back to the livery stable, I reminded him I was attending the Saturday race meeting. I explained I intended to meet the owner of the large breeding farm out near Woodland that I had told him about. I had accepted an invitation to join my new acquaintance and her son, who worked for the breeder. We were having a picnic lunch at the race meet.

I would arrange for us to view the breeder's horses and a few mules. Jonathon asked if he could join me at the races. Reluctantly, I said yes. He was a nice young man, but I thought he was still keen to have it on with me. Jonathon was at the stables early the following morning. He had the same hack, and he offered me a ride to the race grounds. I checked Penny and noted she was regaining her weight from our journey over the Sierras.

When we arrived, the weather was threatening rain. Several racehorses were being led into the fenced enclosure. A few horses stood out. They were old-time horses: sleek, thin-necked, with large bodies reminiscent of the conformation famed by Currier and Ives paintings. It was a visual delight—heaven on four legs. We paid for entrance to the racing venue and found Hattie with the preacher from my boardinghouse. Ha! Hattie was my fellow boarder's friend. We would be a foursome. Hattie had left her children at home with her mother and had prepared a picnic basket for four. It turned out that her son was too busy with the racehorses to join us.

We watched the pre-race parade. This sure was like looking at the old lithographs I saw along the halls of my veterinary school. Long stirrups and tall jockeys abounded. We watched the first two races, and Jonathon was very good at choosing winners.

We laid out the food Hattie had prepared. "I feel embarrassed. I've contributed nothing to the meal." Hattie would hear nothing of it. Jonathon went and bought some drinks for us all. I tasted alcohol. Knowing I was a cheap drunk, I was careful about what I said.

Hattie and I went to the stabling area to see her son grooming horses for his employer. Hattie's son, Lorenzo, was a small but handsome young man. He smiled and continued his duties. A tall, bearded man, who appeared to be my age or slightly younger, strode up to Lorenzo with instructions.

Hattie whispered, "That's his boss, Dr. Merritt."

You know that feeling of something that reminds you of something, but you can't seem to put that something together? I felt I had seen this man before. I would think about this.

Dr. Merritt was a handsome man. He had an air of confidence as he looked over and smiled at Hattie. He finished his conversation with Lorenzo and came over to us. I was introduced, and my work with horses was acknowledged.

"You should visit us sometime, Dr. Harper," he suggested.

"Dr. Merritt, I'm hoping to ride over on Monday. I'm helping a young gentleman procure horses and mules for his mining company. I heard about your stock, and if any horses are for sale, we would be interested in a transaction that would be beneficial to us all."

"Why, we have plenty of stock to meet your needs, most certainly. Of course, my stock is a good cut above what you might pay."

"The money is always a consideration, but I assure you the gentleman has ample resources for this venture." I smiled. What was it about this man? He was so familiar.

"Dr. Harper, I'm not used to doing business with a woman, but I have a feeling we could be good friends. My wife and I would be most intrigued to hear your story. Please accept our hospitality at our humble farm."

"Thank you, sir. I would be most grateful."

"Do you know where we're located? It's a day's ride from here. We'll expect you for dinner Monday night. I must get back to my horses. I have an entry in the Sacramento Cup in an hour. We need to prepare for the race. If you will excuse me, ladies."

"Isn't he nice?" exclaimed Hattie.

"Very," I said, still sensing déjà vu.

The rest of the day was pleasant. Dr. Merritt's horse won the cup. We were invited to a small celebration after the race meet ended. However, Jonathon was almost falling down drunk. He still won enough money from his betting to pay for several of the stock he needed. I walked him back to his horse and buggy. I harnessed the horse and drove it to Jonathon's hotel. I didn't want Dr. Merritt to think of Jonathon as a drunken fool.

I took Penny out for a ride on Sunday. Monday morning sickness was a common ailment of horses. It had several names over the years, including azoturia, meaning nitrogen in the urine. Although by the time I was in college, it was commonly called tying up or rhabdomyolysis. It occurred commonly when draft horses had the weekends, primarily Sundays, as a rest day and still consumed high-grain diets. The first day back to work might produce a catastrophic cascade of events that caused a horse to have a muscle melt-down. Many other metabolic problems occurred with the release of myoglobin into the bloodstream. Death was not uncommon during these times. Although the condition was well known, the actual mechanism of glycogen storage was not understood in the 1800s, so horses were fed the same whether or not they worked. I gave strict instructions not to feed Penny any grain while she was at the livery stable. Out on the street, she felt good. She even crow hopped a few times. I was used to this in my father's breakers, and her bucks were small and easily rideable. Several men saw this and hooted and whistled. I laughed and rode on.

Many people don't like chestnut mares because they are thought to have a bad temperament. Still, Penny was honest and lively and had no malice in her disposition. I petted her neck and playfully admonished her.

We walked around the streets of Sacramento and down to the river. I found a place to get down to the riverbank and gave my little mare a good bath. She loved the water and rolled in it. I had a bit of a swim, with my clothes on, of course. We returned in the late afternoon, and I took her to Dr. Merritt's farm the following day. I would tie her to the buggy for the journey.

Horses came and went when I was a child at my father's ranch. I had my own horse, which I loved, but mostly, horses were with us for only a short time. There was never a chance of forming more than a temporary bond with one. I was falling in love with Penny. So far, I would have no regrets about leaving this time to return to my own, but I would miss Penny.

# CHAPTER 13

J onathon and I left early the next day. We boarded a ferry to cross the river. It was a beautiful day, but it was going to be hot. We wanted to beat as much of the heat as we could. By the time we crossed the river, the temperature was still reasonable. We arrived in the town of Woodland by lunchtime.

We stopped and received directions to the Merritt property and had a bite to eat. I cautioned Jonathon to be reserved and not jump on the first horse or mule he saw. He was contrite for his behavior at the races. He assured me I would make all the decisions about suitability and in negotiations about prices. We drove the buggy along the road leading out of Woodland. An hour south of town, we came across a big entry gate leading to a large house under construction. It was hard to visualize what this was going to look like when it was completed.

A handsome woman came out and introduced herself and two children to us. "Welcome, I'm Jeannette. I think you're Rebecca?"

"Yes, ma'am."

"And I am Jonathon Marks," responded Jonathon. "Is Dr. Merritt about?"

"He's over at our other property. We're having some issues with a few cows. He should be back for dinner. Our son, George, is our ambassador today. He'll show you the stock. I hear you're looking for mules and horses. We have plenty of both. Would you like to freshen up before we begin?"

"Mrs. Merritt, perhaps just some water for our horses would be nice," I replied. "Is there someplace..."

"Lorenzo will tend to your horses. Come up on the porch, and I am going to insist that you at least have a glass of lemonade," Mrs. Merritt commanded. Hattie's son was standing close by and took the horses to lead them away.

While the house was under construction, you could still see it was going to be a mansion. "Sorry for the noise. We want to have the roof finished by fall before the rains come. It was a close call this weekend, but we missed the rain. Not that any rain isn't appreciated. I'm used to the noise of the builders, but I am sorry to burden you with it."

Jonathon replied it was not a problem. He asked if the Merritts had architectural plans, so he could get an idea about the finished house.

"Oh, Hiram would be proud to show you tonight," she replied.

George asked us to follow him into the nearby paddock. He looked like his father. He was probably only eight or nine years old, but he had an excellent command of the breeding lines of both the mules and stock horses. I noticed three heavily pregnant mares had the Cattle Creek Ranch brand. We examined several of the geldings, and I saw enough to fill all of Jonathon's requirements. I stirred them up and watched for lameness. One gelding was lame. I suggested we inspect him. Lorenzo arrived and placed a halter on him. I picked up his leg and palpated the tendons and suspensory ligament, which was enlarged and painful to palpate. I showed Lorenzo, who said he would tell Dr. Merritt.

I wondered about Dr. Merritt's credentials. He didn't seem to practice medicine. Many men assumed the title of doctor without having attended medical school. I wondered where he'd received his degree. We looked at a few more horses, but we had more than enough prospects to meet Jonathon's needs.

Now for the actual negotiations. Dr. Merritt returned in time for dinner. We were quite prepared to sleep rough, but the Merritts would not think of it. Despite the construction, there were two empty rooms to which we were each assigned for the night. Before dinner, we had drinks on the veranda.

The noise from the construction was gone, as were the men housed in long tents behind the main house. Maids, who had prepared large plates of food for the men, were busy carrying the food out to the tents. Dr. Merritt engaged Jonathon in conversation. He excused himself for a minute. He returned to the veranda and laid out the architectural plans for the house, including a drawing for the finished product.

I nearly fainted. I had seen this drawing before. The picture was in my grandmother's house and then ours. It was the family homestead that burned down when my grandmother was a little girl, well before my mother was born. I was a descendant of Hiram and Jeannette Merritt. My grandmother's maiden name was Merritt. That was the reason he was so familiar to me. A portrait of Hiram as a much older man hung in my grandmother's house.

I so wanted to tell the Merritts and even hug them, but I couldn't. This was my past. I could tell the Merritts what became of their landholdings and descendants. I could say that they lived through me and my daughter, Lauren, as well. But I wouldn't, and I didn't. I wondered if I was going to encounter more relatives before I returned to my time.

We had a grand meal, and in the morning, we had the horses and mules sent by stock train to Sacramento. They knew a mule skinner, and they were confident he'd work for Jonathon's company.

I showed Dr. Merritt the horse with the suspensory ligament injury. He had worked in a pharmacy in his youth, and I suggested some lotions he could make up to try on the horse. He asked me how I was so knowledgeable. I explained my husband was a trained veterinarian, and I had learned from him. He asked me to look at several horses with various ailments, which I then examined. He offered to pay me, but I refused. Later, Dr. Merritt recounted his medical training, including a university degree. He mentioned he'd financed his journey from the East by vaccinating people against smallpox. Dr. Merritt was the real deal. He felt there was more money in farming and didn't practice much anymore.

"You are almost like family. I couldn't charge you for work," I said. He was about thirty and two or so years younger than I was, but his deportment was that of a man twice his age. I was in awe. He gave me another letter of reference and several recommendations for my trip to San Francisco. My time in the Central Valley was ending.

"I'm sure your husband will catch up with you. He would be a fool to lose you."

Jeannette asked me to write when I had settled. "You know, with the gold rush, many family members are getting lost. He probably didn't want to risk going over the pass after the pitiful people in the Donner Party. You'll soon be reunited."

I could tell from her tone that she was worried. Many people were killed coming across the country. If only I could talk to her and tell her my problems. I knew she would be a great ally. Realistically, she would probably think me insane or worse. I could not remember which of their children would become my great-something-grandfather, but one of the boys was undoubtedly him. My job in Sacramento was over. I would see a Chinaman tomorrow or the next day and be off to San Francisco.

Or not.

# CHAPTER 14

We were back so late that I could not see Gee Ling's cousin, who might know someone who could help me search for the future. The next day, I made my way down to the Chinatown district. I was sent to a small cabin in the middle of the community, where I was taken to a Chinese woman who told fortunes. Without divulging too much, I asked her how I could find my husband and daughter. She stared hard at the sticks that fell in a pile in front of her on the table. She looked back at me and then at the collection again. After a minute, which felt like ten minutes, I rose. She tapped me on the shoulder and said she could not help me. "Many years before you see, baby. Many years. Need to go back to the rocks." She looked intensely into my eyes. "Back to the rocks and fish," she said and slammed her clenched hand down on the table. "You go now. I have nothing left for you. Go." She swiped her hand toward the door. I did as I was told.

What a waste of money and time — I was so disappointed. I didn't believe in fortune-tellers or any hocus-pocus, but then I didn't believe in time travel, either. Besides meeting my long-dead relatives, I had wasted my time in Sacramento, and I needed to move on. If I would not meet someone who could assist me, I needed to find a job that would sustain me. I thought the more substantial the population, the better my chances of getting work and finding the secret to returning to my previous time.

I caught up with Jonathon one more time to receive my payment. He was so grateful that he paid me much more than our bargain. I was positively wealthy. But the question was, should I go east or west? San Francisco had been my plan, but was it going to aid me in reaching my actual goal?

A phrase that I had often repeated in deciding where Jeff and I would move when we finished vet school came to mind. *Go West, young man.*

I wasn't convinced how this would help, but I felt compelled to head to San Francisco. With a larger population, I might be able to locate someone who could help me find my way home. I ate my last dinner with Mrs. Findlay and said farewell to Hattie. I even stopped to see the whore who helped me with my wardrobe, but she was busy with the mayor.

A day later, a barge left Sacramento that took me down to the San Francisco Bay. I then caught a boat to the San Francisco wharves. It was still summer, but it was cold and foggy. I feared a large ship would hit our small boat in the pea-soup fog. The barge rocked violently, and Penny, who was with the other horses, slid back and forth. One gelding went down under two other horses and was stepped on.

He held his leg in the air when he regained his footing. I steadied Penny as best as I could, but I was becoming seasick myself. We finally docked, and I assisted the man with the injured horse. The skin was not broken, but he still limped. I palpated the limb and could find nothing wrong. *Go get an X-ray in a couple of days if he isn't any better.* Life in the 1800s was so third world. There was a 'horse healer' based in San Francisco, and the owner of the injured horse promised he would seek him out if his gelding did not improve.

I was directed to the boardinghouse that Sam Buchanan had suggested. There were no vacancies, but the proprietor pointed to another one down the same road, which would take horses as well. I knocked on the house door, and an old man with dirty clothes and an unkempt beard opened the door.

"Sorry, this must not be the place I'm looking for. So sorry to bother you." *Nope, not going there for love or money.* Now, where? It was late afternoon, and the fog, which had receded, was rolling in again. I could stay in a hotel, but I was trying to save money.

A couple, who appeared to be in their early forties and looked respectable, were walking down the road. I asked them about finding a place to stay for a few days, and they looked at each other and said, "We might be able to help you." They looked clean and safe.

"I can pay. How much would you like?"

They smiled and said, "Maybe we could do some trading." The couple asked if I had any skills. I told them I was an animal doctor. The man's eyes lit up.

"Oh, I'm Dr. Thomas Walker, and this is my wife, Clara. Please come and at least spend the night with us."

We walked to their home, which was above average for the area. He was a surgeon.

A match made in heaven. I didn't discuss the nature of my travels with this couple. They were devout Christians and had a large family of children. They had several servants and were prominent in the community. I was not the only person they took in off the street. Many of the servants were former alcoholics and opium addicts. The Walkers strove to rehabilitate them. I was almost sure they were trying to get me to join their family in servitude. However, when I was invited to attend a medical clinic with Dr. Walker, I sewed up a laceration and assisted with an appendectomy.

The conditions were less than sterile. I tried to show the doctor some simple techniques to clean the area where he planned to operate. He had iodine and alcohol. It was like jumping ahead fifty years from Nevada and back fifty years from my time. I spent several days at Dr. Walker's public clinic. It was not his regular practice. He worked at a prestigious hospital in the city center, but this was his joy.

Both Dr. and Mrs. Walker were missionary kids. They met in Africa in their youth, where their parents converted Africans to the joys of Christian living. They were sweethearts from the time they were young teenagers. When a neighboring tribal village attacked Mrs. Walker's village, both families returned to Vermont. The young couple was separated for years but continued correspondences and eventually married when Dr. Walker finished his studies in medical school.

Their children ranged in age from four to twelve. I was sure some were adopted. They were all fun, polite, bright sparks. Mrs. Walker, with the aid of two nannies, ran a small school from the back of her property. The one-room class had at least thirty children. Getting sufficient materials for all the children to read and grow academically was a challenge. The Walkers could have been wealthy from Dr. Walker's work at the regular hospital, but they invested much of their money in their street clinic.

I wanted to emulate them when I returned to my time. The Walkers loved each other, and they loved their extended family. They were so involved in their community and church. I attended each Sunday with the family. The preaching and Scriptures did not move me, but it was fun to be in such a caring, loving community. My religion came from within. As a child, I attended church with my mother. When my mother died, so did my family's association with structured religion.

Of course, there were questions. I made sure that everyone knew I was married, and a devoted wife. I explained my husband was traveling to meet me. My story changed to fit the Walkers. He was supposed to be on a boat coming around the Horn. He should arrive in a month or so. It was totally plausible, and I was not questioned.

# CHAPTER 15

A month later, fall was setting in. I couldn't tell, as the famous San Francisco fog made even a summer day initially cold. I had a routine. I helped Mrs. Walker in the morning with the children and the school. Then, I attended the street clinic with Dr. Walker in the afternoon. I became quite proficient in the use of chloroform for procedures performed at the clinic. I was learning a great deal about human medicine. One day a week, I explored the city and sought people who might be open to the idea of time travel. I searched the library without asking for help or directions. I had not found a single individual whom I could trust to help me.

I thoroughly enjoyed my time with both the Walkers. I almost sensed they could be trusted with the truth. I went down to the docks weekly to check for incoming ships. It was a ruse regarding my missing husband. Life on or near the docks was dangerous. The men there were not to be trusted, according to Dr. Walker.

I remembered a *Comstock* episode where some of the Buchanans were shanghaied. They were in a saloon, and a trapdoor opened and dropped them to a waiting crew that would send them to sea. I did not go into any pubs, and I always looked at the floors when I walked along the docks. I know how silly it seems, but how does that compare to this new life I was living? I was taking no chances. No way.

The Walker's middle child was a fair-haired eight-year-old beauty. Her mother braided her hair in long pigtails and spent an enormous amount of time dressing her in fancy clothes. The other children were oblivious to the special treatment little Dorinda received. Perhaps they realized it came with obligations that were not rewarding. This child was a tomboy if there ever was one. The last thing she wanted was to dress up and go to high tea with her mother. One day, she begged me to let her ride Penny.

"Ask your mother." I was definitely not going to cross Mrs. Walker when she had been so kind to me.

Mrs. Walker was not happy about Dorinda riding a horse. I tried not to get involved, but her father intervened, so Dorinda began riding lessons on Penny. Penny was an obliging horse. She could be lively, but she adjusted to the rider's abilities quickly. The riding lessons continued for weeks. Dorinda became dependent on me for company. She'd found me to be her kindred spirit. On several nights, she came into my room and climbed in bed with me. That started a pattern with two of the other children, and soon it was almost nightly. Mrs. Walker admonished me for spoiling the children. Dr. Walker found it amusing, much to the dismay of his wife. One night I heard them arguing about how Mrs. Walker thought I was stealing her children's affection.

That was the night I told the children that I was not feeling well, and they should stay in their own beds, or they could sleep together if they were frightened. I had three howling children and a very furious mother.

"Do you see how you have spoiled them, Rebecca?"

"No. I mean, yes, I do. I'm sorry, I won't let the children sleep with me again, Mrs. Walker."

One night, all the young children ran to my room at the sound of gunfire. Mrs. Walker came in to see what the noise was, and she told the children to get back to their beds. I was chastised for going against her will. I tried to explain, but she said we would talk in the morning.

The following day, one of the Walker children told me their dog, Sheba, was not eating and was panting. She was older and had whelped a litter of puppies three weeks earlier. She drank water continuously. I felt her abdomen and considered she might have a pyometra. I thought I could feel a dead puppy inside her. I looked at Dr. Walker, who shrugged. Maybe it was my turn to show him some of my surgical skills. We took her down to the clinic and anesthetized her. Sheba's muzzle was covered with a funnel attached to a mask. She vomited after the first application of chloroform, but after we cleared her mouth, we tried again. She went to sleep after the second application. Using the clinic instruments, I opened her abdomen, removed the uterus, and stitched up her skin incision. We had no antibiotics and no intravenous fluids, let alone catheters, to administer the fluids. She lay on a blanket on the floor for hours.

I lay with Sheba, and Dr. Walker sat at his desk, doing reports and writing to colleagues about medical procedures. I must have fallen asleep as I was startled by a vigorous shake from Dr. Walker's wife. She'd come down to the clinic. Even Dr. Walker had fallen asleep on a pallet next to me. It was a compromising scene. As God is my witness, we were innocent of any impropriety on any level. Sheba was still quite groggy and had vomited again.

We carried Sheba back home to her puppies. She appeared to be improving. She drank some broth and began cleaning the puppies. Her engorged mammary glands got some relief with five puppies nursing around the incision. I prayed the sutures would hold, and she could fight any infection on her own.

Things were notably tense between Mrs. Walker and me. She hinted it might be time for me to move on and that perhaps my marriage might be over, or worse, a fantasy. I could tell she and Dr. Walker had fought.

Things appeared to settle down, and I was careful to never accompany Dr. Walker without a chaperon. After a year, I decided it was time to move on. I'd found no answers to my quest to return to the future. I'd gained surgical and anesthetic skills that would help me in my endeavors to establish a veterinary practice. I announced my intention to move on. The day before my departure, I answered the door to two constables, who asked for my name. I replied, and they said they were taking me into a station for questioning.

"What for?" I asked, shocked beyond all recognition.

"Theft, ma'am," replied a lanky man in uniform.

"Theft of what?" I demanded.

"Money, medicine, clothes, and jewelry," the stocky man responded. Mrs. Walker was standing behind me now. The younger constable was ordered to go up with Mrs. Walker and search my room.

"Righto, captain," the constable replied.

I almost collapsed when my traveling bag was brought back full of chloroform, iodine, instruments, money, and Mrs. Walker's jewels.

"I think she's dealing in witchcraft. I saw her enter several shops that deal with those kinds of things."

Mrs. Walker, who I thought was my good friend, had a smirky smile on her face. Dr. Walker was out of town and had taken a steamer to Sacramento yesterday. I was headed back to the Sierras. I think she believed he and I might rendezvous in Sacramento.

I was to be taken to court for an immediate hearing. If the judge felt it was necessary, I would be held in jail for trial. The constable took all of my possessions, including the medicine and drugs, for evidence. Mrs. Walker could keep her jewelry and the money. Some of it was mine.

I was destitute and could not post bail. I'm screwed.

As I was escorted out the door, the children watched helplessly, and one cried. "Mrs. Harper, come back," wailed one of the older children. "Mother, please stop them. She saved Sheba, and she promised me a ride on Penny. Please, Mother."

Mrs. Walker had a stern look on her face. "You all stop crying. That woman tried to steal our money."

Two older children shouted, "But that's what you said the last time someone left, and the time before that, too. They can't all be thieves. Father won't be happy."

The door was closed, but I was sure I heard her say, "Your father will never know."

I was taken to a small building several streets from the Walker home. From there, an open wagon delivered me to a sizeable, austere building in the center of San Francisco. I was handcuffed and made to sit with people who were also charged with crimes. I looked straight ahead. Somehow, I didn't think requesting a phone was going to work. Did the accused have legal representation in these times? I could not afford a lawyer without my rightful money. There was no one I could ask for help. The constable read the charges and his initial findings. I was to be confined for weeks until after Christmas, when a judge would hear my case. I asked that bail be considered, which was set at two hundred dollars. Even if I had my own money, it was well below the bond.

# CHAPTER 16

The women's section of the holding jail was wet and cold, with no light other than the daylight that seeped through the vertical, glassless windows near the ceiling. *Thank God I didn't end up in the eighteenth century. I thought I was going to get sick and die in this hellhole. Women all around me were coughing and had lesions on their skin. We had to defecate, drink, and share blankets in the same small cell. There were five other women and beds for two. The other women all knew one another. I guessed they were being held for solicitation. Was that a crime at that time?* I sat in a corner and had my usual pity party. I was healthy and well-fed, but that would not last long. I might not see natural daylight for weeks.

I was removed from my cell and transferred to an even smaller chamber with a table the following morning. A very young, blond, pockmarked man walked in. He was clearly under the influence. "Mrs. Harper, I'll be representing you in January. Unless you have evidence, I suggest you plead guilty, and we can have you moved to the women's correctional institute, possibly by tomorrow." He gave me a stern look.

"How many days would I need to serve?" This might not be so bad after all.

"Days, Mrs. Harper? More like years. Your crimes are grave." He paused and reached into his coat pocket, drew out a flask, and took a sip. I distinctly smelled alcohol. "You would be looking at eight years minimum."

"And if I don't plead guilty?"

"If you are lucky and have a lenient judge, you might get ten, but I would think fifteen." He burped and repeated his stern look. "Mrs. Walker would like this wrapped up quickly. She won't mention that you have made inquiries about witchcraft and the occult."

"I must not understand. Who do you represent?" I asked.

"Mrs. Walker is paying for me to represent you. You're lucky. The last two she fired are still in jail."

"Does Dr. Walker know anything about this?"

"Oh, no, we wouldn't want to bother a man in his position." He seemed to scoff.

*Sure, you wouldn't.*

"No, thank you, sir. I'd rather rot than have you represent me, and you can tell Mrs. Walker she will reap her just desserts when, and if, I ever get out. I'll be representing myself. Get out, you drunken piece of dirt." I may have used another word.

"Mrs. Harper! There is no need to be foulmouthed. We're just trying to help you rehabilitate."

Purposely, I raised my voice. "Here's the deal, buddy. I'm not one of the poor hapless women that Mrs. Walker thinks had an affair with her husband. I'm not stupid. I have two college degrees, and my guess is I'm more educated and know more than the two of you together, and I repeat, I am a married woman. See you in court. And remember, she can do to you what she has done to me."

The jailer returned and shouted, "Hey, what's going on here?"

"Sir, will you please take me back to my cell? This man is trying to slip me some whiskey. You may want to relieve him of his flask."

The lawyer looked shocked. The jailer patted the man's pocket and took the flask. "There will be none of that, Mr. Bishop. His Honor will be very disappointed to hear his son is back up to his old tricks."

"Go to hell. I gave her an option, and she was stupid enough to reject it. My father can go to hell, too."

As I walked back to my holding cell, I queried who his father was.

"Judge Bishop, a right nice and fair judge."

"And may I ask your name, sir?"

"We aren't supposed to say our names in case you come out and retaliate."

"Will I have reason to?"

"Not as long as you mind yourself, Miss."

"Well, I'm Rebecca. Pleased to meet you." I held out my hand, and he looked at it before taking it. "I won't be any trouble."

He left me with my cellmate 'friends.' One never knew who might be of help. I had sixty or so days to go. It might as well be pleasant. I was going to be positive.

I finally had to eat something, and I started with bread. It seemed the least likely to kill me. I knew I'd need something else. I thought if I took small amounts of food, my intestines might slowly adjust to the bacteria. Salmonella and tuberculosis were significant concerns. I talked to the women about this, and they agreed to cover their mouths when they coughed and attempt to wash their hands at least once a day. We were given smocks to wear, and our clothes were taken away and probably burned. I asked if I could write to someone, and the girls all laughed.

The oldest was a pockmarked woman. She was a regular. She was at least five feet eleven and had to weigh close to one hundred eighty pounds. I did not want to upset her. "No letter is gonna be mailed. You'd be wasting your time, and the jailers would read it and use it against you in court."

"So how do I get the word out that I'm in here, say, to a family member?"

There was a chorus of, "You don't." They laughed. They were all regulars and had spent months here over the years. "You do time, or you pay the fine," they chorused again. "At the regular prison, you can send a letter once a month. I ain't never had anyone reply. None of my kin can read."

"I'm happy to write letters for you all." If I could keep them on my side, I might not get killed.

"You an educated lady, ain't you? My son went to school, but he's gone off to fight Indians, the damn fool."

"Is there a way to buy my way out?"

"We will all get out soon by 'paying our way,' but I doubt you'll do what it takes, and I doubt you could, anyway." A plump, red-haired, cheery lady in her late forties knew about a friend of a friend who had worked for the Walkers, who was now in jail. "I heard she got fifteen years."

I thought all was lost. I could not find my way back to the 1980s, to my husband and daughter, or even see the sun on the odd days when the sun broke through the fog. Our cell captured only partial gray light. I could see why suicide in jail was contemplated as an option.

My cellmates eventually left. For one blessed night, I had the cell to myself. That was when the guards wanted to 'offer their services.' I persuaded them to find other sources for their needs by feigning illness. The clap was the best one.

I had my driver's license in the heel of my shoe. I had not looked at it in months. I decided it was too risky to keep it and shoved it in the crack between two bricks. I covered it with slime and dirt from the walls and floors. I pondered what a guard would think if it was discovered before the 1906 earthquake. More of my past was gone.

Raymond O'Keefe, my regular red-headed Irish guard, became my protector. He brought letters from Ireland for me to read to him. I obliged by reading them to him repeatedly, teaching him the alphabet, and eventually read his own mail. I was allowed a private cell most of the time.

As the days wore on, I went crazy. The light was my daily blessing, but the dark stone walls became slimy, and I smelled mold all the time. I asked for something to clean the walls, and the guards said I could use my clothes. Raymond brought me a candle so I could read his letters. He furnished paper, a pen, and then even chalk. I wrote letters to Dr. Walker. Raymond said he took them to his clinic, but I never received a response.

As Christmas approached, I had a visitor ask to see me. It was the same lawyer as before. His hands were shaking, and he asked again if I wanted to plead guilty. He thought time would make me more amenable to this proposition. He received the same reply minus the cuss words.

I prepared for the worst Christmas of my life. No family, no friends, and only the dark eighteen hours per day. Raymond was going to be away for a week to welcome a new child into his family. I fought back the tears, thinking of my beautiful little girl. I wondered if Jeff had moved to the Nevada veterinary practice. Had he stayed closer to his parents instead? Was it really a year and a half for him, too? Had time stood still for them? The tears flowed, and I knew in the dark no one would see them.

I was getting colder, and finally, I realized I had a fever. I was waiting for diarrhea or a respiratory infection that would become pneumonia or tuberculosis. For days, I shivered and sweated, and then I could feel a fever break only to have the cycle start again. I knew food and water would help, but I had no appetite. This was it. I was going to die, and this hellhole would claim another life. For several days, I lay beneath a wet blanket and did not take food or water. My faith would not allow suicide. If I didn't actively try to live, I was convinced I'd still go to heaven. Much to my dismay, I felt better. I could not even die properly. That was to be my out. I failed myself, and I'd live again to rot in this abyss.

Finally, one morning, a day or so before Christmas, the cell door lock jingled. A uniformed guard asked if I was Rebecca Harper.

"Yes, sir," I responded.

"Someone is here to see you."

I was taken to a new room with lanterns, tables, and chairs. Dr. Walker was sitting in one chair, and Clint Buchanan was in the other. My knees buckled at the sight of them. I gasped. I knew they thought I was insane.

Clenching my fists to control and steady myself, I turned away. I felt vile and naked. My hair was greasy and uncombed, and I smelled. My clothes were dirty — no, they were filthy and were less than the Victorian modesty model I had learned was proper at this time. I didn't want anyone I knew to see me like this, but God, I wanted out.

Both men looked down and tried not to stare. "Rebecca," Dr. Walker said quietly, "I'm so sorry. Just so sorry. I didn't know."

I turned back and stared at him, and my eyes flooded. I could not speak. I looked down at the ground.

"Rebecca, Pa was worried. He hadn't heard from you." Clint was clutching the edge of his chair. His knuckles were white from his grip. "He sent me to find you. He asked me to bring you home."

Dr. Walker raised his eyebrows and quizzically looked at me. Sam Buchanan's home was not my home. My home was with Jeff and Lauren. Or was it anymore? "My trial isn't for several more weeks," I said weakly. "I can't leave."

Dr. Walker stood and came over to me. He put his hand on my shoulder. "My darling Rebecca, there won't be any trial. You're free to go. The charges were a mistake and have been dropped. I'm so very sorry I didn't know sooner."

"But how did you find me?" My words were halting and intermixed with gulps and hiccups. The enormity was too much, and I broke down and had another cry. I tried to say they were tears of joy, but my hiccupping interrupted my words and questions. Finally, I managed, "I need a bath."

Both the men and the jailer, who was looking embarrassed, nodded. After an hour of signing paperwork, I was escorted out into the bright sunlight. It hurt my eyes something fierce. I could hardly open them. Each man took an arm, and they walked me to a hotel. A maid was sent to my room. She escorted me to a bathing room, where she offered a tub of hot soapy water. She provided me with hair oils, powders, and scrubbing brushes. The water was stone cold before I emerged. Clothes were left in the room, and I dressed and attempted to fix my hair. It was much longer now. A woman knocked on the door, entered the bathing room, and helped me set it. The cornflower-blue velvet dress was long-sleeved and had a corset and undergarments to go with it. The shoes were too big, but I stuffed paper in them to make them stay on. I fell back on the soft, clean bed with crisp sheets and slept for an hour. The sun was setting when a knock on the door woke me. It was Clint, and he was alone. I smiled weakly with embarrassment. He returned the smile.

"May I have the pleasure of your company at dinner tonight?" he inquired with a bow. I thought he must be in his early twenties at best. I wondered why his father had sent a young man for such a long trip. At dinner, I learned he was off to a technical college, and he was taking a ship around the Horn. It was merely an aside that his father had requested for him to look me up. By pure chance, he saw Penny tied in front of the Walkers' residence and knocked on their door to see if I was inside. The children answered before their mother was aware there was a caller, and they cried. Dorinda told Clint that I'd been taken to jail. Mrs. Walker came to the door and said she had kept Penny awaiting my return, and the children brushed her daily. She told Dorinda to return to her studies and not to talk to Clint.

Dr. Walker walked up the stairs to his house to a scene of crying children, a barking dog, and his wife yelling at Clint to go away. This was when he found out what had happened. He didn't know, and he was sure the children were mistaken. Mrs. Walker told Clint that I'd left in a hurry as a ship had set sail a day early and that I'd gone and given the horse to the children. The children were too afraid to tell the truth, because their mother threatened that the horse and dog would be sent away if one word got back to their father.

"Apparently, you aren't the first, Becky," Clint explained. "If Mrs. Walker suspects her husband is seeking outside dalliances, she finds ways to get rid of the recipients."

"But, Clint, I never in a million years did anything to encourage Dr. Walker, nor he, me. I swear. There's another woman who's in prison now because of Mrs. Walker. I pray someone's going to look into her case."

"He knows that, and he said the same thing. He's hired a lawyer for her. He said he'd learned some surgical skills from you. He also said he taught you about anesthesia. I'm sorry for all this. I sent my pa a telegraph. I leave tomorrow, but I'm sure he will want you to come back to the Cattle Creek Ranch. I'm guessing you've had no word from your husband?"

"No, not yet anyway." I tried to sound hopeful, but I think he sensed I was giving up.

"Becky, I know Virginia City, which has been recently named, is a small place compared to San Francisco or even Sacramento, but you're welcome to stay there while you're waiting. My father would be happy to help you restart your life. You can stay at the Cattle Creek Ranch until you get on your feet. I'm sure there is something you could do. We knew you just for a short time, but we were all quite impressed, and I know my father is genuinely fond of you. He was unbearable when you left."

"Okay, yes, Clint. I'll give it some thought." The food arrived, and I could eat only a tiny portion of what I wanted. My stomach had shrunk, and it would take days before I could eat a proper meal. My eyes slowly adjusted to the constant bright light, but I would have killed for a pair of dark glasses. My lodging at the hotel was paid up for several days. Dr. Walker visited me twice. On the first visit, he brought my few personal possessions. During the second visit, Dr. Walker brought me a large sum of money as compensation for what his wife had done to me. He also gave me two bottles of chloroform ingredients and several instruments.

"Rebecca, why didn't you tell me you're a doctor?"

"I'm a veterinarian. As I explained, I trained with my husband. And yes, I have a husband and a daughter. To be honest, I don't know where they are, but I'll remain faithful to them until I die."

"And I will be faithful to my wife until I die, no matter what she does." We embraced like a brother and sister, and he left the hotel.

# PART 3

## BACK AT THE RANCH 1859

# CHAPTER 18

I received the wire confirming that a stagecoach ticket and travel money were waiting at the stage office. I spent one day walking around the city and seeing the sights. I'd never been to San Francisco in my past life, but I'd seen pictures. This was so rough and unpopulated compared with what I had expected. It was rather dismal. Sand dunes covered much of what I now knew were thousands of houses. I realized that the San Francisco I was now familiar with would be destroyed in the 1906 earthquake. Dr. Walker's children would be alive to see the quake, but he would be dead or very close to dead. I might be deceased — unless I found a way back to my time.

The day was clear and bright. I spent Christmas by myself in the hotel. The lobby was decorated with trees, candles, and ornaments. The staff treated me like royalty at the request of Dr. Walker and Mr. Buchanan, who were known to the management. I saw Fort Alcatraz and several clipper ships from the bayside. I took a hack over to the ocean side and marveled at the waves. I saw the inlet where Clint sailed out of the bay to his destination on the Eastern seaboard and college. One day, the Golden Gate Bridge would span it. I knew Clint would return to the Cattle Creek Ranch in a few years. I hoped I would not be there to greet him upon his return. I planned to be back in my own time. I wondered where I'd be in four or five years.

The next day, I had my trunk delivered to the stage, and I said goodbye to Penny. She would be sent up later in the year. Dr. Walker had arranged for her care and travel to Nevada. The trip back to Nevada was uneventful until I hit the western foothills of the Sierras. The snow was impassable. I was held up in the small mining town of Placerville. I took lodging in another boardinghouse. The rooms were small and sparse. While it was not free of vermin, it beat Miss Jayne's house, hands down.

I passed the time by attending to horses and mules injured or sick from their mining duties. The man who called himself a vet was really a human doctor who found more money in horses. That news was encouraging. The problem was that the doctor was drunk most of the time and unable to attend to the horses. He hired me to do his work. I worked six for seven hours per day. After so many weeks of work, I was getting quite a reputation as Dr. Price's nurse. *Grr.* He was happy to give me half of the takings and drink his half. *Double grr.* It was a man's world in the late 1850s.

A tall man walked into the livery where Dr. Price had his shop.

"Price, you bastard," he shouted. "Where the hell are you?"

I quietly replied, "Dr. Price is under the weather. May I help you?"

"Girly, ain't no one touching this horse but Price. Where is the cretin?"

"Upstairs," I said as I pointed to the loft above.

The man climbed up the ladder and found Dr. Price three sheets to the wind. A string of colorful words followed. He came back down, and for the first time, he turned toward me. Oh my God, it was Lee Marvin. In the flesh. Well, really, it wasn't Lee Marvin. This man resembled one of the characters he played. I thought about it and could not decide who he was playing. It was on the tip of my tongue.

"Again, may I help you? I'm Dr. Price's assistant." I faced him and smiled. I was star-struck. Time travel had its benefits.

He faced his horse to me, and I saw the horse's eyelid was torn. Eyelid lacerations were easily fixed with local anesthesia, of which I had none. This was going to be interesting. Dr. Walker had given me several curved sewing needles. The use of a twitch was uncommon, as far as I had observed. I made one from an ax handle and a rope. The rope was attached to the end of the ax, making a small loop, which was placed around the upper lip and tightened, pinching the nose. I explained it acted differently than one would expect. When I graduated from vet school, it was becoming known that the pressure on the upper lip causes a release of factors that make the horse sleepy. Oh, and it hurt, too.

"What's your name?" I casually inquired, hoping this would give me a clue.

"Name's Ben. Can you fix this?" The name did not offer me a clue.

"I can try. Where you from, Ben?"

"You wouldn't know it. It doesn't have a name."

"Are you sure I wouldn't know it? How is he about touching his head?" I cautiously approached the horse with the needle and thread.

"He'll stand, or he will see the other end of that ax handle, girly."

It came to me when I heard him say that. Paint your Wagon.

It was a job and a half without sedation and lidocaine, but I eventually put the dangling eyelid back together.

"Not as good as Doc Price, but it'll do." He paid me and was off. I wondered how many horses became infected with the bacterium that caused tetanus during these times. Modern vaccines were an unrealized dream, although smallpox virus was now preventable.

In March, there was an extended dry period. Several miners went over the pass and reported a stage could get through. By then, Penny had caught up with me. I wondered if I could get over before the next snow hit. It was rough going, but my sure-footed little mare carried me over the top and down into the lower elevations, where snow would not immobilize me. I made it to Virginia City.

I checked into the hotel and immediately walked to Dr. Sullivan's office. He was sitting in a leather chair, reading the paper once again. He looked up, and a broad smile came across his face. "Mrs. Harper. I hear you have had an interesting time since you left." He looked genuinely glad to see me.

"Ah, yes, about the departure," I pursed my lips together. "I'm sorry, sir. I've come to pay for your services and the food I took." It was snowing lightly outside, and my warm jacket was not holding its own.

"Come in and sit down. How are you? Can I get you some tea or coffee? Sam said you were living with Tom Walker. He and I went to school together. Lovely chap and such a clever surgeon."

"Yes, sir." *Sheesh, is anything a secret around here?* After chatting for a while, I confessed I was tired and needed to get some food and get back to the hotel. He would not hear of my eating alone. Mrs. Sullivan was attending to a child with a burn and would be back to cook dinner in an hour. I was ordered to come back and eat with them this evening.

Jeff often cooked dinner when I was at school. A husband doing 'women's work' was not common in these times. I know my father never cooked until my mother was terminally ill. Even then, Sherry and I did most of the cooking. I thought about the evolution of the role of housekeeping that men in my future time would adopt. I would marry no one who didn't do housework. These men would die if the time travel were reversed. *Spoiled rotten.*

"I must pay you for your services and what I, um, borrowed."

He looked at me squarely. "I'm pretty sure you will make it up in the next few weeks. I don't want your money. It is so nice to have an educated woman in the town. We're excited to have you. You can tell us about your travels tonight."

The meal was delicious, and the conversation was lively. I had a reasonably good idea of the level of practice here in Virginia City. Don't get tetanus or appendicitis, and you might survive to your mid-sixties. Pregnancy was also a worry, but not mine.

# CHAPTER 19

I hummed the *Comstock* theme song to myself all the following day. I would stay out at the Cattle Creek Ranch for a week until I could find a property. I'd seek work doing anything I could to make money and rent or buy a property near Virginia City. I wanted a junker or fixer so I could improve the value.

Alas, without power tools, the task was much more daunting. Jeff and I had fixed our small house back at the university. I did much of the work involved in the renovation and learned quite a bit from my father, who helped while Jeff and I were in the clinics of our veterinary school.

I planned to open a veterinary clinic in Virginia City. Still, I knew that would be a long-term, slow-growing proposition. I might get some difficult or lame breakers from the Buchanans, rehabilitate them, and sell them on like my dad did.

In a month or two, I would explore where I came from, and with Sam's permission, I would continue to explore the beautiful valley. I would not give up on getting back to my time. I would not.

Sam Buchanan and Gee Ling arrived in town around nine o'clock in the morning, and we met in the hotel lobby. I still could not get over how young they both looked. He and Gee Ling both hugged me and asked me how I was. I had my satchel and a small trunk of clothing that I'd sent on the stage. I was wearing a brown traveling dress, and my waterproof coat was ready to take on the freezing rain.

"You just made it. A storm's blowing in. The pass is already closed, and the Cattle Creek Ranch will be covered in snow in a few hours. Gee Ling and I will get supplies, and we should return to the ranch as soon as possible."

"I'm ready to go. I don't have much to take, just this satchel and a small trunk. I can't thank you enough."

"Four of our top mares are due to foal in the next week. You'll earn your keep." Sam took my trunk and placed it on the wagon.

"No work for missy until I get her fat." Gee Ling felt my arm.

"Oh, no. Are you fattening me for the spit?" I saw them look quizzically and said, "You know, the oven?"

I thought I might have offended Gee Ling, as he took it to mean I was to cook.

"The spit is like the grill or barbecue, Gee Ling." He laughed and gave me another hug.

"Very nice to have smart lady at the table. All I hear is boy talk. Now, I hear some lady talk, too."

"This is just until I can find a place of my own. I hope to be out of your way as soon as possible."

"We'll see, Becky. There's no hurry. We're just glad you're safe." Sam looked fondly at me.

"I can't thank you enough. Really, when I saw Clint in San Francisco — well, I probably wouldn't be alive without his help." I felt tears but held them off.

We loaded the buckboard. The boys wouldn't let me help much, but I carried a few sacks of flour and sugar while they carried the heavy crates. We climbed on the buckboard, and they sandwiched me and threw a warm blanket and canvas over our knees. The warmth of the two men and the feeling of security were intoxicating. I fell asleep leaning on Gee Ling as I had on the first occasion when I'd met them on the road.

I awoke as we arrived. The homestead was blanketed in snow. The young boys, Hank and Danny, came out to greet us. They insisted I go in and warm up by the fire. They would not let me bring in any supplies. They prepared an upstairs room for me this time. Clint's room was converted into a slightly more feminine bedroom. I would live there until I was ready to leave.

I was given time to change into more suitable clothing for the ranch life. I was now used to the chamber pot and outhouse. Bathing was not a daily affair, but there was cologne for me to use. Again, I guessed this was from Danny's mother. I was reluctant to use it because smells are so emotive, and I didn't want to use up a small connection to his mother. I could still remember the lavender sprigs my grandmother kept in her bathroom.

Dinner was a feast of roast, soup, potatoes, and more green leaves I had not tasted before — no nutritional deficiencies tonight. Gee Ling had made a beautiful pie with whipped cream. The boys went out to tend the stock one more time. They were concerned that they would not even be able to get to the barn by morning at the rate it was snowing. I offered to come and check out the mares, but they declined.

"Please give Penny a bit of extra hay tonight, but no grain, thanks." She had been tethered to the buckboard and had a good trot all the way up. She knew where she was going and was excited when we turned into the front of the barn.

The boys returned and reported all was well. "Ma'am, we'll call you if we need you. Ain't no way anyone is foaling tonight, and they're probably a day away, if not more."

"Hank, I'm not a ma'am. I'm Rebecca, Becky, or Bec. I'm probably old enough to be your mother, but I'm not. I'm just Becky."

"Yes, ma'am, I mean Miss Rebecca or Miss Becky."

"No, Hank. Just Becky."

"Becky, we sure are glad you're here," said Danny.

"Thanks, Danny, and I'm grateful, too," I returned. "God moves in mysterious ways, doesn't he?"

They left the room and went upstairs, and Gee Ling also announced his retirement for the evening. This left only Sam and me. I knew he was politely waiting for an explanation. I still wasn't ready to tell the complete story. I gave him an outline of my travels and talked a bit about each place.

"I know I owe you a bit more of an explanation about myself. I'm pretty sure you won't believe me, so if you don't mind, can it wait until the snow's gone? When you kick me to the road, I mean out on the road, I might survive." Sam laughed and offered me brandy.

"This will warm your soul," he said.

"I'm not sure I have one anymore. It may have left me a while ago." We sat without talking in front of the famous Comstock fireplace until I dozed for a few seconds.

"Becky, you need to get to bed." He stood up and hugged me one more time. "Pleasant dreams."

"You too, Sam. Thanks again." I went upstairs while Sam stayed and went over his "figures." There seemed to be a lot of that "going over figures" in the television series.

It was snowing furiously outside, and my room was cold, but I was given heated bricks. If my head hit the pillow, I had no recollection of it. I have not slept so carefree since my last night with Jeff.

I had lost my picture of them when Mrs. Walker took my possessions. When Dr. Walker returned the bag with my riding boots, I jumped for joy. My driver's license was long gone, but I had proof of my life before the slide. I pulled it out and saw the now-fading picture. I'd try harder to get back, but for now, I have a new life.

# CHAPTER 20

T he snow continued to accumulate all day. Drifts were above the downstairs windows. I cleaned myself as best as I could and dressed for the cold weather. My room was chilly, but the water had not frozen. The goose-down comforter that had kept me warm the previous night was calling. I felt an overwhelming sense of relief. If I couldn't go home, this might be the next best place to be. I was surrounded by caring, virile men and two young boys who would grow to be the subject of a television series. Maybe this was all taking place inside some screenwriter's head. That was a new idea. *Hmmm.*

Breakfast was the usual feast. Now I sat in Clint's place at the dinner table. I could just about predict the conversation. Both boys were still going to school. They often missed school due to storms such as this one. They had regular lessons given ahead of time, and they had to work at these on snow days, such as today. I had seen the readers they were using in glass library cages in my own time. I should have told them to be careful with their books. They would be valuable someday. I helped Hank with his math, which he called "figuring." Danny needed no help. He was a quick learner, and soon he and I were playing checkers while Sam went through countless records and papers at his desk, planning out the upcoming year. I tried to help Gee Ling, but he would not allow it for the first few days of my visit.

An attempt to reach the barn by carving a path through the now eight- or nine-foot snowbank failed when it caved in. Everyone was worried about the mares, but it was not worth risking human life. In the evening, Sam and I were once again alone in front of the fire.

"Care to talk?"

"Sorry, Sam, I don't think you have enough liquor in your house for me to tell all." I smiled, but I knew I might have to tell him the truth at some stage.

He shrugged. "I'm a good listener, and I would love to help you. I've lost three wives, but I can't imagine what it is like to be separated from your husband and child and not know where to find them."

"Thanks, but it's more complicated than just that. Someday, I'll tell you. For the present, I must learn to live in your world." I knew he would not comprehend the double meaning, and again I was thankful he did not press the issue.

"We have an impressive library here. I even have a wonderful book called *Moby Dick*. It is a story about whaling. I used to captain a ship."

"I know." The second I said this, I could have kicked myself. "I think Clint mentioned it at dinner in San Francisco,"

I quickly explained. Oh, man, I was going to have to watch myself. I thought of Captain Klink in *Hogan's Heroes*: *I know 'nothink.'* I laughed.

Sam cocked his head. "Something funny?"

"No, well, yes. I just remembered something from my past. Again, not enough alcohol." I smiled, and he returned the smile.

I pulled The *Count of Monte Cristo* from the bookshelf. It would keep me busy for a long time.

"I'll start here. I'm a slow reader, and this will keep me occupied for weeks."

"Suit yourself." He held out *Moby Dick*. "It's a wonderful book."

"Call me Ishmael," I replied. "I read it at Dr. Walker's."

"Ah, well, that's a good book, too," he said, pointing to the book I had in my hand. "So glad to have someone here to share these books with. Clint is a reader, but the younger boys aren't that fond of books."

I remembered watching Hank sitting and reading in the house in many scenes on the television series. "Give it time," I said and smiled to myself.

The following day, the snow continued without abatement. Danny and Hank rigged up a slide from the house's upper story to the loft in the barn. They strung a rope from the loft door to the house. Only Danny went back and forth. The snow accumulation on the barn was getting dangerous, despite the slant of the roof. Danny was able to clear some of the snow, but unlike the house, it was not built to withstand the weight of the snow. There was the ever-present danger of a cave-in.

He reported no foals had been born, and he had broken the ice in the water buckets. The horses were not drinking as if they had been denied water. They were happily eating the new hay he had fed them all. Danny went back to clean the foaling pens after another Gee Ling breakfast. I offered to join and help as the rope system could easily support my weight. The men were aghast at my suggestion.

"What?"

"You're a lady."

"So? Hank, I did this with my father for years. It's nothing new, really."

"But still, Pa. The longer I take, the less time I'll have to do my studies."

Sam gave Danny a stern look.

"Sorry, Pa, I only meant...."

"There'll be time enough for both, young man. No, Rebecca will not be allowed on the rope. Does everyone understand?"

There was a chorus of "yes, sirs," and the subject was closed for now.

I had to hide my disappointment. It would be an adventure, and, like everyone, I was getting cabin fever. I didn't have to wait long.

Danny made his way over to the barn the following morning. A shout came from inside the barn. One of the mares was in labor. Danny had been down on the ground floor when he saw a white bag coming out of a bay mare.

We all sat in Hank's room every morning until Danny crossed the snow, using the rope on the handmade sled. He would open the bay doors of the loft, where the hay was stored, and then go down and examine the stock. Danny would come back up and give the all-clear. After that, he would remain in the barn for an hour or two, feeding and cleaning. Once Danny signaled the all-clear, we would go back down to the great room and resume our activities: studying, reading, or, in Sam's case, doing accounts and planning his year's activities.

This morning was different. "Pa, send Becky. Tilly's in labor. Hurry, please." When the urgent call from Danny came, I didn't hesitate to put on my jacket. I retrieved the sled, which had a rope attached to the house, and climbed on, despite Hank and Sam's concerns.

I inched across the snow, which had accumulated to two-story drifts, and climbed into the barn. I wormed my way through the hay to a ladder and descended to the barn floor. I was surprised by how warm it was. The horses and a few cows kept the conditions verging on tolerable. I saw Danny at the end of the row of stalls and opened the wooden gate. The mare was down, pushing. I could see the foal's nose and one leg protruding from the vagina. I'd have preferred to clean my arm, but there was nothing around. I reached in and could feel the foal's second foot just inside the vagina. Teach a man to fish. I asked Danny to reach in and touch the hoof. At first, he was appalled, but he did it.

"I can feel it, but it's slimy," he said.

"That's the amnion, Danny. Just reach under it, grab the leg, and pull."

He pulled, and the elbow, which was caught on the pelvic brim, was free. The foal came out seconds later in a whoosh of fetal membranes and fluid.

"You did it," I exclaimed, slapping him on the back.

"I did." He was so excited that we both slipped on the fetal membranes and went down into a pile of fluids and manure. I laughed and commented that now I had an excuse for a bath. Danny remarked he had just taken one at his father's direction before I arrived. This was much too soon for another. Ah, boys.

He went up to the loft and reported the safe arrival of a foal. We didn't know the sex for a few more minutes, as I suggested the foal not be disturbed so the blood could be drained as much as possible from the placenta. After several minutes, the mare got up and broke the cord. I'd used iodine in a bottle in the barn on my last visit here. We found the iodine and doused the umbilical stump. It was a filly. She was a bay with three white feet. She slipped around on the membranes until we removed them. The filly was standing within minutes. In an hour, she was nursing. I took this opportunity to help Danny clean the stalls, groom the horses, and feed the rest of the stock. The physical work was invigorating. I hoped for another foal this evening.

When I returned via the rope and sled, I was greeted by nose-holding from Hank and an immediate plan to heat water for a bath and wash my clothes. I was given Sam's famous hunter green bathrobe to wear in the meantime. Yep, it looked just like the one on Comstock. Both boys offered to help me by bringing clean hot water, but one look from their prudish father eliminated all their hopes for a sneak peek.

The snow subsided after a few warm days, and I could go to the barn daily to inspect the filly's progress and check the other mares. One more foal was born during the night, a liver chestnut colt who was up, dry, and nursing when we arrived. Unseasonably warm weather followed the late snow, making the creeks run full and the passage to Virginia City dangerous. Any thought of going to town was abandoned. The other two mares foaled, and all four foals were progressing well. I was getting outside regularly, and I even took Penny out to ride up to the breaking pens. The horses were all turned out on the range, and the ranch hands had left for town, the mines, or warmer climates. They would be back in a month or two to break in the next lot of Cattle Creek Ranch horses.

# Chapter 21

I stayed at the Cattle Creek Ranch for a month. My finances did not suffer as much, and I tried to pay for room and board. They wouldn't accept my money. Gee Ling let me help occasionally and taught me how to cook several of his recipes. I tutored the boys and assisted with any veterinary needs that I could. The castrations would not begin for several months. I was not wanted for what had traditionally been men's business. They had predicted losses from this endeavor every year. Basically, the horses were cast and held down with ropes, and the job was performed with no anesthesia. I was dying to try chloroform on one, but that was out of the question.

When I traveled to Virginia City, I heard about a miner's cabin a few miles out of town coming up for auction. It included a couple of horse yards and a small shed I might use as a clinic. A creek ran through the property, and I saw trout in one of the pools. There was enough cleared land for plowing and growing a garden. I requested the expected dollar amount if sold at auction. The figure quoted to me was fifty dollars. I had thirty. I went to the bank to see if I could borrow the extra money. I was approved with the assistance of the Cattle Creek Ranch and the Buchanans behind me.

On the day of the auction, a few folks had gathered at the property. I was surprised because it wasn't really a place where many people would choose to live. One would not make a living out of this property.

The bidding started at twenty-five dollars. I was the only bidder initially. Just as the hammer was going down, someone raised the bid. I went up, and the bidding war began. I had to opt out at sixty, but two people were still bidding until it hit one hundred, which was well above my limit. I was disappointed, but I knew other properties would become available.

Before we left, Sam said he needed to see the auctioneer. I assumed he had other business with the man. I waited by the buggy and looked at the cabin again. It was rough, and I couldn't imagine why anyone would pay that much for this place. I'd studied properties for sale, and I was not prepared to pay that much myself. The creek had been surveyed for gold and silver; nothing was found. Who else wanted this property? I was chagrined, but I held my head high and smiled when Sam returned to the buggy. "Next time," I said.

"You never know," he declared. "There are some great opportunities around."

I was to shift into town tomorrow. I would live in the new boardinghouse. Gee Ling made an extra-special supper. Sam and the boys dressed up, and I wore a dress to add to the festive occasion. After dinner, Sam had a brandy poured for everyone, even the boys. Gee Ling never drank, but he watched on. Sam cleared his throat. "I have a proposition for you, Rebecca."

That was interesting. Sam never called me Rebecca anymore.

"What kind of proposition?" I could see he had more than a casual or fatherly interest in me. I purposely made sure I mentioned my husband every day to remind them I was not available.

"I recently bought a property that I need to sell. I was wondering if you would be interested in it. It has a caveat on it. I'm selling only some of the property and not all the rights."

"Go on," I replied.

"How about the boys and I take you there tomorrow? If it suits you, we can negotiate a sale. We can stop on our way into town."

We had our brandy, and the boys went to bed.

"May I offer you some alcohol?" Sam asked with a grin.

"You can try," I returned. "You know how you think you know someone, but then you really get to know that person? Then, you find out they aren't who you thought they were, and you no longer want to be friends. That's me. I don't want to lose you as a friend. It feels as if I have known you for decades, and I'm counting on you for friendship. I've done nothing wrong, but if you knew my past, I don't think you would want to be my friend. Can we leave it at that?"

"I can't imagine anything would dissuade me from being your friend. I'll leave it to you to decide what and when you think you can confide in me. You know I have resources to help you."

I smiled, and we hugged for a little longer than was just friendly. Sam kissed the top of my head, and I stepped away, blushing. How many times had I observed him doing this with women who rejected him or were never worthy of his love? Here I was, married and still held the hope I would get back to my time and my husband. I knew he would fall in love with many more women over the years, and I'd be a passing fancy. The question was how would my life end and where?

The following morning, a very cheerful Sam, Hank, and Danny started into town. I was packed and sat next to Sam in a buggy. They turned off the main road and headed toward the cabin. I thought another miner's cottage must be nearby.

We stopped at the scene of the auction, which had a sold sign mounted on the gate. We turned in to the property.

"Well, would this do?" Sam and the boys grinned and crowded around where I sat in the buggy.

"I don't understand. Did the sale fall through?"

"It's for you, Becky," said Hank. "Isn't it perfect?"

Danny continued, "It's on our way to town and school. We could stop by and cut wood or help with Penny. Hank could shoe her for you. You could tutor us with our homework, and maybe Hank or I could spend the night once in a while."

I was shocked and honored, but who actually owned the cabin? How was this going to work? Was I going to rent it from whoever purchased it?

"Does someone want to tell me what's going on?"

Sam cleared his throat. "When I saw who was buying it, I realized they wanted the water rights. They would divert the water to the McDougals, which eventually flows to the Cattle Creek Ranch. I bid on it, standing behind your back. I have no need for the property, but I need the water. The cabin isn't worth thirty dollars, but the water is worth so much more. I'll sell you the property for thirty dollars if you allow me to keep the water rights. You don't have to decide today."

"No, I think this is a bargain for us both. I was worried that this was charity, but I see your point. It's a deal. I think your price is rather high, but you have me over a barrel. What will the town say? Here you are, taking advantage of a poor, husbandless woman. If you can live with yourself and the dent in your reputation, it's worth every penny. Speaking of which, I'll need some hay for Penny."

Sam roared with laughter. The boys caught the ire of my admonishment, and they opened the door to display wild spring flowers in a vase on a table, a single bed, and wood stacked next to the hearth.

"Madam, you strike a hard bargain. If I throw in an oven, would you speak kindly to the townspeople on my behalf?"

"If the oven has room for two pots at once, I promise not to besmirch your name."

"You're a hard woman." Sam beamed.

"Hank, if you are allowed, you can come for lessons and pay for it by cutting wood once in a while. Danny, I can use your help as well. Shall we go into town now, so I can buy provisions?"

As we walked out of the cabin, Gee Ling showed up with several wooden crates with flour, sugar, salt, and jerky. He brought curtains that just fit the window and a rifle for bears or mountain lions.

"No need to go into town." I looked at the cabin and grinned.

I reached into my leather purse, which Danny had made and given to me during our snowbound days. I pulled out the money and counted it as I handed it to Sam. While I wanted a paper to make it legal, I was too shy to ask for one. "Everyone here is a witness. I've paid for my beautiful cabin." Compared to the Cattle Creek Ranch, it was only one step up from a privy, but to me, it meant independence and a brief interlude in my journey back to my husband and daughter.

"I'll have my lawyer draw us an agreement on Monday."

"Ben, don't forget to have him include the oven."

"Boys, let's get home before she has us sign over the Cattle Creek Ranch in the deal."

"Right, Pa," said Danny. So predictable. I was going to have to think about what else I remembered from watching Comstock.

I hugged and kissed them all. Gee Ling was particularly pleased, and the boys didn't seem to mind, either. Sam smiled, and I could see he was delighted to have helped me.

The next evening was a church social. I hadn't met many people besides Dr. and Mrs. Sullivan. The Buchanans insisted on taking me into town and supplying supper for us all. For all the nice things about this time, one thing was not. Gee Ling could not socialize with the Anglo-Saxons. Women did not have the right to vote, and they had no tampons either. Life was not fair.

# CHAPTER 22

Thanks to Dr. Walker, I had a beautiful dress to wear, and the Buchanans had given me more of Danny's mother's shoes and womanly extras. I dusted up pretty well. While I was a married woman, I didn't mind having men look. They just couldn't touch.

I had not been to the church, so Sam and the boys introduced me to many townsfolk. Some lovely women knew about me, and I could see that my stay at the Cattle Creek Ranch had some tongues wagging, but I didn't care. I met the schoolteacher, Martha Gilliam. I hoped she would be a good friend. I promised to stop in and talk to her class. I realized there would be opposition to any support for girls to go further in their education. I had to tread a fine line, but I wanted to be Martha's friend. I needed a girlfriend. She was educated, spirited, and single, which was about as close to my status as could be considered. I'm sure there were widows in the town. Perhaps I could become friends with one or two others as well.

After a sit-down meal, the orchestra, comprising two violins and a banjo, played. Danny wasted no time in asking me to dance. I didn't know the dances of the time, so I wanted to just watch. He would not take no for an answer. This kid was already a heartbreaker. I went out on the floor and followed his lead. I watched others and did the best I could. The next dance was Hank's turn. He was not light on his feet, and my toes were taking a beating. After that, Dr. Sullivan asked me to dance. I was exhausted. I sat down for a minute, and much to my surprise, Sheriff Ray Thompson bowed and asked me to dance. I could not take my eyes off him. He was ten years younger than his television character and agile on the dance floor. I knew he was a widower on Comstock, but was that after this time, or had he been widowed before? When did he come to Virginia City? He wasn't there when I first arrived and met his deputy, Glenn Frasier.

"Mrs. Harper, or, should I say, Dr. Harper, you remind me of my late wife."

"Oh, Sheriff, I'm sorry to hear you are alone," I said solemnly. "Please call me Rebecca or, better yet, just Becky."

"I guess you know we sent Sam's foreman, Gil, to the state prison," he said casually.

"Ten years is a bit too short of a sentence, but I'm not the judge," he continued. "So, how are you settling in? Did I hear you bought the old miner's cottage and drove a tough bargain with Sam?" His smile had a kind twinkle that I had seen on television.

"Well, the transaction isn't completed, and I still don't have my oven, but it's early days, and I'm convinced Mr. Buchanan will make good. He seems to be a man of honor."

"If he gives you any trouble, just see me. No one is above the law, even in a civil dispute." He smiled, took my hand and twirled me.

"Yes, sir. I will." Sheriff Thompson was a talented dancer.

The band took a break, and I needed one, too. I was introduced to the town mayor and his wife, the dry goods store owner, and the livery stable owner, along with their wives. They had all heard about me and were eager to meet the infamous woman who stayed out with men on the Cattle Creek Ranch for a month with no female companionship. After more food, liquid refreshments, and an outhouse break, I was back on the dance floor with Danny, the mayor, and others. I was surprised Sam Buchanan had not asked me to dance. He had danced several times with a woman much closer to his age. I thought maybe they were an item. Sam brought her punch and escorted her around for a good portion of the night. I was relieved not to be the object of his attention for once. Or was I?

Someone announced, "last dance." I was exhausted and comforted the night was over. Danny asked me to dance, but Sam tapped him on the shoulder and asked him if he minded. "Sure, Pa."

Sam took my hand, and then slow romantic music began. This was all wrong. I was a married woman. It felt so good to be in his arms, but I knew the plot. He would never find the right woman, and I would not be his fourth wife. That was almost madness. But it was so good. It felt so right, and yet it was so wrong. So wrong.

Nothing was said. When the music ended, Sam bowed politely and asked the boys to escort me home. He was taking the other woman back home and would catch up with them on the trail.

The next day, Sam and the boys picked me up and took me to church. I hadn't met the Reverend Earl Tyler until the church service was over. He was attending to a dying woman and was not at the social.

Out of propriety, I sat with Martha Gilliam, who introduced me to Reverend Tyler when we were leaving. If Burt Lancaster had a twin, I just met him. He was in his mid-thirties and, as far as I could see, single. I was not single, but I considered tossing my ring. *What ring?* I was gobsmacked. *I am not worthy. I am not worthy. So good-looking.*

"Dr. Harper, I've heard so much about you," he stated. "I'm glad you joined our community. We hope this is a permanent arrangement?"

"Oh, thank you, Reverend Tyler. One never knows. As you've probably heard, my husband and daughter are missing, and I have to assume in transit. I have to wait and believe that they are alive, well, and we will all be reunited soon. More people are coming from the east. They may have been held up on their way."

"I'll pray for you."

"Thank you."

Martha and I left together to see the schoolroom. I returned shortly to find the Buchanans finishing up with their social obligations. They took me home, and the boys offered to stay and help me clean, but I needed some time alone. I had so much to do to get ready for any clients or guests, and I needed to start the soil preparation for planting my garden. I planned to order some seeds from the dry goods store's catalog, and I wanted to explore the area.

I felt strongly that if I traveled to this time, I could get out as well. I only had to find an opening somewhere. By my calculations, Lauren was at least five. Did she miss me or even remember me? Did they all assume I'd been killed in the rockslide? Had Julie really been killed, as I thought?

I saddled Penny and took a tour around my new home. I was glad to be independent of any social obligations. I was approximately thirty minutes from the town, an hour or so from the Cattle Creek Ranch, and another hour from the rockslide area. It was the tail end of winter and still cold, even freezing, at night.

The tall pines surrounded my cabin. I could hear the creek gurgling behind the house. There must be a small rapid with the sound of water churning upstream. I loved the smell of the nearby pines. I hoped my senses didn't get too accustomed to it to notice. The clearing where I intended to plant the garden was several yards from the house, but the shed and Penny's pen were behind the house.

I wanted a dog. Of course, that's what I needed. A dog was a beautiful companion, with no obligations or questions — blind loyalty. I would look for one the next day. I'd additionally put up a display sign to advertise my services. Men were the primary horse owners. My competition was the livery stable owner, Mr. Owens, a kind man and an excellent horseman. Still, he was not a good healer. He tarred anything where tar would stick. He used something he called a 'physic' for colic. I didn't know what the ingredients were, but it smelled like paint thinner.

I stopped by the livery stable on Monday. I informed Mr. Owens I'd be glad to consult on any cases for which he would like advice. He looked at me as if I were daft.

"Well, missy, if there's anything that I can't cure, I'll be sure to send it your way." It was apparent that he had no intention of doing anything to give me business. The Buchanans spread the word, and I saw a horse with abscesses under the jaw from last year's hay and grass seeds that migrated under the tongue. The bump had a soft middle, and I opened it with a sharp knife. The pus flowed like lava out of the substantial swelling under the jaw. I flushed it with a basting appliance and cleaned it up as best as I could. I knew the abscess wasn't from strangles bacteria. The horse had no fever. He didn't present with any other characteristics of a horse with strangles, a highly contagious bacterial infection.

Strangles also caused abscesses under the jaw. They could be so large, they cause respiratory difficulty and even death — hence the name strangles. The gelding wanted to eat immediately after the mass was drained. I felt under his tongue and pulled out several putrid grass awns.

I had drawn quite an audience by the time I was done. One old-timer with chewing tobacco in his mouth said, "Well, not as good as a *hangin'*, but it was close," to which several people reacted with laughter. I laughed too. My first actual case. After that, a few more trickled in.

I saw an abscess in the hoof from a nail puncture. The owner, a local miner, had removed the nail but wasn't sure what direction the nail had taken or how deep it had penetrated the sole of the hoof. Now, that was tricky. How could I prevent tetanus or, as they called it, lockjaw? The best I could do was pare out the hoof down to the infection and soak it in iodine and alcohol. *Phew, no lockjaw after three weeks.* I thought I was safe. A few weeks later, the owner paid me in chickens, which provided me with a ready supply of eggs.

Sam came by one day to bring me a fishing pole and tackle. As a fly fisherwoman, I should have been repulsed, but I'm not a purist. He asked me to take him to the water and see how the fish were biting. I willingly obliged. The sun shone through the trees, and the creek was running at a nice pace. I had large, juicy worms from the barn area. Within thirty minutes, I had a good number of rainbow trout on a string. I kept two and gave the rest to Sam.

"You're not bad, for a girl," he commented.

"Okay, mister, let's see how a boy does it." I handed him the rod, and he out-fished me, hands down.

"Becky, I have so much to teach you," he said, handing me back the rod. "You need to practice."

"It would be fun to see how you do with a fly rod," I countered.

"Maybe next time," he suggested as he mounted Cash for the ride home. I handed him the fish I had cleaned and wrapped in leaves and grass for Gee Ling. The Buchanans would eat well that night.

Several days later, a beautiful new fly rod, reel, and a few hand-tied flies were at my doorstep when I returned from a veterinary visit. I smiled, looking at the craftsmanship of the rod. I knew it was from Sam. I raced out the back and ran down to the creek and had a few casts. The third cast was the charm. I laid the fly gently just above a bubble line where I knew the fish would rest. As the fly floated over the line, I saw a fish rise and gently take it into its mouth. I waited for a second and set the hook with a slight jerk. I played the fish for a minute, which seemed like an hour. I forgot where I was and even what year it was. I landed a large trout. I had not lost my touch. It was heaven on a stick, as my mother used to say.

When I saw Sam, I complimented him about the rod and suggested he come by for a session before taking it home.

"It's for you, Becky. I didn't want you to lose your skills in case you need them someday."

"Are you sure? It's a very nice rod. I'm happy to buy it."

He looked hurt. I felt horrible. *How do I show him how much that gift means to me?*

"I don't know how to thank you." I blushed. I hugged him in front of the people in the dry goods store. They didn't know what the conversation was about, but I was sure it caused a stir. I smiled and walked away. I turned back as I rounded the corner and saw him smiling, too.

I made enough money to keep food on the table, and I even had the boys over for dinner when their father went on a horse-buying trip. I really thought the world of them and loved seeing them as young men or boys. When they were helping me plow my garden one Saturday afternoon, Mrs. Gardiner came up in a horse and buggy. The boys shot me a look of annoyance.

"What?" I asked them.

"Do you know who she is?" Hank answered.

"Mrs. Gardiner. Is there a problem?"

"Yes, but do you know what she wants?" groaned Danny.

"Well, she heard you were helping me, and she knows your dad, I mean your pa, is out of town, and she invited us to dinner tonight."

Both boys fell to the ground and groaned.

"What?" I repeated.

"Becky, you got a funny way of talking. Is that how your folks talk?"

"Hank, you would not believe me if I told you."

"Well, the widow Gardiner is in love with Pa, and she invites him or us to supper all the time." Danny looked pleadingly. "You didn't say yes, did you?"

"Maybe." I paused. "Is she the nosy type?" Danny fell down again and did his machine-gun laugh. Apparently, this was something he developed early in his life. It was the first time I had heard it other than on television.

"I'm certain she means well." Both boys looked at me and shook their heads.

"Well, I'm sure she's a wonderful cook." Again, both boys shook their heads. "She mentioned her nieces were visiting. It'll be nice to have some young people, and especially women, to converse with you. Think of it as practice. We're going to have a pleasant night. I fixed up some beds in the loft for you two when we get back."

"I think I'm just heading back to the Cattle Creek Ranch when we get done," said Hank.

"Like hell." I covered my mouth. I doubted they'd ever heard a woman swear. They looked at each other, and both howled with laughter. "If this gets back to your pa, I'll personally remove your," I thought for a minute, "fingernails." *Phew, good save.*

Danny looked down at his fingers and said, "Yes, ma'am."

"Darn right. Hank, is darn a swear word here?"

"No, ma'am."

"Becky," I reminded him.

"No, I don't believe Becky is a swear word, either." Hank knew he'd told a joke and was feeling pretty pleased.

Later that afternoon, the three of us cleaned up as best as possible, and we all rode our horses into town to Mrs. Gardiner's house. Mrs. Gardiner and her two nieces warmly greeted us. The two nieces were much older than Danny and Hank and snobbish. Okay, their noses were so far in the air they were in danger of taking down a plane. *Did I even think about an airplane? I've got to stop even having those thoughts.* Anyway, they were unpleasant.

I actually liked Mrs. Gardiner. The poor boys had to answer a hundred questions about their father. Of course, my stay during the snowstorm was controversial. Still, when all the townsfolk were talking about me, she was defending me. Well, she didn't know me, but she knew her dear friend, Samuel, and was sure nothing untoward would have happened.

"It didn't, dear, did it?"

I was trying to swallow a piece of gristly meat I just couldn't chew and missed her question.

"Sorry, ma'am, didn't do what?"

"Nothing happened?" she replied tersely.

"Nothing happened when?" I responded.

"When you were staying at the Cattle Creek Ranch in the snowstorm."

"Oh, gosh, lots happened." The boys, who had followed the entire conversation, got the giggles. I gave them the look. The phrase 'the look' probably hadn't been invented, but the expression itself was timeless. Unfortunately, this made them snicker even more.

I tried to ignore them, and I clearly did not get the gist of her conversation. "Well, to begin with, I don't ever think I saw snow that high, and we have plenty of snow where

I come from. A foal was born, and I had to slide out of the window to the barn on a rope. Because Danny and I slipped in the fetal fluids and membranes, Gee Ling and Mr. Buchanan had to draw me a bath." I looked at the boys, who were streaming tears, and said, "Oh, boys, I can see you're tired. I think it's best we get you home and to bed. You have so much work to do tomorrow before your father gets home." I said through gritted teeth. "So much work." I spoke with emphasis on the word "so." They got "the look," again.

In a few minutes, we departed, and we all promised to come again with Samuel. Well, actually, I knew she meant just the boys with Sam. When I got far enough away from her house, I laughed so hard that I almost slipped off the saddle. There may have been alcohol involved too.

"Penny, control yourself," I shouted. The boys heard this, which sent them into another round of laughter. "If any of this gets back to your father...."

Saying that sent me into a gale of laughter. "Becky, we swear. Don't we, Danny?"

Danny answered, "Swear? Of course, I swear." Which again sent us all back into the giggles. Now my side hurt, and I almost fell off Penny again.

We went back to my cabin, and I sent the boys upstairs to sleep. The house was open, so there were no secrets. "Hank, do you think we should tell Pa about tonight?"

"Little brother, only if you feel the need for repentance and a hiding."

"Yeah, that's what I thought, too. Pleasant dreams, Becky."

"Sweet dreams, Danny, and you too, Hank." Hank did not reply. He was asleep.

The next day, Sam was due back at the Cattle Creek Ranch, and the boys finished planting a beautiful garden for me and left for home. A few days later, I saw Sam at church.

"I heard you had dinner at Mrs. Gardiner's," Sam mentioned cautiously.

"Oh, yes. We had a wonderful time. Mrs. Gardiner's such an excellent cook, and she's keen on you. You know, Sam, you could do worse." I looked at him with a straight, innocent face. I turned to say hello to my new best friend, Martha, and didn't dare look at him for fear of having another breakdown in laughter.

It didn't take long for visitors to come to my door. Some were welcome, and some were not. There were the human and nonhuman types. While the raccoons were comic relief and just peskier than anything, a bear came regularly and became bolder with each visit. I had my gun ready every night when I went to bed. I had made a secure lock on my door to keep out any humankind, but I wasn't convinced just how far a bear would go.

As a child, I remembered a bear that came to our home in the high country of Montana. It attacked our dog, who was defending our property. The dog died, which gave me a lifelong fear and appreciation of what a bear could do. There had been talk in town of two miners who had been killed in a bear attack a few years before I arrived. I knew Penny was vulnerable.

I was in town a few days after the bear first appeared. Spring was in full bloom, and I was trying to make a fence to protect my garden. I mentioned the bear to Mr. Graves, the dry goods store owner. Mr. Graves gave me some advice and sold me a new door lock.

"Becky, you take care. You're no match for a bear. There's a young tracker in town. I can send him over."

"Oh, thank you, I'd appreciate that, Mr. Graves."

"Hey, isn't it time we set aside the formalities? Please call me Horace."

"Sure thing, Horace."

"Becky, you got some peculiar ways of talking."

"Sorry, I don't know what you mean."

"Sure thing?"

The next time I was in town, I heard several people saying, "sure thing."

Sheriff Thompson had heard about my unwanted visitor and brought along Lance Wohali. I recognized him from one of the *Comstock* episodes. In real life, he was played by Ted Goodfeller, a frequent cowboy character actor. *What am I saying? This is real life, at least for me.* I knew he was basically a nice guy from the *Comstock* episodes that I remembered. I think he was what was called a 'half-breed' in his 1800s television role. Either his mother or father was white, and the other was of Native American heritage. I welcomed them in and offered coffee. I was now at home with the oven, and I was getting reasonably handy at making cookies and biscuits. *Move over, Julia Child.* That was another thing: no Oreos or store-bought cookies. *How do these people survive?*

Sheriff Thompson, who, I have to say, was a bit of a spunk himself, suggested that Lance hang out here and attempt to encourage the bear to move on, and if failing that, kill the beast. Killing sounded better to me, but I didn't voice my thoughts.

Lance agreed to come and stay overnight. He was going to sleep in the shed. I offered him my bed, and I could sleep in the loft, but he said no, it wouldn't look right. Was this prudishness just in my *Comstock* life, or was it the norm in the actual 1850s society? I wondered.

He came back that night, knocked on the door, and was gone by morning. I fed him dinner, which was my payment. We shared pleasant conversations about his growing up in a Paiute tribe and then adjusting to the 'white man's world.' He saw good in both. He cautioned me that the local tribes were mainly friendly now, but some renegades could still try to harm me. Ah, the unwelcome kind of visitor.

Lance's sleepovers were repeated several times until one night 'Cujo,' as I came to call the bear from a book Jeff had read, began visiting, and he was hungry. He prowled around the porch, and I yelled out. Lance was on him quick-smart. As the bear moved away from the porch and toward Lance, a rifle rang out. I saw a flash in the dark. I called out, "Hey, Lance, you all right?"

"Becky, boil some water. We got some lard and jerky to make."

Lance finished dressing the bear by midmorning. We made lard, and I was going to learn how to make soap from Gee Ling. We had a sizeable bear-hide tanning in the shed, and there was enough meat to feed an army. Lance took most of it into town to trade for supplies. He was headed into the backcountry the next day, and he wanted to take his mule and some "vittles" for his mother and half-siblings. Lance promised to come back for dinner when he returned from the mountains with his animal skins, which he traded for supplies during the winter months. He was a nice, gentle, and quiet man, but I already knew that from watching *Comstock.*

# CHAPTER 24

S pring was fading into summer. The snow was mostly gone from the lower elevations. The springs, creeks, and rivers were slowing, and the grass in the higher meadows was lush. I wanted to return to the valley where Julie Smyth had tried to take years ago. The anniversary of the rockslide was coming up. I was feeling the blues once again.

I knew I could not go up there without Sam Buchanan's permission. He was seeing a new woman and was occupied most of the time. I saw the boys frequently. They liked the lady but said she wasn't as fun as I was and did not want to read or help them with homework. I secretly smiled. How could I complain, though? I was a married woman, and nothing was going to make me break my vows. Okay, the hunky reverend was a moral challenge, but even he was seeing my good friend Martha. Unless I got home, I was going to die a widow in everyone's eyes. I plotted my plan to get permission for a trip up to the valley when a loud, rapid knock came from the door.

"Becky, Becky, Becky." I heard Gee Ling's voice. "Please come now, missy," he shouted. "Hank hurt badly and no doctor."

Hank's was not the only serious injury like this one. Dr. Sullivan was run ragged lately and could not keep up. I'd stepped in on a few minor injuries and one birth. I ran for my bag and tied Penny to the back of the Cattle Creek Ranch buggy. We headed to the doctor's office in town, where Sam had brought Hank, not knowing the doctor was hours away.

He was lying on the same bed I'd slept on during my first night in Virginia City. He was moaning, and Sam and the reverend were holding him down. A large shaft of wood was protruding from his pant leg. It was jagged and was at least one-by-two inches, and God knew how deep. I cut away Hank's pants with scissors, which revealed the shaft going down his leg nine or more inches inside his thigh to just above his knee. He was in agony, and the only way to get it out in one piece was to incise over the shaft. If we didn't remove it in one piece, there would be hours of picking splinters and an increased chance of infection. The possibility of tetanus was a genuine concern without vaccination. I asked again when Dr. Sullivan would be back, and Mrs. Sullivan said she wasn't even sure he would be back tonight at all.

"Becky," she said. "I know you can do it. I can help."

"Mrs. Sullivan, can you boil some water, please?"

"It's Flo, dear." We smiled at each other. "Anything else? Whiskey?"

"No, Flo. We're going to use chloroform." I gulped.

"Pa, is she going to pour boiling water on me?" Hank asked with desperation on his sweating face.

"No, son, she's going to save your life."

"Hank, the water is to sterilize the instruments and get rid of the — germs. We don't want any infection." I almost said bacteria. I was still unsure of what terms were appropriate for this time.

I prepared a cone to drip the chloroform anesthetic into Hank's nose and mouth. I boiled the instruments, including a surgical knife, and washed my hands for the third time.

I had Sam and Reverend Tyler hold him down, and Flo dripped in the liquid anesthetics as I directed. Finally, he rested quietly. I washed his leg several times and then incised over the shaft. I was able to remove the wood in one piece. I had sutures from Dr. Walker, who had also sent me additional equipment in the last month. I was able to close the long incision and left a wick in the end for drainage.

As I was finishing the last few sutures, I turned to Flo.

"Okay, you can take the cone away, Flo." Flo had fifteen years on me, but she treated me with kindness and respect.

"It will be a while before he rouses, so why don't you all have a bite to eat and some coffee? Flo and I can clean up and watch him. Maybe come back in an hour."

"But — " started Sam.

I waved my hand in a dismissive gesture. "Go, Danny and Gee Ling need food. They've been sitting out there waiting and may die of starvation."

Danny poked his head through the door of the waiting room. "No, that would be Hank, who might starve." We all laughed. They left with the reverend.

I cleaned Hank up, and Flo brought me coffee and some toast. We agreed that I'd stay by his side as he woke up. During the night, Flo would take over, and I could sleep in the room next door. I sponged Hank's face and arms while he continued to sleep.

I experienced surgeries with horses at the vet school that were touch and go. That release of tension when the horse rolled into recovery was euphoric. That was what I was experiencing. I'd watched and helped Dr. Walker with many cases, and I knew Hank would wake up. I was uncertain about the long haul. Then I remembered. Hank grew up and walked without a limp. I had seen him as a man ten years older than today. Hank would live. The thought brought tears to my eyes. I saved him, and I kept the *Comstock* series alive. I chuckled with relief.

A few minutes later, I felt Hank squeeze my hand. I looked at him, and his eyes rolled. He was on his way back. "You'll be fine. Just sleep for a bit more. Danny can do your chores tomorrow." I thought I saw a hint of a smile.

An hour later, Sam, Gee Ling, and Danny returned. It was late, and Hank was responding to commands.

Danny whispered in his ear that he loved him and to take care. "If you're good, Becky said she'll take us back to Mrs. Gardiner's for dinner." I had to stifle a laugh.

Sam wasn't amused. "Gee Ling, you and Danny go back home. Danny needs to sleep if he's going to do double chores beginning tomorrow."

"Yes, Mr. Sam." Gee Ling patted my head and said I was good luck and could not leave Virginia City, ever. I gave his arm a squeeze.

Sam sat on one side of the bed and held Hank's hand, and I sat on the other. He watched as I washed and dried the sweat on Hank's forehead.

"Becky," he started. I put my finger to my lips, indicating he needed to whisper. "How can I thank you?"

I smiled, thinking of the valley and my desire to fully explore it. "Well—"

# CHAPTER 25

I could tell Hank was on the mend, and life had settled down in the Buchanan family when I reexamined him two weeks later. Hank was eating like a horse and spending some time out in the barn for a good part of the day, overseeing the horses. Sam came to my cabin, and we headed for the valley. The steep, narrow granite passage had not suffered in the winter. The creek flowed rapidly below us. I was nervous about riding past the area where Julie and I had come to grief. Once past that part of the ride, we climbed over the pass and gazed down on the valley. I persuaded Sam to let me go by myself. He would wait up at the summit. We had a bite to eat, and then I descended into the beautiful valley I'd remembered so often since last year. The thought of this sanctuary sustained me in my darkest days in prison. Now, for six blessed hours, I had it to myself.

At first, I rode around the boundary where the cliffs of the mountains' edges jutted straight up from the valley floor. The smell of the pines and the quiet shimmer of the lake when a gust of air touched its surface were becoming familiar. I rode the lake's circumference and searched unsuccessfully for caves or narrow passageways. I got off and let Penny wander and graze while I took off my clothes and bathed in the warm, shallow water out of view. I dressed, picked mushrooms and berries, and walked along a portion of a jagged cliff. I found no escape. The cave I had seen on the previous trip was not deep and required no light to see to the full depth. I tried not to become despondent. After only four hours, I re-saddled Penny and began the climb out of the valley.

I met Sam, who was sleeping in a small grassy area near the top. I looked down and saw that if he had looked, he might have seen me swimming in the shallow water. If he did, he made no mention.

"Find what you were searching for?" he asked.

"No," I looked away. "I kind of think I may never find it."

"You know, sometimes, what you are seeking is right in front of you, but you are so intent on finding something that may not even exist, you miss what does."

"I wish I could believe that." I looked back down in the valley.

"I wish you could, too."

We said little on the return trip. Sam dropped me off and said he was headed into town. He was going to see his lady friend.

I thanked him. Once again, he mentioned he would do anything to help me find what I was looking for. "I don't know what or who it is, but if I could bring him or them here, I would move heaven and earth to give you what you want."

He helped me dismount Penny. He kissed me lightly on the top of the head again and said, "Hope you enjoyed the water. It sure smells good in your hair."

I blushed. "I'm going to the church social tomorrow night. Will you be there?"

"Sarah and I wouldn't miss it." *So, her name is Sarah. I think this must be a new lady friend.*

The next night, I rode Penny into town. Neither of the Buchanan boys came. Hank was still recovering, and Danny stayed to keep him company. Without my dancing partners, I was lost. I danced with Sheriff Thompson, who said he would lock me in the hoosegow if I didn't start calling him Ray. Dr. Sullivan asked me for a dance at Flo's request. I sat out several dances and helped clean and pack food with the single ladies or whose husbands didn't dance. I didn't dance with Sam, and he hardly looked my way. His attention was focused on Sarah the whole night. I had not met her, but toward the end of the evening, she came into the kitchen where Martha and I sipped cider.

"Are you Becky?" she inquired with a look that could kill.

"Yes, I am, and I think you're Sarah Ingle." I smiled and went over to shake her hand. "A pleasure to meet you."

She did not offer her hand. Her lips were pursed. "You just stay away. Do you understand me? I never want to hear about you and Sam riding to your secret places."

"Sarah, I'm not sure what you thought, but I'm a married woman. I'm waiting for my husband to join me. I'm not interested in any men in this state, or even country, except for my husband, Jeff Harper. You'll have no worries from me."

Of course, I had the gift of seeing the future. There was no fourth Mrs. Buchanan in the television series. Sarah was just a passing fancy. *Ha.*

She spun on her heels and left. I turned to Martha. "Where did she get that idea?"

"Gee, I can't imagine," said Martha.

"Martha, they're calling the last dance. Get out there and make Earl Tyler realize what a catch you are."

Martha went out to find Earl, and I was left alone. I stepped out the back and looked up at the stars. "Where are you, Jeff?" I went over to where my beloved Penny was tethered, tightened the cinch, mounted, and rode off.

The following day in church, I sat in the front pew with Martha. That was interesting. The front bench was usually designated for the wife and family of the minister. Martha wore gloves. When we were asked to hold hands for a joint prayer, I felt a ring through the glove. I smiled at her. Reverend Tyler was a catch and a half. For a minute, I was jealous.

I looked at her and mouthed, "When?"

"Last night."

"No, the wedding."

"In a month."

I was so happy for her. I guessed this meant the school would need to get a new teacher soon.

The engagement was announced at the end of the service. Everyone was glad for the couple. Sam gave her a hug and shook the reverend's hand. Even the schoolchildren were delighted for their teacher as the couple stood arm in arm. Sarah came over and slipped her arm in Sam's and looked directly at me. *If looks could kill,* but Sam was oblivious.

Dr. Sullivan and I came out to the Cattle Creek Ranch to remove Hank's stitches and suggest an activity to help rebuild his muscles. As usual, Gee Ling was ready with food and coffee. We did not see Sam, who was out checking some cattle.

"Gee Ling, boy, do I miss you."

"Gee Ling misses little missy, too," he lamented. "It's not the same without you here. All Buchanan men are mad all the time. Everyone happy when you stay with us."

We helped Hank with some handmade crutches. Soon he was heading into the kitchen, mumbling something about how he was starving, and Gee Ling wouldn't bring him any food.

On the way back to town, Dr. Sullivan complimented me on the surgery. "You saved his life, Becky. You really did. You ought to think about going to a school to become a physician. I would love to have you join my practice."

I blushed and thanked him. But I knew otherwise. If I had not been there, Hank would have still lived. What else was going to take place? The Civil War and the assassination of Lincoln were still going to happen. Maybe I would be gone back to the future. The thought was depressing and hopeful at the same time. I knew I would not change history, but perhaps I would become part of it. Missing tampons and Oreos aside, this was not a bad time.

# CHAPTER 26

The arrival of Martha's little girl brought it home for me. I could not believe that a year had passed. The town was growing, and the mines were producing both silver and gold. This took its toll on the environment, and the surrounding hills, creeks, and trails were covered in litter and pits. A new breed of citizens was infiltrating the township. Lawlessness was keeping Ray Thompson busy. He'd hired more deputies, but keeping everyone safe was a day and night task.

My practice was busy, too. I performed more and more veterinary work and moonlighted by helping Dr. Sullivan with surgeries, which meant dripping chloroform on the side. I treated occasional human injuries or illnesses. Hank's leg had healed, and he was back to himself. He and Danny had returned to school. Hank was still not a scholar, and he was about to finish his education. He and his father had struck a deal. Hank would leave one year early, as most boys his age were doing. Clint wrote home that he was enjoying his studies in architecture and engineering. As predicted, Sam had moved on in his quest to find eternal love. In a few years, the television program would begin. Would I find my way back home? I was not there when those years were being documented on film.

As agreed, I made another visit to the magical valley. Sam came all the way the following year. It was later than the anniversary of my arrival in the 1800s due to the snow and long winter. This time, I made him stay on the valley floor and wait while I had my annual swim. Ever the gentleman, he said he didn't peek. I wondered if he was the television Sam or the real-life Sam. We ate the lunch that Gee Ling had packed for us. I walked another long stretch of the mountain cliff face, looking for a cave or walkway that might lead me out of the 1800s. Again, I found nothing, and the predictable melancholy overtook me.

I decided that as beautiful as it was, this hidden oasis was not the solution to my dilemma. I might need to search again. I hated the thought of leaving Nevada and the people I had grown to love. I had a family in my past life, including a husband and a child, and I wanted what Martha had: a loving and devoted husband and child — my child. She would be asserting her will now. She would have curly brown hair like her mother, and if I might guess, she could cast a fly like a pro.

Sam could see the change in my mood. As he lay on the blanket, he casually asked, "Where did you just go, Becky?"

I had to gather my emotions to keep from crying. "It's not where I've gone. It's where I'm from." I thought about it. By now, I knew the rumor that had surfaced about me. The townspeople all thought my husband and child had been killed, and I just had not accepted it. They felt I was in total denial about my past when I said I was still married and would not believe otherwise.

"Becky, I'm always here if you want to talk. I'm not a judgmental man. The Lord knows I have had losses, and it took me years to move on. Each time one of my wives died, I asked God to go back a few days, so I could do something different. If I could have one more chance, maybe I could change the course of what happened."

I'd watched the episodes of the flashbacks in Sam's life to his three marriages. I felt profound sadness for him. The difference was that my husband and daughter were alive. I knew they were.

"Sam, if you could have any one of your wives back, would you be willing to sacrifice the Cattle Creek Ranch and live in poverty?"

"Of course," he replied. He turned on his side toward me and put his head on his arm, half sitting up.

"Well, what if you might be able to see them, but it was not for certain?"

He looked perplexed. "I don't follow you."

"I mean, let's suppose someone told you that if you gave up your fortune and went with him, you might be able to see your former loves, and he possessed some evidence they existed, would you go?"

"I don't know," he answered and turned onto his back and asked, "So what does that have to do with you?"

"I know my husband and daughter exist. That's all. I just don't know how to get to them. It was never about them coming to me, but it is about me going to them. I simply don't know how to travel to them."

"Do you care to tell me?"

"Alcohol, Sam — not enough alcohol." We both laughed.

"There's a whiskey wagon coming to Virginia City next week," he casually observed.

"Yep, that might just be enough." I needed to change the subject. "Have you ever considered building a cabin down here?"

"Funny, Hank asked me that last week. You know, he calls this place 'Hank Heaven.'"

I recalled that episode on Comstock. Hank fell in love with a beautiful woman who was dying. He wanted to build a cabin so they could be married and live there. I probably cried when I watched it. So, this was Hank Heaven. It made me think of some of the pain Sam and his boys were going to experience over the years.

I was falling asleep. Sam let me doze for several minutes. The warm sun and the smell of grass and pines were intoxicating. Then I drowsily remembered the sun exposure and skin cancer association. My knowledge was a curse sometimes.

My eyes opened from the glare of the sun. I examined Sam's hair and ran my hand through a lock. "Jesus, you're getting a lot of gray hairs. You'd better get a bride before you're too old to be a catch." I laughed until I saw his face.

"Rebecca Harper, I'm shocked."

I remembered where I was and said, "Sorry." The Victorian era was in full swing. Women did not swear.

"If you were mine, I'd turn you over my knee."

I remembered the Comstock scenes where Sam would discipline a truculent guest.

"Not going to happen, Sam. Anyway, in a year or two, you'll be too old to get the job done." With that, he got up. I shot up and ran to Penny for protection. She obliged and stayed between Sam and me until our laughter subsided.

# CHAPTER 27

Another church social and dance were held the following night. The Buchanan boys were going, and Gee Ling made the food. He was attending a Chinese version of a social with his various cousins but would return to the Cattle Creek Ranch in two days. He usually came back with more money from his gambling adventures, but not always.

This time, I danced with both boys, and I danced a few with their father. My favorite partner these days was Ray Thompson. That man could dance. He had to leave early due to a fight in the saloon. I had some cuddle time with Martha's baby, Rosie, who could appear at her first social. Martha and Earl were beaming with pride. I really enjoyed holding their bright little baby. Several people commented on how natural I looked. A new member remarked I looked as if I had practiced. Martha overheard and patted me on the shoulder and quickly took the baby while I stepped outside. Sam saw it and came out immediately.

"You okay, Becky?" he inquired. I nodded but did not respond as I struggled to get control of my emotions.

"You know, Sam, maybe it's time I considered increasing the family."

He looked shocked. "Becky, are you thinking what I'm thinking?"

I nodded. "I think so. Your colt is old enough now to breed to Penny. Could I buy a stallion service?"

His look of relief was unmistakable. "Well, I suppose we could consider it. It'll cost you. I'm not sure you can afford my stallion's service fee."

"How much?"

"One more dance tonight. You're the best dancer, and I want to dance," he announced with a smile.

I sent Penny over for her date with Sam's stallion. I borrowed a gelding that had passed its prime and was used only for the occasional guest to ride. He was a plodder, but he got me around, and Penny was gone only for a week.

When twenty days had passed from her last service, I palpated her uterus by sticking my arm into her rectum, which was how pregnancies were confirmed in my time. I did this myself in my shed. I didn't have a glove to protect my arm from the manure, and I had to get my arm dirty up to my forearm. Penny tolerated the procedure beautifully. I felt the uterus and ovaries. There was a perfect enlargement in the uterus just left of the center. "You're preggers, Miss Penny." I went around with my clean hand and hugged her neck.

This pregnancy put a slight crimp in my plans, but it was just in case I couldn't go home. Penny was about twelve years old, and I would need a new mount in a few years. I'd have to stay put for a while.

In the fall, I was invited to attend the roundup. There'd been a significant loss of calves the previous year. The ranchers had me look at the stock. It was cold, but moving cattle out of the high country was a ritual where I'd often helped in Montana. My sister, Mom, and I rode up with Dad and several ranching families to bring the cattle back to the ranches that dotted our community in Montana. The Cattle Creek Ranch cattle were sent to the East or Texas or fed over the winter, depending on Sam's contracts negotiated the previous year.

It was getting colder, and Penny was fresh. She was still quite rideable. The crew all gathered for breakfast. One of the other ranchers brought his wife and kids. He was doing it tough and couldn't afford ranch hands. I tried to stick with the wife as much as possible. There was overt dissent among the ranchers about women joining. I tried to work harder than the men did, take the tough jobs, and give vet advice where I could. I slept outside the camp and often volunteered for the evening watch. Mountain lions had been a problem this year. A sentry was posted, which helped scare away the cats. The other threat was Indians. I was shocked to encounter Indians who were not friendly. I saw two lurking in the bushes beyond the camp one night. I gave the signal, and immediately the men were up and armed. The two ran away, but the ranchers said they were just scouting for a larger party. After that, three men were on duty at all times.

Mrs. Straight, the rancher's wife, her children, and I were down at the creek early one morning when Indians surrounded us. One looked at me, and I realized he had been in town. He grabbed my arm and threw me up on his horse behind him. "Come sick. Many sick. You doctor."

The ranchers were all scattered in the mountains, looking for cattle. No one except Mrs. Straight and her children heard me yell. The Indian sped off while I struggled to slide off the horse and get away from his grip. We rode for miles and entered a glen with tepees and huts and virtually no activity. Only a few people were alive. Sadly, it was easy to see the situation. The tribe was infested with smallpox.

I knew smallpox had decimated thousands of people within the Native American tribes in the early days of colonization. However, I didn't realize it was still active and causing such devastation. I guessed that all but a few Indians were ill or dead. Those still alive were going to be gone soon.

I knew for certain I was immune, having had a smallpox vaccine in my youth. I wondered about polio and measles. Thankfully, my mother made us get all the vaccines we could. I was definitely not going to catch smallpox.

I moved from tepee to tepee and helped with the living. A few healthy young men were lurking just at the perimeter of the encampment. I begged them to leave. They didn't understand me. I tried drawing pictures and speaking to the man who had grabbed me. He was getting sick as well. This had to stay here and not spread. I worked for several days to save the few who were still alive. Several of the cattlemen found me after two days of searching. Sam and Hank were among them, and their anguish and then relief were clear.

"Go away, smallpox, run!" I screamed. Many people were vaccinated even then. I was reminded that Dr. Merritt earned money to travel to California by vaccinating citizens along the way. I also knew that many people had not been vaccinated. I'd made fires all around the village. I burned clothing, bedding, and eventually all the possessions and bodies of the dead. A young man and a slightly older woman appeared to have immunity and did not succumb to the disease. I wondered about the genes these two people carried. Would they get together and propagate, or was this the end of this genetic variation?

I finished cleaning and burning anything that might carry the virus. I took extra precautions to leave the encampment without bringing the virus myself. I stayed away from anyone for two weeks, living out in the remains of the Indian village. The two Indians gave me four horses in thanks. I wish I could have done more.

I arrived home to a cabin full of jerky. My garden had been tended, and there were flowers on the table again. I put a sign on my gate to stay away due to smallpox. I knew many local citizens couldn't read, so I drew a skull and crossbones on the sign. I felt exhausted and demoralized, lonely, and depressed. I went to bed after a few bites of jerky and a biscuit decorated with the sign that Gee Ling put on his cookies. I fed Penny and the other horses enough hay to last for a few days. I was too tired to cry. I just slept. I don't know how long I slept. When I walked outside, there was more fresh food by the gate, and hay had been left for my horses. I stayed in isolation for a month. When I returned to Virginia City, the townsfolk shunned me. Half of them were afraid I would pass on smallpox, and the others were mad that I had treated the Indians at all.

Martha asked me to wait a bit more before seeing her and the baby. She was already expecting her second child. She sent me a note saying how proud she was that I had risked my life to help the Indians. I'd talk to Dr. Sullivan about smallpox. The vaccine had been discovered, but the number of individuals who had been vaccinated was uncertain. I didn't know for sure, but wasn't there an episode on *Comstock* about the vaccine? Maybe it was another show? I didn't want to test the immunity from the vaccine anyone received in the 1800s.

One night several weeks later, a shot rang out. I was in my shed, and whoever fired the rifle had hit my house. I hid in my shed for quite a while. Finally, I heard two horses move away from the property. I slipped back into my cabin and sat with a loaded rifle for the rest of the night. The following morning, I found a sign tacked to my gate reading, "Get out, Indian lover." Indians were living in town. Why was I targeted?

I went into town to see Ray Thompson in the morning and tell him about the evening's activity. He was worried and asked me to stay in town with him that night. I declined, but I thought it was kind of him to offer. He must have told Sam Buchanan. That night, Sam knocked on the door and said that he was tired, it was too far to go home, and did I mind if he stayed in my shed. I knew he was offering protection, and I was chagrined but thankful. This was the man I remembered from my youth watching *Comstock*.

"No, Sam, you can sleep in my bed, and I'll sleep in the loft." He declined and brought his bedroll and laid it out in the hay. Later, we heard a rifle shot ring out, and Sam yelled for me to get down as more gunfire could be heard.

Sam then shot back toward the person who had fired. Sam's bullet went up in the air. I heard hooves moving away. There was no sign on my gate this time. Sam stayed up the rest of the night and left early in the morning after a cup of coffee, bacon, and eggs. After that evening, various men in the town came to sleep in my shed until whoever was menacing me got the message.

The following week at church, I was received back into the congregation. Many people congratulated me on my courage and asked if I was okay. Dr. Sullivan and Flo were particularly concerned. They invited me to dinner, which frequently meant just Flo and me when Dr. Sullivan was out on an emergency or too tired to eat.

I asked Flo how she and Dr. Sullivan could stand the long hours and the continuous pressure of practice. She shrugged and said she was Dr. Sullivan's nurse before they were married, and she knew the life she and Paul had chosen. "It's just what we do. Do you think about the meals you must prepare and eat? It's just part of life. It's not like we sit around, disappointed that we can't socialize and play cards with the neighbors. We have a different calling in life, and Becky, I think you do, too."

I considered this and thought about whether that would have been my life and calling if I was with Jeff and Lauren. The Sullivans had a son who had moved back East and a daughter who had died in infancy.

"Becky, if we save one family from the grief of losing a child, our life and work are worth it. We have prevented many deaths, and every time we give thanks that God has given us the strength and knowledge to do his work."

Where was God when I needed him? Why wouldn't he let me return home? My religious convictions were wavering.

# CHAPTER 28

In the late spring, Penny gave birth to a liver chestnut filly with a white patch on her nose. She was flawless. I was so pleased. Penny was too, and she was not inclined to share her filly with anyone, including me. Many mares had a hormonal change after foaling and passed through a period when they wouldn't let even their owners near their foals. It usually went away after a few days. Penny was typical, and soon she would let anyone come and handle her foal. Both Buchanan boys helped me halter break the filly. They saw several foals each year and rarely fawned over any, but they were so kind to Penny and me.

Hank was finishing his education in a few weeks. He was excited to start a man's work. Danny had a crucial reason for staying in school. I think the biggest reason was called Melody Miller. According to Danny, Melody was sent from heaven. She was petite, blonde, and brilliant. Hank teased him that her other assets were more important to his brother than her brains. Danny became furious when he was teased and stayed with me many times during the winter, so he wouldn't miss school. The teacher who replaced Martha had similarly become betrothed, and a new teacher was starting next fall. She would arrive on the stage with Clint, who was finishing his studies.

Sam was excited that all three boys were going to be home on the Cattle Creek Ranch. I was in town when the stage arrived. I saw Clint greet his father and brothers and introduce the woman. I didn't stop because I thought they would want to be alone as a family.

Clint spotted me and shouted for me to come over and meet the new schoolteacher, Barbara Younger. Danny was taken aback by this mature woman. I watched both Danny and Hank fawn over her. She was oblivious as she had eyes only for Clint. He had matured during his departure and looked more like the Clint I knew in the television series.

I looked at the boys and realized it had been several years since I first walked onto 'the set.' In another year, they would be old enough to appear in the television series. Where would I be? I definitely was not in the series. So, did that mean I was dead, or back in my time, or had moved on? It was so confusing.

I was invited out the next night for dinner at the Cattle Creek Ranch. When I arrived, the boys were fighting over who would sit next to Barbara. I found the whole situation amusing, and I could see Sam did too. After dinner, I went into the kitchen to talk to Gee Ling for a minute. One of his cousins was looking for work, and I'd found him a job. Gee Ling wanted to ensure this cousin was not lazy and would not give his family a poor reputation. I said I would stop by the family who hired him and ensure all was well.

"Of course, that'll cost you, Gee Ling. I think a lemon cake might pay the bill." We laughed, and he promised to deliver the cake when he came to town next week.

I returned to the living room and brought a tray of coffee and a small cake for dessert. The boys were all dressed up and on their best behavior. They were all fighting for Barbara's attention. I wondered how this romance would end. It was not on the television series, so I didn't know if she moved on, found someone else who proved to be worthier, or, gulp, died.

When I left, Sam asked one of the boys to drive me home. I declined as it was an unusually warm evening, and the moon was full. I had sold the Indian horses and had no other mount. I climbed on the horse that had been lent to me while Penny was caring for her foal. I waved goodbye and left. I remember little, but I must have fallen off because I woke up the next day in Dr. Sullivan's hospital room with my leg in a splint. I barely remembered someone picking me up and bringing me in. There was a rumor I may have sworn like a sailor, but I knew that couldn't be true. I was hazy and vomiting and had severe pain in my leg and head. I was given laudanum for the pain, which put me to sleep. I endured this waking and sleeping for days. I remember Flo washing my face. I think Sam and Ray Thompson came by, but not for sure. I may have dreamed it.

I knew a heavily pregnant woman, who I later realized was Martha, came in and asked me several questions. Gradually, I understood I must have fallen on the way home the night of the dinner with the new schoolteacher, and the horse went back to the Cattle Creek Ranch instead of my cabin. The boys all came out looking for me. They found me by the road with a broken leg and a concussion. I was brought to town and Dr. Sullivan's house. He and Flo set my leg as best as they could and kept me drugged until the pain was bearable.

When I realized what had happened and how bad it was, I panicked. How would I take care of myself, Penny, and the foal? How would I pay the bills? How would I start my new plan? It turned out that between the Buchanans, Martha, and Ray Thompson, I would be cared for, as would my mare and foal.

When we were alone, Sam said, "Ever since you operated on Hank, I've wanted to do something for you in kind. You're a tough, independent woman, Rebecca, but you've met your match. You need to let others take care of you for once."

"But, " I started.

Sam put his finger on my lips and said, "No buts, young lady. You're coming home to the Cattle Creek Ranch. I've arranged for a woman to take care of you until you can get around enough to care for yourself."

"Yes, sir." I was relieved, embarrassed, and totally an-noyed. How dare they make all these plans without my permission? Who did these people think they were? *I'm the one who cares for people and solves their problems.* This was not what I intended for my life.

# CHAPTER 29

Loose lips sink ships. With great pain and effort, I was transferred out to the Cattle Creek Ranch under severe protest. The laudanum made me a little free with my words, but no one said anything. I'd like to cancel anything nice I'd previously thought about the Buchanans, the 1800s, or anything regarding my life in Nevada. The comparison between being shifted in a buckboard and a modern ambulance is laughable. According to Clint, I laughed a great deal. According to Danny, I swore like a muleskinner. Sam and Hank made no comment.

The woman they hired to care for me was a monster. She had no bedside manner at all. She was determined that I would be bathed daily despite incredible physical pain. Splinting a leg was far from ideal. Plaster of Paris was a dream unrealized. My only salvation was laudanum.

Back at the Cattle Creek Ranch, I was placed in the bedroom just off the kitchen. The men — and they were becoming men — visited several times daily. Gee Ling was my new savior and protector. He wouldn't even let the nurse into my room when I was sleeping. I'd lost a lot of weight, and he was determined to have me gain it back. I was not in the mood. I was constipated from the pain medicine and nauseated. I realized I had to stop taking it. I stopped, and the pain was incredible. During the second week at the Cattle Creek Ranch, I was able to sleep for a few hours without waking in agony.

Dr. Sullivan said it was a simple break, and he was able to set it with the chloroform on board in such alignment that he was convinced I would not walk with a limp. My thigh was twice the size of the other one. However, after another two weeks, it gradually went down, making re-splinting necessary. The nurse, Gee Ling, and Sam all held me down when Dr. Sullivan changed the splint. *OUCH.*

Things had settled down, and I even felt like reading. Sam gave me a copy of *David Copperfield*, which was popular back then. Of course, I'd read it in school and had even seen the movie, but I feigned ignorance. One night, Sam brought in a liquor bottle, which surprised me.

"Care to talk?" he asked.

"Of course," I said, scooting myself until I was almost sitting. Sam placed pillows behind my back to help prop me up.

"I think it's time we had the talk about you and maybe about your past," he started.

I swallowed hard, my heart raced, and I know my face flushed. "Why now?"

"When you were, shall we say, under the influence, you said things that made little sense."

"I did? Like what?"

"Yes, you did," answered Sam in a manner that meant business.

I was not falling for this. "Oh well, it must have been the laudanum." I tried to dismiss the subject. "I keep meaning to ask. How are Penny and her foal?"

Sam smiled and ignored my question. "Want more alcohol? The time has come, Becky." He paused and waited.

I'd thought about this moment for several years now. I bit my upper lip and looked away. This is the moment I had been dreading since I read the date in the newspaper in Dr. Sullivan's office. "It's complicated."

Sam replied, "I have all night." He sat back in his chair, poured himself another shot of liquor, and tipped the bottle toward me. I nodded, and he poured me a second drink, which I drank immediately. *How do I begin? He won't believe me, but how will he feel about me after I have told him? Maybe it isn't as bad as I thought.*

"So, do you mind telling me what I said?"

"Television, lightbulb, car."

It's bad. "Huh, well, there's an explanation." I thought about trying to say I could tell the future instead of coming from the future. I mulled it over for a minute and decided if anyone would not lock me up or send me to a loony bin, it was this kind, reasonable man.

"You won't believe me." Oh my God. Please let this end well. My heart was racing.

"Try me." He folded his arms and leaned back.

I hesitated. *Do I hit Sam with the facts or ease into my unbelievable story? Just the facts, ma'am.*

"When I first walked into Virginia City, and I was injured, I didn't know what time it was. I knew it was midday, but I mean, what year? A few days before that, I was riding a horse with Julie Smyth. I think I told you about her and the rockslide. I asked you to look for her. I know you don't believe me, and you thought this was an accident. My brain was indeed injured, and I was confused, but all of it was the truth. I asked you to locate her body in a large rockslide. The slide didn't exist, and I couldn't figure it out. When we went there later, I realized why there was no slide. The slide happened in the future. That is where I come from, Sam — the future. I was born in 1949."

Sam did not blink, and I saw no visible emotion. "Go on," was all he interjected.

"I'm married, and I have a child, but that child was born in 1977. My husband and I are both veterinarians, and we were buying a veterinary practice near here. I was visiting the veterinary clinic, and my husband was at home, where we went to veterinary school. He stayed back at our university with our daughter. His mother came to take care of our daughter, Lauren, while I looked over the veterinary clinic in Nevada. That was 1981. That's where I come from." I stopped.

Sam looked at me, and I could visibly see him recoil, although he didn't move a muscle. Again he said, "And?"

"What else do you want to know?"

"If this is true, and I doubt it, how did you get here?"

"For me, the question is, how do I get back? I don't know. That's why I try to visit your valley, Hank Heaven, and attempt to find someone who can help me. I love living here, and I love being with you all, but I really have a daughter and a husband. Do they know I'm alive? Have they held a funeral for me? If I can return, will it be years that have passed, or will it be the next day? I just don't know." Cue the tears and cue the obligatory handkerchief.

Sam said nothing. He patted my hand and just stared. Finally, he leaned forward and quietly asked, "What's a car?"

I laughed. "You would not believe the future. It's amazing. Do you believe me? Do you believe anything I've said? If I were you, I would say no and think it's in my head."

He shook his head. "I don't know. God moves in mysterious ways. I recognized your clothes were quite different when you arrived."

"Can you hand me my boots?"

He did, and I reached down under the lining and pulled out my picture of Lauren and Jeff. I didn't know if he was more amazed by the photograph or the people in the picture. He'd seen photograms on a trip back East. He'd mentioned it once. Despite the fading image, this was so much clearer and more colorful. Jeff and Lauren were dressed so differently that I knew he had to consider what I said was true.

"Becky." He paused and looked at the photograph once again. I saw the pain etched on his face. "How can I help?"

"I wish I knew Sam, but I don't."

There was a great deal more to be said, and whether he believed me or could even think this might be all true was unknown to me. He just stared at the photograph and eventually handed it back.

"We'll talk again. Pleasant dreams." His voice was constrained, and I wasn't sure if he really meant it. He blew out the lamp wick and left me in the dark.

So much in the dark.

# CHAPTER 30

"Missy, what you say to Mr. Sam? He in bad mood. He say you crazy, and then he pack food and say he going and not know when he coming back."

"What? How mad?" Just then, Danny and Hank came in and asked to know what had happened last night.

"It must have been terrible. I don't know when I've seen Pa so mad. And this time, it wasn't my fault," said Danny.

"Oh, really? I'm sorry. Your father asked me questions about my family, and I answered. I can leave if someone helps me. I don't want to cause a problem."

Clint stuck his head in the door. "I think it's too late for a retreat. When Pa's on the warpath, it is best to just step aside until things calm down. From what I saw this morning, I figure he will be back to normal in a year or two."

"Gee, I'm really sorry. I'll leave today."

"No point. Pa said he wouldn't be back for a long time."

"I don't know what you said, but I have a feeling you might not get a dance at the next social."

Well, I should have seen that coming. I probably would have felt the same way. *At least, I didn't talk about the television series in which he stars, and I didn't tell him the things I know, such as historical events, births, deaths, marriages, or lack thereof.* Did he believe me? Did he decide I'm crazy? Was he just mad because he now had confirmation that I was married as he'd seen my family? I didn't know. He was so kind and thoughtful. He deserved someone who could give him all the love and attention that he deserved. I couldn't. Sam's reaction was another reason to start the plan. I was heading east as soon as I could travel. I vowed to tell no one else again. Never.

Dr. Sullivan arranged for me to enter a new school of medicine. I explained my dilemma without mentioning my past or plans for my future. He knew the chance of my return to Nevada when I finished my education was nil and none. Still, he lived in hope. I promised him I would promote his work in Virginia City. Maybe a new grad would come to join and aid him. The second doctor in town had gone the way of the bottle, and all the pressure was on the Sullivans once again.

I moved back to my house a month following Sam's reaction to hearing my description of my past life after my accident. The woman hired to help me traveled with me and assisted me for several days until I could take care of myself. The Buchanan boys helped me almost every day. Penny's filly was ready to wean, and Danny wanted to break her to the saddle in a year or two. He rode over one day, led her back to the Cattle Creek Ranch, and placed her in the herd where she would mature with the other foals of her age.

Penny was beside herself. My beautiful little Penny was my one companion who never complained and who carried me across California and back. I was just riding once more, but I had to return her as well. She'd been on loan. There were no papers. I asked Hank to take her back without disclosing that I was leaving and would not return. I merely said I was going to be away, and would he care for her? He was pleased that I would ask him above anyone else.

My plan was to head to Montana and see the area where I grew up. I also wanted to go to the college where I became a veterinarian. I wasn't certain it existed yet, but the town was there in the 1860s. Afterward, I would head to medical school and start my training. The Civil War was coming, and even women would be accepted in the medical profession to help the victims of war. If I couldn't stop the war, maybe I could help ease the pain and suffering of the young men who would sacrifice their lives and limbs for their chosen side. I was a Union girl through and through. While Nevada was not a state, it was definitely a union territory.

I survived my last winter in Nevada, and I departed for the East in late February. Sam Buchanan and a new lady friend came to a goodbye party the Sullivans organized for me. He hardly spoke to me. The boys were all over me with kind wishes and small but meaningful items for traveling. Ray Thompson said he would miss me, and I returned the compliment. We had a meal together at least once a week. He still mourned his wife's passing, and Ray never suggested his interest in anything but his job. I knew this from watching Comstock. His life was protecting his town. Ray told me that despite what it looked like on the outside,

Sam loved me and would grieve my departure. I knew he was wrong on that count, but I didn't argue.

The stage was early, and the driver wanted to make good time crossing the desert, so I climbed in after hugging about twenty well-wishers. Dr. Sullivan had taken up a collection, and he placed an envelope in my hand. He kissed me, as did Flo. She had become the mother I had lost so many years ago. Her parting words were, "Make everyone proud and, this time, stay out of jail."

*Saddle our horses,*
*Canter away happily,*
*Toward other adventures.*

My tangential trajectory was going to be an adventure, for sure.

# PART 4

## HEADING EAST 1860

# CHAPTER 31

I stopped in my hometown of Mountain Laurel, Montana. *How do I describe it?* Empty, rural, and desolate. And that was the good part. The smell of bare earth permeated the small town. The trees were scarce, and all the while, the wind whipped my hair. I was able to hire a horse for the day. It was hard to figure where my homestead was situated, but I rode up a canyon and found where the ranch would be someday. Nothing manmade existed, but I recognized a large boulder positioned at the entrance to our property. I rode up the mountain and located the site for the cabin. Again, I saw no signs of human intervention yet, but the view of the peaks and valleys was the same as I remembered.

It was my mother's special place. She would take us girls up on horseback, and we would have much-needed respite from our father when he was stressed about his business or some horse that he could not sort out. Dad was a master of horse breaking. Still, when he had a tough one, we all knew about it.

"Hide the belt," my sister Sherry would say. "The chief is on the warpath." Sherry was irreverent. She had Mom and Dad sorted by the time she was four. My sister masterfully assigned blame to her dumb, guileless younger sister. If Sherry was discovered to have lied about a broken window or a saddle improperly stashed away, she got it good. Still, mostly it was I who copped the brunt of my father's wrath. That ended when Mom died, and Sherry headed somewhere in Arizona.

After Mom died, and Sherry vanished, Dad went through an angry drunk stage. One night, he picked me up from basketball practice — drunk off his face — and just about killed me when he hit an embankment and rolled the car, flinging me out. No one wore seat belts in those days.

Our church minister came to the hospital. After deciding that the last rites were not required yet, he took Dad out to the parking lot and read him the riot act. Either he was going to Alcoholics Anonymous with our preacher, or I was going to be re-homed. I never saw Dad drink again. I think AA lasted a month, but he got the message. I recovered from broken ribs and a fractured collarbone but had to give up basketball for the rest of the season. If you think my dad copped it from the preacher, you should have seen the coach. I attended a small high school, where our sports teams were always a player short. Our basketball team played one girl down or borrowed one from the competition on game night. Surprisingly, the opposing team didn't send us their top performers. There was no sign of a schoolhouse in Mountain Laurel now.

A single night in Mountain Laurel was enough. I caught a stage to Denver and then traveled to Cincinnati and then on to New York, where I was to join a small new medical school that accepted both men and women. As I crossed the Mississippi River, I watched for one of the Maverick brothers. I would have dumped Jeff for James Garner. Alas, no Mavericks were seen. My dad didn't like them either. I had to bypass visiting my veterinary school to arrive in New York in time for medical school.

The new medical school was considered quite radical in allowing women to train as doctors. The head of the school was a dear friend of both Dr. Walker and Dr. Sullivan. With my recommendations from both men and an interview that resulted in a consultation for the ambulance horse, they let me in. I paid part of my tuition by caring for the workhorses employed in hauling the rudimentary ambulances used to bring injured people to the clinics.

Medical school was arduous. There were forty men and two women. As women, we were harassed daily by our male classmates, who were incensed that their school allowed women. Charlene Whittier was the other woman. I never knew either way, but I think she preferred women and batted for the other team, as we said at my high school. I didn't care. She was bright and a lot of fun. We roomed together in a small apartment, for which we paid weekly rent by helping to make rum in the basement. The rum merchant had us doing all kinds of things besides making rum. I think he might even have had prostitution on his mind, but a girl has to draw the line. I was firm on that.

I started a small business working on the draft horses used to pull the carts around the town for various merchants, other than our landlord. On Saturdays, after school ended at four in the afternoon for the weekend, I assisted the farrier with some of his complex cases at the local livery stable. Word spread, and I soon had a reputable veterinary business that kept me out of the rum business. Charlene wasn't so fortunate. She didn't possess any other skills and was drafted into liquor distribution, which was scary due to the people controlling the flow of products from one neighborhood to another.

Finally, Charlene won a scholarship. She was awarded a rent-free room on the campus, and I could stay with her. Of course, the boys thought I was her girlfriend. I still had my wedding ring, and I was not happy with this response to our accommodation, but the room was warm and convenient. After graduation, I would never see these men again. Just like in modern society, there were good and bad people. The instructors were demanding, and we women had to get high marks to pass exams. The men passed with no preparation.

The headmaster of the medical school asked Charlene and me to come to his office, where we met Dr. Elizabeth Blackwell one day. She was the first woman physician who had graduated from an American medical school. Dr. Blackwell was well-renowned, but I also knew she had difficulty making ends meet with a small practice for women and children in an impoverished area of the city. She was familiar with Dr. Walker, and she was curious about how I knew him and what I had done to earn his regard. I described his street clinic and what he did at his clinic for the indigent people of San Francisco. She was curious about what I'd learned from him. Both Charlene and I were invited to her clinic, where she employed us, without pay, of course, to help nurse and attend to people with various ailments. I learned to do obstetrics and other surgical pro-

cedures from Dr. Blackwell and her midwife, business partner, and good friend. My veterinary school surgery class was
far above what was being done at this time, and I became a
bit of a legend in the backstreets of New York.

I detested the city's smell and lack of sanitation. Lis-
ter's idea of hygiene was only being considered. Washing
one's hands between patients and surgeries was still only
discussed occasionally. I was surprised by how cavalier the
medical profession was about sanitation.

A physician delivered an address at our college regarding handwashing with lye soap. He was all but booed off
the stage. I knew his name from high school history. I
approached him and thanked him for coming. Dr. Oliver
Wendell Holmes Sr. appeared to be in his late fifties when
I met him. He invited me to dinner the next week with
some of his friends who were in town for a lecture series.
I was introduced to Henry Wadsworth Longfellow and
Ralph Waldo Emerson. Dr. Holmes saw my wedding ring
and politely asked the circumstances. I explained that my
husband and child were separated from me and possibly
drowned at sea several years ago. I had no firm knowledge,
but I remained loyal.

"Oliver, tell her what you wrote about. She is the perfect
example of your thoughts," said Mr. Emerson. Oliver, or I
should say Dr. Holmes, was a poet and was a prolific writer,
as well as a practicing doctor.

"She is, isn't she?" he mused. "My dear, if I may..." Dr.
Holmes stood and placed his hand on my shoulder.

*"Where we love is home.*
*home that our feet may leave,*
*but not our hearts."*

I blushed. My English teacher had recited this same stanza many times to our class. This was the original source. Oh, would my high school teacher die on a cross to be at this dinner? I could hardly breathe for fear of making a complete fool of myself.

Dr. Holmes's son would become a famous jurist and a Supreme Court member someday, but then he was just a polite young man who loved his horse. He was already growing a mustache rivaling that of Sam Elliott. We were the young ones at the table that night. I seemed to capture their attention for one night with my tales of San Francisco and the gold country.

While I was older than young Oliver Jr., we hit it off and became friends. The next day, he took me riding in Central Park, where he introduced me to several of his friends. I became a bit of a novelty because I attended an unspecified veterinary program and studied in a medical school. I was not marriage material for the rich young men, but we all had great fun riding, hunting, and fishing on weekends at their estates. They frequently called on me to help them when their racing horses had tendon troubles or a mare could not conceive. My ability to help them was limited, but they didn't mind since they recognized I knew far more than anyone they had encountered, and I cared.

I was the toast of the in-crowd for the last year of my medical school. John Rockefeller came to my graduation ball after I saved his prize mare, who was in labor and unable to give birth. I delivered her filly with similar tactics I had implemented on my first day at the Cattle Creek Ranch a few years ago. I was then treated as a respected classmate, even if it was our last day of medical school. I was unemployed, and they all had jobs and positions in other schools with surgical appointments for further training. I had letters from both Dr. Walker and Dr. Sullivan, who encouraged me to come home. Still, the Civil War continued, and I realized I could be helpful.

My war days were a blur of blood and bones. The North and South both recruited me, but as a nurse, because I was a woman. I liked the Southern men, but my heart and sensibility were for the North. The fact I knew how it would end may have swayed me as well. The military hierarchy was like any big government. Some individuals were ahead of their time, and my skills, once noticed, took me to the battlefield front lines. I was reassigned as a surgeon with no raise in pay or recognition. I didn't care.

Over the last years in medical school, I realized that finding a way back to my time was not something that I could research. I would never mention my dilemma to anyone ever again. Ever. The reaction of Sam Buchanan, whom I had trusted, was enough to make me recognize I would be considered a freak or an insane woman. I wore the ring and told people my husband was dead. I was a widow. It helped to fend off men and make them respect me. More importantly, it gave me distance. No one had asked me when Jeff had died. For all they knew, I had just recently thrown off the black widow's clothes.

My introduction to battlefield medicine was swift. I was assigned to a medical team that was filled with other women. We became fast friends, and we were efficient. If we saw casualties at noon, we worked until they stopped coming in. We had a system to triage and treat the savable and offer comfort to the unsavable. *M*A*S*H** had nothing on us. I sometimes hummed the *M*A*S*H** theme song when I worked. No one noticed.

I watched hundreds of men die. Like the men and women in our medical camp, we became somewhat immune to death. A surgeon realized he had made a colossal medical mistake on a grueling day. We all made mistakes in the heat of the battle, but this quiet, kind man had amputated a perfectly savable limb and had left the unsavable one. He didn't hesitate to take the other leg, making this man a double amputee. After a long night, the doctor went out and shot himself. Life was not fair. In another time, this doctor would have forgiven himself and moved on with life. In the pressure cooker and with continual misery, he'd just had enough.

The suffering and hardship these young soldiers endured were heartbreaking. I sat with many men who knew they were dying or going home without limbs and comforted them as best as I could. Their mothers, sweethearts, and even young children would never see them again or would perceive them as broken men.

It got to even the strongest and the best of us. Many of the medical doctors and nurses turned to drink as a coping mechanism. I found salvation in prayer, but even prayer was not enough sometimes. I held the hands of at least two hundred dying young men. I wrote countless letters to families to help ease the pain and suffering of the young men who wanted to leave one last note for their families.

I looked down one day, and my wedding ring was gone. I took it off frequently to scrub before surgery. I placed it in the pocket of my uniform, where it must have slipped out of a small hole I discovered when I went to retrieve it. The medical team had retreated during a long battle, and I was half a mile away from where I must have dropped it. This was the moment I really gave up on getting back to my family. This day had been a long time coming. Our casualties had been horrific that day, and everyone thought the work had finally gotten to me. I sat in the tent's corner and cried.

A young soldier sat down and patted my shoulder. "Ma'am, I know how hard this is, but I want you to know that I saw green grass coming through the mud today, and I saw two hawks soaring above this tent an hour ago. This land and country will survive, and so will you."

He got up and walked away, and I never saw him again. I would survive. I was moving on. I intended to find a purpose for my struggles and my life, and I would find joy in this life and in this time. This time. My time.

While I was stationed in Gettysburg, I was asked to be available for a special dignitary who was arriving to dedicate a cemetery for the fallen soldiers. If he, or any members of his entourage, experienced medical needs, two other doctors and I were required to be stationed close by. We were not officially told who would speak for security reasons, but we all knew it was the president. However, I was the only one to know the speech and its significance in history. "Four score and seven years ago," I mouthed the address as I stood behind the podium. Oh, how I wanted to yell, don't go to the play, Mr. President. I never tried to significantly change history. I may have played around the edges and advanced medical care in the rural places where I worked. Still, I altered none of the critical historical events.

I was in the surgical tent on one frigid, snowy day, tending to several casualties. A tall, well-appointed lieutenant came into the theater looking for Dr. Harper.

I was finishing a suture line while the nurse aiding me yelled, "Here she is." He strode by and looked over my shoulder at an amputation. I heard him gasp as he hurried away.

"Ma'am, you're needed in the horse pens."

"I'm sorry, sir. I think you can see I'm busy." I wrapped the stump of my most recent amputee. I requested that the recumbent man be taken away and the table be cleaned to prepare for the next casualty.

"I'm sorry. I have my orders," the lieutenant insisted.

"And, as you can see, there are men who need me far more than a horse does," I said with obvious irritation.

"Ma'am, General Grant insists you attend his horse. I have my orders," he said, stepping in front of the table and blocking my access to the next patient.

His voice was familiar. I glanced up at him and saw a man resembling the actor Jimmy Stewart. He outranked me. "Either you come with me now, or I will carry you. Your choice."

I knew this man and his determination. He was the star of the Civil War movie Shenandoah. Well, he looked like him, anyway. I didn't remember the name of the man that Jimmy Stewart played in the film. I was star-struck. I looked down and shook my head. *What a life.*

I smiled and opened my arms. "Lead the way, sir." I followed him out to the line of horses tethered to a rope. One horse stood out. He was seventeen hands tall and towered above the other horses. He was well-mannered and had a very swollen leg. I felt for a pulse and used a hammer to test for tenderness on the sole of the hoof. An arterial vibration could be likened to the throbbing one might feel when a finger is hit with a hammer. Hammering on the sole of the hoof elicited no increased palpable pulse or reaction. I flexed his leg firmly and perceived minimal response from that stimulus either.

"Lieutenant, can you trot him for me?" The behemoth was not lame. I knew the calvary men had poultices. "One of your men should stand him in cold water for twenty minutes and then apply a poultice. I think he must have broken a blood vessel. He should be fine. He's huge. What's his name?" I asked.

"Cincinnati, ma'am. He's General Grant's personal horse. General Grant leaves for a new front tomorrow. Is he safe to ride?" asked the lieutenant.

I recalled the statue of General Grant and his horse, but I didn't remember his horse's name. I knew General Grant would be President of the United States sometime after Lincoln died. The one fact I remembered was the perennial question on television quiz shows. *Who is buried in Grant's tomb?* I laughed to myself, remembering veterinarians and students comment while auscultating horse's abdomens. They would describe the paucity of abdominal sounds as

*'Grant's tomb'*, indicating no intestinal motility — a bad sign.

"Excuse me. Just one more thing." I walked up to Cincinnati and put my ear to his flank. He had excellent motility, not Grant's tomb.

I looked around, and in the distance, I saw that General Ulysses S. Grant must be looking over at us. I did not wave or indicate I saw him. I returned to the surgical theater and began a long, arduous succession of surgeries to repair an endless number of injured soldiers. I never saw either the lieutenant or General Grant again. I think Cincinnati survived the war.

If the battle wounds did not kill the soldiers, dysentery or other maladies would rage through camps and claim many lives. My ability to treat both humans and horses was a significant benefit to the battalions. I was often on the front, treating horses with broken legs or ambulance horses with Monday morning sickness, commonly known as tying up. Horses that were rested between battles were abruptly expected to go out and work.

The glycogen in their muscles caused a toxic effect. The muscles would cramp, and as I was taught, "melt," spilling myoglobin into the bloodstream and eventually to the kidneys, which could cause significant renal damage. The urine from the affected horses was red to brown. If they went down, they rarely got up again. This was primarily a problem in the draft horses that pulled the cannons. I was never left wondering where and how I could be of help. Horses and humans were always in need of medical attention.

The war finally caught up with me when I contracted dysentery. I was cautious and observed all the modern precautions, but I was almost wading in diarrhea. One day, I felt feverish and nauseated, which was followed by explosive diarrhea. I was removed from the front line and sent back to a small hospital reserved for the medical team. I arrived, and the smell in the infirmary was overpowering. The next thing I remember was a beautiful nurse bathing my forehead. I could barely talk, and my hydration was critical. I smiled through cracked lips and requested water. She said I could not have water on the doctor's orders.

"What's your name?" I asked.

"Clara. Clara Barton, Dr. Harper. Yes, I know who you are. The medical director ordered me to save you at all costs. His mules need you."

"Clara, if I told you I know things that no one here knows — that hydration is the most critical factor for saving soldiers with diarrhea like I have — would you believe me?"

"No, I wouldn't."

"Okay, then let me die in peace. But, just so you know, someday you will be famous all over the world."

Right then, a doctor came up and asked Clara how I was. "She's delusional, sir, and she wants water."

"She looks like she's dying, anyway. Give her the damn water."

Clara Barton returned with a jug of water. "Thank you, Miss Barton, and you must believe me. You'll be famous for more than a century." I thought about the Red Cross, which she is credited with starting.

"Don't expect me to clean up what you expel, Dr. Harper."

"No, ma'am."

She cleaned up the vomit and diarrhea, and she bathed my forehead for days.

I survived, and she became famous.

At the end of the war, I was paid sixty dollars and issued a clean dress. Many other medical professionals and I were set adrift.

# PART 5

## BALTIMORE 1866

# CHAPTER 33

The Civil War was over, Lincoln was dead, and I was unemployed. I'd done my duty for my young country and played a small part in holding this beautiful nation together. My participation would never be in the history books or the movies. Field surgeons were held in high regard, but women surgeons were an anecdote to the cause.

I was mentally exhausted, financially bankrupt, and, like many men around me, soulless. I didn't need to perform another amputation, enucleation or put some poor young soldier's intestines together ever again. I needed a quiet life and a home.

Traveling by ship from Charleston, South Carolina, I arrived in Baltimore, Maryland, to the sight of a maelstrom of men returning home. There was no joy, except for an occasional cry of recognition when a family saw their loved one come off the boat. I lingered as I was not in a hurry. No one would greet me. I was in Baltimore to interview for a job at the central hospital. These jobs were rarely given to women, so I wasn't holding my breath. After the war, surgeons were a dime a dozen. We all were scrambling for work, and the jobs went to men as they were supporting families. My prospects weren't good, but I had no other offers.

I disembarked and went down to the dock. There was a bench, and several men got up to offer their seats. I still had my uniform and insignia to show I was a surgeon. Infantrymen were respectful. I sat down to reconnect my brain and feet on solid ground. I heard a distinctive voice and looked up at Clint Buchanan, facing away from me while gazing toward my ship. He was talking to another man. I hesitated and looked down at my shaking hands and drab clothing. I was not sure I wanted to acknowledge his presence. It was him. He was older. He was heavier, and his receding hairline was graying. So was mine. I glanced up again, and he was gone. I stood and searched in both directions.

"Becky?" I heard him call. "Is that you?"

I turned and smiled. "Hello, Clint." I was at a loss for words.

"It's been a long time. What are you doing?" He still had that beautiful smile.

I answered haltingly. "I just arrived. I'm here for an interview at the hospital. I just got off the ship. Is this your home? Are you based here, Clint?" I knew about his father and brothers, but there was no word about him in the television series, so I didn't know what had become of him.

"My home is wherever I am at the moment. I live a nomadic life."

"No wife or children?" I thought that, given the way the television program finished, Clint would be the last hope for an heir to the Buchanan name.

"What kind of marriage would it be if I was out at sea all the time?"

"Well, I don't think your mother or grandparents minded at the time."

He looked perplexed. "How do you know about them?"

*Oops, sprung again.* "Your father told me about your mother and his life as a captain." *Liar, liar, pants on fire.* At least I knew this prevarication would not catch up with me.

He asked where I was staying. I'd been given the name of a hotel near the hospital. "Can I walk you there?" he inquired.

"That would be lovely, Clint. How's your family?"

"Well, I have some bad news," he started.

I'd heard about Hank's death as well as the tragic deaths of Danny's wife and daughter.

While Dr. Sullivan had passed two years earlier, Flo and I stayed in contact with yearly letters.

"Can I buy you lunch?" I think he sensed my lack of funds.

I didn't hesitate. "Yes, you can. Thank you." I smiled.

We were on a corner, and Clint pointed out the hospital, which loomed as a massive structure two blocks down from the spot where we stood at the hotel. "The café is just down here," he said, pointing in the other direction.

We ate and discussed old and current times. He was a charming man, and the stories of his life away from the Cattle Creek Ranch were filled with adventure.

I told him about my life after leaving Nevada. "Do you ever regret leaving, Clint?"

"Oh, sometimes, but mostly not. It can be difficult to return to old ways. I made the right choice for me. I know the burden is now on Danny. Pa has stepped back a bit from the day-to-day operations of the ranch. Who would have thought my little brother could run such an empire? But he's doing well, and the Cattle Creek Ranch is expanding."

"Do you think either will ever remarry?" I asked. He looked at my hand, which no longer displayed my wedding ring.

"A Buchanan marrying?" He laughed. "Look how long it took Danny to find the right woman. Maybe in another ten years. As for Pa, well, Becky, I think you know you were the last love of his life, but then, you were taken. Are you still taken?" Clint looked again at my bare finger.

"Nine plus years and counting. I've lost track. You must acknowledge I'm a loyal wife, if nothing else. It's too late for me. I'm becoming an old woman, and I've lived a wonderful life, but maybe it's time to move on. My work is my family now, Clint. I hope this is my new family in Baltimore. I can only be married to one thing at a time."

"Becky, do you mind my asking, did you ever hear anything about your husband and daughter?"

"No, I still look in crowds and wonder if they moved on in their lives. Maybe one day I'll run into them. It's so complicated. Clint, I don't know where I'll be living if I get a job here. If you are in town again, will you look me up? I'm exhausted and must get some sleep before my interview tomorrow." I needed to leave. This reunion was so good and yet so painful at the same time.

"Of course, Becky. I leave at dawn. I'm sailing to England, but I should be back in six months or so. Can I buy you dinner then?"

"Hopefully, I'll have a house and can cook you a meal. You know, Gee Ling taught me to cook many of his dishes. How is he?"

"He has severe arthritis, but he still rules the kitchen. His cousin does the cooking for the crew. He mainly cooks for Pa and Danny."

"Please pass on my regards to your family, Clint. I miss them. I think about Virginia City often. I feel as if that's home."

"Becky, I know they would love to have you back even for a visit."

"I'll remember that, Clint. Maybe this is where I belong now. You know I'm married to my work." We hugged, kissed, and parted.

# CHAPTER 34

I sat in a small room the following morning with five other candidates, all waiting for an interview. We viewed one another with suspicion. Only two positions were on offer, with no camaraderie among us. We all needed this employment. One fellow stood out. He was elegant, had long fingers, and was immaculately dressed. He spoke with a British accent. I guessed he did not have any war or trauma experience. The others were average, and I thought I might have a chance. They'd been in the war and knew how to perform an amputation. All had good solid medical educations and were confident.

When my turn came, the man conducting the interview requested that another female be present while talking to me. The head of surgery had an emergency and was not available for the interviews. An older matron sat next to him as he inquired about my history. I told him I had first studied veterinary science and then transitioned into human medicine. The interviewer described another hospital in a smaller Maryland town that was linked to the big central hospital. I could see where this was going. He asked me a few more questions, but I knew I had a job, although it was not in the center of Baltimore. I preferred the idea of a smaller town. I was born and bred a country girl. I liked the atmosphere of a small town where I would get to know the citizens. The more remote the city was, the more cases I would see and do myself as well. I liked the idea of being the captain of my own ship.

I received a notice from the hotel lobby. I had a visitor the following day. The head of the central hospital, Dr. Benjamin Meyers, asked if I would look at his horse. He was supposed to have interviewed me the previous day but had been called away. The horse had been suffering from colic for more than a week. Considering the horse had survived for a week, one potential cause was easily found out. I would probably blow my chance at a job by doing this, but I asked him to remove everyone from the barn, except for the two of us, and I took off the top of my dress. I fashioned a makeshift twitch and stuck my bare arm through the anus and beyond to examine the intestines. On the left side of the abdomen, the spleen was sitting low, and I was pretty sure the horse had a nephrosplenic ligament entrapment. The large colon had flipped over the ligament that lay between the kidney and spleen.

There was hope. After I cleaned my arm with soap and water and redressed, I initially suggested running the horse. He was slightly dehydrated, but his pain level wasn't too bad. I asked to borrow another horse to lead the colicky gelding while riding at a canter. Since it was a city, I chose an unpaved street and led him up and down at an ever-increasing pace. I waited an hour, but he didn't improve. My next trick was rolling him. I could use chloroform, but the liverymen were adept in casting horses for castration. We put him in hobbles and dropped him to the ground, then we rocked him back and forth. This time, I undressed with three men present.

While the horse was on the ground, I repeated a rectal exam by lying flat on the stable floor. He couldn't kick as his legs were bound, but it was still terrifying. Man, I wanted that job. When I was satisfied that the displacement had been rectified, I again cleaned my manure-covered arm and dressed. The men were both in awe and embarrassed.

The horse stood up when the ropes were released and passed a considerable amount of gas. He walked over to the trough and drank. The barn floor on which I had lain was musty and wet. My dress was a mess. I still had to return to the hotel to change. Dr. Meyers offered to take me to his apartment to get clean, but he was a widowed bachelor, and he had no clothes suitable for a woman. He rarely used the apartment. I gave him the key to my room at the hotel, and Dr. Myers retrieved the clothes I requested. We quietly snuck out of the livery stable and went to the hospital's back entrance, where I was shown to a room with a bowl in which to wash and change my clothes.

I had noticed little about him until we were sitting in a café near the hospital, where he took me to eat after I was presentable. He was blond, tall, and devastatingly good-looking. We're talking about the spitting image of Richard Chamberlain. I mean, a total hunk. He had sideburns I didn't like, but what a visual delight. I could see he was enthralled and probably repulsed by my actions. He had to be ten years younger than I was.

He came from a wealthy family nearby, and his father was a retired doctor. He'd signed up for the war, but the hospital needed a surgeon. They persuaded the army to release him to ensure the people of Baltimore had a reliable, skilled surgeon. He said he felt guilty that he had not done his part in the war effort. He opposed any form of slavery. His good friend, who had lived with him and maintained his parents' residence, was the son of a former slave.

Benjamin asked about my background. He wanted to know about the West and the level of medicine practiced there. He'd heard of Dr. Walker and his work but hadn't heard about the Cattle Creek Ranch or the Buchanans. We talked for an hour and then returned to the stable. The gelding had passed manure by then and was calling for food. All the men congratulated me, and I was asked to examine several other horses with various ailments. I spent the afternoon at the livery stable. Benjamin asked me to join him and his family for dinner at his parents' house.

We were driven to his parents' mansion in an upscale area of town. Streetlamps abounded, and it was almost like daylight. Our carriage turned onto a circular driveway, and we were delivered to the front steps. This home was almost more prominent than the hotel where I was staying. Off to the side was a beautiful circular barn. I'd thought the carriage that transported us was a rental, but after dropping us at the front steps, it was driven around toward the barn. The grounds were immaculately maintained and looked like a city park with large trees and shrubbery. A tall black man greeted us. An elderly couple, attired in the fine clothes of the day, followed behind.

Benjamin warmly greeted his friend. "Hello, Grayson."

"Sire," Grayson returned jovially.

"Hey, I have been explaining to this saint of a woman that we freed you last week. She'll get the wrong impression." He turned to me. "Dr. Harper, this is Grayson Beadle. Grayson is not my manservant. He is my good friend who is temporarily helping me with my family, and this is my mother, Anita, and father, Homer Meyers."

"Hello. So nice to meet you all. I'm Rebecca, but my friends call me Becky." I shook everyone's hands, starting with Grayson. He appeared to be the same age as my host or younger. His hand was warm and soft.

Mrs. Meyers said, "Well, finally, I have some female company. So nice to meet you, Becky."

"Likewise, Mrs. Meyers."

"Oh, Becky, I may be old, but I don't stand on ceremony. Please call me Anita."

About then, I heard the clatter of feet coming down the hallway. "Father! Father, we built a rabbit pen today. Come and see."

Three boys came bounding down the porch stairs and into Benjamin's arms. *Déjà vu all over again.* "Becky, these are my boys, Thomas, Marcus, and Leonard. Boys, this is Dr. Harper, who we hope will work at the hospital with us."

"Oh, Father, when will you bring us a new mother?" the youngest cried. The other two looked up, questioning.

"I went to the place where they sell mothers, and because there wasn't one as good as yours, we'll have to wait until there's a good one. Of course, there were some mean mothers, but I thought we should wait and choose a nice one. What do you think?"

There was a chorus of disappointed "Okays."

"Father, may I show Becky the rabbit pen?" asked Marcus.

"She's Dr. Harper to you, young man."

"Benjamin, I don't mind if they call me by my first name. I'm not a formal person."

It sounded as if I'd gotten the job in the central clinic, not the smaller branch, after all. Either way, I was employed. I was almost out of money. I hoped the position would start soon. I was quickly pulled around to the back of the property, where there were three other smaller houses and another barn with a milk cow and a goat. The boys took me to their rabbit pen, which was next to the chicken pen.

"Did you know our mother?" they asked.

"No, I'm afraid I didn't. I'll bet your mother was beautiful by looking at you three boys."

"She was so beautiful, Becky. She died, though. Father was so sad. Can you help him be happy again?"

"I'll try my best, but sometimes it takes a long time after someone you love dies." *Oh, how I know that.* "We better get back."

"Can you come to see Tinker? She's our pony. She has sore feet. Father says she can't be ridden anymore." We took a lantern to see the pony. Inside the stable, there were lanterns hung everywhere. I could tell how easily these places caught on fire. I saw the pony, and I felt for a pulse in each foot. They were bounding, indicating acute founder or laminitis, and I saw a large bucket of grain in the manger.

"You know, boys, too much candy — I mean sweets, aren't good for you. The same thing is true for ponies. How about we take out this extra food? I'm guessing Tinker will be better in a few weeks if she is only fed hay." I wrapped her feet in some soft cotton. She moved better with padding on her feet.

We returned to the house and had a wonderful dinner, which was served by two maids. Grayson sat at the table with us. It was tremendously satisfying to witness a bit of racial equality at this time.

All the boys asked to sit next to me. I rotated to different chairs, so they all got a chance, and I had a ball talking to them. I was asked about my family and history. Over the years, I had developed an answer that usually satisfied the curious and stopped further questioning. I told people that I had been married and had a daughter, but I had lost them both many years ago. It was rare that the conversation continued. At some stage, I stopped counting. I think I was forty, or late thirties at least. I might have been that old, but I no longer keep track. If Jeff were alive, he would be in his fifties, and Lauren would be approaching her teens. Did time move at the same rate for them as it did for me? I wondered if Lauren had a picture of me. My photo of them was so faded, I could hardly see their faces.

After the boys were in bed and I'd read them a story, the adults asked me to join them in the library. It was bigger than any private library I'd ever seen. They offered me an after-dinner drink. Benjamin told them about his horse, which he kept in the city for emergencies, and how I'd removed my blouse to palpate the horse via the rectum. Anita looked at me and tried not to frown.

"Benjamin, tell me you didn't look while she was undressed."

"Mother, you know me better than that." He acted offended, but I saw him wink at Grayson.

"The sight of an unclothed woman at my age would have killed him, so I think we can safely say he saw nothing." I laughed.

Dr. Meyers patted his wife's arm. "Oh, I might have to take exception to that."

Grayson took me back to the hotel. He was a well-educated man and fun to talk to. He explained his parents had been slaves, but they had escaped many years ago. He'd been raised in Baltimore and lived in a house down the road, where his parents had worked. They were both dead. He and Benjamin had become friends when they were young. Benjamin's parents treated him like a son, but Grayson's parents had not been happy. They had often told him that someday Benjamin would abandon him, but even in marriage, Benjamin was loyal to Grayson.

"He's a good man, Becky. You could be good for him."

"Ha, Grayson, I think he already has a wonderful mother."

# CHAPTER 35

The following morning, I presented for inspection. I was to perform surgery with the Dr. Kildare look-alike, Dr. Meyers, and his associate.

They were excellent surgeons, but I had years on them and numbers, thanks to my medical war days. We powered through several simple surgeries and consults. I learned from them. I taught them. We had a few laughs, which was such a novel experience for me. I had not laughed like that since medical school. How had I become such a sourpuss?

Life was looking better all the time. I knew if I lived the rest of my life on this trajectory, I would probably not experience another war. Understanding how the average age of death in these times was much lower than in my former time, I figured I wouldn't see the first World War. So, a few epidemics and maybe the San Francisco earthquake aside, which was the only looming event I could remember, I might just live a purposeful life.

I was hired, and the best part was I was offered one of the modest houses on the Meyers' estate. I would live next door to Grayson, who lived on the estate, as well. I had the Meyers' horses at my disposal, and the trade-off was spending time with the boys. Because I was really too old to be their mother but too young for the grandmother role, I was happy to split the difference.

The day I moved in, there were three vases with hand-picked flowers with a note from the two older boys and a picture from little Leonard. They wanted a "sleepover," and would tonight be too early? I asked their father about a sleepover on our way to work the following day. He laughed and said I would be lucky to even get home, tonight or any night. It was true. I slept many nights at the hospital. The understaffed mail-war hospital had little money, which meant the doctors performed many of the duties that nurses typically would. I was accustomed to such conditions from my war days and had no issues with either long hours or the menial work balked at by many of the male physicians.

I spent evenings and days off with the boys. Their pony eventually recovered, and I was their hero. I particularly loved young Marcus, eleven. All three boys were blond copies of their father, but Marcus was a serious boy and posed questions beyond his age. Did I believe in God? Did I think about my daughter much? What did I think of the new President of the United States? And of course, the big one — how are babies made? That was easy to answer: "Ask your father."

They all took turns riding the pony, and even I had a go. I was still small, and Thomas, at twelve years of age, was taller than I was. Tinker was a kind pony. Despite being on a diet, she did not spend her time under saddle trying to eat. She smartly trotted and cantered around the arena that was behind the barn. The boys loved her and took great pride in showing their grandparents how well they rode.

Dr. Homer Meyers had retired from active practice several years earlier, following a minor stroke. I could only see a slight tremor in his hand and would never have guessed he was not fit for practice. The elder Dr. Meyers and I got on well. He knew Dr. Walker from my San Francisco days. Dr. Meyers was amazed to hear about Dr. Walker's philanthropic efforts with his street clinic. I sensed he missed practice very much.

Benjamin and I were never off simultaneously, so when I was home for a meal, I often ate with Grayson. I enjoyed his company and felt a great kinship with him. He rarely ever complained about his treatment as a black man. Still, occasionally, he would offer me an example of his second-rate citizenship. I casually mentioned that it would get better with time, and he looked at me and shook his head. "Becky, can you tell the future?"

Oops, I thought. "Well, no, but I'm sure it will. It has to." It was rare I made a mistake like that anymore. I reminded myself to be more vigilant in the future.

"Grayson, do people play baseball here?"

"Yes, but it isn't popular. Why do you ask?"

"I saw a game played and thought it would be fun to see another one."

"I've never seen it played, but there is a place that men go to play."

"Do women play?"

Grayson looked at me and cocked his head. "You are a strange woman, Becky Harper."

I got a ball and bat for the boys. I got my fix that way. We played for hours until the cold of winter arrived.

I loved my life in Baltimore. I attended a few concerts with the older Meyers and the horse races with Grayson. Although we had to sit in the black section, I didn't mind. If I had no choice, I think my sentiments would be different. In the summer, Benjamin and the boys sailed, and occasionally I joined them. We went crabbing and caught lobsters, which the boys detested. I'd never eaten lobster but quickly determined that it was my favorite meal. Life was good. I had a friend or two from the hospital, but my involvement with the boys was enough to satisfy my motherly needs. Despite my age, I longed for intimate companionship, but I could have happily died living as I did there.

Marcus didn't feel well one day and asked to stay in bed. He'd slept over in my house on a small cot. The boys alternated, but Marcus would have moved in if he could have. I felt his forehead, and he was burning up. His father had already left for the hospital. I found Grayson, who rode to the hospital to inform Benjamin. Two servants carried Marcus back into the main house, where I barricaded everyone from entering if Marcus was infectious. His grandfather and I were the only ones allowed in the room. We did an ice bath because his fever would not abate despite all available treatments. At least we were not bleeding him.

Benjamin arrived home two hours later and helped with the bath and assumed other nursing duties. The three of us cared for him for two days. One of us would sleep while the other two used alcohol, ice baths, and other medicines, but life was slipping away from the boy.

Marcus wanted to hold my hand. For the last eight hours, I never left his side. His father sat by his other side and repeated how much he loved him and how proud he was of his son. Around midnight, Marcus sighed twice and slipped away.

Even though many school children were gravely ill with this influenza-like virus, only three children passed away. Thomas and Leonard did not become sick, but the elder Dr. Meyers was deeply affected and suffered another stroke. His recovery was not as fast or as complete as with his first stroke. Grayson took over as a caregiver until Benjamin's father passed away five months later.

This profoundly affected my life, too. I had experienced death thousands of times. Because I wasn't there when my mother physically passed, I found Marcus's death the most challenging loss I had ever experienced. Life is not fair. In my time, Marcus would have most certainly lived.

# CHAPTER 36

The years passed, and I could find little joy in either my work or home life. I found myself at the hospital more and more. Benjamin went home more frequently to stay and care for the boys. Benjamin's mother was faltering. She was much younger than her deceased husband had been. Still, she was exhibiting the signs of dementia. She forgot to dress and often asked the boys why Marcus was not at the table. Quietly, this infuriated Benjamin. He didn't want to remind the boys of their dead brother. She and I discussed her deterioration when she was lucid. She sat on the divan in front of an enormous fireplace. I used to stare into the fire and be transported back to the fireplace at the Cattle Creek Ranch. I thought about them as an old dream. I knew they weren't real, just as this was not real. What was real?

Viruses were sweeping the Baltimore area, and the hospital was full. Surgeries were limited since most of the nursing staff members were treating the sick. I rarely became ill. I guessed my childhood immunizations and illnesses had prevented the replication of the viruses in my body. I counted myself lucky. *Well, almost lucky...*

In March, I had just completed a forty-eight-hour shift and felt the overwhelming exhaustion that was a regular part of my life. Two of our doctors had become ill and had gone home the day before. Nine nurses and I took care of fifty or more hospitalized patients. I toted bedpans, changed sheets, and sponge bathed the ill, along with the nurses. Medicine to treat fevers was in short supply. Intravenous therapy was a dream whose time had not come. Dehydration was a common cause of shock that led to death.

I went home to my little cottage and lay down to sleep. The next thing I remember was Benjamin waking me and telling me I was burning up, and prescribing me a day off. He had Grayson come in with a concoction, which I was to drink. I detested the taste of this quinine-laced broth. Apparently, I lingered for days. I don't recall.

I knew it was important to consume fluids. I remember waking up and sipping broth and other drinks, and then I was gone again. My dreams were bizarrely delicious. I dreamed I was back in vet school or back on the ranch with my father and helping him break horses to ride. I also dreamed I was on the Cattle Creek Ranch and swimming in the shallow end of the lake in Hank Heaven.

"Becky, can you hear me?" Benjamin had come home and was shaking my shoulder.

I roused and looked at him. I was completely out of my mind, and I answered, "Oh, Dr. Kildare?"

"Becky, it's Benjamin," he responded. "You had a visitor today who left a note. His name is Clint. I think the nurse who saw him thought he was related to you. Becky, are you hearing this?"

"Can you read the note, please?" I asked.

Benjamin unfolded the note.

*Dear Becky,*

*I am so sorry to hear you are unwell. I know Danny and my father would be too. They send their love and greetings from the Cattle Creek Ranch. They wanted you to know that Penny is still alive and has three offspring. Gee Ling wants you to come for a visit before he dies, which he is sure will be this winter unless he can teach his cousin to cook. I am heading back to San Francisco in a few days and would have loved to have met with you. Alas, the nurses said you were too ill but appeared to be recovering. I will pass this good news on to my family.*

*Yours,*

*Clint Buchanan*

I was crying. I hardly exerted any control over my bodily functions, and now I was a blithering idiot. Benjamin stroked my forehead and tried to soothe me. Eventually, I regained my composure. "Penny was the horse given to me when I visited the Cattle Creek Ranch. We traveled hundreds of miles together. She must be in her late twenties. I can't believe she's still alive."

Horses didn't live long in those days due to several factors, including parasitism, lack of vaccines, and virtually no antibiotics. I'd thought of Penny often when riding the Meyers' horses to and from the hospital. She was not as fancy as them, but she was so loyal and steady.

I fell asleep and did not wake until the next day. I could feel a shift. My fever had broken, and my soul had been touched. I was going to live, and I would return to work. I would find joy in small things, and soon the young Meyers boys would knock on my door. While I was sick, they had left dried flowers on my doorstep. Spring was coming, and they would soon be replaced with live flowers. I would be replaced as well. Benjamin had found a new love: Maria.

# Chapter 37

It was time to move on. I had played my part in giving the growing Meyers boys some normality and fun, but they were going to have a new mother. Like Benjamin, Maria was tall, young, blonde, and the antithesis of me. Benjamin and I shared a camaraderie in our professional life, but neither was attracted to the other outside of work. I would miss the boys terribly. They were the children I would never have again.

I moved closer to the hospital. I bought one of Benjamin's nicer mares and settled her in the livery stable where Benjamin kept his horse when he came to work. My new residence was occupied by a collection of eclectic men and one other woman who worked in the city. Like me, they were dedicated to their work. I suspected two were homosexual. That couple was my favorite. Dinners, on the rare occasions I was present, were fun, but the food was only marginally better than the hospital food. The two men took me out frequently to establishments where their lifestyle was not frowned upon. I enjoyed their company immensely. Both men worked in banks, and if found out, would be fired immediately. Their circumstances gave me a bit of confidence in possibly revealing my life without fear of reprisal. I would think about that possibility.

The other female boarder was a nurse who worked at the new hospital, which was under renovation. She was in her early twenties and a rare beauty. Men were attracted to her, and she knew it. She laughed about this burden. "I guess when you are born with a curse, you just have to make do," she told me one day.

"I guess. I have no personal experience with that problem," I replied and laughed.

"Are you joking? I can see you were a beauty in your day," she answered thoughtfully.

"Nope." that was not a term used much, if at all, in those days, but they all understood its meaning. We became good friends, and she was a source of information and entertainment about inner-city life.

I was experiencing second thoughts about my work. I missed the small-town atmosphere. I had amassed a fortune since the Meyers did not collect rent, and my needs were so few. I thought about opening a practice in a small rural town. I missed the friends and interactions I experienced in Virginia City. I knew people from all walks of life, and I took care of many horses, as well as cows, dogs, and cats. I could be a one-stop health shop. I would consider it. Ours was a cutting-edge hospital for surgery, and my skills were increasing with Benjamin's guidance. A great deal of what I had learned would be lost in a small town. I'd lived in Baltimore for several years, but it still didn't feel like home.

I no longer sought a way back to my own time. If a portal opened to me, I would not hesitate, but I had accepted I now lived in another time. The thought of Lauren and Jeff no longer brought tears to my eyes. She would be a young woman, and by now, I was certain Jeff would have remarried and probably had more children. I was sure my father was dead, but I wondered if my sister had escaped her wild lifestyle and settled down.

I plotted my move to a town where I could have chickens, a garden, and maybe even a dog. When I graduated from veterinary school, our old dog, Pepper, had died. We waited to replace him until after we moved. That was so long ago. It was time.

I took some time off to travel to remote towns in Maryland to see what it was like in smaller cities. They mainly were farming communities. At some point, I realized I missed the mountains and then thought about Montana, where I was raised. I knew the terrain and felt that it might be an excellent place to start. I put my plan into action. It would be an escape and a new adventure. The weather was brutal, and the growing season was short, but it was home. The people who remained were ranchers. I would be an outsider for years, but I would always be an outsider in Baltimore. I needed a home. I needed to belong. Maybe I could be buried with my family when I died, although it would be a hundred years before they joined me. The thought made me laugh but brought me comfort. I was lonely for family.

I ventured out with my friends to the Fourth of July celebration in Baltimore. We'd prepared a picnic basket to be eaten in the park. It was a rare day off for me. In two days, Benjamin was to marry, and I would assume the duties as the senior surgeon for two weeks straight. Today was my time to relax and enjoy the festivities. I was dressed in my Baltimore finery, as were all the women I saw.

The crowd was enormous, and we were lucky to find a place to sit on the grass under an immense oak tree. My hat was heavy, and I removed it. We had chicken with corn on the cob and a bean salad. The band music was traditional post-Civil War songs. They played for more than an hour. My friends were in fine form. They went down to the dock as a clipper ship had come in. I stayed and guarded the food and blanket. The band took a break, and I lay down on the ground and closed my eyes. I dozed. In the distance, I occasionally heard firecrackers. From a long way, I heard someone whistling a familiar tune. I could not quite place the melody, but I knew it. I smiled. It was on the tip of my tongue. The man whistling stopped and then started a second one. I shot up.

The melody was *"I Want to Hold Your Hand"* from the Beatles' album *Meet the Beatles!* I looked in the music's direction. I jumped up and raced toward the source of the music. It had stopped, but it had to be from someone close by. I searched the crowd and inquired if anyone knew who was whistling. They all pointed in different directions.

I attempted to whistle the tune myself to attract the whistler's attention, but my mouth was dry, and I couldn't make a sound. I walked among the picnickers, but no one struck me as different. No one seemed to know where the man was. I said the words to the song, but then the band started up. I was drowned out and gave up. I walked through the general area for several minutes. Someone was from at least the 1960s in this crowd. Were there others? I had given up on ever returning to my time, but maybe a path existed? I was disappointed but still heartened by this revelation. Perhaps I should stay in Baltimore.

I spent off-duty days walking in this park and through crowded streets, humming the same tune. After a month of effort, no one ever acknowledged me. Either the fellow time traveler had left, was a figment of my imagination, or was as scared as I was of declaring they were from a different time.

I left for the west in March. I would finish this last year in Baltimore and go to some place in a more rural environment. I gave notice in November. Benjamin had married and was expecting his next child. Grayson was courting a woman who was teaching in a school for 'colored' children. I mentioned that someday children of all colors would learn together. Benjamin, Grayson, and their women looked at me as if I were crazy. I said no more.

The boys were in love with their new mother, and the elder Mrs. Meyers was sinking into cognitive oblivion. She might recognize the boys one day and not the next. She never knew me anymore. That was a relief — one less person to leave. That ship had sailed several months ago.

In February, the hospital had its annual influenza outbreak. Of course, only I knew it was a viral infection. Everyone knew it was deadly and highly contagious. Many people died, and any signs of illness were genuine causes for concern. I stayed at the hospital, trying to minimize the ravages of the flu on the elderly and the young. The new Mrs. Meyers and the boys were forbidden to leave the house. Benjamin stayed at the hospital with me, and Grayson remained at home to guard the Meyers' mansion, stopping all visitors.

The elder Mrs. Meyers was sequestered in one of the cottages because of her now-nightly ravings and wanderings. It was common for dementia patients to become worse at night. She was watched by the staff, which had grown with the pending arrival of Benjamin's new baby.

I tended a child with appendicitis. He had surgery the day before and was feverish. We weren't sure if it was sepsis or influenza. He was a beautiful, black-haired boy with freckles that stood out from his pale skin, giving it an iridescent, three-dimensional look. His mother had run home to check on her other children, and his father, who was taking over the boy's care, was late. I said I would watch him until his parents returned. It was mid-morning on my day off. No one was truly taking time off. A day off might mean light duties, at best.

As I changed the ice pack we used to reduce the boy's fever, a nurse came up and announced I had a visitor. The only person I could think of was my boarding-room friend or maybe Clint Buchanan. Without looking up, I asked the nurse if it was a man or a woman. She said she was simply asked to pass on the message. She hadn't seen the person. I asked her to take over with the boy, but she said Dr. Meyers had called her to the next ward. I had to let the visitor wait. It must have been two hours before anyone could relieve me. The parents still had not returned, but I could see the boy's fever was decreasing, and he was becoming less restless.

I guessed whoever had been waiting had left. I could not get word to the main lobby, where my visitor waited, explaining I could not come down. I looked in the mirror. My hair straggled, and my dress was rank from lack of bathing. If it were Clint, I would stick my head in the lobby and tell him to go away for a few hours, and I would meet him for dinner later. I descended the stairs and turned the corner. Sam Buchanan was sitting patiently on a bench.

He was looking out toward the street. He was older, and his hair was white. He still appeared strong and well-groomed. He may have lost some weight, but besides his hair and a few wrinkles, he had not aged as much as I had expected. My heart raced. Why had he come here? I could not imagine. The last time I'd seen him alone, I was in his guest room, which had to be over thirteen years ago. I'd told him the truth about myself, and that was the last time we talked privately. He had left the following day in what his family said was a near rage, and he'd said he would not be back until I was gone. I'd seen him a time or two shortly before I departed from Nevada. Still, we'd never spoken privately or addressed one another since that fateful night.

He looked up, and when he saw me, I was partly smiling and partly in shock. I had undoubtedly aged. My hair was still more brown than gray, but there was definitely gray. While my face had stayed somewhat youthful, it carried the wrinkles of age, and I was reasonably sure I looked like a wild woman. I knew my eyes were puffy from lack of sleep. In short, I was a mess. For an instant, I was going to retreat before he saw me, but it was too late.

He stood up and walked over to me. He approached, and I stepped back. He stopped, unsure of the meaning of my gesture. "Hello, Rebecca," he mumbled.

"Hello, Mr. Buchanan," I replied. "I may be contagious."

He looked around the room filled with coughing people and smiled. "It may be too late for that, don't you think?"

"It's nice to see you, but why are you here?"

"May I talk to you somewhere in private? Maybe outside of here?" Again, he looked around. People from all walks of life filled the benches. Children were coughing, and an older woman was moaning. A man was rocking a little baby back and forth.

"I can meet you later. Is dinner too much? I can get away in an hour and go to my boardinghouse to clean up. There's a café two blocks down the road." I pointed to the street. "I could meet you at six o'clock, or if you're already engaged, I could meet you tomorrow." I didn't want to sound too excited, but I was on so many levels.

"Dinner at the café sounds perfect. I'll meet you there. Is six o'clock too early?" He was looking at my disheveled state. I laughed and agreed six-thirty might be better.

"It's nice to see you, Becky."

"You too. How many years?"

"Too many. I'll let you get back to your work." He turned and left the building.

My heart was racing. This was the best thing that had happened to me in a while. I wondered what had made him come to visit. I hoped all was well with him and his boys. Maybe he had bad news. I'd never received a letter from him during all the time I'd been gone. I knew from the television series that during that time, he had fallen in love with several women and almost married many times. They were all beautiful, tall, young women. He could have whomever he wanted. It was not me he wanted. Perhaps it was my expertise? In a few hours, I would know.

I entered the café at six thirty and glanced around. Sam had chosen a small booth in a private area. It was dark, but I knew we could talk without interruption. A bottle of wine and two glasses were on the table. He got up and ushered me into my seat.

We both smiled and talked simultaneously. We laughed, and Sam said, "Ladies first." *Ever the gentleman.*

I'd put on a fashionable dress I purchased a few years ago. Baltimore was still cold, and it had snowed yesterday. I removed my cape, and Sam could see my actual figure, which had not changed with age. I still had the same relatively flat chest and weight.

"Well, I really don't know what to say. I guess I'm wondering what brings you out East and the reason you would see me, as well."

"Becky, our town has missed you." I felt a slight pang. The town? "Gee Ling and Danny have missed you." I thought I knew where this was going. He paused. "And I have missed you." I tried not to smile like a fool, but I'm sure he spotted my pleasure.

"I've missed you all, too, along with Virginia City," I returned. Okay, *Bec, don't sound overly enthusiastic,* I reminded myself. I guessed he wanted me to move back to Nevada and become the town doctor. I had thought about it many times. Aside from my life in the 1980s, that was my favorite time.

He continued, "I received a letter from someone I don't know. The sender wanted me to pass it on. When I saw the contents, I thought it was best given to you directly." He reached into his pocket and pulled out an envelope. From the envelope, he handed me a letter. I had reading glasses now, but I could still read without them. I squinted in the dim light, however, and Sam moved a lamp closer to me.

*Dear Dr. Harper,*

*I don't know if you remember me. I was the guard at the prison where you were kept many years ago. You taught me to read and write so I could write to my family back in Ireland. I am forever grateful. I enrolled in a small school for adults, and now I teach others to read and write. I have become a teacher for inmates in the women's prison. I am now very well thought of. My family is all well, and my wife is so proud of me and what I do. You changed my life. Several months ago, I was assigned to clean out one of the cells in the area where you were kept. I gave a bucket, scrub brush, and mop to the prisoner and said I would be back in a few minutes. When I returned, she handed me this paper. She said it was in between two bricks, and when she scraped away the dirt and grime, she could see it. I just kept it. She could not read and could only see the photograph. It took me several days to realize it was the beautiful woman who had taught me to read. I was not sure where to send it. I remembered a local doctor, but I didn't remember his name. I looked up your details, which took several weeks, and found a Clint Buchanan had signed you out. From there, I sent it to the address he gave. I hope this letter finds you healthy and prosperous.*

*Kind regards and salutations,*

*Raymond O'Keefe*

I looked at Sam, who reached into the envelope. He pulled out my driver's license. It had a picture of a very young me. It had the state seal, my date of birth and height, weight, the color of my eyes, and signature. I just stared.

"Well," was all I could say.

"Have you told anyone else?" Sam held the envelope as we considered the sender.

"Well, I guess Raymond knows now. I'm not sure he would be smart enough to put it together, though. But no. I was afraid. As I remember, your reaction was pretty over the top, as we used to say in my time."

Sam blushed and looked away.

"Not that I blame you. How do you think I felt when I figured out where and when I was at the time after the accident? It's taken a long time, but I have accepted it. I'm not going back. I'm just trying to find a place to live out my life, be of service, and find some small joy in what's left. I take joy from my work. Maybe that's enough?"

We said, "Cheers," and we took the first sip of the wine. The waiter came to explain the menu. We ordered, and I sat and waited.

"Becky, when you told me about yourself, I didn't believe you, and I think you can understand. But when you showed me the picture, I was confused. I have seen other photograms since, and now I know it is real. Back then, I thought you were crazy. I thought about it all that night and decided you might actually be from the future. I was enamored with you, and when I realized how committed you were to your family, I knew I had no place in your future. I just needed to go away. That is the best I can give you as an explanation, and I'm sorry for abandoning you. You deserved better."

"Sam, I should have stuck to my guns and insisted on lots of alcohol." We both laughed.

"May I ask you a question?" Sam took another sip of wine.

I nodded.

"Did you know about Abraham Lincoln and the assassination?"

I nodded again. "Yes, and the war."

"Is there anything else?" He gazed at me.

"Sam, I'm not a student of history, but I know there will be a big earthquake in San Francisco and two world wars, but I think we will both be dead by then. I know nothing else about you, or me, or our friends and families. I know general things. The steam-powered transport in which Hank wanted to invest will replace horses. They are called cars or automobiles. I remember you asked me about a car before. Electricity will run-on lines from house to house. There will be glass bulbs powered by this electricity, which will illuminate homes. You will flick a switch, and poof, there will be light." I expanded my fingers to emphasize the example.

The waiter came to bring our dinners. I didn't expand any further. I didn't want anyone to overhear this.

"I'm afraid of the consequences if anyone knows what I know. Do you understand?"

He nodded. "I should tell you that several years ago, I adopted a son," he began his story.

Of course, I knew from the television series. I would tell no one about this aspect of my knowledge.

"Oh?" was all I said.

"His name is Johnny. He's joined the army to see the world. He's a fine boy and, in some ways, has filled a large hole in my heart left by Hank's death."

"I'm so sorry." I took his hand. Losing a child is the worst possible loss. I thought of both Lauren, whom I would never see, and my beautiful Marcus. At least, I felt Lauren was still alive or would be in the future. Well, it was confusing.

"You know, last year, I heard a man whistling a tune that I recognized from my time. I was in a large crowd, and I assumed he was searching for others."

"Did you find him?" Sam asked.

"No, but I started humming this tune wherever I went. I never located the man. That was when I decided not to look anymore and to make do with what I have. I'm living an adventure that few women are lucky enough to experience. I'm finally at peace with my life and where I am. I don't need to go back anymore." I smiled.

Sam took my hand. "Then return with me to Virginia City. I know your work here is important. But if you leave, there'll be ten doctors to take your place."

I was disappointed. So, Sam just wanted me to come back and work? I had sensed something more. I said nothing.

Sam took another sip of the wine. "I know this is sudden. I'm sure you need time to think about it."

I ate without responding for a minute. I didn't inquire about the details. Where would I live, and what would my salary be? Would I just go back to Virginia City and hope people would accept a woman doctor who could also take care of their animals? Was I about to fall into the Buchanan curse, another woman who almost caught a Buchanan?

"Sam, I'm not sure. I need to think about it. I was already planning to leave. I just don't know about returning to Virginia City. I need time."

Sam looked down and then retook my hand. "I think I may not have been clear. I'm an old man, but I'm healthy. I've missed you terribly over the years. If you even come back as a friend, I would be happy to share an occasional dance or a meal like tonight. I've missed our trips to Hank Heaven. I've missed my fishing partner."

My heart skipped a beat. *That would be enough.* I didn't need any more than that. I already knew my answer, but I said, "Tomorrow, I'll be attending church next to the hospital. Will you join me, and we can talk further? Is that okay?"

He smiled warmly and nodded. We finished dinner, and he walked me to my boardinghouse. He took me in his arms and kissed my forehead. "Pleasant dreams, Becky."

"Sweet dreams, Sam."

Although I was exhausted, I could hardly sleep. I went to the church the following day but could not find him. I looked around as the service progressed, and he never showed up. Had last night been a dream? I had the envelope with my driver's license and knew the previous night was real. Had he been injured or called away? I had to return to the hospital in a few hours. At his hotel, I asked if Sam Buchanan was a guest. The clerk said he could not confirm it as the register had been taken to the back office for accounting purposes. I described him, and a worried look came over his face.

"Was that the man who was taken to the hospital early this morning?" He asked as he turned to the bellboy.

I didn't wait for a reply. I hurried out of the hotel, down the street, and into the hospital. I ran past the admissions desk and into the men's ward. Sam lay there, flushed and shaking. His eyes were closed, and he was hyperventilating. Benjamin Meyers saw me and looked up from the patient he was examining.

"Dr. Harper?" We were very formal in the wards.

"He's an old friend, Dr. Meyers."

Benjamin saw my anguish. "His vitals were poor when he was admitted, but he's stable now."

"I guess we don't have a private room, do we?"

"Not that I know about, but I can inquire." He whispered, "How good of a friend?"

"He's the man who owned the big ranch near Virginia City. Sam Buchanan."

"Oh, that good." Benjamin smiled and went to see if he could find a room.

I wondered if Sam could hear this conversation. I didn't think so. He was gravely ill. He had a fever, and he labored to breathe. I gave him the few safe drugs that were available and kept the phlebotomist at bay. I packed him in ice to reduce the fever and attempted to keep up his hydration with sips of broth and water. I administered salicylic acid, which was the forerunner of aspirin. Two days later, I could see a change. His breathing became more regular, and he sweat profusely. The fever had broken. I was cautiously optimistic. I still had to fend off any secondary bacterial infections. *Oh, I would give my left hand for penicillin.*

When I took his pulse the following morning, he squeezed my hand. He opened his eyes, looked around, and then focused on me. "I guess I'm going to live then."

"I think so. God must have decided he couldn't deal with you yet. He didn't have enough roughriders."

Sam smiled, "Thanks, Becky. Sorry, am I too late for church? Does this change things? Have you had time to decide? The town needs you." There was a pause. "I need you. We all need you."

"Yes, Sam, I've decided. I need you all, too. I'll come back to Virginia City. How things go from there, we'll just have to see." Then, I did something quite unprofessional. I kissed his forehead. "Get some sleep, my friend. I'll be back later. I need to clean up, and I have work to do. You might be surprised to hear some patients are actually sick and in need of my attention."

# CHAPTER 38

After a few more days, I walked Sam back to his hotel room. Ever the gentleman, he did not let me into his room without accompaniment. These Victorians were so prudish. He slowly regained his strength. We eventually dined in the hotel restaurant and even went out for walks around the town.

He asked me to hum the song that had been written in the 1960s. With much embarrassment, I did. That became our walking anthem. He was not partial to "*I Want to Hold Your Hand.*"

"I can't believe that's popular," he kept repeating.

"Big-time," I replied, and he laughed at that phrase as well.

"What will the world come to?" Sam shook his head.

"You have no idea," *You really have no idea.* There was only a tiny amount of foreknowledge I would share with Sam. I taught him a James Taylor song and a few more from various eras. Just the tune, not the words. We discussed

Sam's departure and when I would come over. I wanted to stay for the birth of Maria and Benjamin's baby. I was adept at performing cesareans, and I wanted to ensure the safe arrival of their baby.

Sam was leaving in a few days, so he could prepare for the arrival of the new doctor and help with the spring calving, which would start soon. He would travel by rail on the transcontinental railway and then by stagecoach.

My fondness for Sam increased. The pending separation, which would be for several months, dampened our happiness in the time we had together. There was nothing formal or stated. We were just good friends. We shared no more intimacy than a brother and sister would share. I didn't know if it would ever go beyond that. As I thought about my life, a platonic relationship was good enough for me and more than I'd ever expected.

We hugged, and he boarded his first train in the early morning. I wanted to kiss him but refrained. I had finally found someone with whom I could share my entire life. He knew it all. I told him about my parents and sister, my education, and even my married life. He told me his life story. Although I had seen it on television, I mentioned nothing about that. I never would. Occasionally, I would say a name or an event that I could only know by watching *Comstock.* I would cringe internally when he would look at me and cock his head, trying to figure out how I knew something, such as Hank's venture into motorized cars. I might say that Clint had told me. *Oops.* Adding that would complicate things. It was not real. He might not be real. What was real? If I admitted this, would it all go away? At this stage, I hoped not. This was a good life. I didn't need another anymore.

A month later, Maria went into labor. I attended her, but Benjamin was right there as well. The birth was long and exhausting for us all. Maria naturally delivered a beautiful girl. They named her Anita, for Benjamin's mother. His mother was in full-blown dementia and, when presented with the baby, tried to keep it for herself. The boys, who were many years older in mind and body since I met them, were doting brothers. They promised to write. I doubted it, but people were letter writers in these times. Grayson was about to marry and had moved to Boston to be near his fiancé and her parents.

It was time to go. I gave my mare to Thomas, who had outgrown the pony, and packed my trunk. Benjamin took me to the train and kissed me goodbye. He insisted on giving me a book for the travel. I didn't know, but he had placed several hundred dollars inside the book. We'd shared many good years and experiences. We'd both lost family members. Our beautiful Marcus was as much a son to me as he was to his father. We had learned from each other. As I boarded the train, he stopped me. "Becky, I have a confession. On that day when I met you, and you removed your dress top to examine my horse." His face reddened, and he stammered. "I looked." He blushed.

"Oh, really." I laughed. "Happily for you, the sight of an older woman didn't harm your eyesight."

"Not at all. You were beautiful, and you still are now. I just wished you were looking for more back then. I knew you weren't."

We kissed each other once again and parted.

# PART 6

## BACK TO NEVADA 1876

# CHAPTER 39

The trip home was eventful and arduous. Damaged sections of rails and other dramas interrupted the train journey several times. Train robbers even held us up. We were at a junction to replenish the coal and water. The passengers stepped off the train when a group of about six men wearing bandanas galloped up to the train. When they were close to us, they raised their guns, and two fired into the air. The train engineers halted and tried to run back to get their weapons, but the robbers stopped them. The masked men lined us all up and ordered us to empty our purses and remove any jewelry.

Sam had warned me not to carry money or anything of value on myself. My valise contained the money Benjamin had given me. It was hidden under my bed, and the door was locked. As the men were going down the train carriages, we all heard gunfire coming from the other side of the train, which sounded like the U.S. cavalry. It really was the cavalry. I looked for Rin Tin Tin and Rusty, but they weren't there.

The robbers ran to their horses and galloped off in the opposite direction.

The prevailing story was that it appeared to be a new gang. I saw the bandits, but of course, their faces were covered. I suggested Jesse James and the Younger Brothers, but no one had heard of them. Maybe this was their first robbery? I think they suspected me because I could name these men. Several soldiers questioned me. I just said I had heard about them from a penny dreadful that was published in Baltimore. They then realized I didn't know who the men were. The troopers were furious that they had wasted time talking to a dime novel reader.

*Phew, close call.* By the time the Younger Brothers were known, no one would recall that I had named them well before they had become famous. *Reminder to self: keep my mouth shut.* As we crossed the Mississippi, I once again looked for James Garner or the Maverick brothers. Sadly, no one knew them.

I went as far as I could before boarding the stage. In the cramped space shared with several people, I kept noticing one individual. I was convinced I recognized him. I didn't want to expose myself as a time-traveler and wasn't sure if he was well known, but I remembered him from a *Comstock* episode. We all introduced ourselves and mentioned where we were traveling. Yes, the man said he was Sam. He was headed for San Francisco. I said, "Oh, I was there several years ago. Yep, the coldest time I ever spent was a summer in San Francisco."

Samuel Clemens, better known as Mark Twain, looked at me and laughed. "I'll remember that." Of course, I was the only individual on the stage to recognize the honored guest. He then asked me where I was headed.

"Virginia City," I answered nonchalantly.

"What takes you there?"

"I'm a doctor, and I'll be working there."

He sat up and looked at me. "I worked for their town newspaper for a few months."

"Oh, I think I heard about that." That was featured on a Comstock episode. Did it really happen or not?

"If you meet a family there named Buchanan, please pass on my regards."

"Yes, I will." No sense in complicating things. We had a pleasant conversation about life and the politics of the day. We parted when I caught a different stage headed up toward my destination, and he continued west. *Pinch me now — what an adventure!*

On the second leg of my stage journey, we encountered Indians. Once again, we were attacked, but this time, the man riding shotgun turned them away. In the race that ensued, we broke a wheel, and the stage went over. One of the passengers was killed outright. I was bruised but not seriously injured. However, the horses took off. The man killed was traveling to Reno. He had not conversed with us much. The stage driver went through his belongings. He appeared to be a salesman, and he had unusual medicine in his bag. They showed it to me. It was tablets with an unfamiliar label.

It read, "Penicillin," which they pronounced pen eye killen. I was shocked, and I asked to look through the rest of the trunk. I discovered more modern drugs, including anesthetics and other antibiotics. The drivers wanted to throw it all out. I suggested I could keep it and see if it might be of any use. Oh, my God. I looked through his papers, and nothing suggested he was from another time. *Where did he get this?*

It took several days to repair the coach. We all took turns guarding it against further attacks until the horses had been rounded up, and we were once again on our way. I just could not believe my luck. Not only did I have precious, futuristic drugs in my possession, but I also had actual proof others like me had brought items from the future.

We brought the man's body into the next stopover. He was identified as a regular who had recently been on a wanted poster for petty theft. I wondered from whom he had stolen this. Was there more? I didn't comment, and no one asked me. Again, I changed stages. This one would take me to Virginia City.

My arrival should have been several weeks earlier. There was no way to advise anyone I had been delayed or when I was finally going to arrive. No one was there to greet me. I was disappointed, but I understood.

The town had changed. It looked far more modern. I remembered one of the later episodes where a woman set fire to many buildings, and it was to be rebuilt. I didn't recognize anyone. The church was still the same, but the hotel had been rebuilt, as had most of the main street. The saloon was busy as usual. Women were still banned unless, of course, they 'worked' there.

I went to the post office, but the postmaster was new. I inquired whether there was any mail left for me. There was a letter dated ten years earlier from Dr. Walker. I took it and then went to the sheriff's office. Glenn Frasier was now the sheriff. Ray Thompson had retired. I'd met Glenn only briefly before I left many years ago.

"Well, I'll be. Dr. Harper. We've been so worried about you. The townsfolk just about gave up on you. Sam Buchanan has been to all the stage stops, looking for you. He even enlisted Ray to help. Oh, he'll be so relieved."

"Where is Sam?" I asked.

"I don't rightly know, ma'am," he said, scratching his head. "He comes into town every day. Did you come in on a stage today? It's here early. He may have gone down to Carson City, searching for you."

"I see. What time does the stage come in normally?"

"Usually around noon. I'd expect Sam to be here soon if he hasn't ridden down the line. If he isn't here, Danny will come in, and maybe Gee Ling. Can I get you something to drink? You must be tired. May I take you to the hotel, ma'am?"

"Yes, that would be lovely." I now used that word regularly. "Can you point me to the doctor's office first?"

"Yes, ma'am. I can take you there. The newest doctor is living there. The town asked him to stay until you came. It was getting difficult since he was expecting to leave last month. He sure will be glad to see you. He was just stepping in."

We walked to the doctor's office, which had a fresh coat of white paint. I walked in and got the shock of my life. Dr. Walker was treating a young girl being held by her mother.

He looked up and grinned. "Finally. Aren't you a sight for sore eyes? We were thinking you weren't coming. If I don't get back home to my wife, she's liable to throw us both in jail, and you know she can do it." *Still a fox and still so married. What is it about older men?*

He finished bandaging the girl's arm. She wiggled out of her mother's arms and gave Dr. Walker a hug. He rose and embraced me. "Welcome back, Becky."

All I could say was, "Thank you."

"I want to hear all about your life and work. I'll bet you can teach this old dog some new tricks."

"Hardly, you're the master."

"Not anymore. My time is almost up. I only have my street clinic now. I need you to teach me what's new, and I'm leaving in a few days. We need to get you to work. Can you start tomorrow?"

I was exhausted from my travels, but I owed this man my life. "Of course." I sensed he was hiding something more sinister, but I didn't ask.

We left, and Glenn took me to the hotel. It was new, clean, and highly contemporary for a relatively small town. I checked in, and my trunk was brought up to my room. I cleaned myself as best as I could and changed into a new dress I had purchased. I still hated wearing dresses. After living back East, I resigned myself to the societal norms and adapted, but I longed for blue jeans and T-shirts. Not going to happen. Not going to have Oreos, and thankfully I was finding the need for tampons diminishing, too.

I lay down on the bed and fell asleep. I must have slept for hours. It was late afternoon, and a knock on the door awakened me. Sam, Danny, and Gee Ling were all there. Danny, or just Dan — as Sam had mentioned — now had rapidly graying hair, as did Gee Ling. We all had aged. Immediately, I was enveloped in their arms. I was teary, but the men politely ignored it. I was invited downstairs to dinner. As usual, Gee Ling could not join us. He went to have dinner with relatives. *I will struggle with this convention until I die.*

Dr. Walker joined us. We enjoyed both the food and wine, and I recounted my adventures minus a few details I would only share with Sam. After dinner, both Dan and Dr. Walker left. Sam and I walked in the cool of the late summer. He took my hand and wrapped my arm around his, as was the custom at that time. I could tell Sam was nervous, as was I. He showed me the reconstructed shops and a new library. There was a lull in the conversation.

"Becky, I've missed you," he finally confessed.

I squeezed his arm and admitted that I had missed him as well. Virginia City had a scent of pine trees and a bit of stale beer mixed with the new aroma of freshly cut lumber and, of course, Sam's pipe tobacco. It was a smell I would remember forever after as it accompanied Sam's first proper kiss. I returned the kiss but had to stand on my toes to reach his lips. It was soft and gentle, and I had a surge of pleasure at that moment I did not remember existed.

"Welcome home, darling," he finally said.

"Thank you. I think this is my home."

He kissed me again.

"Sam?"

"Yes, darling?"

"If this is going to be a regular occurrence, I'm going to need to buy a step stool."

Sam looked down at me. "I'll build you one."

He walked me to my hotel and said he would see me the next day. In the lobby crowd, we were both self-conscious and simply shook hands, which made me giggle. He laughed, turned, and left.

*He called me darling — be still, my beating heart.*

Dr. Walker was busy with patients when I arrived in the office the following morning. He had a boy with a deep splinter, a woman with advanced breast cancer, and a young woman close to term. She was experiencing some bleeding. I took her into a room and examined her. I decided she required bed rest for the last week or two of her pregnancy. This was her first pregnancy, and her husband worked in the mines. A receptionist was now employed by the clinic. Mrs. Clayton knew everyone in town. She remembered a young girl who had recently lost her parents and needed support. She would arrange for the young girl to come and stay for the expecting mother's confinement.

Dr. Walker, or Tom, as he insisted I call him, discussed the ongoing cases he could remember. Medical records were sparse. Most of it was just memory. We discussed some of the newer techniques I'd been taught, but I still had much to learn from this brilliant man. In the late afternoon, he and I drove a buggy out to the Cattle Creek Ranch, where the Buchanans entertained us. I packed an overnight bag in case Tom was called out. The town doctor couldn't hide, even when he or she was hours away. Gee Ling prepared a wonderful dinner, after which I had a few games of checkers with Danny while Tom and Sam had a chess game. Danny invited me to come out to the barn to see a horse injured by a cow protecting her calf, and we left the men. I suspected he wanted a quiet word with me.

"Becky, we're all so glad you're back," he started. "I think you might be able to restore some joy in our lives." It had been a few years since his wife's death, but he was still emotional about it. "All I ask is, please don't leave this time. I think you can see how my father feels about you."

"Danny — "

Danny interrupted my response. "We all feel the same, Becky. Gee Ling was intolerable when you left so many years ago. We can't afford to lose his cooking. We might all fade away." We laughed.

"Danny, I mean Dan, I have no intention of leaving. Back then, it was different. I'd just been separated from my husband and daughter. It was all new and so raw. I think you now can understand a parent's desire to do anything to be reunited with their child. Anything," I repeated. "I've accepted they're gone. I'm quite fond of your father. I have no firm plans, but I'm not leaving. Virginia City is my home. Home — it's such a wonderful word, isn't it?"

"It is," he lamented, and we entered the barn. We looked at two horses by lamplight. I said I would examine them tomorrow in the daylight and check for lameness. We returned to the house in time for Dr. Walker to say his goodbyes. He was going fishing in the morning, and Mrs. Clayton had been instructed to send for me in case of any emergencies. The office was closed for the day.

Dan went to bed, and Sam and I stayed up another hour talking until I dozed off. "Am I that bad of company?" Sam joked. I was embarrassed, but he put his hand on my shoulder. "I'm surprised you lasted this long."

"Yes, I'm a bit of a lightweight these days."

"Is that another one of your expressions?"

"It's not a swear word."

He laughed. "Well, you know what happens to women who swear, now."

"Not gonna happen, Sam. That isn't done in my time." I thought about it. "I mean, my other time."

"You're in my time now, Bec. I wouldn't want to test that theory." We both grinned like teenagers.

"Our time, Sam, our time. Trust me, the theory will be tested. I don't think you have ever seen me riled. If needed, I have a vocabulary, and I'm a modern woman."

I would have kissed him good night, but he just smiled and offered his standard, "Pleasant dreams." I knew where a modern woman would have ended up that night. I think he did too.

"How about some brandy?"

*Oh, this man is testing my limits.*

# CHAPTER 40

In the morning, I awoke to the smell of a Gee Ling breakfast. The aroma of pancakes, sausage, coffee, and biscuits overwhelmed my desire for more sleep. I dressed in riding gear and descended the stairs to find a table covered with Gee Ling's efforts.

"You too thin, missy," he announced. "Gee Ling will fatten you up."

I laughed and gave him a hug. He smelled of spices that had always been a part of him. "You can try. Many have, and many have failed." I was about to explain the genetics of my family but stopped short. I knew Mendel had discovered the basic inheritance laws by the late 1800s but was not sure exactly when. Even after all this time, it was hard to remember what I should know and what I should not. I felt safe alone with Sam, but I would never share this with anyone else.

After breakfast, Dan escorted me to a small pen behind the barn. There was my beautiful Penny. Sam was brushing her and smiled when I saw her. Yes, she was old and had a swollen hock and front fetlock. She came over to the fence immediately, and I entered through the gate and threw my arms around her neck. Her muzzle came down on my back. I started to tear up, and Dan placed his hand on my shoulder. "We were hoping you would return to see her, Becky. Pa's always made us take special care in case this day came."

I looked at Sam, who turned away for a moment. I'd noticed during the years that men get much more emotional as they age. "Thank you all. I'm overwhelmed and so grateful," was all I could say.

Sam walked away around the barn. When he returned, my saddle was on what looked like a slightly younger version of Penny. "This is Penny's daughter. We named her Copper. She has a daughter as well, but for today, this will have to do. I want to take you on a ride. Sam extended the reins to me. I hugged Penny once more and mounted Copper. She was the same color as Penny but had two white hind legs. Sam mounted a younger version of his old horse, Cash, who had died a few years ago.

"What's he called, Sam?"

Sam shrugged. "Cash." We laughed and headed out with a lunch prepared by Gee Ling. I thought we were going to Hank Heaven. Instead, Sam took me in a different direction over the ridge. After two hours of climbing, we came to the top of the mountain and a grassy meadow with a view of Lake Tahoe. We loosened our girths and tethered the horses.

Sam had a blanket, which he spread out on the grass. We ate some cheese and apples and had wine and water. It made me sleepy, and Sam commented that when it came to alcohol, I was a lightweight. "Is that what you call it?"

"Pretty much," I said, closing my eyes but smiling. I would have to acclimatize to the elevation once more.

I dozed for a minute, then a fly landed on my nose, and I jumped. "Nap over!"

"Is that it?"

"Yep, I usually just need a minute. Batteries charged. Now, I can go for hours. It's a gift. It sustained me through the war and in several epidemics."

"Batteries?"

"So much to teach you, so little time."

Sam stood up and extended his hand. I could see he was nervous. I took his hand, and he pulled me up.

The way he looked at me made my heart race. He took both of my hands and looked directly at me.

"Becky, I'm not a young man anymore. I don't know how many years I have left, but I would be honored if I could spend them with you." He smiled, but it was a nervous smile.

My heart raced. "Yes, I would be honored, too."

"So, will you marry me?" He reached into his pocket and pulled out a ring.

I thought my heart would jump out of my chest. "Yes, I will, Sam. I'll try to make you proud."

Sam slipped the ring on my finger. The indentation of Jeff's ring was long gone. The new one was much bigger. The large stone was set flat in gold. It slid around my finger, and we both realized it would have to be resized.

"Should I keep it until I can have it fitted?"

"Try taking it off. I may be small, but I can fight like a cougar."

He took me in his arms and kissed me. I don't think I ever have felt so safe and loved — ever. Even knowing the Buchanan curse, I didn't care. This was the happiest moment in my new life. He sat down again, and I sat between his legs and leaned back on his chest. He pointed out landmarks that showed the extent of the Cattle Creek Ranch. We discussed my need to work, and he agreed that this would not be a traditional 1800s marriage. I would continue to work. He was very old-fashioned, but in many ways, he was a modern man. We would have to sort out many issues, but that would come later. I smiled to myself. Knowing how strong-willed we both were, some head-butting was in our future.

We returned late in the afternoon. Dan was out working on a timber contract and would be back before dinner. Sam took me to see Penny's progeny and a few other horses. The black stallion was out with the herd. He had proven to be the perfect fit for his mares. Two younger colts had been bred and were currently the main breeding stallions. There was a new bull in the pen that would be turned out with the cows when the roundup was over.

Sam turned to me. "Let's surprise Danny and Gee Ling. Do you mind taking off the ring until I tell them at dinner?"

"Perfect. That'll be great fun."

Dinner was a slightly less extravagant affair compared with the night before. Gee Ling had ordered his cousin to use some of the leftovers. The dessert was new. After the meal, Sam stood up and brought Gee Ling to the table. As he had planned, I put the ring back on my finger under the table, after which I brought my hand out and casually covered it with my other hand. Sam announced there was to be a new addition to the family. He discussed a new stallion, and Dan looked perplexed. "Oh, and Becky has agreed to marry me."

Both Dan and Gee Ling jumped up and hugged me. Dan said, "I've always wanted a mother. I can hardly wait to call you, 'Ma.'"

"Over my dead body, Danny, 'Becky' will be just fine, young man," I sternly responded. "Am I even old enough to be your mother?"

"When's the wedding, Pa?"

I was curious as well. I hadn't even thought about it. Because we both had been married before, this wedding didn't need to be an extravagant affair.

"I was kind of hoping to wait until Clint comes in April. We might even get Johnny back from the cavalry for a few days." Sam glanced at me for assurance.

"That's a wonderful idea," I said, and I meant it. I was in no hurry.

Gee Ling was up in arms. How could we do this so quickly? He needed time to plan. Off he went in his native tongue, ranting about the required planning and preparations.

Later, when Sam and I were alone, he asked me if it was all right that we wait. "Yes, of course, it is. Maybe I can get Martha Tyler to come, and her children could be at the ceremony. Maybe she can be my matron of honor," I suggested. I thought about how old Lauren would be if time had not stood still for them. I also thought about Hank and how Sam must feel.

This time, we kissed good night. "I love you, Becky Harper, but it will sound better when you're Becky Buchanan."

"I love you too, Sam Buchanan. Becky Buchanan sounds good to me, too."

# CHAPTER 41

The next day, I returned to Virginia City as a soon-to-be-married woman. There were genuine well-wishers. I finally saw Ray Thompson, who kissed me and invited me to dine with him when I stayed in town. He was overjoyed at my return and the news of my pending marriage. "Next to me, I can't think of a better match."

"Well, Ray, I'm not married yet. Come up with a better offer, and I'll consider it."

"I can't compete with Sam," he replied.

"Aren't you younger, Ray?

"By six months. Hmm, maybe I can."

Some Virginia City citizens were genuinely unhappy. Mrs. Gardiner, who invited the younger Buchanan boys and me for dinner many years ago, was one of them. She spread gossip about my occasionally staying out at the Cattle Creek Ranch. We ignored her, as did most of the citizens of Virginia City. A few individuals refused to talk to me. Many men would go to the male doctor several hours away to avoid my examination of their private parts. Still, during the next few months, the practice grew due to my good deeds and reputation.

The months passed, and preparations for the wedding continued. Martha had been contacted, and she promised to be my matron of honor. The children were too old, although she ended up with six in total. The youngest was nine. So, a ranch hand's daughter was going to be the flower girl. Dan and Clint would be the groomsmen. Johnny had not replied, and I knew it bothered Sam.

During the winter, I didn't see Sam for weeks at a time. Each time, I fretted, thinking of the Buchanan curse. Was I to be yet another woman thwarted in marriage? When we met, however, the same giddy feeling of new love always surfaced. I felt like an eighteen-year-old. He would take me in his arms, kiss me passionately, and tell me how he had missed me and what was happening at the ranch.

The last Saturday in March was the date we decided upon after Sam received a letter from Clint confirming he would be home a week before. This gave us a month. The spring was exceptionally warm, and Virginia City was booming with a new silver mine opening. Men were coming in droves. The town and my practice were growing. Sam was in town for a meeting of the Cattlemen's Association. We planned to go to dinner following the meeting. We walked to the hotel, and as we turned the corner, I heard a familiar sound coming from the saloon. The piano was playing a song that brought back memories. I stopped short and just about fainted. It was the Nat King Cole song "Unforgettable."

Sam felt me tense. We both knew the significance of this melody. I listened and then looked at him. I could see his face darken. I peered into the bar and saw a man whom I had observed once before in the general store. He hadn't stood out then. It would never cross my mind that he could be from my old time — the future.

He looked my way and smiled but continued playing the distinctive melody. Sam urged me on, and we passed the saloon and entered the hotel. Dinner was forgettable. We hardly talked. I smiled and tried to make conversation, but I could tell that he was upset.

"It's probably just a coincidence. Maybe it was an old song that was revised later. Maybe he's the original song-writer. It doesn't matter, anyway. I'm getting married to you next month. That's final."

Sam smiled and took my hand. "I love you."

"I love you too, Sam. Nothing will change that. I promise."

I didn't see the piano player again until he came to the clinic with a smashed finger. He introduced himself as Nat Cole. I was reasonably sure it was not his name.

"It's not career-ending," I assured him. "I don't even think it's broken," I said, manipulating the finger back and forth to determine his level of pain.

"Too bad there are no X-ray machines," he casually men-tioned. I looked shocked, and he got the reaction he was seeking.

I quickly recovered. "I don't know what you mean."

"I kind of think you do, Dr. Harper. I'm pretty sure you know exactly what I mean. I've played that song for two years, and you are the only one who looked as if you knew it."

I stammered, "Well, it was rather unforgettable, wasn't it?" I wrapped his hand and said no more.

Several days later, I saw him again at the bank. I walked past him and inquired about how his hand was. He replied it was healing slowly, and he was back to playing the piano. I smiled and got in line to deposit some money. Two days later, I was sitting on a bench near the town hall, taking advantage of the sun and unusual warmth. The piano man sat down on the other end of the wooden bench.

"Do you know how I got here?"

"Pardon? I don't know what you mean. Stage or horse-back, I assume."

"Guess again," was all he said.

"Mr. Cole," I began, but he interrupted me. "Actually, it is Bob. Bob Barker or John Kennedy or Lyndon Johnson. Take your pick."

"I don't know who you are. And frankly, I don't give a damn. Please go away."

"Suit yourself, but where I come from, and more impor-tantly when I come from, may interest you."

I got up and walked away. My entire body was shaking.

As I left, he shouted, "And I can tell you how to get there."

Right then, Ray Thompson rounded the corner and saw me. He smiled and asked if I wanted to have a cup of coffee. "That sounds lovely, Ray."

Ray glanced over at the man and inquired if anything was wrong. "Is he bothering you, Becky?"

"No, he hurt his hand, and he showed me how it's doing," I said rather unconvincingly. Ray looked back at the man, who was now walking in the other direction.

"Funny man. He plays these songs that are kind of catchy, but none of us have ever heard of them." I suspected Ray had more than a casual interest in the piano man.

# CHAPTER 42

Two nights later, Sam was back in town. He'd seen Ray, and I think Ray might have had a word with Sam about the piano player. We were having dinner at the hotel, and when we were alone, Sam asked about him. "Is he from another time?"

"I won't lie to you, of all people. I think he is. I want nothing to do with him. I made my peace. My life is with you, Sam. My life is here and now." I touched his face. I didn't care if it was inappropriate now, but I wanted him to know I had chosen him over anyone alive.

"Thank you, my dear Rebecca." He kissed my hand. We ate the rest of our meal in silence. A young man came up to us and said his wife was in labor, and the baby wasn't coming out. Sam smiled and said, to go. I left and followed the man out to his buggy. The trip was a short distance, and I arrived in time to see a beautiful little boy as the midwife placed him in his mother's arms. I returned to the hotel, but the waiter said Sam had gone over to the saloon. I hoped he was just having a drink before returning to the Cattle Creek Ranch. I heard the piano player playing those tunes that were so familiar — Neil Diamond, Hall and Oates, and one that made me laugh, Roy Rogers and Happy Trails. I had to hand it to him. It was a great way to communicate with fellow time travelers.

With only a week left before the wedding, I was getting nervous. Clint was late, and Martha had to back out because her entire family was sick with chickenpox. The local dressmaker created a wedding dress that fit like a sack of potatoes. Gee Ling was in a dither, and Dan was not back from a trip to take the cattle to the mountains.

I saw the piano player one day when I was gathering wildflowers in a meadow near the town. He had not bothered me since Sam had visited the saloon. I figured Sam must have spoken to him. "Dr. Harper, how are you?"

"Fine, thank you," I returned while I gathered the flowers to take to the church for the service the following day.

"I think we got off to a poor start. I'm sorry. It's just that we have so much in common. It would be so nice to talk about things."

I looked at him and realized he was probably as frightened and bewildered as I was when I arrived here.

"Yes, I suppose we do. What year were you born, Mr. — what is your real name?"

"Frank Lash, 1954, and you?"

"A lady never tells her age. How did you get here, anyway?" I deflected his question.

"Ah, that's the simple part. The hard part is whether I want to go back?"

I raised my eyebrow. "You can return? Like, go back and forth? Have you returned?"

He nodded. "Yes, several times."

"To the time you left. You have gone back and forth, really?"

"Yes, well, time did not stand still. I went back once, and it was the exact time I had spent here. A month had passed in both places. So, if you left there — several, say ten years ago, that time also passed from where you left. The ten years would be gone from there as well. How many years has it been, Dr. Harper?"

"I stopped counting. Fifteen at least and maybe more."

Frank Lash let out a long whistle. "So, about 1980 or so. A bit has changed."

"How about you, Mr. Lash?"

"I've come and gone over the years. I teach history, and I like to conduct actual research."

"Really. Where do you go when you're here?"

"Well, I always start here. This is my portal. I've met other time travelers, as they are called, and they have various portals. I've used theirs, and I ended up in a different place, but mine is near here. I'm going back next week. You're welcome to join me."

I was shocked. "No, no, nope, not me. I'm getting married."

"Did you have family back in the — was it the eighties?"

I didn't answer. I looked away, and the memories came flooding back.

"Dr. Harper, I didn't mean to upset you."

"It's in the past, Mr. Lash. For years, I tried to find a way home, but then, a few years ago, I just gave up and settled for what I had."

"Settled?" His eyebrows raised as if he had found a hook.

"I didn't mean it like that. I'm quite happy in this life. It's been so many years, Mr. Lash. I'm sure they think I'm dead. What good would it do to go back? For all I know, they're all dead too."

"Dr. Harper, in case you've forgotten, they haven't been born yet."

He was right. *What an annoying man.* The day was getting away from me. We had a church social tonight, and I needed to prepare. "Thank you, Mr. Lash. I must go."

I returned to my office, where two people were waiting. Sam was sitting on the bench with a young boy and his injured dog. Sam kissed me hello and said, "Duty calls." He pointed to the boy. I laughed, opened the door, and invited the young boy to come in.

"Gee Ling made us some food for tonight."

"Is Danny coming?" I asked.

"No, it's still painful." Sam stared away, hiding his grief. So many losses in this family.

"It took me a decade. The day's young." I directed the young boy to follow me.

"Longest wait of my life." Sam laughed. "Shall I come back in an hour?"

"Perfect. See you then." I'd attended two socials since becoming engaged. I enjoyed dancing, but dancing with Sam was the only time I could legitimately make body contact in this Victorian society. I'd entirely stopped even imagining intimacy in the last several years. Now, I craved human touch — his touch.

The dog had torn a toenail, which was dangling and hitting the ground, causing pain. This was not an anesthesia job, but it was close.

"How strong are you?" The boy appeared to be capable.

"Very strong, ma'am." He puffed up his chest.

"Okay. Put your right hand around the muzzle and hold the leg out with your left hand." I showed him the position that I wanted. He held the dog as required. With one sharp yelp and a jerk from my pliers, it was over. We bandaged the foot. I had the penicillin I'd taken during my stagecoach ride back to Virginia City. I'd told no one — not even Sam. This dog would not get antibiotics. I'd encountered a few cases of tetanus in people back East and several in horses. All wounds were washed diligently to prevent the clostridial bug from colonizing. I thought about the tetanus vaccine. What vaccines would I bring back to this time if I could?

It was time to get ready for the social. I sent the boy home with instructions to keep the dog's paw away from dirt and with a small vial of iodine to redress the claw in a few days. The boy asked about payment. I suggested that the following week he could come to the clinic and do some weeding for me after school. He agreed and was off. Sam picked me up, and we walked to the church hall, which was a short distance from the office. He offered me his arm, and I gladly took it. We stopped to put the flowers in vases inside the church, which was always open.

"Next week, this will be covered in flowers," Sam remarked.

"Longest week of my life, darling."

"Mine too." Sam took my hand and kissed it.

He took me in his arms and held me. We stayed like that for a minute.

"Becky, you're shaking. What's wrong?"

"Nothing. You're imagining it. I'm fine. Let's get to the dance. I'm starving." Sam was right. The talk about time travel disturbed me. I could not decide if I should tell Sam. How would he react? I was getting married, and nothing was going to stop that. But knowing or thinking that I could move between both worlds was both disturbing and intriguing. That was putting it mildly.

We ate fried chicken, potato and egg salad, and other small dishes Gee Ling's cousin had prepared. The dancing began, and Sam and I danced several dances. I needed a break. "I know Mrs. Gardiner would love a dance. Maybe that would make her happy," I suggested. He looked as if I'd gone mad.

Just to prove it to me, he asked her. Mrs. Gardiner was a rotund woman now, and she wore a bright orange dress. She accepted his offer, and I observed her quietly whisper in his ear about something. He looked surprised about whatever she was saying. They finished the dance, and he returned. He gripped me by the arm and said we needed to talk.

"What's going on? Was there more gossip?" I could not imagine what she could have said.

Sam was furious. "Did you spend the afternoon with the piano player?" he asked in a restrained voice. "When you're married, or even about to be married, there should be no secrets, Rebecca. None." He was holding my arms in a tight grip that forced me to look at him.

I hissed, "I have no secrets that are of consequence. None. Yes, I spoke to him. He told me about his life to some extent. He told me about traveling back and forth. He wanted to show me how I could do it, too. I did not, and I repeat, do not, want to know about it. My past is my past. You and your family and this town are my future. I'm not going back, and I will live whatever time we have together with you and you alone. I love you. I have a past, and you have a past as well. We can't change that. We can only live and make the best choices we can for our future."

I looked at him, and despite my great effort, the tears came. I'm such an emotional control freak, but this man has brought me to tears so many times. These were tears of anger. Or were they? Did I regret my life? Did I subconsciously want to go back and just have a peek?

Just then, Ray Thompson walked out of the hall and rolled and lit a cigarette. To break the tension, I chided him, "Those will kill you, Ray."

"We all gotta go some way, Becky," he replied. "Hey, you two, in a week, you will have all the time you want to be alone. I want a dance with the bride before the night's out." Did he sense our fight? Ray had spent his life defusing dramas.

"Ray, it's getting harder and harder to share her, but I guess I'll let you have one dance." Sam released my arms, took out the obligatory handkerchief, and wiped my tears. "Go back in, darling. I'll be back inside in a moment. Ray and I have a few details to discuss for the ceremony." Because the Tyler clan wasn't coming, Ray had offered to officiate at the wedding. I suspected his conference with Ray concerned something else.

# CHAPTER 43

S am asked me to go for a ride after church on the following day. We headed up the mountain pass toward Hank Heaven. I had not been there in years. It was as beautiful as ever. As we descended into the valley, we saw a bear and two cubs cross in the valley's far end. The grass sprouted early this spring. There were still small snowbanks in the shadows of the peaks that surrounded the valley. The bears were slow, but the cubs had survived their first winter. They might be slow, but we both knew they would be hungry.

Sam took me to the center of the meadow and asked me to dismount. He tethered the horses. There was no picnic. We had a short time to stay before the day would turn toward night, and it was still chilly up here in the early spring.

He took my hand and led me to the edge of the clearing, and there it was: Hank's grave. I didn't know he was buried there. I was not one to visit the graves of the dead. After my mother died, I never went to the cemetery, and my father didn't, either.

I kneeled down and cleared off some branches that had fallen in the winter. It was such a beautiful, peaceful spot. I was finding it hard to swallow or speak.

"Becky, I want to talk to you about Hank. You know it was sudden, and we didn't know it was coming. I have few regrets in my life, but not talking to him the day he died is probably the biggest. I would give anything to return to that day to talk to him — anything. I've had many losses in my life, as you know. But losing a child, even as a grown man, is the worst." There was silence. I knew what was coming. "You need to go back. If you don't, you'll resent me and everything here for the rest of our lives. I couldn't abide that. You'd regret it for the rest of your life. Go back, Becky. I love you too much to keep you here."

I looked up at him standing above me. He was right, but he was my rock, and he was now my love. Yes, Jeff was a wonderful man, but I knew he would have moved on by now — but Lauren?

I said nothing for a while. I stood up and put my hands around Sam's waist. I pulled him toward me and cupped his chin in my other hand, and kissed him as passionately as I had ever kissed anyone. It was a tender kiss, but the feeling was pure sorrow and joy at once.

"All right, but I'm coming back. You can count on that." We both knew it might not be true.

We rode out in silence. As we arrived at the summit, I turned and memorized the vision. I would soon visit this valley at another time.

I went to the Cattle Creek Ranch that night instead of returning to Virginia City. A young doctor was coming to work for me while I prepared for my wedding and honeymoon. Sam and I were going to San Francisco after the wedding.

I looked at Dan and Gee Ling and said nothing that would alert them to the parting. I planned to leave just after the wedding. I watched the fire and chatted with Gee Ling about his life, and I would like to say I let Dan beat me in checkers, but sadly he whipped my butt several times. *I'd better not say "butt" in front of Sam.*

Dan offered me more coffee. "Becky, you aren't here tonight. Where are you? Does the idea of marrying my pa have you that rattled?"

"Well, he's a force to be reckoned with, Dan. I have to plan my strategies for husband wrangling. He must behave, but I don't want to break his spirit in the process."

Sam looked up from some papers he was reading. He smiled and shook his head. "You're dreaming, Bec."

"Oh, am I?" I suspected Sam sensed my fake laugh, but Dan didn't.

"Hey, Pa, does this mean we need to clean up for dinner every night and behave ourselves?"

"No one should put on good clothes for me. Remember, I was raised on a horse ranch. And don't expect me to dress every night."

Dan responded, "Dress or dress up, Becky?"

"You know what I meant. Remember to be respectful to your elders, young man."

I went out to see Penny. Her time was coming. She nickered and came straight over to me. "I'll be back, old girl, I promise. Hang around longer, will you?" I scratched under her mane, where I knew she liked the stimulation. She arched her head toward my thigh and reciprocated by rubbing her nose on my leg.

"Hey, I'm not sure I like to think of your horse rubbing my wife's thigh." Sam had snuck up on me. He put his hands around my waist and pulled me back into his chest. Ever the gentleman, he did not go further.

"Just so you know, I'm expecting a bit more when we're married," I laughed.

"Just so you know, you will get a lot more, young lady." He squeezed harder. He turned me around, and we kissed.

"Are you going to talk to the piano player tomorrow? What's his real name?"

"Frank, Frank Lash. Yes, I will. He says he can go back and forth easily. I won't be gone long, I promise."

"I know, but let's just wait and see. I just have to figure out what I'll say and do while you're gone."

"Oh, I think Mrs. Gardiner could keep you occupied," I joked, trying to keep the mood light. And that was it. I received a swat on my bottom.

"That's a warning." He turned and took my hand, and we walked into the house. My backside stung, but in a good way. It made me laugh.

# CHAPTER 44

I returned to Virginia City the following morning with Gee Ling. He was preparing for the wedding reception. His cousin came too, and they dropped me at the office. It was early, and the office was closed, but Mrs. Clayton opened the door as I entered the clinic.

"Hi, Dr. Harper. Did you hear about last night?"

"No, what happened? Did I miss a birth or death?" That was the difficult part of being a vet or a doctor in a small town. You could never relax.

"The piano player was in a fight with the bartender, who accused him of stealing the tips. Glenn was called, and the piano man departed. No one can find him. There was a terrible fight, and the place is all broken up."

"Was anyone hurt? You knew where I was, didn't you?"

"Oh, sure. The piano player might have been hurt, but he's in hiding or moved on to the next town. Good thing, too. He gave me and everyone else the spooks."

Well, that put a wrinkle in my plans and kind of gave me an excuse to continue with my intention to marry and spend the rest of my life as Mrs. Samuel Buchanan. But in truth, I was dying inside. I barely got through the day. The new doctor showed up, and I gave him the tour and discussed all the current patients. He was green as green, but he had excellent medical training, although rural practice was different. I knew I was going to be there to help him get started. Or was I?

Late that night, there was a soft knock on my door. Sam and Ray had tried to get me to carry a small gun and to be cautious of strangers at night. At least I'd locked the door.

"Who is it?"

"It's Frank Lash, Dr. Harper. I need your help."

I opened the door, and he was standing hunched over with his hand wrapped in a towel. He put his hand forward.

"Good thing you don't make a living with your hands," I remarked as I examined his mangled hand.

"But will I be able to play the piano?"

"Could you play the piano before?" I couldn't recall where that came from, but it was not from the 1800s.

"Dr. Harper," he started.

"Becky. Call me Rebecca or just Becky," I said while turning his hand over. Several bones were broken.

"Before you say anything, did you steal the money?"

"Would it make a difference?"

"I don't know. It might."

"No, no, I stole nothing. I grew up with Roy Rogers and Gene Autry. Need I say more?"

"No, I suppose not." I said nothing else about the events the previous night.

"You need surgery. The best I can offer would not be as good as you could have in the future, but I think you know that." I had to admit this life and time had its limitations. "So, what are your plans?"

"That's why I'm here. I have to leave tonight. I need help to get there. If you come, I can take you with me. I promise you can return. At least I can show you how to get back into your time."

"You realize this is not really the past? It is my imagination. The Cattle Creek Ranch or the Buchanans did not exist in the past. It was a television series. This is all in my head. How can you be sure I can come back?"

"How do you know there wasn't a family called Buchanan with significant land holdings, cattle, and timber operations? I'm a university professor of history, and I can't say it didn't happen. This is not my first trip into the past, and it won't be my last."

"Okay, what do you need from me?" I splinted the hand as best I could and made a sling. I wasn't convinced he didn't have a hairline crack of the radius. His entire arm required support.

"At least come with me to the place where I go, and you can come another time. Just help me get there. You've been there. I know."

"How would you know?" He pulled out a locket that I had worn on my neck for years. It was my mother's and her mother's before her. I gasped. I'd forgotten about the locket, but now I remember losing it. I knew where Frank had found it. We could ride there, and I'd be back by daylight. "All right, let's ride."

I saddled two horses that I kept for traveling to distant patients. Both horses were spooky in the dark, but both had carried me many times to the dying and women in labor. We headed out of town on the back row of houses on a quiet road. The dogs that lived in the various dwellings along the way were accustomed to my nightly travels and did not bark. We headed up to the mountain, where the slide had occurred, and toward Hank Heaven. The wind blew cold, and the pine trees sighed in the dark. The granite shelf on which we traveled seemed solid.

As we approached the area where I knew the slide had occurred, he looked down into the ravine. He pointed, "Down there."

I could barely make out a large pool in the stream that ran below. "You jump in the pool, and when you surface, you're back in your old time."

"Is that it?" This was crazy. We would freeze to death in the spring waters.

"Becky, please come with me. Please. You can come with me and return to all this." He waved his arm, indicating our present time and location. "To your home, if this is what you want, and you can help me find a doctor to fix my hand and be on your way."

"Frank, I don't know anyone there. What am I supposed to do? I can't just show up in these clothes." I had on my traditional riding clothes of the time, with culotte pants and a corset with a frilled shirt. No way was I going. We carefully worked our way down to the water, and he dismounted. I took the reins. He kneeled down and tested the water. "Shit, it's cold." I thought of the last time I had used that word. It must have been during the Civil War. I could make the infantrymen blush in those desperate times. Thankfully, Sam wasn't around me then, or Jeff, for that matter.

"So?" I asked, looking at Frank.

"I think I'll wait until just before dawn. That way, when I get there, it will be morning as well, and I'll dry off in the sun."

"It's spring. How do you know it's not flooding with the spring thaw?"

"I don't," Frank confessed.

I dismounted and sat with him, waiting for daylight. I thought about how old Lauren would be and where she would be. I didn't know if Jeff took the veterinary practice or not. If not, where was he? Was Lauren in college? Did Jeff remarry and have more children? I had serious doubts about the time travel phenomenon. It might be okay for Frank, but the likelihood that I would find my family close by was remote. *And how do I explain my absence in their lives?* No, I was not going. The relief of this decision was overwhelming. I was not leaving the man I loved, his family, or the town I had grown to love.

"Frank, I'm not going. Not now or ever."

"Are you sure?"

"Yes, very. If you ever decide to come back, can you look up my husband and daughter and maybe send word to me about my daughter? Her name is Lauren."

I was about to give him her details when a tremendous roar came from a rock above the pool. Two mountain lions crouched and looked like they were about to pounce on us. We both jumped back and fell into the pool. The shock of the cold water took my breath away.

I'd gone in over my head. I surfaced, and the water was rushing far more than it was when I fell in. I could not see the two mountain lions, and Frank was next to me, gasping. His arm was hurting and not allowing him to swim. I grabbed his other arm and pulled him to shore. Our teeth were chattering so strenuously we could hardly breathe. I felt as if I were paralyzed by the cold. We hugged each other for warmth and watched for the return of the cats.

I don't know how long we stayed like that, but at some point, we saw the sun. The snow was all around us. Snow-covered the rocks and trees above the creek banks. This was crazy. There was no snow when we fell in.

Frank was the first to realize that we had time traveled. He looked over and saw the remnants of the rockslide that had propelled me back in time. As dawn broke, I gazed up, and the trail had been remodeled into the cliff face. A railing had been added to the track above. We were wet and cold. Frank finally got up and climbed to some bushes. He pulled them apart and found a plastic sack with his clothes. He gazed over at me, and I turned away as he removed his wet clothes and dressed in his dry ones. Well, at least one of us was warm.

He threw me a sweatshirt and said to put it on. He looked away while I took off my shirt and put on the dry top.

# PART 7

## BACK TO THE FUTURE OR NOT, 2001

# CHAPTER 45

Frank and I climbed up to the trail that led either to Hank Heaven or back to the trailhead where, many years ago, Julie Smyth and I started on our fateful ride to see her favorite oasis, away from her hectic life. It was challenging to make headway in the snow. I was freezing, literally. As we walked along the granite trail, I looked down on a valley with cattle in large, fenced sections. There was no snow in the valley, but the fields had not greened up as I'd observed last week, over one hundred or so years ago. Off to the side was an old ghost town. There were no signs of activity, but I was observing from far away.

We made our way to a paved area, marked with white lines, indicating parking bays for horse trailers or smaller ones for cars. One car looked as if it had been there for months.

"My girlfriend brings it up and leaves it in case I come back."

"You have a girlfriend? Someone knows what you're doing?" I was a bit taken aback.

"Well, she thinks I'm looking in old mines. She and her son drive it up on the weekend and pick it up a few days later. You know, I'm not gone that long normally. Crap, I hope it starts."

*Me too, minus the c-word, I thought. I don't want to go back to my 1980s vocabulary.*

*Phew, it started.* "What kind of car is this? Where's the heater?" I was still shaking from the cold. My legs felt like ice, and I was wet from the waist down.

"It's a Mazda. You may want to catch up on a bit of technology." He grabbed a small handheld device and flipped it open. It eventually glowed, and he punched numbers and talked to someone. I assumed it was his girlfriend.

I had explained to him I wanted to go to the clinic, see my family, turn right around, and return to the river. His girlfriend was several sizes larger than I was, but her clothes were better than what I was wearing. She was at work. He would borrow some and take me to Kmart to get me something that would fit. He would then go to the hospital to have his hand examined.

"Bring on the blue-light specials." It wouldn't hurt to have a quick look.

"They don't have blue-light specials anymore."

"Seriously, what's the point?" *What's happened to the world?*

After driving for ten minutes, it was apparent he was in too much pain to drive a car, so we switched places. It was a stick shift. I silently thanked my father for making us learn to drive a manual. After all those years, it was not as bad as I thought. I only almost killed us twice.

Since I had no money, I had to rely on Frank. He agreed that my medical services were worth one set of clothes and a jacket. I stayed at his house when he went to the store to buy my clothes. He brought them back, along with McDonald's food. He left me at his apartment. Frank's girlfriend picked him up while I hid in the bedroom, and they headed to the hospital and then to her apartment for the evening. There was no Victorian protocol in the twenty-first century. We decided that there wasn't a reasonable explanation for my presence, and I needed to hide.

I stayed in his apartment and had a bath. It was pure luxury. I'd go look at the vet clinic to see Lauren and possibly Jeff, then head straight back to the river and the pool. I missed my fiancé and my life. I wasn't comfortable in this modern world anymore. The entire experience was a foolish mistake. I wanted to go home —this century was not my time anymore. I had only a day, and then I had to be back for the wedding. Sam must be beside himself worrying about me.

I woke up early the following morning. Frank came back and brought me a telephone book. I looked up the clinic and saw it still existed, but it did not list Jeff as the owner. Frank told me he had a specialist appointment, and he would be back soon. He had switched to his friend's car, which was automatic and didn't require two hands.

I turned on the television and quickly checked what was on. The morning shows did not interest me. I searched for a *Comstock* episode, but Frank had just five channels. I remembered when cable television became popular in the

1970s, but I never had it. I flipped it off and waited for Frank to pick me up and take me to the veterinary clinic. It was cold and snowing even at this lower elevation. We were lucky to get out alive.

Frank finally returned mid-morning. I wasn't happy. "Where have you been?" I snarled. "I'm on a time schedule. I have to be back in two days."

"Have you looked outside? Apparently, this is the biggest snowstorm to hit this area in recorded history. You aren't getting back today."

I was devastated. The Buchanan curse strikes again. Sam and I would not be getting married as planned. I wondered if I could get back at all. I just stared at the surroundings. With all the electrical appliances a woman could hope for, all I wanted was a woodstove.

I needed to smell the spices that permeated Gee Ling's kitchen. I wanted a big open fireplace at the Cattle Creek Ranch, with my horse in a stable behind my house. I had a purpose and was an asset to my community. I didn't know about what level human or veterinary medicine was happening now. I was sure I was too far behind the times to practice in this day and age.

"Can we at least drive to the veterinary clinic?" I asked.

"I already called them. It's closed except for emergencies. I asked them if Jeff Harper worked there. The receptionist didn't know who he was."

"Maybe I can do some research for you," said Frank as he walked over to the black television screen and pushed buttons on a white box next to it. It was a modern com-puter. Frank explained the concept of the internet, which was not available in 1981, or at least was unknown to me in those days. I was gobsmacked. He searched for Jeff Harper and found at least fifty. He searched for Lauren Harper and discovered about forty. He narrowed his search to Jeff Harper, DVM, and found three, all back East. My heart sank. Jeff was probably one of those three.

With a bit more sleuthing, Jeff Harper, DVM, was found working at a private research facility in Kentucky. It looked as if he worked for a drug company. He was married to someone named Sherry and had three children . Is this my sister, Sherry? The names of the children were not mentioned. He was a deacon in his church and was an avid fly fisherman. That was Jeff. There was an email address, which Frank explained was a form of communication currently in use today. It was an electronic letter.

I thought about it and composed a letter in my head.
*Dear Jeff,*
*Hey, it's me, Becky. Sorry I haven't been in touch.*
Or
*Dear Jeff,*
*Good news, I'm back, so let's just get on with our lives.*

Frank wanted to get some food before the storm really set in. I stayed and did more internet searching. It was kind of addicting. "Hey, can you buy some Oreos?" I asked before he left.

I tried to look up my father, but I suspected he was not on the internet. I looked up our nearest town. From there, I located the obituaries. I typed in his name, got up, and walked away before hitting the search button. I peered out at the snow and thought about just how much I wanted to know. If I were back in the 1800s, my father would not be born yet and would still have had an entire life to lead. I walked back to hit the search button. Nothing came up. Is he alive?

I then remembered Julie Smyth and the rockslide. I went to the local news archives and notable deaths in 1981. Julie Smyth's obituary popped up on the screen. I used the date of our accident and Julie's name to search the archives. I discovered a short story about Julie Smyth and the search for her and a companion's bodies after a massive rockslide had caught them both. No bodies were found. I searched for a few days after the slide. The report was that Julie's body had been identified, but the companion was still missing. "A recent veterinary graduate was presumed dead. Her husband had arrived from the East and was searching for her body. He was reported to be devastated." The bodies of the two horses were discovered in the rubble. The search was ended due to the precarious situation. The trail and area were sealed off to hikers and horsemen until the site could be cleared.

I searched for my name and obituary notice. I was not listed at all. I went back to the site for my university. I found my veterinary school graduation photo and a note "presumed deceased." I don't think so. Should I be exposing my family and friends to the pain of finding me and losing me again? I was not staying. Clearly, they had moved on. Showing up and trying to explain my absence from their lives, only to disappear again, was unfair.

I pondered this while Frank was gone. Maybe I could use him to at least find me a picture of Lauren. When Frank returned, I explained my concerns. He gazed into the darkening sky. "Hmm, if you're sure you're going back, you have a point."

I considered my dilemma and took another bath. A girl could get used to hot running water. As I examined the hairdryer, which was not that different from my old one, the lights went out.

"Damn. Sorry, Becky," I heard from the living room. I actually laughed out loud. I had not experienced electricity for more than a decade, and now I was supposed to be sorry for its fallibility.

"Don't worry. I'm fairly used to it." I took a towel to dry my hair and heard him chuckle.

The power was out for the rest of the day. Frank didn't have a fireplace, and we huddled in the apartment under separate blankets. His handheld phone still worked, but he mentioned it would die by morning. Frank called his girlfriend and explained that a colleague was in town, and he would not attempt to drive across town tonight. I think he may have forgotten to mention I was a woman who was several years older than he was — no one needed to worry. With his hand now in a cast and surgery scheduled for next week, he was in no mood to do anything more than eat and sleep.

I looked longingly at the computer. It was a genuinely brilliant invention. I wanted to research electricity, herbal medicine, and how to make penicillin before I went back.

Frank and I devised a plan to get a story from my surviving family and a picture of Lauren. He was going to call Jeff and say he was a reporter for the local newspaper and was planning a piece on the 1981 slide. He would say he wanted an update on Jeff and Lauren. Maybe I could talk to her without letting her know who I was.

Frank spent the day writing notes about his recent trip to the 1800s. He was particularly interested in mining at the time. His apartment was small, and stacks of papers lined the walls. Books written about the 1800s were piled everywhere. I thumbed through them and found some references to a few of the places I'd visited.

They were all reasonably factual, except no mention of any Buchanans. Well, the history of Virginia City showed no mention of a Cattle Creek Ranch, either. Sutter's Fort and the newer hospital in Baltimore were mentioned, but my old hospital was not. Mostly, I slept. I was still tired, and the shock of being extremely cold for so long took the life out of me.

The roads were covered in snow the next day, and not a snowplow was seen. Frank said they didn't usually have snow here, and he had never seen a snowplow. His landline phone still worked, but his handheld phone was dead. He called his girlfriend, who said it was the same on her end of town, and the small college in which they taught was closed.

Frank dialed information and got Jeff's office number. He called to talk to Jeff as I listened in, but we got a message recorder. I shook my head and mouthed, "Don't leave a message." I didn't want to spook him. It was his voice, and my stomach or some visceral organ surged. It might actually have been my adrenal gland, in hindsight. We checked, and his own number was not listed. We tried one for Lauren, and there was no number either.

We sat in his tiny apartment talking, reading, and sleeping for two more days. It was getting colder, and I mentioned the papers would make an excellent fire. Frank disagreed.

The neighbors were all abandoning their apartments to walk or ski to other places.

On the third day, the lights switched on, and the heater kicked on, too. The temperature rose outside, and the snow melted. I was on that computer before you could say, "Bill Gates." We looked up the main office number for Jeff's workplace. Because it was early in the morning in Nevada, we knew it would be midday in Kentucky. When a pleasant woman with a very Southern accent came on the line, Frank asked to speak to Jeff Harper.

"And what would this concern?" she asked.

"It's personal." Frank tried to sound like an old friend.

"Well, Dr. Harper won't respond to personal calls. I'm afraid you all will have to be more specific," she drawled, with a strong emphasis on 'doctor.'

"My name is Frank Lash. I work at a community college near Reno. I'm writing an article for the local newspaper, The Argus, on a rockslide that claimed the life of his first wife."

"Oh, I didn't know that. Well, anyway, Dr. Harper's on sabbatical, and I'm not sure where he is at the moment. He's due back next month. I guess I could leave him a message for when he gets back."

I swear there were three syllables inserted in the word "back." I almost cried, but Frank was a good sleuth. "How's Lauren doing?"

"Oh, she's good. Do you know her? I guess not. Well, she's in her first year of vet school. Dr. Harper and Sherry are so proud of her." A lump formed in my throat. I turned away and looked out onto the snowy landscape. "You know, she is the spitting image of her mother. Oh, wait, maybe not. Are you saying she's from a mother that died?"

"Ma'am, do you know where I can reach Lauren?" Frank asked.

"Oh, I couldn't hand out that information to a stranger. You are just going to wait until Dr. Harper gets back. Excuse me, I have another call on the line. Do you want me to put you on hold?"

"No, ma'am, you've been quite helpful. Thank you." As he hung up, he looked over at me. "Which vet school?"

I shrugged. When I was in school, Kentucky didn't have a veterinary school. A quick search of veterinary school applications in Kentucky showed a large number went to Auburn University in Alabama. We searched the school for photographs and information. There wasn't much information for the public. Most of the material was under restricted access, including classes and social activities. There were lists of instructors and clinical researchers. Some of the instructors had pictures of students holding animals. None were Lauren. I would have recognized her. So close, but so far.

We searched for her name in the online white pages and found her, but the number was unlisted. We called the veterinary school, and again a receptionist with a strong Southern drawl answered. She said she was unable to connect us to Lauren as the students were on a holiday break. She would leave a message, but the school vacation break had just begun, and the students weren't due back for two weeks. Frank left his name and number. My timing stank.

My wedding date had passed. I looked at my ring and wondered how Sam had taken my disappearance. There were no impediments to remarrying. Rebecca Harper had been declared legally dead. I knew it would be weeks before I could get back to my new life, if ever.

"Excuse me while I go slash my wrists," I lamented. I went back into Frank's second bedroom, where I was sleeping on the floor. The house was warm, and the snow was melting. I was despondent. I wondered what Dan, Gee Ling, and the townsfolk were thinking. Had I stolen away, fearing my impending wedding? Had Frank kidnaped me to get away? Had I gone to attend a sick or injured person and been killed in an accident? Only Sam would suspect I'd traveled to the future, and he would tell no one. That was for sure.

I asked Frank to take me to a library where I could study herbal medicine and perhaps get a jump on some of the advances in both human and veterinary medicine. I needed to know how to use what was available in the 1800s when I returned. No one would know me here or recognize me. I was almost twenty years older. Aside from a single picture of me that had been broadcast when the accident happened, I was legally dead.

I didn't have any modern currency, but fortunately, Frank was more than charitable. He took me to some secondhand clothes shops, and I purchased a bra, extra knickers, and another set of clothes. Pre-made clothes were a luxury, but the quality and fit were not incredibly flattering.

We went to a shopping mall so I could see how things had changed. Actually, not much, if this mall was an example. Frank said it wasn't. We went to a library, which had just a few books on medicinal plants and none of the history of the Nevada side of the Sierra Madras. I saw one on the

California side. With Frank's status as an instructor, we were able to check it out of the library.

We headed home and ate fried chicken from a drive-through outlet. It was not a patch on Gee Ling's fried chicken. I read the books and made notes, which I was pretty sure would not survive the trip through the water. I didn't want to bring anything that was unnecessary. I raided Frank's cabinet for antibiotics. He had some out-of-date tetracycline. Since he was scheduled for surgery in Reno in a few days, we stocked up on food, and I practiced driving in a big city.

The snow was not melting in the mountains above the town, and new snow fell in the lower elevations the night before the surgery, but it didn't stay on the ground. I took him to the hospital and dropped him off. I wondered what the girlfriend, whom I now knew as Heather, thought. I was to pick him up the following morning and bring him home.

He called early the following day but explained things had not gone well, and he was not coming home yet. Heather was by his side at all times, and he quickly asked me to play the role of his cousin when he came back to his apartment.

"Please, I really like her, and I don't want her to be jealous."

"Frank, all she has to do is look at me, and she will see she has nothing to worry about."

"Please, Becky?"

"Okay, but you owe me. Speaking of which, is there something I can do for some quick money? We're going to be out of food soon."

"There's some cash in my sock drawer in the tallboy. Help yourself."

I drove down to the grocery store and walked in, safe in the belief that I would not be noticed. I walked around, amazed at the variety and quantity. No one even looked at me. It was pure bliss.

As I walked down the cookie aisle, I heard, "Hello, Dr. Green," but I didn't look around. The greeting was repeated, and there was a tap on my shoulder. An older woman with Down syndrome said, "Do you remember me? I'm Rosa Smyth."

I was shocked and so surprised. I just answered, "Yes, I remember you."

"When are you coming to work?" she asked.

"Oh, I'm not sure, but soon." I said goodbye and walked to the counter. I bought the items I needed for two nights and left wondering where that would go. Would Rosa understand the significance of seeing me? Would she be believed or not? That was a bit of a gut punch.

I noticed she didn't mention her parents. I had read about the passing of Rosa's father a few years after the rockslide. Did she have some savant-like memory for faces? I recalled when I showed up on my first day at her parents' clinic that her mom called me 'green' based on my lack of experience.

As I returned to the apartment completely rattled with anxiety, the phone was ringing. I dared not answer it. Frank had an answering machine, but the caller didn't leave a message. When I did talk to Frank, he said it wasn't he who had called. I wondered if it could be Jeff or Lauren. Sitting in this dreary apartment was torture. I wanted to go home and my life.

It was two more days until Frank was ready to leave the hospital. His hand was infected from the surgery, and he was on antibiotics. His arm was swollen and in a sling. I met Heather, who suspected nothing. She taught English to freshmen. She was busy with student meetings and dropped Frank and left. I was asked to get the antibiotics at the drugstore. I was amazed at all the products and the array of pharmaceutical drugs that were now available.

The perfume made me sneeze, but the men's cologne was delish. I picked up his drugs and headed back. *Dare I go to the vet clinic to see what's new?* Probably not, but oh, did I want to go there?

I cooked a simple dinner of lamb, carrots, and rice with Gee Ling's spices. I liked Frank, but as usual, he was too young, and I was engaged. I would never betray Sam, and he knew it. I was about to test his love and patience.

# CHAPTER 46

The following morning, the phone rang early. Really early. A very groggy, Frank answered.

"What is it?" he demanded of the caller. I was awake in a second and picked up the other line.

"May I speak to Frank Lash?" a sweet, Southern-accented young woman replied.

In a heartbeat, both Frank and I knew it was Lauren. "My name is Lauren Harper, sir, and I think you're trying to reach me."

"Yes, we, I mean, I'm Frank," he replied while watching me making come on and keep it going circles with my hand and wrist from the other room.

"Lauren, thank you for returning my call. Uh." Frank paused, and I gave him an extremely exasperated look. "Lauren, I'm writing a story about an accident that occurred when you were very young. I'm sure you don't remember it, but your mother was killed in a rockslide in Nevada. You probably have heard about it or seen pictures over the years. I was attempting to reach you and your father about the incident. He appears to be away."

"Yes, sir, he and my momma are on a fishing vacation in New Zealand."

"Oh, is that so? Well, do you have any memories you care to share with me? I think you were too young to remember her, but do you keep a picture of her with you? And I hear you are in vet school. What influenced you to go down that path?"

"My father is my biggest influence, and of course, my momma  — I mean, my aunt, too. I think of her as my mother. According to Dad, he was going off the deep end until she stepped in. She saved us both. We love her to pieces." She paused. "I have some photos of my mother, but they're back home. I can send you one of me. Do you want me alone, or maybe with my horse or boyfriend?"

I made a circle motion with the hands again. "How about sending them all, and I'll select one for the story? So, you have a boyfriend? It would be nice to show you have a normal life. Could you tell me a bit about him? Is he at Auburn too?"

"Yes, sir." Oh my God, she is so polite, and I love the accent. "Dwight is older than I am, but we get on so well. My daddy said my mom — I mean, my bio mom — went for the older guys. I guess the acorn doesn't fall far from the tree, sir. Anyway, he's a senior, and he graduates in June. He's going to Texas. We hope to study reproduction."

"Oh, so he's in vet school too?"

"Yes, sir, he's like me. We're both into horses. My dad says it's a genetic thing, and there is nooo cure."

"Well, if I give you my email address, could you send me the pictures?"

"Yes, sir, let me find a pen. Sorry for the early call, but I have to get to work."

"Oh, what kind of work do you do?"

"Waitress, sir." I nodded and pointed to myself from the other room. I was crying and trying to be quiet. Email addresses were exchanged, and she hung up. I was a basket case. My daughter was perfect.

I made coffee and got the antibiotics for Frank's hand. I couldn't see under the cast, but his fingers looked less swollen, and he said his hand felt better. As the coffee was brewing, the phone rang once again.

"Mr. Lash? This is Lauren Harper again. Sir, if you are doing a story about my mama, talk to my grandpa. There's the real story, sir."

"Is he alive?"

"Well, according to him, he's dead, but the rest of us know better. He lives in a nursing home in Montana, where my mom and aunt grew up. He's the one who looked for my mother's uh," I think she was going to say body, but she stopped. "He searched for my mother all summer and every year after that for I don't know how long. He was sure she was alive. He wanted proof she was dead. Since they found nothing, and they found the other lady, he just kept looking."

"Lauren, does he, I mean, is he all right?"

"You mean, does he have his marbles? He definitely does, sir. He gives them holy heck at the nursing home. He begs me every time I call, or my mom, my other mom, I mean, calls and pleads with us to get him out so he can do more searching. I used to stay with him sometimes when I was little. He taught me to ride, and we spent a lot of time at his cabin in the high country. I rode, fished, hiked, and had a grand time. I have the number of the nursing home if you want to talk to him."

"Oh yes, please."

There was a flood in the other room. My tears could not stop. My throat was getting sore from trying not to cry out loud. Frank took all the details, and I sat in the living room, just trying to focus on what had transpired. Even Frank was near tears. Frank thanked her and hung up. "All those long years, Becky."

I knew what I had to do. I realized it would be weeks before I could get back to the water safely and return to my time. I was going to see my dad. I didn't care what the circumstances were or what the outcome would be. I'd travel to Montana to see my father.

The email with pictures arrived later in the day. She was gorgeous and athletic. I could see she had her father's height and my brown, curly hair. I was overwhelmed with pride. I had no influence on this young woman, but I gave her half her genes. Frank printed the photographs for me and offered to have small copies for me when I returned.

# CHAPTER 47

The first problem was I had to have identification to purchase a plane ticket. Compared with years of time travel, that was an easy problem to solve. Frank had a friend. Frank wasn't wealthy, but he had a stable job. He took money out of his bank, bought the plane ticket, and gave me enough money to get a junker and drive to my father's nursing home. If I were lucky, there would be enough to feed my father and me for a week. Old people eat little, and I was a master of surviving on hardtack now. I considered springing him from the nursing home and taking him up to his cabin in the high country for one last look. After that, I would take him back to the nursing home and prepare for my return. It was an option. I would decide when I saw him, if it wasn't too late.

Frank took me to the airport in Reno. He said there was a restaurant nearby that was popular. He wanted me to see it and eat one last good meal. The Wagon Wheel's parking lot was almost empty, a bad sign, but it was mid-afternoon.

We entered and were seated in a booth with soft, cushioned seats. Frank insisted I order the chicken fried steak, and he ordered some, too. I drank milk, and he had a beer. We discussed how I could repay him. He wasn't worried, but I was.

The food arrived, and Frank was right. It was delicious. I was almost in a stupor. I noticed Frank sitting upright and peering over my shoulder. "Somebody's looking at us," he remarked, gazing at the table behind me.

"Who?"

"I don't know, but he's looking our way."

"Who?" I turned, but Frank gave me the look.

"Don't turn. Don't look."

"It must be you, Frank. No one would know me."

"Here he comes." Frank attempted to appear casual.

The man approached our table. "I don't usually do this, but you're just so familiar. Do we know each other?" He gazed at me intently. "Did we work together? I'm sorry if I don't remember you. I'm Alex. Alex Conrad." Was I supposed to know who this man was?

"I don't think so," I mumbled and blushed. I was praying the man didn't recognize me as an older version of the woman who went missing long ago. He was an elderly man with a receding hairline. He kept staring at me and turning his head from side to side, trying to elicit a memory.

"I don't forget a face. Sorry to bother you. I was so certain we had a past."

"No problem, sir," I said casually. We shook hands. If a lightning bolt ever was transmitted in a handshake, that was it. I could tell he felt it as well. He turned and walked back to his booth, where I guess his wife and another couple sat.

I got up and went to the bathroom. When I returned, the man smiled and waved to me. To me! The man and his entourage all stood to leave. Even Frank was shocked.

Frank whispered, "Do you know who they are?"

I shook my head. "I don't think so."

"He's the real Mr. Comstock. He and Colin Chandler were the creators and producers of Comstock. He studied the area's history, wrote the scripts, and produced and directed many of the episodes."

It was unnerving, to say the least. We left without talking, and Frank dropped me at the airport. I hugged and thanked Frank.

I was off to see my dad. I thought about the upcoming reunion. Would my reappearance after so many years shock and kill him?

# CHAPTER 48

Montana was stark and cold compared with Nevada and the Tahoe area. It was also another home — my first home. I landed in Billings on my second flight and walked two miles in the cold to a used-car lot. I found an old station wagon that, if necessary, could accommodate my dad. I wasn't sure any of my plans were possible. I could see springing dad from his residence without being recognized by any locals. I had a wig and a scarf, and I thought I looked reasonably different from the Becky anyone would recognize. Maybe I could drive him to the home ranch, but getting him up to the cabin was going to be interesting. I didn't know how his health was. I doubted he could ride. I didn't think there were any horses left at the ranch. I wondered if he still owned it.

I slept in the car, which was uncomfortable, to say the least. In the morning, I drove along the long road to the nursing home. It seemed like a pleasant place from the outside. I could be happy here. When I entered through the glass doors, I noticed that there were security locks. Exiting was not as easy as coming in. Several older men and women were in the lobby. They seemed happy. Many were in wheelchairs or had walkers. It smelled okay. I walked up to the glass-encased reception. "Hi. I'm here to see my uncle, Jack Lauder."

"Oh, Mr. Lauder. Oh wow, uh, can you wait here?" The receptionist left and returned with a nurse.

"Who are you?" asked the nurse.

"I'm Uncle Jack's niece. My name is Karen Lauder. My dad was his brother."

"I'm afraid Jack isn't doing well. He doesn't respond to people. It may be a bit of a shock. He eats and sits up, but you need to be prepared that he won't communicate," she warned. "He is a bit, um, shall we say, cantankerous, even at the best of times."

"Oh, that's certainly my uncle for sure." I followed the nurse to a private room where my father sat, staring out of a window. He was frail and had aged more than the many years since I last saw him at my graduation. He had to be in his mid-eighties. He looked ancient. His hair was white and thin. His complexion was not the tanned, hardened skin I knew. He had several bruises on his arms — typical of aging.

The nurse saw me look at them and explained. I waved my hand. "I'm a nurse. I know how fragile old people's skin can be."

"Hi, Uncle Jack. It's Karen, Jim's daughter. How are you?" Dad stared into space. There was no response.

The nurse could see I had doubts about my visit. "May I bring you a cup of tea or coffee? We're so happy when relatives come to visit. Please stay as long as you want."

"Thank you. No, I'm fine. I'll just talk to Uncle Jack and tell him what's happening in our family." I casually glanced around the bright room. A dresser displayed pictures of Sherry and Lauren and one with Jeff, Sherry, and the other kids. I felt a pang of jealousy.

I noticed a node in the ceiling that looked like a camera, which was facing Dad. I suspected this was how they kept tabs on the patients who were in bed all day. The view from the window was of trees that had not quite leafed out. There were tiny green buds. A bird was flitting from branch to branch. I positioned myself between the camera and Dad and looked him straight in the eye. I lifted the wig enough to reveal my curly brown-gray hair.

"Dad, look at me, Dad. It's me. It's Becky. I'm back, Dad. I'm back."

He did not move or flinch. He barely blinked.

"Dad, I know I've been gone a long time, but I came back to see you. I love you, Dad, and I want to help you." I paused. "I can't help you if you don't tell me what I can do." He stared ahead without recognition or change in his eyes. He just stared at the bird flitting back and forth from branch to branch on a nearby tree.

A nurse came in and inquired if I was alright. "Oh, yes. I'm just chatting to him about our family and about our horses. He would remember Crazy and Molly and even Tank."

"How's Snake Oil?" he asked. The nurse gasped, and I smiled.

"Just as cantankerous as ever, Uncle Jack."

This made the nurse laugh and nod. "Well, I'll leave you two to catch up. We're so happy you're here, Karen."

"Me too. You have no idea."

When she left, I looked at him and cried. He reached out and took my hand. "Is it really you?"

"Yes, Dad. It's me."

"Becky, where on earth have you been? I looked for you for years."

"Dad, it's a very complicated story. I'll explain it all. But first, how can I help you?"

"Get me the hell out of here, girl. I want to go home. I want to go to your mother."

I was alarmed. Did Dad mean to Mom's grave, or did he think she was alive, too?

"What do you mean about going to Mom, Dad?"

"I want to go up to the cabin. Your mother's buried up there."

I was right. Dad was not all there. "Dad, Mom's buried in the cemetery. We were there when she was buried. Don't you remember?"

"Becky, only one other person knows this, but she isn't there. We took her out of the coffin and put rocks back in to maintain the weight of the coffin. I took her up to the cabin, and she's buried up there. I want to be buried with her, darling. Please get me there. I'm an old man, and I don't have much time."

I had to plan my father's escape. I figured I could drive Dad to the ranch. However, I doubted I could safely get him to the cabin, which was up a thousand or more feet and accessible only by horseback or walking. I knew he couldn't ride. Well, they had doubted he could talk.

I returned the next day when the staff greeted me like a hero. Dad was a new man. He was up and out of bed for the first time in a month. Dad was using a walker and was eagerly awaiting my arrival. He introduced me as his niece, which made me realize that he definitely had all his marbles, and probably then some. He begged me to take him outside to the smoking area. "Uncle Jack, you don't smoke, do you?"

He winked and said he needed fresh air. No one was smoking out there, anyway. He led me to a small table, and a nurse brought us both some coffee. He sat close to me and quietly handed me a number. "Do you remember Sheila?"

"Sheila Robinson or Trent?"

"Robinson, you idiot. That Trent woman is a traitor." I didn't recall why Dad didn't like her, but I think it had something to do with Mom and her bridge club.

"Okay, what about her? What's the plan?"

"Call her. Tell her you are busting me out of this joint. She'll know what to do."

"Where're you staying, anyway?" he inquired.

"Sleeping rough, Dad, just like you taught me."

"Why don't you stay at the ranch?"

"Do you still own it?"

"Well, I'd better, damn it." Dad sat up and slammed his fist on the table.

"Is anyone up there?"

"How the hell would I know? Your sister has me stuck in this hellhole."

"Dad, I'm sure she's doing the best she can." Who was I to talk? I had been of no help for years.

"She could have moved back," he growled.

"Dad, you know that would never happen for her or me."

"Well, this is how you're going to make it up to me, Becky. I'm going home to your mother, and I'll be buried with her. Do you understand?"

"Yes, sir." That was my dad. Nothing remotely subtle. Nothing.

I was supposed to call a phone number. Dad's plan was for me to ask the staff for permission to take him out to lunch in a few days when Sheila had her part organized, and he would never return. Never.

I had wondered about Sheila after Mom died. She was alone, and Sherry was convinced they were having it off when we were in school. I guess something must have happened for him to have her number.

I didn't have a handheld phone. I had to drive quite a distance to find a payphone. I needed to get coins to make calls.

I dialed the number. "Mrs. Robinson, hi. This is Jack Lauder's niece. No, Mrs. Robinson. He's fine. He told me to call you about the plan."

Sheila thought I was calling to report his passing. "Well, all right. Tell him hello for me."

"Yes, ma'am."

Sheila knew precisely what the plan meant. She would recognize me if she saw me. I wasn't sure how this was going to work. I loved my father and wanted him to have his last wish, but not at the risk of upsetting my daughter at this stage of her life.

That afternoon, I returned to the nursing home and went straight to my father's room. I was a celebrity now. Even the doctor came by and introduced himself. I didn't want publicity. No, sir.

I went to the front desk and requested permission to take my uncle out of the home for an afternoon drive. "He really wants to see his ranch. I'll have him back after dinner." Keeping him alive and kicking was in their best interest. My family paid good money to keep him there. With this rejuvenation, they might even get another year or two and more money from the estate.

"Well, it's irregular, but I'll see what we can do. You really are a miracle worker." The middle-aged nurse was so pleased.

"I've heard that before," I replied. *I need to get out of here.* "Does my uncle have any medication he'll require if you let him out for the day?"

"He is on a few heart meds. I'll see what we need to do for the afternoon."

"Great, I would kill to give him one last visit." Okay, maybe not kill, just do a minor elderly abduction — another resurgence of my criminal past when I stole clothes off a line in the 1800s.

The following morning, I got enough food for a few days at the cabin. I went to the ranch, which had been cleaned out to prepare for a sale. There were still a few things around that might come in handy. I found a tarp and some old blankets.

The weather was warming, and the creek was running. The ice was gone. I still didn't know what 'the plan' entailed, but I knew I had to disguise myself from Sheila. I went to a cosmetics store and bought some hair dye and some over-the-top makeup. I still put on my red wig when I picked Dad up.

The nursing home was more than obliging and even helped me get him in my car. I stole something, though. When the nurse was off her station, I casually went in and borrowed a few more heart meds just in case we were delayed in getting Dad back tonight, or ever.

"So glad I taught you and Sherry to drive properly." He smiled and put his hand on mine, which was on the stick shift.

"Me too." But I thought in a week or two, I would never shift again, and I smiled.

"So, where are we going, Dad?"

"Becky, we're going home, darling girl. We're going home. Now, get the hell out of here before I take a switch to you." He meant it too. He was definitely a hand-on-bottom disciplinarian. It made me think of Sam. *Maybe I'm attracted to men of authority? I think it's the challenge that attracts me.*

"Go to the ranch and let me out for a minute. You stay in the car."

"Yes, sir, but can you walk all right? You haven't walked for weeks, Dad."

"Don't be an upstart, missy. You do what I say."

"Yes, sir." Oh, this was going to be fun being bossed around for the next few days. I knew it wouldn't last. He would be back in the home and living on this last hurrah. I could do this and know he would die a happy man. I knew I could get Sherry to make sure his ashes were taken up to be with Mom. I was mad that Dad hadn't told me about Mom's actual grave. Frank would sort out the details for me after I was gone, and Dad was back at the rest home.

I parked the car and turned off the motor. I waited and waited, and finally, I felt I'd better come and see what had happened. He wasn't there. Fresh hoofprints led from the back of the house into the paddock and over toward Sheila's house. The cabin was nestled in the mountains in a different direction. It would not be difficult to figure out where he'd gone. The police would find us from those tracks in a heartbeat. A single horse tied to the hitching post was getting anxious about being left behind. *For God's sake, Dad, this is crazy.*

The trail to the cabin was steep and slippery. I wondered how Dad mounted a horse and how could he stay on? A note left for me instructed me to wait an hour before I was to follow. He and Sheila had business! If the horses were still at the cabin, I was to stay away until Sheila left. *This is ludicrous. How old are they?* My dad had not changed a bit. I wondered how he and Sam would have got on. Ugly.

I poked around the cabin a bit more and checked in all my old hidey-holes for forgotten treasure. I found an arrowhead, Mom's comb, and a silver dollar. I knew Dad had buried money when we were kids that was never reported to the feds. I searched around and saw a freshly dug hole. That old coot probably paid Sheila in more ways than one. I was flat-out annoyed. However, when I lifted a wooden box, and discovered old newspapers about me and the rockslide and his annual quest to locate me and bring me home. I swallowed. How could I deny my father this last fling?

After an hour, I tightened the girth on the little bay gelding and headed up to the cabin. I arrived to find three young men standing with the two horses just over a rise where I couldn't identify them nor they me. They had what appeared to be a small, motorized mower with a trailer attached. I guessed they probably put him in the trailer to haul him up the mountain. There was a fire in the fireplace and one in the oven. I smelled coffee, and my father was sitting by the window looking out over a vast range.

"I may die tonight." He tried to adjust his thin frame in the chair to view the range and trees better. "It's worth it, though." He laughed. "I wonder how long before the word gets out and they search for me?"

"About now," I replied. "Where's Sheila, Dad?"

"Sheila? Did you think Sheila was coming? She broke her hip last year. She's been bedridden ever since. They're her grandkids, Becky."

"By tomorrow, someone will be up at the ranch and follow the tracks, and you'll be hauled off the mountain by lunch."

He smiled. "I don't think so, miss smarty-pants." He closed his eyes and laughed. Really laugh. It started a coughing fit, which led to him gasping. What did it matter if he was going to be dead in the morning?

"Those tracks are where Sheila's boys were going hunting. You should see the bull they shot."

"Dad, it isn't even hunting season."

"Wanna bet? You think I'm so stupid. There's a special elk season this year. The boys have tickets, and they are on private land — my land. Tomorrow morning, they'll be down at the stockade milling around when the sheriff comes. They'll be able to say they stayed in the hut last night, and no one was there, no one, let alone a poor old bastard like me, who could barely get around a nursing home, let alone climb a mountain. Ha! I got 'em all fooled."

"What about my car, Dad?"

"What about it? It'll be locked in Sheila's barn tonight and beneath several tons of hay. Becky, let's not fight. I haven't seen you for almost twenty years, and I want to talk to you. I want you to know about things, too. I want to hear where you've been and why you left us. Now, that is the question that needs an answer."

The day was ending. The men who brought Dad up took my horseback to their ranch. I never saw them face to face. Thankfully, the dye job was a washout type, and it would be gone in two or three washes.

"Hey, Bec, I kinda like your hair. It reminds me of your mother. You know she had beautiful hair." And thus, it began. He started with his story, and over two weeks, he told me all about his youth until I went missing. We would eat. I would clean the cabin and help him clean and dress, and then we would sit on the porch and watch the wildlife and the change of the last of winter to the full green of spring. He would retire at about sunset. I would stay awake, and by lamplight, I would record the stories he told me. Once a week, we would get a deposit of food and the newspaper. His health seemed to improve every day.

We ventured into a small meadow. In one corner, with his bony finger, dad pointed to a barely raised line of earth. "Your mother's in there," he said, pointing to the spot. "I want to be right next to her. Can you dig?"

I closed my eyes. "You want me to dig a grave for you next to Mom?" I winced at the idea.

Over the following two weeks, he told me about my disappearance from his perspective. He arrived two days after the slide. Even though the rockslide was unstable, he began combing through the rocks, seeking anything to verify that I was in there.

When he found nothing, he rode in ever-increasing circles to see where I may have wandered off in search of help. For the first two years, he made the journey. Mac Smyth, Julie's husband, lent him a horse. The two would ride around the area looking for anything that would indicate I was in the rubble, or that I had escaped and fled the scene. After Mac passed, Dad said he became friends with a dude-ranch owner. Dad used their horses in trade for some stock reeducation. "You know, Lauren came and rode with me. You did good with that girl. She's in vet school. She's a bit of a hand with a horse." He told me things about her I would never have known. It made me cry.

Dad related stories about particular horses he broke and trained on our ranch and training problems that were both familiar to me and unfamiliar. He told me about clients and young men who had worked for him. There were many stories about my mother and her assistance with the horses while raising us. I didn't know that she had had several miscarriages following my birth, or that she was hospitalized for several weeks due to an undiagnosed infection a few weeks after I was born.

I dutifully wrote it all down. At times, my dad would read what I had written and chuckle to himself. Finally, he was done. I'd written his story. He would not be forgotten after his death. Dad ordered me to send a copy to my sister and to each of the grandchildren upon his death. I didn't have the heart to tell him I would leave, and he would have to die alone up here or back at the nursing home. Summer was approaching, and I had to return to Nevada and the creek with the portal back to my time. "My time" was not the 1900s — it was the 1800s. I was worried about Sam. I knew he wouldn't move on, but what if he died or became ill with something I could cure if I were there? I missed his reassuring voice and touch.

One morning, Dad looked at me. He'd finished a breakfast of bacon and eggs. "Now, girl, it's your turn. I ain't leaving this planet until you tell me where you've been. But first, you need to dig."

"Digging what?" I asked, pretending to have forgotten.

"My grave. I already told you."

"But, Dad, you're healthier than I am," I lied.

"I want you to get a start on it. After lunch, you're gonna tell me why you've hidden for all these years and why you haven't seen that beautiful girl you bred."

So, I dug with an old shovel. It was creepy and hard work. Every few days, I would bring my father out to the meadow and inspect the site. It was too short, too narrow, too shallow, as if I didn't know that, and not close enough to Mom. It was slow going, and I worried I would run into her. The thought made me mouth vomit. In the afternoons, I told him about my life. Initially, I didn't mention the dates. But slowly, I told him the truth and left nothing out, except for the names that would make me look like a delusional idiot. I gave the Cattle Creek Ranch and the Buchanans different names. Some I kept the same, and some I changed.

"I know this is hard to believe, but it's the truth."

He didn't speak. It was only at the end that I explained the time travel. I could see he was trying to make sense, yet it was just too much of a stretch for him.

"What about that rock on your finger?" I looked at it and smiled.

"Well, let's hope the man who gave it to me still wants me."

"Hell of a rock, sister."

"Hell of a man, Dad." *God, I miss Sam so much.*

In late July, our last grocery delivery had the local newspaper with a story about my father's disappearance. The family had come and conducted a memorial in his honor. They placed a plaque next to his wife's grave in the cemetery. The Robinson boys had scoured the mountains several times for any trace of Jack. Still, they had no evidence suggesting he'd gone up to his property.

"Good old Sheila," was all my dad said. He chuckled to himself as he read and reread his obituary. The woman who had taken him away was not mentioned. I think the nursing home was too embarrassed to admit they had let him go with a stranger. My guess was it had been made perfectly clear he did not have a niece named Karen.

I completed digging the grave and ended my story. Dad asked about the horses I had ridden and the quality and the saddles, bits, and harnesses I'd used over that time. I repeated a few things and added some details that interested him. I told him I was going back to live out my life with the man I loved, and I was not staying, so there was no point in disturbing Jeff, Sherry, and especially Lauren. She was in excellent hands.

One morning, Dad wanted me to describe Penny once again. He wanted more detail and asked me to bring him a piece of paper. He sketched a figure.

"Right hip, Becky?" He drew the brand on Penny's hip. It was the Cattle Creek Ranch brand. I didn't remember ever discussing this with him.

"Dad, why did you want to know about her brand, and how'd you know what the brand looked like?" He had never watched the *Comstock* series. He used to give Sherry and me holy heck about idolizing this fictional drama about horses when we had the real deal in our backyard. I think we could watch because my mother was in love with Clint.

"I dreamed about a sorrel mare last night just as you described. She came to me in my dream and told me it was time to join the herd."

"Huh, well, don't get any ideas, Dad. We still have a week's worth of groceries."

We enjoyed a nice dinner of sausage, potatoes, and fresh greens. Dad had a glass of whiskey from a bottle that he'd hidden many years ago.

"Are you jumping off the wagon at this late stage, Dad?"

"I was never on it, sister. Why do you think I spent so much time with Sheila?"

"Well, there are several reasons to spend time with a lady. I guess Sherry and I got that wrong."

He laughed. "You sure did. I was never unfaithful to your mother."

When I woke up the following morning, my father was dead.

# CHAPTER 49

I buried Dad with the belt buckle he had won in his youth at a local rodeo, his finest western shirt and pants. I left his wedding ring on. I covered the graves as he had requested. I walked out of the mountains and down to the ranch with the manuscript and nothing else. I wondered who would discover enough evidence to recognize Dad had been there for almost three months after his daring escape from the nursing home. I left no plaque or stone to indicate the location of the gravesite. The cabin, which had been built in the early 1900s, was actually in the national forest. Upon his death, the cottage, which was deeded to him, reverted to the Forest Service.

He'd left a letter under his pillow. He knew his legacy and inheritance did not constitute a windfall for anyone. Still, his will had directed that anything of value go equally to any surviving children, meaning Sherry. I was happy with that. He left me a note saying he realized I had sacrificed my time for him, and he wanted to make sure I had enough money to get back to wherever I was going. A small map illustrated where additional money was buried on the ranch. I followed the map and found a can with about six hundred dollars in it. I had to dig it up at night. The property had been sold while we were up at the cabin. The new owners were moving in during the day. He also included a map to Sheila's place, where my car was hidden. I went to see her. She was not well and didn't recognize me. She gave me the keys and asked if he had passed. I nodded, and she thanked me.

"I loved him from the time I met him, but he never stopped loving his wife. He was a good man." Sheila looked away and had tears in her eyes.

The tank in the car had been filled. I was out of the mountains and back on a plane three days later, with another three hundred dollars for selling the station wagon. I stopped at several small towns on the way down and got scripts for various ailments. The biggies were penicillin and tetracycline.

I returned to Nevada and called Frank.

"Jesus, I thought you died. Where the hell have you been?" I told him the story, and he let out a slow whistle. "You pulled it off, you little kidnapper."

"Yep, I did." It was a happy but sad moment. I had to detox before going back.

"I need another favor. My dad asked me to write his stories, kind of like a memoir. Can you type them up and send them to my sister? Can you send the locket you found in the creek, too? Just say that my father found it, and that's why he stopped coming to look for me, and it should go to Lauren. Will you do that? Hey Frank, want to go on a hike?"

"Can't, fellow time-traveler. I'm heading to Hawaii with my girl."

I hitched a ride from the airport and arrived at Frank's apartment. He was packing for a traditional romantic vacation.

"May I borrow your car?"

The following morning, I drove up to the unloading area where, many years ago, Julie Smyth and I unloaded our horses and took that fateful trip along the creek. I'd borrowed a backpack and sleeping bag and headed up the trail to Hank Heaven. It was now called Miner's Meadow. It was a five-hour hike, or three hours on horseback, from the trailhead.

I walked past the rock pools. A large pool that would send me back to my time reflected a passing cloud. Things had changed slightly, but again, after the cloud passed, I could discern the shadows of two trout feeding in the pool. I looked over the edge of the granite path. The pools were greener than I remembered. The creek had snaked its way around the slide, which was still obvious below. I saw a plaque that bore Julie Smyth and my name with the date of our supposed demise. The guardrails had warning signs of falling rocks.

Several hikers were returning from a trip to the meadow. We passed as I made my way up the pass to the summit. I looked at my beautiful valley. Colorful tents dotted the grassy valley this time. I could see most of the trees had survived the ravages of time, and I thought I spotted two people fishing in the lake on the valley floor. The lake was blue that day, reflecting the sky. No more clouds could be seen, and I observed rock climbers as they scaled the cliffs around the valley.

It took an hour to work my way down to the valley floor. I walked around the perimeter and discovered that a few minor slides had done little to change the confluence of the valley and towering rock walls. The rock climbers acknowledged my presence, and I returned their greetings. I walked to the valley center, trying to avoid the hikers. Something new was erected in the pines. A cabin that had been constructed many years ago was now standing among the conifers. Its design suggested it might have been built in the 1800s. It had undoubtedly stood the test of time. When no one was around, I looked where I thought Hank was buried. Pine needles covered the area. I had to dig down a bit to find it, but there was a tombstone that had been laid or had fallen flat. I could barely see the name Henry, which was Hank's proper name, but the Buchanan was ground out. I was about to get up when I felt another piece of rock or granite.

I removed several inches of dirt and pine needles. The stone was flat with smooth, rounded edges. I could barely make that name out. I saw Samuel, and below capital B. Time had erased the rest of the word. I could see the start of the dates, but I purposely did not look. I kept clearing the pine needles and soil, expecting to locate one for Dan. Instead, I identified the first letter: R. Was it me? Was this my forever resting place? I didn't read anymore. I quickly replaced the dirt and pine needles.

After finding an isolated place to camp, I rolled out my sleeping bag and lay down, looking up at the sky. It was so blue and warm. I remembered my first night staying here when Sam rescued me from his cattle-thieving foreman. Seventeen years or more had elapsed. There was no chance of an au naturel swim. I would need a proper suit for sure. I laughed.

That night, I dreamed about the Cattle Creek Ranch and Penny. I woke in the morning with the sure knowledge she had passed. I hoped it was quick and painless. She'd served me well, and I prayed she'd taken my father to a meadow as perfect as this, where he could be reunited with my mother. It was time for me to rejoin my family. It was time to go home.

# CHAPTER 50

I returned to the apartment and prepared to travel back to the 1800s the following day. How would I be welcomed? I was reasonably sure that Gee Ling had put a bounty on my head. I just hoped they didn't think I was dead. I knew Sam would understand.

I placed the riding outfit I was wearing when I escaped the mountain lions in plastic bags. I added the antibiotics and a picture of Lauren that Frank had printed while I was abducting my father. I left a note for Frank that I had taken the car and where the keys were hidden, as he had done previously. The following day, I waited until it was warm and sunny. I hoped it would be the same when I surfaced. The water level in the creek was low. Despite the freezing temperature of any mountain stream, I prayed it was survivable.

Traffic along the granite trail was heavy, and I had veered off the path several yards ahead of the old slide and rock pool. As I arrived at the creek, I noticed several hikers above me looking down. I waved to them, and they waved back. I had to wait an hour before I could dive unobserved into the water. I felt the creek water, which was cold. I was too old for this. I grabbed my sealed plastic bag and waded into the water. It was a shock to my system. I plunged down, attempting to stay underwater for a few seconds, and then surfaced. I looked around, and it appeared nothing had changed. I looked up, and there was the guardrail. I plunged again, trying to go deeper. I resurfaced, and still, there was the guardrail. I was frantic. I waded over to another area of the pool and tried again.

I surfaced, and that was when I saw him. A forest ranger walked up to the water's edge to ask me what I was doing. I was fully clothed and holding a large plastic bag, and to any sane person, I looked like I was trying to drown myself.

"Ma'am, I'm going to ask you to come out of the water." He instructed me to wade over to him, and I climbed out, shivering and wet.

"What are you doing?" He had a fishing rod, and I suspected he mixed work and pleasure.

*Think fast, Harper.* But what logical explanation could there be for my actions?

"It kind of looks as though I'm trying to kill myself, but I'm not, so let's get that straight." Nothing like the truth to sway an argument. "I don't have a logical explanation for this, sir." Again, the truth. "I was told that if I jumped into the water, I might time travel." More truth. "But since you and I are here, I figure I'm wrong." The first lie.

"Well, you aren't the first person to think that, which is why I patrol this area almost every day. The legend started about twenty years ago when a girl was killed in a rockslide, and her body was never found. They say she left this time for another. You wouldn't even be the first person this year seeking a portal, but you're the first I've encountered in a while. The pool several yards down is the pool most people try." He pointed down the creek to another set of water pools. "So far, no one has escaped, but many have tried."

"Oh, really?"

"Boyfriend problems? Running from the law? Or just an adventure?"

"Ha, just an adventure. Do you know much about the cabin in Miner's Meadow?"

"Oh, now that has an interesting history, which may be why you heard about the time thing. The story goes that in the 1860s or 70s, a rancher was stood up at his wedding, and he thought his fiancée had left for the future. To prove his love for her, he built the cabin so that when she visited the meadow, she would be reminded of that love and return to him."

I swallowed hard. "Romantic. What a great story! He must have loved the woman very much."

"She probably ran off with a traveling salesman, but who knows?" he replied casually. "I need to get going. You might try the pools down the way, but my suggestion is that you go home and find some joy in your life in the here and now. Good day, ma'am, and because you aren't breaking the law, I won't take you in. Safe travels."

I sat and waited. When the ranger was truly gone, I made my way down to the next set of pools. Oh God, please let this work, I prayed. I was wet and cold and wanted to get home. It would be late when I arrived. If I arrived. I'd brought a peanut butter sandwich and a few Oreos.

"Goodbye, Nabisco, you have been kind to me, but you are not worth losing my only love."

I found a pool, which was almost identical, and took the plunge, so to speak. I surfaced, and the water level had risen significantly. It was overcast, and rain threatened. Yet was it my time or another? I looked up, and there were no signs of a rockfall in the distance and no barriers on the narrow granite shelf. I was back.

# CHAPTER 51

I still had the plastic bag. The antibiotics were dry. My riding outfit was not too damp, and my picture of Lauren as a grown woman had been laminated in plastic so it would survive. I changed out of my modern wet clothes. I let them dry. While they dried, I took a nap. I overdid it, and it was late when I woke up. I had a three-hour walk to the Cattle Creek Ranch. I decided it was best to just stay the night, and I built a fire to use for protection against any wild animals. My modern clothes had dried, and I placed them in the plastic bag with the antibiotics. I buried them before any dew would wet them again and cause mildew, which would ruin them. I never planned to leave, but who knew what might happen. I would come and get the drugs later. I kept thinking about the Miner's Meadow cottage story. That was definitely Sam. Nice story if it were true.

At dawn, I fashioned a stick to use for safety and began the long trip to the Cattle Creek Ranch. I encountered no bears or mountain lions. I saw an old Indian woman whom I had attended when she was ill. She smiled and waved in recognition. That was heartening. When I arrived at the outlook area, which turned to either the Cattle Creek Ranch or Virginia City, I eyed the valley below. It looked like I had expected. There were no signs of modern civilization. I was relieved, and I turned toward the Cattle Creek Ranch.

As I approached the house and barn, all looked the same. Dan's gelding was tethered to the hitching post, indicating he was present. I didn't see Sam's horse, and I noticed the pen where Penny had been cared for now had another horse that I did not recognize. I walked up to the house and knocked. I was apprehensive about my reception. *Please, dear God, let everything be the same and allow Sam to be alive and well.* Dan opened the door. He looked at me, and I could see a puzzled look come across his face. He stood in the doorway and just stared. He didn't seem happy to see me. "What are you doing here, Becky?" Dan was abrupt. He blocked the entryway.

"I'm here to see your father. Is he here?" I could see hostility and resentment building.

"He said you must be dead. We spent months looking for you. Where've you been?"

"I can explain, but I must see your father first." At that moment, Gee Ling came around the corner and saw me. He flew into, I'm guessing, a Cantonese expletive stream and raised his chin without smiling. His eyes became even more narrow than ever, and his lips were tight. "Dan, is your father here?" I was panicking.

Gee Ling responded. "You not see Mr. Sam. You broke his heart too many times. We not like you anymore. I have big plans and food for wedding, and you not even bother to say you not coming. You not welcome in this house."

I helplessly looked at Dan. "Danny, where is he?"

"He spends most of his time up at Hank's grave. He doesn't talk much, and he just comes and goes. I don't want you doing any more harm, Becky. He's had enough loss in his life. We all have."

"May I borrow a horse? Is Copper here? I, um, am guessing Penny...."

Dan cut me off. In a moment of kindness, he quietly said, "No, she died a few weeks ago. Pa had us bury her out behind the barn. I don't know why he was so fond of that mare, but he told us to bury her. Copper isn't here. She's at the clinic. You can take the gelding in Penny's pen. He's her grandson, anyway. He bucks a bit. If you can stay on for the first mile, he'll be fine." He was giving me no quarter, and I asked for none.

I mounted, and the gelding did not buck. The gelding was actually a well-trained and responsive horse. He showed no tendency to react. "Huh," stammered Dan, "and here I thought he was a good judge of character." The meaning was not lost on me.

Gee Ling handed me a large sack of food. "This for Mr. Sam." Then, he grumbled again in his native tongue. He did pat my leg when Dan looked away.

"What do you call him?"

"Jack, just Jack. Although some may have referenced a donkey with that name, too." Dan walked away.

*Jack Ass,* I laughed to myself.

We had lived in parallel universes and times. But now, our lives were going to join forever. At least, I hoped.

# CHAPTER 52

It was mid-afternoon by the time I was able to reach the peak. I crossed the pass and looked down onto the valley floor. I could hear hammering in the far distance and saw the blue reflection of the lake from a clear sky. I saw no deer or other wildlife in the meadow. I descended into the valley and rode to the area where Hank was buried, where there was a newly finished cabin. It was solid. Time and the elements had not marred the wood. It was the one that would still stand in the twenty-first century. I could hear hammering inside the cabin.

Cash was roaming freely. I dismounted and loosened Jack's girth. He'd sipped water as we crossed one of the many rivulets that dissected the meadow. Because neither horse whinnied, Sam was unaware of my presence. He was humming a tune that was from James Taylor. I knocked softly. Sam stood up and paused without looking. He bent down again, and I quietly said, "I'm home."

He turned, looked at me, and just stared. I could not tell his reaction. Was it anger or relief?

"Hello, Rebecca. It's been a while."

He approached me and took my hand, and walked me to a log on which we had often sat. Then, without talking, he walked farther over to where we had a view of the lake.

"Want to tell me about it?"

"Yes, Sam. Yes, I do." And with that, I recounted everything. I told him about Frank, the mountain lions, the snow, and the apartment. I told him about the telephone and computers and the electronic pictures that could be sent instantly.

I paused before telling him about Jeff, Lauren, and my father. It was an hour before I stopped. I didn't cry when I told him I had decided not to see Lauren in person. I laughed when I talked about stealing my father from the nursing home. But I shed a tear when I told Sam about my dad asking about Penny and describing his dream the day before he died.

At some point, Sam, who was sitting by my side, put his arm around my waist. When I was done, he placed his hand under my cheek and, tilting my face toward his, kissed me softly. "Welcome back, Becky. I've missed you."

"I've missed you, too. Am I forgiven?"

"There's nothing to forgive. When you left before the wedding, I have to say I was a bit upset. Ha, Dan and Gee Ling called it wild. But then I decided if you weren't coming back, I would leave you a message. I built you a cabin, so if you came up to the meadow anytime, you would know that our family and town were not a dream."

"Sam, it's still in the meadow. Your cabin has survived more than one hundred years." I didn't tell him about the hikers, tents, and how people used the cabin. I didn't describe the gravestones either. I was not forecasting the future for him or anyone.

He stood and pulled me up, and while I was still standing on the log to meet his height, he wrapped his arms around me and kissed me passionately. It was a long kiss, and when it ended, he caressed my hair and back. "It's late, but my darling, I'm not waiting any longer. Let's head back to the Cattle Creek Ranch to pick up Dan and Gee Ling, head into town, and wake Ray up. I want to marry you, and I'm not standing on ceremony any longer."

I smiled and nodded. "No more waiting, Sam."

We saddled Cash and tightened Jack's girth. We mounted and walked side by side up out of the valley and over the pass.

"Who offered you Jack?"

"Dan did. He said this horse has other names."

"I bet he did. How'd you get on with him?"

"Fine," I responded nonchalantly.

"Hmm, he might be your new horse if you can stay on. Dan must still be rather mad at you."

"Wonderful horse — no problem at all." I laughed to myself. I knew he might be a challenging ride. My last seventeen or eighteen years had been a challenging ride. This guy was literally a walk in the park.

"Sam?"

"Yes, Becky."

"You know you're marrying a modern woman, don't you?"

"And?" he responded with his authoritative voice that made me sit up straight in the saddle.

"Obey, Sam. Not going to happen. I won't say obey in my vows."

He smiled. "You don't have to, my darling. You are marrying me, and that's implied."

I thought about that for a minute and laughed to myself.

"Sam, regarding that discipline matter. That's not gonna happen either."

"Good, I was worried you would give me cause, but it seems you understand how marriage works today. There won't be any need."

# EPILOGUE

I'm looking for a puppy, and I have issues. Can you believe it? Dogs aren't allowed inside the house at the Cattle Creek Ranch. These men have met their match. They just don't know it yet. Negotiations are in progress, and the cowboy reeducation program continues. They say you can't teach an old dog new tricks, but I'm a living example that you can. The men, not so much.

If you're reading this 'epilogue' for the details about the wedding and the after-wedding 'celebrations,' forget it. I live in your *Comstock* dreams, and despite overcoming the Buchanan curse, I'm a traditionalist.

So far, so good. I've given up swearing. It's a self-preservation thing. I'm still working as a vet and a medical doctor, but not as much as I did before the big night.

I'm now breaking in a few horses on the side. My dad taught me well. The men are a bit put out about this, but the results speak for themselves. I work on Penny's progeny.

Oh, Jack did eventually buck me off several months later, but no one knows, and I won't tell.

Married life is great. I'd forgotten how nice it is to have someone who lights the lamp in the morning and gets the fire going. I made myself some blue jeans, which I wear around the house, much to my husband's dismay. Levi-Strauss doesn't make jeans in my style yet. Mostly, I wear dresses. Boy, would my dad laugh at that.

Gee Ling has finally relented and is teaching me more of his recipes. I enjoy his company. Yep, I still go for "mature" men.

So, cue the music and credits and thank the screenwriters or whatever brought me here.

Beck

I hope you enjoyed the book. Let me know. Would you like to review this book? Here is a link. Scroll down and review the book.

# ACKNOWLEDGMENTS

I wish to thank several people for their encouragement and suggestions in this first book in a series about the life of Dr. Rebecca Harper, veterinarian and time traveler extraordinaire.

Shelley Herbert, my daughter and first critic, read the first chapter and said, "You should keep writing about this." My sisters, Jeanie Olson and Jane Gropp, who would never pull a punch with me, have championed my writing and guided me to avoid offending the general population. Many other friends have encouraged me by reading early versions with hundreds of typos. I would like to acknowledge my long-time friend, Quincy Andrus, who, with only a few weeks to live, took time to read the book and encourage me to continue before her life on earth ended.

The two primary readers, who have driven me to write day and night between my work as a full-time horse vet, are Julie Laughton and Jodee O'Leary. I write for the endorphin release that I receive from their daily responses to the chapters of sequential books in this series. Many other friends and relatives have read this book and the other books that will follow. Thank you all for your advice and encouragement.

My editors, Kimberly Hunt and especially Marilyn Anderson, have been masters in reacquainting me with the written language.

Natalie Keller Reinert gave me invaluable information on the publication of this book as well as creating a beautiful cover design. This is a work of fiction. Authentic historical characters are portrayed, but the primary characters and the television series are all fictional, one cowboy aside. If you see yourself or anyone you know in this work of fiction, it is dreaming.

# Books by Elizabeth Woolsey

**Horse Doctor Adventure Books:**

Small Town Secrets
**The Travels of Dr. Rebecca Harper Series**
Book 1 A Matter of Time
Book 2 Troubled Waters
Book 3 Lauren's Story
Book 4 Past and Present
Book 5 A Time to Part

---

**Catch and Release series**
Book 1 Catch and Release
Book 2 Catch and Keep
Book 3 Match the Hatch

A Man's Worth

---

Other books
Custody Down Under
Parkside Veterinary Clinic: I want to be a Vet
Horse Doctor: An American Vet's Life Down Under
Jack's War: Letters Home from an American WII Navigator
AI poetry from a Horse Doctor's Life


Note: The first chapter to all the books can be found on
elizabethwoolsey.com
Amazon links to all books
https://bit.ly/4jba85s

# ELIZABETH WOOLSEY DVM

Elizabeth Woolsey, DVM, grew up in postwar California. Sure, she was the daughter of Roy Rogers, she spent her youth emulating him. Sadly, DNA evidence has proved her wrong. Thus, she followed in her other father's footsteps  into equine veterinary medicine. She subsequently migrated to Australia, where she practiced near Adelaide, South Australia, until her retirement in December 2020.

She began writing about her experiences as a horse vet and published her first book, Horse Doctor-An American Vet's Life Down Under, in 2005. A few years before her father's death, she discovered a treasure trove of personal and historically significant letters. She knew this would make an influential book not only for her family but also for WWII enthusiasts. She published Jack's War: Letters to Home from an American WII Navigator in 2015. While veterinary medicine has been her passion, fly-fishing, horse-back riding, and writing occupy her leisure time. Her new books include stories about women in equine practice. Small Town Secrets: Horse Doctor Adventures 2021 is her latest book. She now lives in North Georgia, where she follows her passions.

She loves to hear from readers! ewoolseydvm@gmail.com

Elizabeth is available for book clubs via Zoom.

https://www.facebook.com/elizabeth.woolseydvm

https://elizabethwoolsey.com/

https://amzn.to/3dPAoGc

# PREVIEW BOOK 2



**The Travels of Dr. Rebecca Harper Troubled Waters**

First things first. I am officially Dr. Rebecca Buchanan. Marriage is often a dance with giving and taking. We are both older, and because we have been waiting so long between dances, so to speak, we have had to adjust our habits. Three guesses who gives and who takes ... There still are no dogs allowed in the house. Despite my best efforts, Sam still smokes a pipe, and Gee Ling still smokes in his room.

It took a while, but both Gee Ling and Danny, or Dan as I now call him, have forgiven me. I don't know what Sam gave them as an explanation. However, we are now all a happy, loving family that gets along like a house on fire. I lie. You can imagine having someone move into your space and disrupting your boys' club.

Despite all that, I'm one lucky girl. I'm around fifty, and I still think of myself as a girl. I'm relatively healthy and active. I now travel to Virginia City and work in my medical or veterinary clinic for two days on and two days off. My associate, Dr. Alfonzo Webber, is becoming a highly competent rural doctor. You must know a bit about everything, from birthing through to dying. He and I work well together. He sees the men for their ailments, and I primarily treat the women. We both see the inbetweeners.

Winter is approaching, and travel can be difficult, so poor Alf will bear the brunt of the work when I'm unable to get to town. Ah, youth, but welcome to my world. When I'm in town, I stay in a boardinghouse next to the clinic as Alf and his wife, Darcy, have moved into Dr. Sullivan's living quarters adjoining the clinic. The Sullivans, who ran the practice for eons, had encouraged me to seek further training to become a doctor. Both have passed, and I miss them a great deal.

I regularly dine with Ray Thompson, the retired Virginia City sheriff. Ray's finally opening up to me about his life and his wife, who'd passed years ago. He has grandchildren from their only daughter, who lives in Carson City. Despite being retired, he still monitors the town and has stepped in many times when Sheriff Glenn Frasier needed extra help and guidance in managing crime.

Mrs. Sullivan, or Flo, was my closest female companion. I've had several women friends over the years since arriving in the 1800s, but they quit. Finding kindred spirits of the female variety is not easy. My first close friend, Martha Tyler, was the schoolteacher when I first stayed in Virginia City. She taught Dan and Hank when they were young. She ended up marrying Burt Lancaster—I mean the Reverend Tyler—but then he was sent to another parish where they remain. Because married women with children generally may not teach, she started her own tutoring business on the side once their children were all in school. At first, she took no money, but then a few parents banded together, and she began an after-school program and was paid a small amount. This helped, as the pay of a preacher is not that terrific. After one year, the school board relented, and when the last teacher left, they gave her the job. She's now the teacher, principal, and janitor of her school. We write regularly, and I read about the children, the trials of being the preacher's wife and the town teacher.

My greatest joy, husband-wrangling aside, is my new avocation. I'm breaking in a few horses on the Cattle Creek Ranch, which mostly are Penny's offspring. Penny was my trusted mount when I first arrived in the 1800s. She died last year of old age. I implemented the tactics that my father taught me. My dad was a tough father, but he was kind and gentle with horses. My sister would say, if dad had a bad day with a horse, watch out. He never took it out on the horse. Dad came into the house, and you could tell that you should tread carefully to avoid his wrath or belt. We both got it regularly, but the horses had no fear of my father. He changed his methods to adjust to the individual horse. I learned a lot from him, and I have to say, so far, it's paying off. Eyes turned to the sky. Thanks, Dad.

Domestic life, when you have cooks who also clean, is easy. Out of necessity, I'm learning to sew. I require pants for riding. My traditional riding apparel, which was the norm for women in the 1800s, is beautiful but not very practical. When I'm working on the breakers, I need to move and swing onto the saddle without my culottes or pantaloons catching. Sam is not impressed. He thinks they show too much. I purposely make them loose, so no one is aroused by my fifty-year-old body—as if. I humor him and try to be as modest as I can. Of course, it's perfectly acceptable to show cleavage in my proper dresses, but dare I show a bare leg? Men!

I have a puppy now. Skeeter, who is only four months old, sleeps in the barn. I think I'll get another dog to keep her company. I was raised with kelpies. They're Australian sheep herding dogs. My dad bought them from a veterinarian in California in the 1960s. They're intelligent and quite good-looking. My mom used to say they were six years of hell, followed by six years of pure bliss. The California vet saw our dogs when he and his daughter were fly-fishing in our district. He told us the history of the kelpie. To date, they haven't been invented, and still, who is getting a dog from Australia? He inspired me to become a veterinarian in the 1970s or in the future. But that's another story.

I'm a fortunate woman. I'm married to a supersmart man who is respected near and far. The average man at this time would never let his wife go out and work, let alone spend nights in town. Sam often reminds me he's proud of my work. He knows he's married to a modern woman, which is how he gives, and I take. I can't imagine not working or contributing to our community. A day or two apart doesn't hurt this marriage.

We have established a small infirmary on the Cattle Creek Ranch, our ranch, where we treat the men who work for Sam and Dan and their families. Free healthcare benefits—how progressive is this? I take care of a few neighbors and even local Native Americans. Traditionally, they are still called Indians at this time.

Being older, we are both light sleepers. We require less sleep than we did in our youth. Sam often gets up extra early in the morning and reads his books down in the great room. I'm a middle-of-the-night kind of insomniac. The one time you don't want to disturb me is during my first hour of sleep. Ask Sam. If someone has an emergency, first, I don't hear the knocking on the door. Second, I'm told I might take a swing at the person silly enough to wake me. I'm reasonably sure this isn't true. After one all-nighter, I returned home to find Sam sporting a bruise on his cheek.

"Wow, what got you?"

"You don't remember?" Scowling at me and feigning pain, Sam rubbed his cheek.

I shrugged.

"You really don't remember?"

"Did you run into a door or something?" I inquired, trying to remember.

"Let's just say, the next time there's an emergency, I'm going to wake you with the end of a long broom."

"Oh, bull," whoa, near miss. Even that was not exactly polite.

Sam raised his eyebrows at me.

"I'm really sorry if I did that to you, darling." A quick retreat was in order.

"I'm sure you can think of a way to make amends."

Now, I raised my eyebrows.

Our private sanctuary from the outside world is Hank Heaven. As winter came, we wanted to make one last trip to the cabin before the snow would keep us away. As Sam and I made our way, climbing the trail along the cliff face, I looked down into the swirling water of the pool that would take me to my other time—the future. I had no need for the portal to another time.

I'd stopped by the portal pool shortly after the wedding to retrieve the antibiotics I'd brought with me when I once went back to the future. They were securely stored in Sam's safe behind his desk. He was still the only person I ever told about where and when I came from. I was home. Yes, I missed my daughter, Lauren, terribly, but I was dead to her, and at least I had a picture and had heard her southern accent. Does this make me a bad mother? I wrestled with this frequently.

Sam and I were free from the daily dramas of running an empire and a medical and veterinary practice when at the cabin. Sam often sat at Hank's grave and read, and I fished and collected plants used in indigenous and more modern human medicine. I became a bit of a naturalist out of necessity. It was difficult for two people like us to sit back and relax, but we were learning. We stayed in the valley only for a night or two, but it brought us both inner peace.

That about sums up my life during the last few months. Yes, we had 'disagreements,' and yes, we were both strong-willed, but we were finding our way in our time together. We won't have the benefit of a long relationship or raising children. We hoped for grandchildren and growing old together. We had a deep, abiding love that didn't waver. Well, so far...